THE VINYL DETECTIVE

VICTORY DISC

Also by Andrew Cartmel and available from Titan Books

Written in Dead Wax
The Run-Out Groove
Flip Back (May 2019)

THE VINYL DETECTIVE

VICTORY DISC

ANDREW CARTMEL

TITAN BOOKS

The Vinyl Detective: Victory Disc
Print edition ISBN: 9781783297719
E-book edition ISBN: 9781783297726

Published by Titan Books
A division of Titan Publishing Group Ltd
144 Southwark Street, London SE1 0UP

First edition: May 2018
10 9 8 7 6 5 4 3 2 1

A CIP catalogue record for this title is available from the British Library.

Printed in Great Britain by CPI Group (UK) Ltd, Croydon CR0 4YY

Did you enjoy this book? We love to hear from our readers.
Please email us at readerfeedback@titanemail.com or write to us at
Reader Feedback at the above address.

To receive advance information, news, competitions, and exclusive offers online,
please sign up for the Titan newsletter on our website:

www.titanbooks.com

For Lucy Kissick, lover of music and language.

PROLOGUE: SCREEN SHOT

Welcome to my new website, '**Historic Homicide**'!

My name is **Jasper McClew** and I am a local historian here deep in the English countryside on the beautiful coast of southeast Kent.

But, despite its alluring beauty, this is a coastline as jagged as the knife of a brutal killer… a coastline shrouded with murder, mystery and mayhem, which is as menacing and treacherous as the deadly sea fogs that roll in from the ancient, haunted waters of the English Channel…

Here you can read the story of a notorious and vicious sex crime that took place during the bloodshed and savagery of the Second World War and resulted in the death of a beautiful young woman.

But you can also read how that crime stretched its icy, skeletal, bloodstained fingers into a new century and plunged them deep into the living flesh of our own era…

…and recently claimed helpless new victims.

Because murder solves nothing, and the dead do not rest in peace, and the evil that man does lives on…

Just click on the link below and, for a modest fee, you can read the entire story!

(Payment information: PayPal, Credit Card, Bank Transfer accepted.)

1. HIDDEN TREASURE

We were in the kitchen. I was making coffee and Nevada was feeding the cats, when suddenly she looked out the window and said, "There he is now. At last."

"Who?" I said, measuring the freshly ground beans as I poured them into the filter.

"Your friend Tinkler."

"I see," I said. "So he's *my* friend now."

"Finish feeding these two, would you? I'm going to deal with him." She wiped her hands and hurried out of the kitchen just as the front gate clanged, signalling Tinkler's arrival. Nevada had been waiting for days for just this moment—her chance to pounce—but now it had arrived, she played it very cool. Opening the door before he had a chance to ring the bell, she was as nice as pie. "Tinkler! Hello." There was the sound of her smooching him on the cheek and then she led him into the kitchen, her arm twined around his. "Darling, look who's here."

She was laying it on a bit thick, I thought. "Hello,

Tinkler," I said. I'd finished giving the cats their breakfast—Aberdeen Angus ox cheek, served raw and laboriously chopped up with the kitchen scissors while Turk tried to snag pieces from me, with her razor-sharp claws and great dexterity, and Fanny merely contented herself by getting underfoot and making lots of imploring noises—and returned to making the coffee. "You want some coffee? It's the good stuff."

"I'd expect nothing less," said Tinkler. His face had an unaccustomed touch of suntan and he was grinning happily. He had no idea what was in store for him.

"How was France?" said Nevada.

"Great. It was just Mum and Dad and Maggie and me in this huge *gîte*. That's a kind of farmhouse—"

"Of course it is," said Nevada, who was fluent in more languages than Tinkler had had hot baths. "But why don't you come in and sit down and tell us all about it?" Tinkler made a move towards a kitchen chair, but Nevada steered him away from it. "No, come into the *sitting* room," she said.

Here it comes, I thought. She took him by the arm again and guided him out of the kitchen. He was beaming, enjoying all the attention, the poor sap. "And while you're at it," said Nevada from the next room, still at this point appearing to be the sweet voice of reason, "perhaps you can tell us *what the fuck this is*."

I left the coffee and hurried through. I wasn't going to miss this for the world.

Nevada and Tinkler were standing there looking at a tall black object that dominated the room.

It was taller than an upright piano, and deeper. A vast, grim-looking box of unvarnished wood painted a matte, obdurate black, its top third consisted of a broad rectangular opening. It completely dominated the lounge, taking up most of the space between the dining table and the sofa and blotting out a great swathe of light from our high, sunny, south-facing windows.

The object was almost as tall as I was. It was big, and it was ugly.

"What is this thing?" said Nevada. "And what is it doing in my living room?"

But if she'd expected contrition or remorse from Tinkler, she was out of luck. He stared at the black monolith and sank down on his knees before it, like one of the hairy humanoids in *2001: A Space Odyssey*, a look of beatific satisfaction on his face. "It came," he murmured, almost prayerfully. "It's here."

"Of course it bloody came," said Nevada. "Of course it's frigging here. The question is, *why* did it come? *Why* is it here? As opposed to being around at your place. Taking up all the room there."

"It had to be delivered while I was away," said Tinkler. He had risen from his knees now and was standing beside the huge black box, caressing the side of it as if it were the flank of some monstrous black horse. "And somebody had to be at home to accept it and sign for it. Which was you guys. I told you to expect it."

"Actually," said Nevada, "you told Agatha to tell us to expect it." It was an index of her anger that she was using

Agatha's real name here. "And she duly told us."

Tinkler looked at us, all innocence. "So what's the problem?"

"So the problem is that she told us to expect a small package which was being sent here for you. Which we were more than happy to do. *A small package*." Nevada's extravagant hand gesture in the direction of the black behemoth was entirely redundant.

"I didn't say that to her."

"No," said Nevada, shaking her head. "You didn't. You told her that we should expect a speaker for your hi-fi. A speaker!"

Tinkler patted the crudely painted black wood with the pride of new ownership. "That's right. A speaker. And here it is."

"But she thought that you meant what any normal person would have meant by a speaker. And she translated that into a small package, and that's what she told us to expect."

Tinkler shrugged. "Well, that girl just doesn't know her exponential horn-loaded loudspeakers, then, does she?" His nonchalance fooled no one. We all knew he was talking about the girl he loved, or at least lusted after, with a longstanding and no doubt hopeless passion.

Turk came wandering into the room, having devoured her breakfast, and jumped up with an effortless leap onto the top of the black box, where she crouched peering up at Tinkler. "Hello, Turk," he said, rubbing her under the chin. "Do you like my new speaker? I know you prefer the horn-loaded designs. All the girls do." Then he smiled brightly at us. "At least it gives the cats a new place to play."

Nevada nodded in my direction. "I thought *his* speakers were ridiculously gigantic. But compared to yours they are just dainty adornments." I gazed fondly at the Quads in question. Just looking at them made me want to listen to music.

"That's because the sorry fool prefers electrostatic technology to the noble horn," said Tinkler.

Nevada headed for the kitchen to serve the coffee, which was beginning to smell good. As she went, she said, "Come away from there before I give you the noble horn."

"Sounds attractive," said Tinkler. But he moved briskly away from the speaker and followed her out. I found my Luiz Bonfá album—on Verve, with arrangements by Lalo Schifrin—and put it on loud enough to be heard in the kitchen. It was one that Nevada loved and it always chilled her out. Sure enough, by the time they returned with the coffee, she had begun to mellow. Luiz's guitar was working its magic. She and Tinkler set the coffee things down on the table and I went to join them, sitting in the sunshine. This took a certain amount of careful manoeuvring of the chairs—to avoid the baleful shadow of the monster speaker.

Tinkler finished stirring sugar into his coffee and said, casually, "So where are the cables?"

"What cables?"

He frowned at me. "Don't tease me. You know I can't stand it where serious matters like hi-fi are concerned."

"I'm not teasing you," I said. "What cables?"

"They were part of the deal."

"What do you mean?"

"The deal. On eBay. When I bought the speaker for what I let this guy think was an extortionate price but actually, although of course I didn't let on to him, was a snip."

"A snip," said Nevada, staring at the giant ugly black box.

"That's right. This beauty here is worth a couple of grand more than I paid for her." Tinkler sipped his coffee, discovered it was still too hot, and set it aside.

"'This beauty'," repeated Nevada, shaking her head. "There's something creepy about you referring to it as 'her', too."

Tinkler ignored her and kept on with his story. "I even convinced this guy to throw in a set of cables, too. It was a really sweet deal. And I want my cables!"

Nevada shrugged, "So, what's a set of cables more or less?"

Tinkler sighed the long-suffering sigh of an audiophile having to explain things to a civilian. "They were *silver* cables. Solid silver. They were worth almost as much as the speaker. And he threw them in for nothing."

"Or perhaps didn't," I said, and Tinkler winced.

"Silver?" said Nevada. "You mean silver wire instead of copper?"

"Yes."

She looked at me. "Does that make a difference? To the sound, I mean?"

"Christ, yes," I said. I'd gone from thinking Tinkler was making a fuss about nothing to suddenly and poignantly sharing his pain. I turned and looked at the speaker. "You're sure the guy's not sending them separately?"

"No, he said they were definitely coming with the speaker."

"Maybe the blokes pinched them," said Nevada. "The blokes who delivered the speaker. They looked like ruffians. Would they have known how valuable they were?"

"I don't see how," I said. "They looked like ruffians."

"But couldn't they have seen that they were silver?"

"No." Tinkler shook his head sadly. "On the outside they just looked like boring ordinary cables with a red and blue dielectric."

"Dialectic?" said Nevada.

"*Dielectric*," I said. "It's the insulator."

A mournful silence ensued as we all contemplated the loss of Tinkler's silver cables, their snazzy dielectric and all. "There was nothing else?" he said. "Nothing else with the speaker?"

"Nope," I said.

"Not an envelope, or—"

"Nothing at all." Then I thought about it. I stood up and went over to the speaker and inspected the top of it where Fanny, ever the opportunist, had supplanted her sister and was lying in a patch of sunlight. I put my hand on the warm black wood. Nevada and Tinkler were staring at me.

"What is it?" said Nevada.

I ran my hand over the wood. Fanny feinted at me with her paw. She thought I was playing.

Then I found it.

Or felt it, rather. A small scrap of adhesive tape. It

was black electrical tape and almost invisible against the black wood. The tape was at the front edge of the top of the speaker, and ran down over the lip of the large opening. My fingers traced it inside. "There was something taped here," I said.

Tinkler was already on his feet. He came over and inspected it. "If the cables were in there…"

I said, "Hanging in the mouth of the speaker…"

Nevada came over and joined us, peering into the shadowy maw of the giant box. "You think they're *in* there?"

Tinkler murmured, "They fell inside…"

I nodded. "It's possible. If the clowns who delivered it were careless."

"Of course they were careless," said Tinkler. I could see he had seized onto this hope and was clinging to it for dear life. "They were ruffians. They were clowns. They were ruffian clowns." We all stared into the mouth of the speaker. And saw nothing staring back at us but darkness.

I went into the spare room to look for a torch and came back with two small, powerful LED flashlights that gave off an intense red beam. For reasons too complex to go into here, we'd once had to rob a grave in the middle of the night, and Nevada had purchased a large amount of ancillary equipment for the endeavour, including these.

"I recognise these babies," said Tinkler happily, taking one of the flashlights. He'd been there in the graveyard with us, in the cold dark Kent night. Though he'd done precious little of the digging. But he was a keen participant now, as we shone the red beams of light down into the mouth of the speaker.

We could still see nothing, except the smooth tapering flare of the horn. "They could be at the bottom of the enclosure." Tinkler looked at me. The childlike eagerness in his face was touching.

So, while Nevada sat blithely drinking coffee and watching us with a slightly superior smile, we got down on our hands and knees on the floor in a grovelling posture and inspected the base of the speaker. On three sides the wood was a solid, flawless piece of cabinetry without so much as an indentation.

But on the fourth was a small access panel about the size of a magazine cover. Recessed in each corner of the panel were Phillips cross-head screws. I went back into the spare room and got my tools, including an electric screwdriver and a drill, in case we had to drill out one of the screws. Tinkler began to sweat at the very suggestion of this—drilling a hole in his beloved. But it looked to me like the screws hadn't been turned for decades and might be hopelessly frozen in place.

"How old is this speaker?" I said, lying on the floor with a manual screwdriver in my hand, trying to find an angle where I both had access to the screws and room to manipulate the tools.

"Over fifty years," said Tinkler. "Be careful there. You'll spoil the paintwork."

"Spoil the paintwork? It looks like a blind man with a brush in his mouth did it in half an hour while drunk."

"But it's still the *original* paint job."

I got the head of the screwdriver seated in the top left

screw and moved around on the floor to free my elbow so I could begin twisting it. Nothing. No give at all. I moved on to the next one. I worked each of the screws in turn, and on the second attempt they started to rotate. With a warm feeling of triumph, and Tinkler crooning encouragement, I switched to the electric screwdriver. At the sound of it, the cats peered down apprehensively from the top of the speaker. Then, when they realised that the noise wasn't actually coming from an electric cat-killing machine, they both hopped down to study it more closely. Tinkler was on his knees beside me and the cats were crouching between us.

Nevada came over and regarded us ironically. "Need any help there, boys?" she said. Then she bent down and caressed the cats. "And girls."

"Could you get the Hoover, please," I said. There was sweat running down from my hairline onto my face, and I considered asking my beloved to get a towel and swab my brow for me while I laboured nobly, like a surgeon in an operating theatre with his loyal nurse at his side.

But I decided I'd better not push my luck, and just settled for the Hoover.

The first screw came free and fell ringing onto the floor. Fanny pounced on it instantly and batted it across the room, chasing it and moving like quicksilver. Tinkler in turn was chasing her. "That's the original screw!" he cried. While he was retrieving it, I got the other three original screws out, falling one after the other musically onto the floor. Unlike her sister, Turk made no move to intercept the little bouncing objects. Instead, evidently bored by the whole enterprise, she disappeared out the cat flap into the garden.

Tinkler came back with the rogue screw and I gave him the other three. Then I swapped the full-sized Phillips screwdriver for a miniature flat-headed one and carefully inserted the narrow leading edge of the flat blade into the hairline gap where the panel met the rest of the speaker. Tinkler said, "Be careful not to—"

"Damage the original paintwork," I said. "Yes, I know." I used the screwdriver to gently pry the panel open. It gave way with a pop and a stale smell of dust, revealing a large hole in the base of the speaker cabinet. Tinkler aimed the flashlight inside.

We saw it right away. There in the thick dust of decades, a fat blue curl of cable like a nesting snake, and the gleam of a phono plug. "Where's that Hoover?" I said.

Nevada bustled in. "Coming right up."

We switched it on and Fanny fled from the noise. Nevada held the nozzle by the base of the speaker as we drew the cable out, catching a rich flow of dirty grey dust and fuzz. The vacuum cleaner consumed it cheerfully, preventing it from becoming an airborne health hazard. As a result of these ministrations, the cables arrived shiny and pristine in Tinkler's eager hands. "Are they the right ones?" said Nevada. "Your precious silver cables?"

"Oh, yes," said Tinkler happily, stroking them. "My pretties."

Nevada switched off the Hoover, and Tinkler and I were just discussing the possibility of giving the cables a test run in my system—"They've never been used. We'll have to run them in for a few hours before they start to sound good"—when Fanny came streaking into the room.

She took one look at the inviting new opening in the bottom of the big black box and, before we could stop her, shot straight inside.

Our cat was inside the speaker.

"Fanny!"

"Wonderful," said Nevada. "Now we've lost one of the cats." She turned to Tinkler. "Your speaker has *eaten* her. You're taking this with surprising equanimity," said Nevada. "Aren't you worried she'll damage the delicate electronics inside?"

"It's a horn," I said, in unison with Tinkler. He shrugged, as if to say, "You explain." So I did. "There isn't anything inside except air."

"Air in a cunningly shaped enclosure," added Tinkler smugly.

I went and kneeled on the floor by the speaker and listened to the mysterious scrabbling within. Nevada joined me. We tried to coax Fanny out, but she seemed entirely happy to remain in her cosy new dwelling place indefinitely. Tinkler sat on the sofa and watched our hapless efforts as if it was an entertainment being laid on especially for his benefit. "Have you got any grapes?" he said. He wanted to eat as he watched.

Eventually, by using a saucer of catnip as an enticement, we just about managed to lure Fanny out. I say 'just about' because when she poked her head and shoulders forth from the opening we tried, rather precipitately, to grab her and drag her the rest of the way.

But the nefarious cat managed a sinuous U-turn, twisting around in our grasp, and promptly scrambled back inside again.

"Professional cat-handlers at work," said Tinkler behind us, watching the proceedings.

I managed to hold onto Fanny's hind legs and, in a protracted and rather undignified fashion, succeeded in dragging her out. As she emerged reluctantly from the speaker, backwards, her front paws were the last thing to appear, desperately striving to retain a grip inside.

Which is why she was, in turn, dragging something else with her.

Between her paws was a square brown cardboard sleeve with a circular hole in the centre. Through the hole a bright maroon label was visible.

"Holy shit," said Tinkler. "Is that a record?"

2. SIGMUND FREUD

It was a record all right, a 78rpm disc. Tinkler had picked it up off the floor as soon as we'd got it away from Fanny— snatched it up, actually. He was staring at it, holding it so close to his face that it was almost touching his nose. "How the hell did this get in there?"

I said, "The same way your silver cables did."

Someone, over the years, had dropped the record inside the speaker.

Tinkler carefully hefted the 78 in his hands as if assessing its weight—which would have been considerable, compared to a modern record. "But how is it still in one piece?"

"What do you mean?" said Nevada.

"It's a 78," I said. "It's made of shellac."

"Oh well, that explains everything," she said.

I reached out my hand for the record, but Tinkler wouldn't give it to me. I turned to Nevada and explained, "It's a brittle substance. Much more brittle than vinyl. When you drop an LP on the floor it generally doesn't break.

Drop a 78, and it invariably does. Let go of your favourite recording and basically it's dustpan-and-brush time, as many a disgruntled music lover discovered."

"That's why they invented vinyl," said Tinkler.

"Well," I said, "it's one reason."

Fanny, who had now apparently forgotten all about her adventures inside the loudspeaker, wandered off. I put the panel back in place over the hole in the side, though, just to prevent embarrassing repetition.

Tinkler didn't offer to help. He was studying the label on the record. "Who is it by?" I said, lying on the floor, operating the screwdriver.

"Some jokers you've never heard of." He showed it to me. "The Flare Path Orchestra. Those exciting music stars of yesteryear." But he must have seen something in my face, because he changed his tune right away. "You're kidding," he said. "No way. You mean they really *are* exciting?" I didn't answer immediately. I got up and went over to the record shelf. I wanted to be certain.

But I knew I was right.

Nevada and Tinkler were watching me now as I found what I was looking for. A collection of airshots by the Glenn Miller Army Air Force Band, a double album in a gatefold sleeve. Nevada, unfortunately, recognised it.

She said, "Is that the one the Danish nymphomaniac gave you?"

"Swedish," I said. I opened the sleeve and quickly scanned the notes inside, which described the career of the Miller band in England during World War Two.

"Why do you always get to meet the nymphomaniacs?" said Tinkler. "You're dating *her*." He nodded at Nevada. "Nymphomaniacs are completely wasted on you."

I found what I was looking for. I was right. I set the Miller album aside and picked up the 78 again. "It's them," I said.

Tinkler came over and scooped up the Glenn Miller cover and began poring through the liner notes. "What's them? Them who?"

I said, "The Flare Path Orchestra was considered to be the finest British swing band of World War Two. It was made up of air force personnel."

"Hence the name," said Nevada.

"Exactly. And they played on a couple of occasions in a 'battle of the bands' with the Glenn Miller Army Air Force Band, who were the finest *American* outfit, when they were serving over here."

"Army Air Force?" said Nevada. "Surely that's a contradiction in terms."

Tinkler was reading the sleeve notes and whistling. "He's right. They were this fantastic British jazz and swing outfit. Apparently they kicked Glenn Miller's khaki-clad ass on at least one occasion in those battles of the bands. They were great. Legendary, in fact. And it says here that almost none of their recordings survive in any form." He looked hungrily at the 78, which I had now slid carefully from its cardboard sleeve.

The surface of the shellac was thickly matted with dust, but other than that it looked positively pristine. Tinkler came and peered over my shoulder as I flipped the record and checked the other side. It appeared just as good. Tinkler gave me a look and I nodded. We were off to the races.

Nevada came over and joined us. "It's worth something, then?"

I said, "I suspect it's worth quite a lot."

Tinkler chortled happily. "I'm such a lucky boy."

"What do you mean?" said Nevada. "Why are *you* lucky?"

"Finding such a rare record. And because that speaker's mine, and that record was in the speaker, the record is also mine." He paused to see if we followed this complex chain of legal reasoning. "All mine, do you hear me! And I'm going to sell it. And make lots and lots of money. My profits will be obscene."

"Wait a minute," said Nevada. "You never would have found that rare record in your speaker if it wasn't for our cat." She went over and stroked Fanny, who had wandered back in to see if she could wreak any more havoc. "Don't try and pull a fast one, mister."

"I love it when you call me mister," said Tinkler.

"I insist on a cut of your obscene profits. For Fanny."

"Oh, for Fanny, of course."

"I think thirty-five per cent would be fair."

"I suppose I could give you *one* per cent."

"Dream on," said Nevada. And they began negotiating in earnest. While they haggled I went in the kitchen to make some more coffee and to think and—I must admit—gloat. The record was a real find. When I went back into the sitting room with the coffee, Nevada and Tinkler had come to an amicable settlement and she was looking at the 78.

"Why don't you play it?" she said.

"I can't play 78s on my system."

She looked at me sceptically. "But your turntable has a 78rpm speed option. I've seen it." It was true. I'd been teaching Nevada turntable skills on the Garrard, and she was beginning to know her stuff. But a little bit of knowledge can be a dangerous thing.

I said, "I can spin the record at the right speed, all right. But if I tried to play it, it might damage our cartridge and stylus, to the tune of about a thousand quid."

"Ouch," said Nevada. "So you need to get a different cartridge and stylus?"

"That's right." Maybe a Stanton, I thought.

Tinkler said, "They used to play 78s with cactus needles."

Nevada laughed, then looked at me. "Really?" she said. "He's not pulling my leg?"

"Nope," said Tinkler. "It was an earlier, simpler, and more innocent time."

I looked at the record in my hands, cold and heavy and terribly fragile. "That's right, simpler and more innocent," I said, "with the entire world at war."

In the end Tinkler and I pooled our resources and bought a suitable cartridge from Lenny at the Vinyl Vault, who was something of a 78rpm specialist, and we were able to play the record.

"Lenny?" said Nevada. "Is he the chap who served us the lovely Chablis?"

"Served *you* the lovely Chablis."

"It was Grand Cru."

I said, "He's also the chap who asked me if I would ask *you* on his behalf if you would go away on a romantic holiday with him to a Greek island. For some reason I declined to do so."

"How selfish of you. Which island?"

"Mykonos."

"Pity. It's lovely there."

Nevada and Tinkler and I squeezed together onto the sofa, joined in short order by both the cats, and listened to the 78, using Lenny's cartridge. It was in astonishingly good shape for its age, and it sounded great. I began to reluctantly realise that at least some of the claims made for the audio quality of shellac were true. It was a different sound to vinyl, sharper yet also somehow smoother. However, each side of the rapidly spinning disc only lasted about three minutes.

Side one was the great Mercer/Arlen composition, 'Blues in the Night'. Side two was 'Elmer's Tune', possibly the finest dance number ever written by a mortician.

The playing of the Flare Path Orchestra was virtuosic, both bluesy and swinging. They also sounded startlingly modern. I might have been listening to a Ted Heath recording from the late 1950s. It had the same assurance and densely organised quality. But there was a quirkiness to the instrumentation that put me in mind of Spike Jones and, from a later era, Esquivel. It still sounded fresh today, first-class British jazz played by a bunch of young guys who were fighting, and dying, in a war against the forces of darkness.

We agreed that I would blog about the discovery of the record on my website. A lot of high rollers, big dealers and specialist collectors made a point of checking my site, and a mention of it there would actually drive the price up when Tinkler eventually came to auction it.

"It's like insider trading," said Nevada happily.

She took a photo of Tinkler's speaker, with Fanny posing on top of it, and I included that on the blog. She also wrote a first person cat's-eye point of view account of the discovery of the record and signed it with Fanny's name. This I didn't include. I told Nevada that the presence of talking cats on the website wouldn't exactly reinforce my reputation as a leading authority on rare records.

She took my point.

The page went live at midnight on a Friday and, by Monday, things started to happen.

The doorbell rang, and I opened the door to see a young man standing there in a black tunic and black trousers. It was a well-cut outfit, almost but not quite a uniform. In his hands he held a flat black cap. He had short blond hair and sunglasses and looked lean but athletic.

He gave me a noncommittal look and said, "Are you the Vinyl Detective?" His accent sounded South African. I told him I was and he nodded. "Would you mind waiting here a minute, please?" Then he walked off, leaving me bemused. It was a warm spring morning, so I didn't mind standing there in the open doorway, but I was baffled as to what the hell was going on.

Just then I heard the back door slam and Nevada came hurrying through the house to join me. "I was out in the garden," she said, "and I saw everything. Were they asking for directions to the Abbey?"

This was a common enough occurrence, and given the steady flow of wealthy high-fliers who ended up detoxing there, the most likely explanation for a liveried flunky turning up at our door. I shook my head. "No. Someone is looking for me."

Nevada did a little controlled Snoopy dance of excitement.

"Someone with a chauffeur! A genuine, honest-to-god chauffeur."

She fell silent as the young man came back. This time he was preceded by a woman. She was, I guessed, in her sixties or seventies. Well-preserved and clearly well-heeled, wearing a chic and expensive-looking black-and-white checked business suit and some gleaming, simple shoes which I saw Nevada eyeing enviously.

The woman was making agonisingly slow progress, leaning on a cane in her left hand while the chauffeur followed, walking a careful and polite step or two behind her, ready to intervene if she slipped.

She didn't slip.

I could see why the chauffeur hadn't wanted her to

make the trip to our front door until he was sure I was at home. The woman smiled at us as she drew near. "Good morning," she said. "I apologise for this ludicrous thing." She indicated the cane. "I hope to be off it soon, when the new hip has settled in." She smiled at us toothily. "I trust this isn't too ungodly an hour."

"No, that's all right," I said. "We're dressed, just about." Nevada gave me a sharp nudge. She scented money and didn't want me putting anyone off. "Why don't you come in and have a coffee?"

"Thank you, that would be lovely." She paused, leaning on the cane, and extended her right hand. "I'm Joan Honeyland." We shook hands. Her fingers were long and cool and had a dry, papery feel. She turned to the chauffeur. "Thank you, Albert. I'm all right now." Albert nodded and left, heading back to the car presumably.

I was quite interested to see what that car was and, as soon as we were inside, with the door shut and the coffee on, I left Nevada making a fuss over the woman and slipped out the back door. Fanny followed me as I crunched across the gravel and mewed at my feet as I took a furtive look over the back wall. There was a gleaming black vintage Mercedes parked in the street. It was old, but immaculate.

Like the record we'd found.

I went back inside to find Nevada and Miss Honeyland sitting at the table with coffee. "What a lovely place," she said, looking up at me as I came in. "So full of sunlight."

"It is when it's not full of huge ugly loudspeakers," said Nevada. Presumably for the benefit of the absent Tinkler, who had finally hired a van and some local goons and moved the damned thing to his place in Putney. He was going to have to remodel his house to make room for it. It was a measure of our shared obsession that this seemed entirely sensible to me, laudable even.

I sat down and poured myself a coffee. I noticed that Nevada had also set out our finest assortment of biscuits. She was smiling at the woman. "That's a lovely scarf," she said. "Is it Hermès?"

"Yes. It belonged to my mother."

"Is it silk or cashmere-silk?"

"Cashmere-silk."

At this point we were spared a detailed disquisition on neckwear because Fanny followed me in from the garden and headed straight for our visitor, rubbing herself around the legs of her chair. "What a lovely cat. May I pat her?"

"Of course," said Nevada. "Be our guest." She shot me a happy, we-just-got-lucky look. The woman was obviously a prospective client, and the kind who came from a long line of Hermès scarf wearers. The woman stroked Fanny, who dodged around under the table, circling her chair, always apparently fleeing but always ultimately returning to get a little more attention.

"How sweet," said Miss Honeyland. "Do you know what Sigmund Freud said about cats? He said, 'Time spent with cats is never wasted.' They are such lovely creatures. I wish I could have one myself."

"Why can't you?" said Nevada. It obviously wasn't a question of being able to afford the odd tin of tuna. The woman smiled and stopped stroking Fanny. She showed us her hand. There was an angry red rash across her knuckles.

"Allergic, I'm afraid."

"Your poor hand," said Nevada. "Can I get you some ointment?"

"No, please don't worry. It will soon fade." She leaned down to caress the cat some more. "And it's certainly worth it." At this point Fanny decided she'd had enough and headed for the kitchen, to see if her bowl had magically been filled with food. Miss Honeyland sighed and folded her hands on the table in front of her.

It was time for business.

She said, "I would like to hire you to find some records for me. Some very important and very valuable records."

3. LOCUST PIE

"My father was Lucian Honeyland," said the woman. "Perhaps you've heard of him?" I couldn't say that I had. Nevada clearly also drew a blank. The woman smiled with the satisfaction of someone pulling off a successful conjuring trick. "He was rather better known by his nickname—Lucky. A nickname he received during the war when he served in a bomber squadron. Commanded it, in fact."

I felt a ripple of premonition.

"On one memorable occasion he flew back from a mission with three out of four engines on his Lancaster destroyed and half of his crew dead. But he successfully landed and returned to his command. He also continued to fly active bombing missions over Germany, although the duties of command prevented him doing as much of this as he would have liked. Just as it prevented him from spending more time in his role as the leader of a band called the Flare Path Orchestra."

There it was.

She smiled at us. "Now, I understand you have found one of my father's records."

"God bless the Internet," said Nevada.

"Exactly. I read about your discovery online. And as you know, my father's records are quite hard to come by."

I said, "If you want to buy it—"

"I actually want to *employ* you," said Miss Honeyland. She smiled again, revealing her many impressive teeth. They might have belonged to a healthy horse. "To find as many of my father's recordings as you can." At the word 'employ' Nevada went into a kind of blissful trance state, sighing over her coffee as her eyes glazed over. I must admit, I was quite pleased myself.

"You see—and I apologise if this is a rather discursive explanation—my father used to do all his writing in a garage at our house. It was quite a large, detached garage, a small building in its own right. He took it over and turned the cars out. Rather fine and expensive cars. He exposed them to the elements. Can you imagine? Our old Wolseley out under a tarpaulin in all weathers. Anyway, he converted the garage into a kind of office and study, and it was there that he wrote his books." She smiled at all of us. "All of his beloved books."

I hadn't known that Lucian Honeyland had also been an author. But at this point I assumed she was referring to some tiresome volumes of military memoirs, or, at best, his musings on music. Perhaps privately printed as the old airman's vanity project.

So I just nodded.

"Now we intend to turn the garage into a museum, so people can see where the books were written. There is a great deal of interest, of course."

"Of course," I said politely.

"And the museum exhibitions will cover all phases of my father's life. Including, naturally, his air force career and his wartime years and his band activities and his love of jazz. So I desperately need some of his records—as many as we can get our hands on. And, as I've said, they are in short supply."

"Rare," said Nevada, as if she was suddenly an expert on the subject. "Very rare."

Miss Honeyland smiled at me. "Which is where your specialist talents come in."

I summarised what I thought she wanted: "You'd like me to, if possible, find one copy of each of his records?"

"Not just one copy. I am very eager for duplicates. As you know, these 78rpm records often turn up in a damaged state." She'd obviously done her homework. "Ideally I would like to be able to choose among multiple copies of each recording, so that I can select the ones with the best sound quality, which I will have digitally transferred and preserved. The spare copies can be used for display purposes in the museum." She smiled. "So it really is a case of the more the merrier."

"Are you suggesting paying us on a per-disc basis?" said Nevada, who had now obviously emerged fully from her trance.

"If you find that satisfactory. And it isn't just 78s we're

after. Any kind of recordings you might happen on. I believe there may be what was called a Victory disc or V-Disc."

I nodded. Some great jazz had been recorded on V-Discs during the war. It had actually been an early 12-inch vinyl format, though played at 78rpm. "I would also be very grateful if you put me in touch with anyone you discover in your travels who knew my father at all well. We are absolutely on the lookout for all anecdotes and stories about him from people who knew him in those days. Fellow musicians from the Flare Path Orchestra, for example."

"And would there be a fee structure covering any such discoveries?" said Nevada. "In addition to whatever recordings we find."

"Naturally. And a bonus payable on a successful conclusion of our researches."

"Hang on," I said. "Just wait a minute…"

Nevada sighed. "Oh, this is where he gets all hot and bothered and puts his foot down about some small detail. Please ignore him. It's just a ritual he has." Miss Honeyland laughed.

"Okay," I said. "But it has to be said. My area of expertise is finding vinyl records, from a later period."

"Some of my father's records are on vinyl," said Miss Honeyland mildly.

"Yes," I said, "but mostly they are 78s, on shellac. And they're more difficult to find. They generally come in anonymous sleeves, they're likely to be misfiled—where they are filed at all—and on top of everything else, they're extremely fragile. We might find them in small pieces, or most likely not find them at all."

Nevada winked at Miss Honeyland. "He just likes to have his say."

I said, "Look, I'm the *Vinyl* Detective."

"And now you're the Shellac Shamus," said Nevada. And Miss Honeyland chuckled again.

And that was that.

Just before Miss Honeyland left she confided that she was indeed interested in acquiring the record we'd found inside the speaker. Tinkler's record.

"It will be the first of our finds for the museum," she said. I explained that it belonged to a friend of ours and he would be thinking of auctioning it. "Then please have a word with him and see if he can be inveigled to part with it. I will happily pay him an advantageous pre-emptive bid to forestall any auction. Tell him to name his price." Then she left.

As soon as she closed the door, Nevada turned to me and said, "Advantageous. Pre-emptive bid. Name your price." She did another little dance. "You've got a job! Let's celebrate."

Our celebrations consisted of buying some even better than usual wine and food, including some diced lamb for the cats, and inviting Tinkler around for supper. We had to talk business with him anyway, about the record. And, for his pleasure and ours, we also invited Agatha DuBois-Kanes, known to her friends as Clean Head, a nickname she'd acquired because of her fashionably shaved scalp. She was a good friend and the nearest thing we'd ever have to a chauffeur of our own.

Clean Head drove a London taxi.

Although not when she was drinking, which we did a great deal of that evening, working our way through the bottles of Rhône red that Nevada had so carefully selected, in descending price order. "Always drink the best stuff first," said Nevada, "while you still have a palate with which to appreciate it."

I turned to Tinkler, who was trying not to make big mooncalf eyes at Clean Head—and failing. I said, "You'll never guess who our new client is the daughter of."

"Deceased World War Two aviation hero and band leader. Boring. Heard all about it."

"Deceased aviation hero, band leader and beloved children's author," said Nevada. "I looked him up online and discovered he was actually *the* Lucky."

"Really?" said Tinkler and Clean Head simultaneously. This seemed to impress them both.

"*The* Lucky?" asked Clean Head.

"Yes."

"Locust pie!" said Tinkler.

"Crunch crunch crunch!" said Clean Head.

"'Ugh,' said Farmer Henry," said Nevada.

I looked blankly at them all. "Okay…"

"You mean you never read *Farmer Henry Versus the Locusts*?" said Nevada.

"Or any of the other books by Lucky?" said Clean Head. I shrugged. "Apparently not."

"What were you reading when you were eight years old?"

"Probably Miles Davis's autobiography," said Tinkler. "It would be all 'motherfucker' this and 'motherfucker' that."

* * *

The following day, as a direct sequel to this conversation, Nevada gave me a present. She'd found it in a charity shop while hunting for designer clothes at low, low prices. It was a children's book. A dog-eared old copy of *Farmer Henry Versus the Locusts*. The author was given as 'Lucky' but the copyright notice on the publication page—the book had come out in 1955—listed Lucian Honeyland.

I was curious and I read the book. It didn't take long. It was lavishly and luridly illustrated—not by the author—with brightly coloured, semi-abstract images of the characters, all of whom were cartoonish and some of whom were downright scary. It detailed the story of Farmer Henry who was the only agriculturist in the peaceful land of Green Valley who recognised the danger of the coming plague of locusts.

In a surprisingly accurate, though simplified, account of insect swarming behaviour, Farmer Henry explained how apparently innocent grasshoppers could, if their numbers swelled to a critical point, turn into an evil, ravening horde of locusts. Everybody ignored his warnings and, sure enough, the population of locusts exploded and went on the rampage. All the other farms were wiped out and Farmer Henry's was the last bastion against the attackers.

With the help of a friendly cast of farm animals, including pigs, horses, chickens, dogs and cats—all of whom could speak, of course; Nevada's version of Fanny would have fitted right in—Farmer Henry fought a plucky last-ditch defence against the evil hordes of hideously ugly rapacious insects.

It was a gory and protracted battle, but in the end the good guys won.

Farmer Henry and the animals found themselves knee-deep in dead locusts. They had to be got rid of somehow, so what the chickens couldn't eat was taken into the kitchen and a big feast was prepared. All the animals sat down with Farmer Henry at his table for the celebration dinner. But the big gag was the farmer didn't know what was in the pie.

So he bit into it innocently. Cue: *Crunch crunch crunch!* And: *'Ugh,' said Farmer Henry. Locust pie!*

The end.

I could see why kids loved it. It read like Roald Dahl with the moral governor removed.

That evening Miss Honeyland was scheduled to come around and collect the record that Tinkler had quickly agreed to sell—as well he might, given that he was being paid a small fortune for it and he wasn't really interested in 78s anyway—and which he had left with us after our celebration dinner.

I was in the kitchen, getting ready to make tea of all things. This was for Miss Honeyland. Nevada had somehow discovered that, although she'd politely sipped our expensive and dwindling supply of finest coffee, the old bat would actually have preferred a cup of tea. As zero hour drew close, Fanny suddenly came scooting in through the garden cat flap. A moment later the back door opened and

Nevada hurried in. "My god," she said. "Their car."

"What is it?" We all bustled back outside, Fanny zipping along at our heels as we tried to peer over the garden wall without being too obvious about it. I understood what Nevada meant. The gorgeous gleaming Mercedes we'd seen the other day was no more. It took me a moment to even recognise it as the same vehicle.

It looked like someone had worked it over with a giant sledgehammer.

The side panels were caved in, the chrome shattered, the paintwork scarred. I was amazed that it was even roadworthy, it looked like such a wreck. We ducked behind the wall as the door popped open and Albert the chauffeur stepped out. He had a bandage around his head. As he helped Miss Honeyland out of the car we hurried back inside the house.

"What the hell?" I said.

"Did you see that?" said Nevada. Then, "Is the tea ready?"

"I think I've forgotten how to make it. It's been so long."

The doorbell rang. "Oh, for god's sake," said Nevada. "Here, let me do it. You go and let her in."

I let Miss Honeyland in and guided her to a seat at the dining table while Nevada wrestled with tea-making. "We saw the car," I said.

"Oh, did you?"

"What happened?"

She sighed. "Someone tried to run us off the road."

"What?"

"A Range Rover. It came up behind us, then passed us

on the inside and swerved and hit us, and very nearly drove us in the path of an oncoming lorry." She studied me, her eyes bright. "If it hadn't been for Albert's excellent reflexes, that would have been our lot." Things had gone very quiet in the kitchen while Nevada listened to this. Now she came through and sat down with us.

"So, naturally enough, we were rather shaken and we pulled over onto the side of the road. And then who should pull up just ahead of us?"

"The Range Rover," I said.

"Yes. There were three men inside. We thought they'd come to offer help, or to apologise. At least, that's what I thought. Albert got out of the car to remonstrate with them. And then they got out. All three of them. There was something about the way they were standing there. I leaned out of the car and called for Albert to get back in. I was too late, though. The men had already surrounded him. And there was a scuffle."

"My god," said Nevada.

"Now, Albert can acquit himself quite handily in almost any situation." There was a note of quiet pride in her voice. "But with odds of three to one against, even he was in trouble. Luckily, at that moment a police car was passing, and it slowed down to see if there had been an accident. The three men immediately got into the Range Rover and drove off. By the time we were able to explain to the police what had actually happened, they were long gone. I don't suppose I could trouble you for a cup of tea? Or coffee would be fine."

"No, no, we have tea," said Nevada, hurrying out to resume her interrupted preparations. Miss Honeyland looked at me.

"They did find the Range Rover. Abandoned. It had been stolen a few hours earlier. The theory of the police, in so far as they can be said to have such a thing, is that the whole incident comes under the three broad headings of 'joyriding', 'hit-and-run', and 'road rage'." She studied me with her pale, intelligent eyes.

I said, "But you have a different theory."

"That's right."

Nevada came back in with a teapot and three cups on a tray. I hoped she wasn't going to serve me any of the stuff.

"I think the incident is considerably more complicated, and more serious, than that. For example, Albert is the least paranoid soul, but he says he thinks he glimpsed one of them holding a gun. One of the men."

I said, "You think you were singled out. That you were a deliberate target."

"Yes, I'm afraid I do."

"Why do you think that?" said Nevada.

The old woman picked up her teacup and held it carefully in both hands, as though warming them. "I'm afraid I haven't been entirely candid with you."

"How so?"

She set the cup down, her tea untasted. We probably all would have been better off with coffee. "Well, everything I told you was absolutely accurate, as far as it went. But what I left out was the background, so to speak. I am indeed desperately looking for my father's recordings to go into the museum we're building. But I didn't tell you why the museum is so significant. You see, I am the executor of my father's literary estate, and his heritage is entirely in my care. And I have reached a point in my life where I want to be certain that the future of his work, and his reputation, is assured. So I have set about the museum project, but I also have started looking for a buyer."

"A buyer?" said Nevada.

"For all his literary properties." She picked up the cup again and this time took a sip. I could smell the gentle fragrance of the tea now. It smelled nice enough, but it certainly wasn't coffee. She looked at us over the rim of the cup. "You may have heard about what became of the literary estates of A. A. Milne and Beatrix Potter and Enid Blyton."

"They were bought by big American media conglomerates, weren't they?" said Nevada.

Miss Honeyland nodded. "Yes, for the most part. The Americans recognise the value of timeless children's literature. And they are willing to pay a fair price for it. Some of the estates I mentioned were purchased for eight- or nine-figure sums." She let this sink in as she took another sip of tea, then lowered the cup. I was thinking, *Nine figures. A hundred million dollars. Yes, people have been killed for less.*

"And that is the kind of price I intend to secure for my father's work. From a major and reputable buyer. I'm rather hoping the Disney people will prevail."

"Disney?" said Nevada.

"Yes, or DreamWorks, but the point is that there are also

many other parties who would be happy to acquire the rights to my father's books. And not all of them are reputable or willing to pay a fair sum. Of course, I have been seeing off such time-wasters in no uncertain terms." She smiled thinly. "But if I was to suddenly and unexpectedly pass away, my father's estate would fall into the hands of lawyers who aren't as scrupulous or motivated as I am and who might also be rather impatient and greedy. They might not be willing to go to the trouble of a painstaking and protracted negotiating process of the sort I am currently conducting."

I said, "You think they might go for a quick sale."

She nodded. "Yes. For a quick profit. Luckily I am still here, to prevent something like that happening."

Nevada said, "But you actually think someone tried to deliberately run you off the road and—"

"That is what I suspect, yes. But that's all right. Because now they've made their move. And failed."

I said, "What makes you think they won't try again?"

She smiled at me. "Because I have just issued a press release, stating that if I should die before negotiations are completed—"

"Heaven forbid," said Nevada.

"Heaven forbid, if I should die before negotiations are completed, then my father's entire estate—lock, stock and barrel—goes to one of our largest and most robust charities." She nodded with satisfaction. "And then no one will see a penny from it."

"Except the charity."

"Except the charity." She suddenly stood up. I was

expecting her to reach for her cane, but she seemed determined not to use it as she took a few careful steps around the room. Her walking seemed to have improved since I'd last seen her. She sat down on the sofa and picked up the book that was lying on the coffee table. It was *Farmer Henry Versus the Locusts*. She studied it fondly for a moment, then looked at me.

"Have you been reading this?"

"Yes. Somehow I missed it when I was a kid."

"What do you think of it?"

Nevada shot me a warning look. I said, "Well, I…"

Miss Honeyland leafed through the book. "I know, I know, so gruesome and bloodthirsty! All those descriptions of locusts being crushed and crunched and spurting goo and split open and baked in pies." She closed the book and set it down again. "I suppose it was the war. I mean, my father's sensibilities were inevitably shaped—I imagine 'coarsened' some might say—by the violence and the bloodshed." She smiled impishly. "But children love it!"

"No kidding," I said. Nevada refilled Miss Honeyland's teacup and took it over to her.

"Yes, they absolutely love it. And it's the gruesome gore that they love best. Thank you, dear."

Nevada handed her the cup and sat down beside her on the sofa. "He must have been quite a character, your father."

"Oh yes." She looked at me. "You would have got along like a house on fire. He loved jazz, too. When he was off duty he could generally be found roaring around England on his motorbike, whizzing down country roads in the blackout, racing off to hear jazz being played in some godforsaken place. Bomber Command gave him a special permit so he'd get waved through at checkpoints." She smiled nostalgically, nodding.

"His boss, Bomber Harris, intervened personally when there was talk of my father being reprimanded for listening to German broadcasts featuring a particular Berlin swing band that he adored." She drained her cup and set it down. "And he could have got into a great deal of trouble for that. His sister, my aunt, had been a notorious Nazi sympathiser before the war—sort of a Mitford in a minor key—and the stink of her reputation lingered, damaging his career."

She stood up decisively. "Still, I mustn't bore you with ancient history."

"You're not boring anyone," said Nevada.

"You're very kind. But I must be off. Albert has an appointment at the doctor's." She smiled, showing her many healthy and sizeable teeth. "And the Mercedes has an appointment at the garage."

After she was gone, Nevada said, "Nine figures. Maybe I should write a children's book."

We caught the news that evening and it gave the official version of Miss Honeyland and Albert's close encounter—joyriders, shockingly dangerous behaviour, a stolen vehicle abandoned without a trace of the culprits.

4. SHEDS

I said, "The problem is, I know about vinyl. All my sources are for vinyl."

Nevada smiled a superior little smile. "You always say something like this, you always have to have your moan. And then you buckle down to the job at hand, and it turns out you actually know exactly what to do. Who to speak to."

"To whom to speak," said Tinkler. He was sitting opposite me at the breakfast table, polishing his cutlery with a paper towel. This was one of his annoying habits. I think he'd once seen a movie about Howard Hughes.

"Fuck off, Tinkler," said Nevada. She looked at him, eyebrows raised in studious enquiry. "How was my grammar there?"

"Spot on."

She sat down at the dining table, and I went into the kitchen and finished sautéing some mushrooms while they bickered. I added asparagus, cooked earlier, to the pan then poured in the eggs. As they began to set I stirred in sweet butter and truffle oil. Scenting that things were hotting up, Nevada came in and started making toast. I served up and we rejoined Tinkler, who couldn't conceal his delight at the arrival of food. We all sat down.

"What was I saying?" I took a sip of my coffee.

Nevada started to eat her scrambled eggs, realised they were too hot and shoved them aside for the time being. "You were making excuses about not being an expert on 78s and shellac and all that. But you must know someone who *is* an expert."

I sipped my coffee. It was just a little too cold. I considered trying my eggs but I suspected they would be just a little too hot. Something's never quite right. "Well," I said, "I suppose there is Leo Noel."

"The human palindrome," said Tinkler. He had already enthusiastically started his eggs. I tried mine but they were indeed still a little too hot. This didn't seem to deter Tinkler, though.

"The human what?" said Nevada. Then, "Oh, I see."

"But I'm trying to avoid that option at all costs."

"Why?" said Nevada.

"Yeah, why?" said Tinkler. "You're so negative."

"Tinkler, it's ten in the morning. What are you even *doing* here?"

He looked contrite, but kept eating. "I heard you were making the scrambled eggs with the truffle oil. I couldn't stay away. I'm sorry."

"How did you know…" I looked at Nevada.

"Yes," she said. "Sorry."

I shook my head. "We could be having a nice quiet

breakfast on our own, you know."

"We have to keep old Tinkler sweet. We may need a ride in his car sometime."

"That's right. You might need a ride in my car sometime." Tinkler stirred the eggs with his fork. "Ah, you've used the thin little asparagus spears this time. They're *much* nicer."

I said, "I'm so pleased."

Nevada said, "Now, about the 78s." She was all business. "Didn't you say that nice chap Lenny is a bit of an expert? Lenny at the Vinyl Vault?"

"Nice chap?" I said.

"Nice to me. Gave me some nice wine. Wanted to take me to the Greek islands…"

"Just one island," I said. "The problem with Lenny is that he only collects classical and opera. Not jazz or swing."

"Well, surely it's still worth giving him a ring?"

So I gave him a ring, explained what I was looking for, and he laughed derisively. "I don't collect that sort of stuff. How long have you known me? Ten years? More? And you still don't know that I only collect classical and opera."

"Is that right, Lenny?" I said patiently.

"Why don't you try our old friend, the human palindrome? Did you think of that?"

"Yes." I suppressed a sigh. "But I'm trying to avoid the possibility."

"I know what you mean. By the way, that friend of yours, Nebraska…"

"Nevada. Girlfriend actually. She isn't going on holiday with you, Lenny."

"Pity. You can't blame a bloke for trying, though. Anyway I've never heard of those pillocks. What were they called? The Flared Pants Orchestra?"

"The Flare Path Orchestra."

"Never heard of them."

I went to Styli, a record shop located just off Tottenham Court Road. It had once been a great establishment under its old owner, Jerry. Since his untimely death it had gone subtly but emphatically into decline. Tinkler tagged along with me. He had once bought a staggering collection of original Chess blues LPs from the place and he had never quite got over it. Now he was like those tragic water fowl you read about who keep returning to their wetland habitat long after it has been transformed into a shopping mall, hoping somehow that the good old days will recur.

They didn't recur today. I asked about 78s and had to listen to a long-winded explanation about how Jerry had been the shellac expert, which I knew. And that he was dead. Which I also knew. I also knew who had killed him, or at least had a pretty good idea.

Which is more than most people could say, including the police.

"So nobody here specialises in 78s anymore?" I asked. Solemnly shaken heads all round. "So what happens if somebody comes in with a big collection on shellac?"

"We send them to Lenny at the Vinyl Vault. But he only buys classical and opera."

Tinkler and I said our goodbyes at Putney. When I got home Nevada saw how glum I looked and instantly inferred that my mission had come to nothing. She picked up Fanny and sat down beside me and said, "Why don't you try your friend the human anagram?"

"Palindrome. All right. I suppose it has come to that."

We caught the train to Enfield Town and then walked to Leo's house. This involved going along Willow Road, past Peartree Road and Orchard Way. It had been a long time since the willows and pears and orchards had been here— if indeed they ever had. But there was still a surprising number of plane trees lining the street, and the big houses had equally big gardens lurking in the shadows behind them.

I surprised myself by remembering the way, and we didn't have to consult Nevada's smartphone at any point. We walked past high hedges up to the house, and I rang the doorbell. As we waited for Leo to let us in I said, "I've arranged for him to play us a record before we look for anything. Just so you can hear what a 78 sounded like on an old phonograph. Get the whole historical shellac experience, so to speak."

"That was sweet of you."

"That way at least we have achieved something by coming here."

Nevada shook her head. "Tinkler's right. You are negative." Then she smiled as the door opened and Leo Noel let us in. He was a tall, thin man in his late thirties, though he looked older. His blond hair was thinning while still managing to be unruly. He smiled as he shook hands with us, but his watery blue eyes were wary. Leo had lived in this house alone since his mother had died and he didn't get out as much as perhaps he should.

He had dressed for company, though, and looked improbably dapper in flannel cricket trousers, white shirt, white cricket sweater and navy cricket blazer. A gleaming blue and yellow striped tie was loosely knotted at his throat. I suspected it was the club tie that matched the badge on the blazer.

Leo didn't actually play cricket. All the clothes had belonged to his father. They fit him quite nicely, though.

"Would you like a glass of Perrier?"

"Oh, yes please," said Nevada, who had been briefed for this eventuality. Somewhere Leo had got hold of the notion that Perrier water was the ultimate luxury to proffer to your guests. This also, of course, got him neatly off the hook for making tea and—more to the point—coffee for anyone who visited. He did quite a nice job of presentation, though, serving the Perrier with ice and a slice of either lemon or lime. Today it was lime.

We sipped and carried our cool, tinkling glasses through to what had once been the family sitting room. But now all the furniture had been removed except for a varied horde of small tables of all different shapes and sizes. And on every table was an old-fashioned gramophone. It was like a museum, although no museum would have jammed its exhibits so close together. You had to edge through the crowded room, finding a route to thread your way between the tables. Sometimes you had to walk sideways.

Leo knew the path, though, and we followed him.

First he went to the far side of the room. There were bookcases lining all the walls of the room, and of course these were full of not books but 78rpm records. They were stored in anonymous, generic brown cardboard sleeves but each one had a computer-printed label on it, full of cryptic information. Small rectangles of coloured paper stuck out from the shelves of records at intervals. There were numbers and letters written on the slips of paper. I had no idea what his cataloguing system was, but it was clearly nothing as straightforward as alphabetical order.

In any case, Leo knew what he was looking for; he set his drink aside, went straight to it and took it down from the shelf, his eyes gleaming. "Good choice," he said, turning to us.

Nevada looked at me. "You chose a record especially for me?"

I had indeed rung Leo the night before and suggested what he should choose for his demonstration disc. "Something I thought you'd like."

"Oh, you'll like this," agreed Leo, winding his way back among the tables. We followed.

"How sweet," said Nevada.

Leo chose one of his gramophones and put the record on its turntable. The gramophone had a large, florid horn. He tapped it. "Note the fact that the horn is made out of steel," he said, "an immediate indication that this is a proper vintage machine and not a modern counterfeit cunningly fabricated on the Indian subcontinent. All the so-called 'Bombay Fakes' have *brass* horns of course."

"Of course."

"And naturally the brass they use on them is shiny and new because they can't be bothered to go to the trouble of making it look properly aged. A proper counterfeit would involve treating the brass to make it look like it had verdigris and the proper patina of age."

Finally, lecture concluded, he played the record for us. It was old and scratchy and tinny, but it sounded wonderful. It was 'Black Bottom', sung by Annette Hanshaw, recorded in 1926. It wasn't really jazz, despite the presence of Red Nichols on the session, and it was way too early for me. And yet...

I'd heard Annette Hanshaw on the radio once and immediately fallen in love.

Nevada listened, rapt. I found myself swaying in time to the music. Leo regarded us happily, the master magician watching his illusion unfold. As the song came to an end, Annette signed off with a pert spoken aside. "That's all!" she said. From another world, from another century, she was alive again in those mischievous words.

"That's all!" repeated Nevada delightedly.

"It was kind of her catchphrase," I said. "She says it at the end of quite a few of her songs."

"I can find out the exact number," offered Leo. "I've got my annotated copies of the Brian Rust discography next door."

"That won't be necessary, Leo. But could we hear it again?" Leo cheerfully played the record again and Nevada listened, spellbound. I was tapping my feet. Even Leo was nodding in time to the music. It was a good rhythm number. Again it ended and Annette Hanshaw declared, "That's all."

"That's all!" said Nevada. She looked at me. "What a charming performance. She's lovely, isn't she?"

"Yes," I said.

Leo was inspecting the tonearm on the record player, frowning at it. "Time I changed the needle on this." He glanced at us. "You have to change the needle virtually every time you play a record, otherwise they become blunt and you risk damage to the playing surface. It means one gets through a great many needles."

"Why don't you use cactus needles?" said Nevada.

Leo gaped at her. "You know what? That is exactly what I was planning to do. How unusual to meet a girl—I mean a woman—who knows about such things." He grinned at her, enchanted. I wondered glumly if invitations to an Hellenic idyll would be forthcoming. He saw that Nevada's glass was half empty and he took it from her and rushed out to refill it.

Nevada turned to me. "What a lovely song you chose for me." She kissed me. "Although one must have reservations about the lyrics, with their unforgivable period reference to 'darkies'. I wouldn't be in a hurry to play it to Clean Head, in case she might throw it out the window like a Frisbee."

"While giving the Black Power salute," I said.

* * *

Leo sat us down beside his computer, a surprisingly modern PC incongruously perched between two ancient gramophones, while he looked through his database for anything recorded by the Flare Path Orchestra. He did several different kinds of searches, using different fields. It was clearly an elaborate piece of bespoke software. A sudden suspicion came over me. "Where did you get your database, Leo?"

"Tinkler designed it for me. I swapped him some John Mayall albums I found at a boot fair."

"Typical."

He shook his head as he studied the screen. "Sorry. It looks like I've got nothing at all by them." He turned and smiled at us. "We can still look out in the garden, though."

"The garden?" said Nevada.

"Yes. Only a small part of my collection has been catalogued on the computer. The bulk of it is outside." We followed him out the back door into what had once been a very large garden.

I suppose it was still large, it just didn't seem that way because it was now as densely crowded with small sheds as his dining room had been with tables. Unlike the tables, though, the sheds were all of a uniform design—virtually identical, in fact—and arranged in neat rows. Between the sheds were thin bands of grass planted with crocus and daffodil bulbs, which were just beginning to come into blossom, small splashes of yellow and purple and blue.

"The flowers are a nice touch," I said.

"Thank you. I wouldn't want it to seem like I'd given

the garden over entirely to my collection."

He led us to a shed and opened the door. Inside it was cool but dry—ideal conditions for storing records. Leo clicked a switch, and a glaring fluorescent ceiling light flickered on, providing ample illumination. Except for a shallow entrance area, the entire shed was filled with shelves. And on every shelf were stacked boxes. Squat, cylindrical boxes like a stack of film cans or biscuit tins. Most of them were tattered and faded but they had clearly once been cheerfully coloured in a variety of designs, floral or geometric.

"Are they hat boxes?" said Nevada. Then, half to herself, "They'd have to be damned small hats."

"No," said Leo. He took one and opened it. Resting snugly inside was a stack of dusty, brownish-black 78s. "They were purpose-built to hold these."

I said, "Where did you get those boxes, Leo?"

He closed the box again. "They're jolly hard to find. But luckily I've managed to secure enough of them to store my overflow collection in while I'm cataloguing it. Of course, once I move the records indoors they'll all have square cardboard sleeves and they won't fit into these boxes anymore."

"Because you can't square the circle," said Nevada. "Or circle the square."

He hooted with laughter, rather overdoing it, I thought. "Precisely! It's a shame, but it can't be avoided." He turned to the wall beside the door where a fat red book was sitting on a small purpose-built shelf. He picked up the book and leafed through it. There were alphabetical tabs on the edges of the pages. Each page was densely crammed with handwriting in blue ballpoint pen. He flipped to F and studied each page carefully. "No. Sorry. Nothing by the Flare Path Orchestra." He put the book back and switched off the light. We stepped out of the shed, back into the garden. It was a mild spring day and the flowers seemed to be glowing in the soft light.

If we hadn't been crammed into a small space by tall looming sheds that hemmed us in on every side, it would have been quite pleasant.

Leo closed the shed behind him and said, "I'm going to do a recursive clockwise cataloguing project. By recursive I mean I work my way in a clockwise fashion through the four blocks of sheds, but also through the four sheds in each block. Thus, starting with North West Zero One I will work my way through to North West Zero Four, then on to the next block with North East Zero One and so on until I reach South West Zero Four."

I liked the way each shed had a zero in its designation, in case he needed to add ten more. "That sounds like quite the project, Leo," I said. "Where are you at with it at the moment?"

He frowned thoughtfully. "By the summer I estimate I'll have completed the cataloguing of NW Zero One." He nodded at the shed we had just been in.

"So you haven't even done the first shed?"

"I've made a start. I've made a very good start." There was the sound of a telephone ringing—an old-fashioned landline, of course—from within the house. Leo turned his head eagerly towards the sound. "You'll have to excuse me for just a moment. I've got some bids in at an auction in Scotland, and that's probably news of them now. I'll be right back." He turned and scampered towards the house.

When he was gone, Nevada said, "Auction?"

"Of 78s."

"Of course." She looked around at the sheds surrounding us. "Because he doesn't have enough already."

"Leo has a bit of a problem. Unkind outsiders might call it an obsession."

"No kidding. Has he ever had a girlfriend?"

"Oh sure," I said.

"No, really?"

"A few years ago he was with this Dutch girl he picked up on a train."

"You're joking," said Nevada.

"No, it was quite a passionate affair. They were banging each other's brains out."

"You're joking!"

"She wasn't bad looking, either."

Nevada glanced towards the house to make sure our gossip was secure, then eagerly back at me. "What happened?"

"They split up after a couple of months."

"The passion just burned itself out?"

"No, actually. What happened was he was wearing his cricket gear when he met her on the train—all this stuff that he inherited from his dad."

"He looks quite natty in it," said Nevada. "One can see how it might turn a girl's head, especially if she's sporty."

"Well, she was sporty. That was the problem. She took one look at Leo and thought he must at the very least be an extremely keen amateur cricket player, if not a full-blown professional. But then she found out that he didn't even know which end of the bat to hold."

"It took her a couple of months to find that out?"

"Apparently whenever the conversation turned to cricket he'd just nod sagely. And that worked pretty well, as far as it went."

Nevada glanced back towards the house and sighed. "What a shame. If he'd just taken the trouble to learn a bit about the game, things might have turned out differently. He might still be with her. I mean, all he had to do was spend a little time looking up cricket online."

I said, "As far as Leo is concerned, any time not spent listening to 78s is time wasted."

"With the honourable exception of banging Dutch girls."

"With that honourable exception." The back door opened and Leo came back into the garden. He looked pleased with himself.

I said, "How did the auction go?"

"Rather well. Very well in fact. I managed to get both the lots I was bidding on."

"So there will be more 78s arriving?" said Nevada.

"Yes, a couple of large crates." Leo didn't actually rub his hands together or anything like that, but he did grin happily at the prospect.

"Where will you put them?"

"I think there's some room in South East Zero Three."

Inside the house, the phone started ringing again. "Will you excuse me? That will be the auction house again, to arrange shipping." Leo hurried towards the house, calling over his shoulder. "Feel free to start looking."

"Start looking?" said Nevada.

I gestured towards the sheds. "These aren't catalogued. That means we can't just look in a little book. We'd have to sort through every record in them. And Leo thinks we're going to."

"Well, aren't we?"

I said, "Oh, come on."

"Oh, come on what? You don't mean to suggest that we've come all the way out here and we're not even going to try and look?"

I shrugged. "Okay. Be my guest."

Nevada stared at me for a minute, then turned to the nearest shed and opened the door. I joined her as she switched on the light and stood staring at the shelves.

"Right," she said. "Let's get started."

We each chose a box, opened it, and started looking through the records inside. This involved laboriously taking them all out and then putting them carefully back in. I found a recording of 'Two Tiny Finchs' (sic) on the Bel Canto label and Miss Florrie Forde singing 'It's a Different Girl Again' on the Zonophone label. But no Flare Path Orchestra. By the time we'd each started on our third box, Nevada sighed and looked at me.

"It's hopeless, isn't it?" she said. I shrugged again. She put the records back in her box and put the lid on it. I did the same. We switched off the light and stepped out of the shed, back into the daylight, which was just beginning to fade towards evening. Nevada stared at the grid of sheds, standing all around us.

"That's all!" she said.

With nowhere else to turn, I tried the Internet. And I came up with quite a promising website devoted to the wartime bands. It featured a link to an enthusiast who specialised in none other than the Flare Path Orchestra, or *FPO* as it was unhelpfully abbreviated. I clicked the link and it led me to a website page that was under construction.

But there was an email address.

And a list of records for sale.

My initial spasm of excitement subsided when I realised that the 'records' in question were actually CDs, but by this time I was just about ready to settle for anything. I thought if I could give Miss Honeyland some CD transfers of her father's recordings, that at least would be a start.

So I sent a message saying I would like to buy copies of all the CDs. Then, as an afterthought, I included an enquiry.

These are the original recordings by the Flare Path Orchestra, aren't they?

I got a prompt reply.

Sorry, all modern re-recording by a local big band. Original FPO records are as scarce as hen's teeth!

I wrote back that I was becoming painfully aware of this. But I asked if he might have any of the original 78s in his personal collection that he might be willing to sell, or to have copied.

Again, a swift reply.

I wish. Sorry. All I have are the modern CDs and a photograph.

Well, that was that. I sent him a thank you message, then I went into the kitchen, intending to make some coffee. But instead I went back to my computer and opened up my emails again. I typed another message.

What photograph?

5. GROUP PORTRAIT

"So that photo," said Tinkler. "It's a picture of the orchestra? The whole orchestra?"

"Yes," I said. "It's like one of those photographs you get of an entire football team."

"Or an entire class in a school photograph," said Nevada. "Don't we have to turn off the motorway here?" She shifted in the back seat, looking anxiously out the window.

Tinkler glanced at her in the mirror. "If I wanted a woman to tell me where to turn, I'd switch on the satnav."

"And they all had their names written neatly there," I said, to forestall what I saw as being a long and fruitless discussion or, to be frank, a quarrel. "Beside all those tiny faces in the photograph." They had looked terribly young, staring up at us in black and white from the lethal depths of a war in another century.

Tinkler began to signal a left turn, and we eased across the lanes to the approaching motorway exit. He wasn't a bad driver, surprisingly.

"So you just took those names that were written there and looked them up on Google or Facebook or something," said Tinkler. "And found the members of the Flare Path Orchestra who were still alive. As simple as that."

"There was nothing simple about it," I said. "When you consider that most of the names were things like 'Leading Aircraftman J. Smith'."

"I can see how that might be a problem," said Tinkler. "What does a leading aircraftman do, by the way? Is he the man who leads the aircraft?"

I said, "Or like, 'Sergeant H. Brown'."

"Yes, yes, don't labour the point. I get the picture."

"Which is why," said Nevada, "we're on our way to visit one Gerald Wuggins."

The Wuggins house was located on the outskirts of Sevenoaks. I'd never been in this part of Kent before and it was intriguing. We drove past ancient stone walls and then a futuristic-looking children's school made of what looked like giant blue pipes. We drove up and down hills, skirted the centre of town, and then all at once we were there, at the end of a long tree-lined street that was densely crowded with parked cars.

There was absolutely nowhere to park. We had to leave Tinkler's little blue Volvo a fair distance from the house and walk it. This was no hardship. It was a warm, pleasant afternoon and the air smelled good. Somewhere birds were singing like they meant it. There were low stone walls on either side of us, and high hedges. The cars were all expensive models. BMWs, Jaguars, a couple of Rolls Royces and a Bentley. "There's no shortage of money around here," said Nevada with approval. The Wuggins place had a large ranch-style gate of red metal.

"So are they expecting us?" said Tinkler, as we approached.

"I don't see how they could be. Every time I rang his number it was either busy or I got the answer machine."

"Tell me you at least left a message."

I shook my head. Nevada said, "He's become very paranoid about these things."

I said, "I thought we could just drive down here and take a chance."

He said, "You mean you thought that poor old Tinkler could just drive you down here and take a chance."

"Oh shit." Nevada suddenly stopped walking. "I left something in the car. Give me the keys, Poor Old Tinkler." He handed her the keys and she trotted off, back the way we'd come. Tinkler and I kept going, through the ranch-style gate and onto a gravel driveway.

It was only once we were inside that I realised how big the place was. Shielded from the street by tall dense hedges, it must have been three or four acres at least. The house, too, was large. We could see its roof looming over a cluster of evergreens. We followed the driveway, which was on a gentle hill and gradually sloped upward as it curved, towards the trees and the house. The gate disappeared behind us and we passed flower beds, a small pond, and a cluster of gnomes with fishing rods.

"Gnomes; good," said Tinkler. "Always a promising sign. I'm being sarcastic by the way." And then suddenly, standing in front of us was a little girl in a white dress with flowers in her hair.

As soon as she saw us her face turned bright red and she pointed at us and screamed, "Here they are!" There was the sound of feet crunching urgently on gravel. A young man came running around the curve towards us. He glanced at Tinkler and me, then at the little girl, and grinned fiercely.

"Well done, Janine," he said. There were more footsteps and another four young men came running. They stopped in front of us with the first guy and the little girl.

"Nice one, Maxie," said one of them to the first guy.

My initial impression was that they all looked enough alike to be brothers. But this was mostly the result of the way they were dressed. They were all wearing highly polished shoes and smart dark trousers, black or navy blue. All had white dress shirts worn open at the neck and one of them had an untied black bow tie hanging floppily from his collar. All wore their hair short or carefully styled with gel.

A waft of sweat, aftershave and hair gel emanated towards us from them. Their faces were flushed from recent exertion. They were all big, muscular and athletic and had a look of ugly excitement about them. They stared at us and grinned.

I had no idea what was going on but I immediately began to get that 'Oh, shit' feeling.

"I found the wedding crashers," said the little girl proudly.

"Yeah, Janine, sweet."

"Nice one."

"Good girl."

Janine basked in the praise from the young men.

"We're not wedding crashers," I said.

Maxie sneered at this obvious canard. "We just chucked out a couple of your mates."

"Yeah," said one of the other guys. "We gave them a thump and sent them on their way."

Maxie looked at us with satisfaction. "They said you might be turning up."

"Well, that was very good of them," I said. "But we don't know what you're talking about."

"We aren't wedding crashers," said Tinkler.

"Yes you are," said little Janine in her piping high-pitched voice. "You're just a couple of losers who sneak into other people's weddings trying to get off with gorgeous single girls."

There was the sound of footsteps in the gravel coming uphill, behind us. Nevada appeared at my side and took my hand. She smiled her most charming smile. "He's not allowed to get off with gorgeous girls. He has to settle for me."

Janine stared at us and then turned to the first guy. "You moron, Maxie. He's not a wedding crasher. Why would he be, when he's going out with someone like her?" The little quisling had made a rapid volte-face.

It was impressive how instantly the situation defused. The five beefy lads literally seemed to wilt and deflate. They suddenly looked younger and smaller and much less formidable. Their demeanour had changed from uniform hostility and a blunt readiness for instant aggression. They now looked variously drunk, dazed, bored, disappointed and mildly annoyed.

"I might still be a loser trying to get off with gorgeous girls," said Tinkler hopefully. "Where are they, exactly?"

Everybody ignored him.

"We're here to see Mr Wuggins," said Nevada.

"Which one?" said Maxie.

"Gerald," I said. "Gerald Wuggins."

"They want to see granddad," piped Janine.

"Someone go get him," said Maxie, looking at the other four. But they seemed much less inclined to follow his lead, now that the prospect of trouble had receded.

I said, "Tell him we're here to ask him about the Flare Path Orchestra."

Maxie shrugged impatiently. "Somebody tell Granddad somebody wants to see him about the Fair Trade Something."

I could see this was going nowhere fast. Nevada stepped forward and smiled and said, "Just show him this."

It was the photograph. One of the lads took it and trotted off uphill. He seemed glad of an excuse to leave.

"That's what I went back to the car for," said Nevada.

"Good thinking."

"Where are the gorgeous single girls?"

"Shut up, Tinkler."

"We didn't mean to interrupt a wedding," said Nevada.

"That's all right," said Gerry Wuggins. Within ten

seconds of meeting us he'd clearly established that we had to call him Gerry. He was a big man with a smooth plump red face and hands like bunches of bananas. He was wearing a silver-grey silk suit that had been tailored to fit his bulk and a cricket sweater and a cricket club tie. *Not another one*, I thought. Though with hands that size, it would make sense. He'd be good at throwing and catching. "It's just the reception," he said. "For one of my granddaughters. Don't ask me which one. I've got about three dozen."

He led us away from the noise of the wedding reception on the lawn outside and into the cool shadows of his house. Despite its traditional English mansard roof, the house was ranch-style and built in modern blocks on different levels, intersecting each other. If Frank Lloyd Wright had been asked to do a cowboy movie it might have turned out like this.

"Sorry to drag you away," said Nevada again.

"I'm glad to get a bit of respite. Would you like a cup of tea? I could murder a cup of tea." He led us into the kitchen, which was Mexican themed, with a red tiled floor, wooden work surfaces and lots of hanging implements. A long table was covered with large plates of brightly coloured food. "Please help yourself to anything in the way of grub."

"Really?" said Tinkler.

Gerry gestured casually with a big hand. "Oh yeah, get stuck in, mate." Tinkler took our host at his word and enthusiastically applied himself to the free food. It wasn't as good as the gorgeous girls, but it would have to do. While he was piling a plate perilously high, Nevada and I sat down with Gerry at a small circular table in an alcove that overlooked a shady corner of the garden devoted to what looked like vegetable beds. There wasn't a shed in sight, which was a relief.

Gerry held the photograph delicately in his big hands and peered at it like a man looking through a window at a distant vista, which I suppose he was. "Where did you get this? Off the Internet, I imagine. Everything's the Internet these days."

"That's right," said Nevada. "You certainly look dashing in it."

Gerry chuckled contentedly. "The birds used to love it. The young ladies, that is. If a feller was in a band. In uniform *and* in a band. We could do no wrong."

I said, "What did you play?"

He looked at me, pale eyes surprised. "What instrument, do you mean? I didn't play anything. I was no musician. I was what you'd call the roadie! I used to carry all the equipment and music stands and all that."

I felt my heart sink. The writing on the photograph hadn't given any indication of what instrument anyone played. And none of the men were holding their instruments. They were just standing or sitting, shoulder to shoulder, in neat rows in their best uniforms.

"They included me in the picture, though. I was definitely part of the orchestra. And it still got me the birds—didn't it just!" He sighed reminiscently, looking at the picture. Then he glanced up at us. "No need to mention that last bit to the wife."

I said, "If you didn't play in the band, I suppose that means you don't have any copies of their records."

He looked at me. "I never said I didn't have no records." My stomach did a little flip of excitement. "I think I've got the lot," said Gerry.

"That's great," I said.

"Oh yeah, I couldn't play an instrument but that don't mean I didn't love listening. I loved the music. I had all the records. Still got most of them. Got a copy of us playing 'In the Mood'. 'In the Nude' we called it, which was ever so apt, given the number of lovelies who ended up in the nude as a result of hearing the band play it. No need to mention any of that to the wife, either."

I explained about Joan Honeyland and her search for the records. "This is Lucky's little girl, Joan?" said Gerry.

"That's right."

He shook his head. "Isn't that wonderful? Building a museum for her old dad."

"Apparently he was quite a successful children's author," I said.

"Oh, really? I didn't know nothing about that. Clever bloke. Not just a pilot and officer and musician, but a writer too. He was a good sort, Lucky, considering he was a toffee-nosed aristocrat."

"This chutney is amazing," said Tinkler, pausing between mouthfuls. He'd sat down at the counter opposite us, his plate in front of him. On it he had bread, cheese, three pieces of chicken, an indeterminate number of sausages, a cluster of bright pink king prawns, smoked salmon, potato salad, chips, some sort of curry, and a mound of coleslaw. "What is it?"

"Green bean, mate. That's the green bean chutney. Did well with our beans last year." He gestured towards the window and the vegetable garden beyond.

"This green bean chutney is amazing," said Tinkler, returning to his plate.

"If god made anything better he kept it for his self," said Gerry. "Actually, god didn't make it. I did."

"And luckily you didn't keep it for yourself," said Nevada.

This was all very nice, but I felt it was time to cut to the chase.

"Anyway," I said, "we represent Miss Honeyland. And she'd be very interested in acquiring any records you have by the Flare Path Orchestra."

"You can fleece the old crone," said Tinkler cheerfully, gnawing at a chicken wing. This was perfectly true, if a bit mean-spirited, but it didn't seem particularly relevant. Sitting here in the big kitchen of his big house, Gerald Wuggins didn't look like he was hurting for money.

"Yes, well, I'm sure we can work something out," said Gerry, waving one of those big hands in the air in a vague gesture. "I've got all those old records up in my attic just doing nothing. Haven't even got anything to play them on any more. The gramophone—can you imagine? It's all iPods now." I began to get a warm feeling inside.

"They'll be going to a good home," I said. "And Miss Honeyland can make digital copies for you." I didn't know that she would, but it seemed like a reasonable request. "So it will be like you still have them, the records." Of course it would be nothing like that at all, as far as I was concerned, trading the original shellac—on which the music actually existed, physically etched there by the very sound waves that had been emitted when it was played—for a phantom digital version to haunt your MP3 player. But most people would go for the latter every time.

Tinkler finally paused in his eating. The pile of food on his plate had got the better of him. He looked around. "I don't suppose there's anything here I could use as a doggie bag?"

"Tinkler!"

But our host just chuckled indulgently and returned to looking at the photograph. "There he is: Lucky. I was with him, you know. On the big night. The night when he flew us back on one engine." He shook his head. "He won the DFC that night, he did."

"Distinguished Flying Cross?" said Nevada.

"That's right. And he bloody well earned it. We'd been shot to pieces. The co-pilot was dead, hit by a cannon round. Tail gunner was dead—poor Tosh, he never had a chance. He couldn't operate his guns. It got so cold in those Lancasters that you froze. Literally. His fingers were literally frozen. He couldn't bring the guns to bear. Not in time. Then we lost our navigator. What was he called? Maurice something, or something Morris. Hit by shrapnel. There was blood everywhere and the wind was ripping through us, we were so full of holes. We were down to two engines, and as we were coming in for our final approach we lost one of those. But Colonel Honeyland still managed to land us in one piece. On a single bloody engine! And they gave him the

DFC. Yes, he bloody well earned it that night."

He set the photograph down and looked at us. Straight at us. Yet somehow it was as if we weren't here. Or perhaps *he* wasn't here. He was back in that moonlit night, flying over Europe. "We was on our way back from Berlin. Berlin was a bugger. It was deep inside Germany, you see, a long way in. The only time you could fly a long-distance mission like that was when the nights were long. In other words, in the middle of bleeding winter. So the weather was always filthy. There was this bloody big cloud looming over Berlin. You couldn't see nothing. You had no idea what you were bombing. And the anti-aircraft fire was diabolical. But that night it wasn't too bad. We didn't take a single casualty going in. It's funny, it was often like that when Colonel Honeyland flew with us. That's why we called him Lucky. Whenever he flew a mission with us, it seemed we came back without a scratch." He laughed. "Of course, the boys wished he could fly with us all the time. But it wasn't allowed. It was a miracle he flew with us as often as he did. Most commanders didn't fly any missions, not a single one." His smile faded and his face darkened. "They sat on their arses safe at home while they sent us boys out to die." He brightened again. "But not Lucky. He flew bombing missions. And he was like our good luck charm. When he was flying a mission, we knew we'd all come back in one piece."

"But not that night," I said.

"No, you're right, mate. Not that night. We were on our way back from Berlin. We'd dropped our load, mission complete, and we were in the bomber stream coming home.

All that was behind us: the searchlights and the anti-aircraft batteries. We were approaching the coast. And suddenly this night fighter spotted us. Got us on his radar, I suppose. Or maybe he was being directed by ground radar. Or maybe he just saw us. Anyway, our number was up." He sighed.

"It was a Junkers. A Ju 88C. Twin engine night fighter. Three 20mm cannons in the nose. And three 7.9mm machine guns. He got on our tail and just started shooting us to pieces. Tosh was the first to go. Then Maurice something, or something Morris. The Junkers was taking his time. Accurate, measured fire. He was in no hurry. Blowing us to bits. And that would have been the end of us if Lucky hadn't—" He paused and gave us a sharp look. "But you don't want to be hearing my war stories."

"Yes we do," said Nevada, at her most honeyed and persuasive. Of course, Miss Honeyland had asked us to try and collect anecdotes about her father. I'd completely forgotten this until Nevada had chimed in. The thought of records in the attic had entirely filled my attention. Now I was grateful for her help.

I had the distinct sense Gerry was going to tell us something significant and had deliberately stopped himself. I nodded eagerly. "As well as any records, we're also very interested in any reminiscences about Lucky."

He hesitated. I felt he was making up his mind whether to tell us. He opened his mouth to speak.

"So this is where you are," said a voice.

A woman came into the kitchen. She was in youthful middle age, smartly dressed and well-groomed. She had blonde hair, which no doubt later Nevada would tell me was natural or not, and disconcertingly large and alert blue eyes. "We thought you'd run off. And with the cake-cutting still to happen."

"Oh no, love," said Gerry. "I wouldn't run off, not with the cake-cutting still to happen. I was just talking to these folk here. You know my old records of the Flare Path Orchestra? These nice people are interested in them. They reckon there might be a few quid in it for us—or at least some glory."

"That's nice, honey," said the woman. "Can I have a quick word with you?"

Gerry gave us an anxious glance in which one could suddenly see the guilty schoolboy of many decades ago, and rose from the table. "Back in a tick," he said, and followed the woman out. She was clearly his wife, although she looked about half his age. He returned promptly and clapped his big hands together.

"Well, folks, it looks like the records in the attic will have to wait. I've just been read the riot act."

"I'm so sorry," said Nevada. "It's all our fault."

"No, no, it happens all the time. We've got a lot of grandchildren, and all of them are girls and all of them are getting married, at least so it seems. We always have the receptions here and I always spring for it—of course I do. But it gets a bit much, and I've taken to sneaking off when I get the chance." He shook his head ruefully. "Trust me, this wasn't as bad as the time she caught me watching cricket on the telly." He chuckled. "Actually, Sheryll was pretty good about it. It's just that she's really hot on family occasions and all that. Makes a special point of it."

"Second-wife syndrome," said Nevada.

"Yes," said Gerry. "Exactly! There are two ways the second wife can go. She can try to cut you off completely from all your old mates and your family, chop all those ties and have you all to herself. Or she can go overboard in the opposite direction, making herself part of the family and being in everybody's good books. You know, remembering every bloody birthday. Like Sheryll. She's hot on family, oh is she ever. Every time one of the grandkids farts we have to have a party to celebrate." He shook his head. "She's worse than Doreen ever was."

"The French have a saying for that," said Nevada. "*Plus catholique que le pape*. It means 'more Catholic than the pope'."

"More Catholic than the pope! I like that."

"Doreen was your first wife?"

"Yeah, lovely girl. Her ticker just blew." For a moment he was lost in thoughts about the past. Then he shook his head, as if clearing it. "Anyway, I've got to get back to the wedding."

"Of course," said Nevada.

"Of course," I said, trying to conceal my bitter disappointment.

"Don't worry, mate, you'll get your records. We'll go into the attic and get them this evening." Gerry grinned at me. "You and me together. You can hold the torch."

"Are you sure?" said Nevada.

"Oh yeah, come back later. Then this mob will either be gone or too drunk to care. I'll be a free agent again, and we can sort it all out. Just kill some time and come back here." He nodded his head and smiled as if he'd thought of something. "Tell you what, why don't you go to Dover?"

"Why would anyone want to go to Dover?" said Tinkler, who had attended secondary school in that fabled port town.

Gerry reached down and picked up the photo from the table. He prodded it with a large finger.

"Because he lives there."

6. DOVER

We drove down a winding hill past Dover Castle, which was very impressive, looming on the hill against the moody grey sky in angular grandeur. "Nice castle," I said.

"It wasn't enough," said Tinkler. "Believe me, growing up here, it wasn't enough."

"You've really got it in for poor old Dover," said Nevada.

Tinkler glanced in the mirror to catch a last glimpse of the vast Norman battlements as we drove downhill, away from the castle. Then, thankfully, returned his eyes to the road. The one-way system seemed to be routing us inexorably towards the docks. I assumed he knew where he was going.

"Still, you're right," he said. "It is a nice castle. Clean Head would like it. I should bring her down here and show it to her."

"That's your plan?" said Nevada. "You're going to try and get into her knickers by showing her the great castles of England?"

"Her knickers," said Tinkler happily.

"Keep your mind on the driving, Tinkler."

We crawled through the town centre. There was a lot of traffic. Perhaps a ferry had just arrived. Then we turned left and began to wind our way uphill again. The little blue Volvo climbed past playing fields and then a gateway leading up a steep slope towards a big ornate building on a hill. "There's the old school," said Tinkler, glancing at it as we passed. "My alma mater. What does that mean, by the way? 'White mother'?"

"Nurturing," said Nevada. "Nurturing mother."

"You see the school gates there? That's where old Smithy got beaten up. Two boys in the year below us. I think they were brothers. They waited for him after school one day and beat him up. He came in the next day with a black eye and split lip."

I said, "So it wasn't very nurturing for poor old Smithy."

Tinkler bobbed his head. "The funny thing was, he wasn't some kind of loser. He was one of the school's alpha males. So I wondered how he was going to get them back. I waited for the showdown." Tinkler signalled and turned left. "But nothing happened. He got beaten up, he took his lumps, he never did anything about it. Time passed and no one mentioned it anymore and that was that." Tinkler shrugged.

He glanced at us. "It turned out that in this respect life was different to any number of Clint Eastwood movies."

"What happened to him?" said Nevada. "Smithy?"

"He's a doctor now. Loads of money, big house, nice family."

Nevada glanced at me. "Why couldn't you be a doctor?"

I said, "I'm too busy looking for fucking records."

* * *

Ever since we'd left Sevenoaks we'd been travelling under a vast, minatory charcoal sky that had promised at least storm and rain and quite possibly the apocalypse. But now, as we parked the car on a hillside slope in a row of small houses, the clouds broke open and sunlight poured through. We were sitting on a steep gradient, so Tinkler turned the tyres at an angle and applied the handbrake before we got out; Clean Head would have approved.

We stood blinking in the radiant afternoon. "Gorgeous day," said Nevada. "Breathe that fresh air. I bet it's lovely down by the sea." She looked at us. "We can go for a walk along the seaside before we drive back."

"Can I kill myself instead?" said Tinkler.

We walked up the sloping street. There was a minivan parked at the top. It was a classic hippie vehicle, rusting and highly decorated. On the side facing us was a giant smiling yellow sun shedding slanting rays across a pale blue background. In swirling purple lettering it read: *Mr Sunshine is giving us some golden love today*. Thirty seconds ago it would have been a bad joke. Now it seemed eerily, almost prophetically apt.

As we reached the top of the hill and the van, Nevada glanced to the right, where the residential dwellings gave way to a small parade of shops meandering back downhill. "Look," she said. "My god, there's a clothes shop. A second-hand clothes shop."

Tinkler rubbed his hands together. "And who knows what bargains these gullible locals might have on offer?"

"Don't encourage her, Tinkler."

"I'll join you in a minute. Number eighty-seven, isn't it? I'll be right back." Nevada gave me a quick kiss and then was gone. Tinkler and I walked in the other direction, along the brow of the hill, towards number eighty-seven. The houses were crowded together, narrow and quaint, with miniature gardens that had mostly been paved or covered with concrete. Our destination had a sad little square of grass outside with a yellow ball lying on it. The paint was chipped and flaking on the wrought iron gate, which creaked and clanged and presumably alerted the owner, because he was at the door to greet us before we could ring the bell.

Charles Gresford-Jones opened the door and smiled and waved.

On the photograph his name had been unhelpfully, and inaccurately, rendered as 'C.G. Jones'. If I'd known what he was really called I might have been able to track him down. That didn't matter now, though. Gerry had phoned him up and made the introductions for us. Gresford-Jones was wearing a maroon-checked sleeveless vest over a black turtleneck sweater, a neatly creased pair of blue jeans and a scuffed old pair of bedroom slippers. It was as if in his dress-style he was torn between bohemian and nerd. He had a narrow, deeply seamed face and a few wisps of dark hair densely streaked with grey. There were liver spots on his thin white hands. But on the whole he was, like Gerry, fairly well preserved, despite being headed for a hundred years old. It was as if, having survived the horrors of the war, nothing could now kill them.

He waved us indoors and we followed him inside, doing an intricate little dance in the tiny hallway to make enough room to close the door behind us. We went through to the parlour, which was a little more spacious. There was a sofa, two armchairs, a bookcase, half of which was devoted to books and half to CDs, and a fairly serious-looking hi-fi system. Being a musician, he probably wanted music to sound like music, or as near as you could get with CD.

"Gerald rang and said to expect you. It was pleasant to hear from him; it's been a while. We used to see quite a lot of each other at the squadron reunions. But we both stopped going." He smiled at us. "They're a bit of a depressing business these days. So few of us left, you know." His smile faded a little. "Gerald said there was going to be three of you."

"Yes, my girlfriend spotted a vintage clothes shop and couldn't resist the allure."

"Oh, yes, Bernadette's. She'll find something in there. Do sit down."

Tinkler and I each chose an armchair. The room was shabby but comfortable, and gave the impression that the objects in it were appreciated and cared for, if none too tidily. There was fresh paint on the window surround—a less than perfect job—and I surmised that the cushions on the sofa and chairs had recently been refilled, because there was a shallow pile of white stuffing still lying on the carpet by the window, glowing in the sunshine.

I nodded at the Pioneer CD player and amplifier that

were stacked on wall shelves beside my head. "Are those the Tom Evans modified models?"

His eyes lit up and any reserve in his manner dropped away. "Yes, that's right. Don't they sound marvellous?" I agreed that they did and he sank down onto the sofa and relaxed. We were now brothers in hi-fi. "I don't have room for a large system in this tiny place, but I do quite well. I miss teaching, though. I used to have access to the music room of course."

"You taught music?"

"Naturally. One of the few ways a musician can earn a living."

"My friend here went to your school."

He glanced at Tinkler, and nodded politely. Another bond of fraternity. "Oh really, an old boy? Many years after my time, I fear. Yes, we used to have a lovely system in the music room when I was there. Vinyl, of course. Played on Quad speakers."

"I've got a pair of Quads," I said.

"Of course you do. I would, if I had the room. And we had Quad amps and a superb Thorens TD 124 turntable." He sighed. "I often wonder what became of that turntable. I actually went back to the school one day and asked about it. They said they still had it somewhere, in a cupboard. But then they went and looked and it was gone." He sighed, mourning the loss of the Thorens.

My gaze was wandering around the room and came to the pile of stuffing on the carpet in the square of sunshine. I suddenly realised it wasn't a pile of stuffing at all. It was a cat.

An emaciated and strangely flattened white cat. There was no sign of breathing or any other movement. It was in the posture of a sleeping cat, but it didn't look like it was sleeping.

It looked like it was dead.

"I was just about to eat," said our host. "Since I was expecting you, I made provision for guests. Would you like some sardines on toast?"

"No, that's fine," I said. "I'm fine."

"I'll have some," said Tinkler. I remembered the huge stacked plate he'd addressed himself to in Gerry's kitchen. Could he conceivably be hungry again? It didn't seem humanly possible. Yet he appeared perfectly willing to send this frail ancient fellow off to cater for him.

"Tinkler, for Christ's sake," I murmured.

"What? I'm hungry. I've been burning calories."

"When?"

"While driving."

"How do you figure that?"

"It's brainwork. The brain burns a surprising number of calories."

"Not yours," I said.

"Excellent," said Gresford-Jones with the brisk manner of a man who had spent many decades concluding arguments between bickering schoolboys. "I'll prepare sardines on toast for two, then." He glanced at me, a little reproachfully I thought. "If you change your mind later, there's plenty. I was planning to provide for three of you." He went out.

As soon as he was gone I looked at Tinkler. "A Thorens TD 124 turntable," I said, keeping my voice low.

"Yes," he said. He had seemed strangely uninterested during our hi-fi discussion. Elaborately detached, in fact. "Just like the one you've got," I said.

"I suppose so."

"You never did tell me where you got that."

"Didn't I?"

"Tinkler, did you steal your turntable from your old school?"

"My lips are sealed. What's the statute of limitations on turntable theft, anyway?" Suddenly Tinkler noticed the pile of white fur. "Is that a cat?"

"I think so."

"Is it dead?"

"I think so."

There was the metallic clang of the gate opening. From the back of the house Gresford-Jones called, "Is that your lady friend? Could you let her in?" I went to the door and opened it. Nevada smiled at me and stepped in. I sensed something behind the smile, though.

"Find anything?" I said.

"A couple of decent items. And there was a really lovely Hermès scarf."

"Was it silk?" I said. "Or silk-cashmere?"

"The latter," she said. "But it's all academic, because some vile little teenage slut beat me to it."

So that's what was bugging her. I led her into the parlour and let her take the armchair where I'd been sitting while I perched on the arm of the sofa. "What a shame."

"They're like that around here," said Tinkler.

"My god, is that a cat?" said Nevada, staring at the thing on the floor.

"I think it once was."

"Is it dead?"

"It didn't seem polite to ask."

Tinkler got up and went over and sniffed the air above the recumbent white form. "No tell-tale odour of corruption." He bent over and prodded the cat.

"Tinkler, don't touch it!"

He prodded it again. It didn't respond. There were no signs of life. Tinkler shrugged. "Maybe it's been stuffed. By a taxidermist."

"Wouldn't he have had it stuffed in a more lifelike pose?"

"Maybe this is a lifelike pose."

"Good point."

"Where has he gone?" said Nevada, looking around the place. "Charles Gresford-Jones?"

"To get us sardines," I said.

"And toast," said Tinkler.

Gresford-Jones came back carrying a tray. He had, as promised, brought sardines on toast for himself and Tinkler. And an unopened tin of sardines on a big white plate. I introduced him to Nevada and she reassured him that she didn't need any sardines. Tinkler had meanwhile seized his plate and begun to eat with enthusiasm hard to credit in one who had so recently gorged himself. Our host seemed, if anything, gratified. He daintily consumed a small mouthful of his own serving, then turned to the tin on the plate. He set the plate down on the floor by the sofa and began to open the tin.

At the sound of the sardines being opened, the apparently dead cat suddenly rose to its feet and approached us. It moved in a strange angular dance, making abrupt shifts of direction. It was like Charlie Chaplin pretending to be drunk. Tacking thus, it came across the room and slumped down again, its chest across the white plate and its face nose down in the contents of the tin, which were a bright, shocking red. The cat began to eat enthusiastically, its whiskers jutting from the tin on either side of its small face.

"Abner likes the sardines in tomato sauce," said Gresford-Jones, nodding with approval as the cat hoovered up the gory mess. With astonishing speed the tin was empty and left, like the plate, sparklingly clean. When Abner finished licking the last drops of sauce, he turned and went back to slump down in the patch of sunlight again.

"We have two cats at home," said Nevada. She looked at me. "We should try feeding them sardines, dear."

"If we did, they'd probably sue us."

"How old is Abner?"

Gresford-Jones considered. "Well, I've had him for several years and he must have been hanging around for a good long while before that." He shrugged, as though the calculation was just too difficult. "Now, I understand you have a photo?" I handed him the picture and he nodded. "I have a copy of this upstairs."

"Our client might be very interested in any memorabilia you have," said Nevada. It seemed as if, by mutual unspoken consent, everybody had decided to get down to business.

"Excellent. And you would like to hear my reminiscence of events?"

"Definitely," said Nevada. "Do you mind if I record it on my phone?" She looked at me. "I should have thought of doing this when we talked with Gerry Wuggins."

"Yes, you should."

"I'll do it when we go back. For our second visit. This evening."

"Do you suppose they'll still have that food?" said Tinkler. He'd finished his sardines. Nevada took out her phone, but our host shook his head.

"No, no, I will record everything and make a copy for you." He took out a serious-looking microphone and set it up on a small table in front of us. A cable ran back from the microphone to some black boxes I hadn't noticed, stacked in the corner beside the sofa. It looked like some kind of solid-state recording system. I remembered again that he was, or had been, a professional musician. He adjusted the microphone so it was in the middle of our small group. His manner was all business now. He looked at us.

"I understand that I am to be paid for these recollections?"

"That's right," said Nevada. "And as I'm sure my other half here was just about to remind us, we are also looking for any records of the Flare Path Orchestra."

I said, "Any 78s, V-Discs, anything."

He nodded. "Yes, I have one for you." I felt a hollow thrill of excitement. But the old bastard obviously wasn't about to elaborate further at this point. Instead he said, "Just speak in your normal voices and the mike should pick you up all right. Who'll start? Well, shall I? I am, or was, LAC Charles Alan Gresford-Jones."

"Sorry to interrupt," said Nevada. "What does LAC mean?"

"Leading Aircraftman."

"Sorry to interrupt," said Tinkler. "But what does a leading aircraftman do? We were talking about it earlier. Does he lead the aircraft?"

"I was a rigger," said Gresford-Jones with exaggerated patience. "I looked after the airframe on the Lancasters." He was starting to get a little annoyed with the interruptions. He obviously had a prepared speech that he wanted to get through. "Do you mind if I start again? I am Leading Aircraftman Charles Alan Gresford-Jones. I was proud to serve in Bomber Command in the RAF during World War Two. I was also proud to serve with the Flare Path Orchestra, as bass trumpet and latterly deputy leader, arranger and orchestrator. The Flare Path Orchestra or FPO came into being in the following way…"

I glanced at Nevada. We were obviously in for the long haul here.

"We were a direct riposte to the American Glenn Miller Band, which was performing in England at the time. This was the so-called Army Air Force Band. You see, the US Air Force did not become a separate service—like the RAF—until 1947. However, in itself, Army Air Force is a misnomer. It was originally designated the Army Air Forces Technical Training Command Band. But the word

'Technical' was dropped in 1943, because of the merging of Technical Training Command and Flying Command."

It sounded like he could go on in this vein indefinitely, so I said, "What was the music like?"

He blinked at me like a man coming out of a trance. Despite having carefully arranged the microphone to pick up all of our voices, he seemed nonplussed that anyone other than himself had dared to speak. "The music? Why, they were the greatest swing band in the world." He glared at me. "Do you know what swing music is?"

I said, "Dance music with a big injection of jazz."

He paused while he tried to find fault with this definition, reluctantly failed to do so, and continued. "We didn't want the Yanks stealing all the thunder."

"Or all the women," said Tinkler. But he ignored this.

"So the powers-that-be decreed that the RAF should muster a band to give them a run for their money. And thus the Flare Path Orchestra was born. It was the brainchild of Colonel Lucian Honeyland, DFC, affectionately known to those who had the privilege to serve under him as Lucky." He paused for a moment, lost in his memories. "We used to say that *we* were the lucky ones, to be under his command. In any case, our Colonel Honeyland, like Glenn Miller, had been given carte blanche to pick the finest musicians available anywhere in the service. So we ended up with some very distinguished players. And, like the Miller organisation, we were very much an arranger's band. We had the great Daniel Overland writing charts for us, and my own humble efforts, and then, of course, there was Johnny

Thomas." His voice trembled oddly as he spoke the name.

Gresford-Jones paused for a moment, then cleared his throat and said, "Which brings us to the murder."

"The what?"

"The murder. It's rather odd that you asked me about it, because—"

"We didn't ask you about it."

"I'm sorry?" He blinked at us. "Didn't you? I thought that was specifically what you wanted me to discuss."

"No. But do go on."

7. GILLIAN GADON

"As I mentioned," said Gresford-Jones, "I was one of the arrangers in the Flare Path Orchestra." He sighed rather forlornly, as if he was running out of steam before he'd even properly begun his narrative. "I have to be honest and tell you that I wasn't remotely of the stature of the other two. Danny Overland, an Australian, is world renowned for his work. He's recorded with Shirley Bassey, Tom Jones, Jack Jones, Matt Jones, I mean Matt *Monro*, Frank Sinatra—I should really have started with Mr Sinatra, shouldn't I? The biggest name in the list. Imagine arranging and conducting for Sinatra. I believe that was at the Sands in Las Vegas. And Tony Bennett, I think, and Mel Tormé, I believe…"

Nevada gave me a look. I knew what she was thinking. Our host was in serious danger of wandering off-topic here. Hardly surprising, given that he was a nonagenarian, spry or not. I wondered if I should try and get him back on track.

Nevada was starting to look impatient. *Tell us about the fucking murder*, was the subtext there.

"And the third arranger for the Flare Path Orchestra was, of course, Johnny Thomas." Again there was something tremulous in his voice when he said the name. "If he had lived he might well have achieved a success comparable to that of Danny Overland."

I said, "If he'd lived?" Gresford-Jones stared at me, unblinking.

He nodded. "That's right," he said mildly. "He was very gifted. It was genuinely a tragedy."

"What happened, exactly?"

"Well," he said, "you remember I was telling you about the Glenn Miller band? At the time, here in England, their radio broadcasts were *huge*. Listened to by *millions*. But, it was decided by our powers-that-be that Major Glenn Miller shouldn't have all the running, and consequently we—we being the Flare Path Orchestra—were pitted against him in a Battle of the Bands."

I remembered that I owned some of those Miller broadcasts, immortalised on vinyl, and realised that I was in danger of becoming interested in his long-winded tale.

Gresford-Jones began to smile a nostalgic smile. "And so it came to pass that we were scheduled to play against the Miller organisation in the grand inaugural Battle of the Bands at the Corn Exchange in Bedford." The smile faded and the light in his eyes dimmed. "And that was the first time she turned up."

"Who turned up?"

"Gillian Gadon. As soon as I saw her, I knew she was trouble."

* * *

"She was in the audience that night and made a point of coming to meet the orchestra afterwards. In fact she followed us onto the band bus. Sometimes girls did. It was quite a scandal, what went on."

"That's what Gerry told us," said Nevada.

"Yes, he would," said Gresford-Jones dryly. "He had more than his share of participation in such goings-on. Anyway, this particular girl started turning up at all of our performances. And she threw herself at various band members." There was a petulance in the way he said this that suggested he hadn't been among the lucky targets.

"She was a groupie?" said Nevada.

"Effectively, yes. Although we wouldn't have used the term at the time."

At this point Tinkler woke up. "Groupies?" he said groggily.

Our host didn't dignify this with a response. "Anyway, contact with her led to the death of a dear friend of mine, a comrade in arms, and a fine musician who should have gone on to great things."

"Is that three different people or all the same guy?" said Tinkler.

"All the same guy," said Gresford-Jones coldly. "Dead."

Then, presumably because he just couldn't keep his mouth shut, Tinkler said, "Still, you must have lost a lot of your friends, your mates, your comrades in arms. I mean, it was the war and all that."

Gresford-Jones's voice was clipped and icy. "Your point being?"

"That you… must have got used to it?" suggested Tinkler timorously.

Our host shook his head. "Oh, he didn't die in combat."

"Didn't he?"

"No. Johnny Thomas was *hanged*. He went to the gallows."

I said, "Why did they hang him?"

Gresford-Jones sighed. "Because of the murder."

"Who did he kill?"

"A girl called Gillian Gadon," said Nevada.

Gresford-Jones nodded.

"He killed the groupie," said Tinkler.

Gresford-Jones's shoulders slumped and he sank back in his chair like a man accepting defeat. I suddenly saw how frail he could be. He closed his eyes and simply nodded. "What happened?" said Nevada gently. He shook his head.

"It was a ghastly sex crime. She drove him to it, of course. Before *she* came along, he was a good steady family man." He picked up the photo we'd brought to him and stared at it. I realised that his eyes were glinting with tears. But his voice remained firm. "It was a tremendous cause célèbre. The gutter press gloated over all the gruesome details. The *way* he killed her. Their torrid sexual liaison…"

He wiped his eyes on his sleeve and looked at us. "They won't leave it alone even today. They won't leave poor Johnny alone. Poor old fellow. Just last year there was this disgusting ferret of a local historian who revived the story. After it had all been decently forgotten, he insisted on reviving it for his own glorification. Digging it all up again, all the filth and innuendo. Every sensational detail." His head drooped wearily. "Every drop of suffering."

"Local historian?" I said. "So it happened around here, the murder?"

He nodded. "Yes. In Kingsdown. It was a terrible business."

"I'm sure it was," said Nevada, leaning forward. She was at her most sympathetic and persuasive. She clearly wanted to hear more.

"They were staying at a pub there. An illicit rendezvous. He was on leave. A weekend pass. He'd gone down to meet her. He should have been with his family, his wife and children, but instead he was in bed with her. That's where they found her, her body, in the bed where they'd spent the weekend. He tried to run. They caught him of course." He seemed to make an effort of will and straightened up in his chair. "And he went to the gallows. But Lucky was magnificent."

"Sorry?" I couldn't follow this abrupt shift of meaning—or of mood. Gresford-Jones had suddenly changed. Now he seemed almost cheerful.

"Colonel Honeyland," he said. "He was magnificent. Stood by poor Johnny to the end. Went to see him in his death cell. Spent the night there with him. The night before the execution. He was always going down to see him. Trying to offer some crumbs of comfort to young Johnny as he sat there in the shadow of the gallows." He smiled as he thought about it. "Our commander-in-chief, good old

Bomber Harris, he got Lucky a 'Cabinet Priority' badge for his motorcycle. So they cleared the way for him wherever he went. And he would go zooming down to see Johnny whenever he could. Right up until the end."

He fell silent. There was a long silence in the room. Then a moist, grisly, sibilant sound emanated from the cat. "I'm sorry," said our host. "Poor Abner suffers from wind after he eats sardines."

That seemed to put paid to any reverential silence. I said, "Were there any recordings made of those radio broadcasts?"

He looked at me. "Broadcasts?"

"The Battles of the Bands. Between the Flare Path Orchestra and Glenn Miller?"

He shook his head quickly and emphatically. "No."

I said, "No?" It seemed preposterous. "Why not?"

"Couldn't they tape them?" said Nevada.

Gresford-Jones seemed to seize on this. "Hardly. Tape recording didn't exist yet. At least among the Allies. The Germans had developed it by this point. And it came back from Germany with our victorious armies. In a sense this new technology was the spoils of war."

"All right," I said, trying to be patient. "They didn't have tape, but they could record it some other way. They had transcription discs."

He nodded happily. I was a star pupil. "Exactly. We had transcription discs or, as they were called during the war years, Victory discs or V-Discs." He looked at me. "And many performances by the Flare Path Orchestra, including those Battles of the Bands, were recorded in just this way.

Unfortunately a priceless stack of these transcription recordings were dropped and broken, utterly destroyed."

"Broken?" I said.

"Yes."

"But V-Discs weren't made of shellac. They were made of vinyl."

He smiled at me. "Indeed they were."

"And vinyl doesn't shatter like that."

Gresford-Jones nodded. "Correct, and what's more, transcription recordings were actually made of a layer of vinyl that coated an aluminium disc. And aluminium itself is highly durable." He stopped speaking and looked at me. The expectant blankness in his gaze suggested that I was supposed to say something at this point to confirm my own intellectual shortcomings.

I said, "So, what was the problem?" It sounded like the damned things were indestructible.

He squeezed his eyes shut happily and smiled. This was clearly the right question. "Ah, you see," he said, "the problem was that during the war years there was a great scarcity of metal. All of it was being used in the war effort. So at this point in time instead of aluminium the discs were made of *glass*. With the result that these transcription recordings suddenly became very fragile indeed."

"Oh shit." I winced.

He nodded in a pedagogical way, satisfied with having made his point. "Yes, 'oh shit'. Indeed. All the recordings were stored at Bomber Command Headquarters in High Wycombe. To keep them safe. And they were quite safe as it happened. For the duration of the hostilities. The problem came when they were *moved*. Shamefully, some ham-fisted private was entrusted with the task of gathering them up and transporting them to Colonel Honeyland who was going to supervise their release, after the war, in what would no doubt have been a bestselling series of albums of wonderful swing classics." His scrawny fingers bunched into fists. Even after all these years it still made him furious. "When the discs reached him, they were in *fragments*."

"I hope the private was shot," I said.

"He certainly deserved to be. Those recordings were utterly irreplaceable. Immensely valuable." His voice thickened. Tears glinted in his eyes once more.

And who could blame him?

But I didn't particularly want to watch an old airman start blubbering. I cleared my throat. "You said you had a record?"

He blinked at me. "Sorry?"

"You said you had one for me."

He came back from miles away. I had his full attention. "And you said you would pay for it?" Suddenly we were all business again. "A generous price, I believe you said."

"Our client will be happy to," chimed Nevada. "Yes. Indeed. Absolutely."

"Well then, let me go upstairs and get it." The talk of money certainly seemed to have energised him. He rose from his chair and went out. His slippers shuffled up the stairs. There was a pause, and then they shuffled back down. He was holding a 78rpm disc in a plain cardboard sleeve. I was pleased to see the sleeve. It suggested that the record might have been well looked after. I felt the old excitement expanding inside me. I couldn't wait to see what it was.

His hands trembled a little as he gave it to me, though whether that was with excitement at his imminent payout, or was just the result of the wear and tear of the years, I couldn't tell.

I looked at the label. It was exactly the same 78 we'd found in Tinkler's speaker. Of all the records it could have been, it was the same damned one.

He must have seen the expression on my face. "Don't you want it?" he said, querulously. I thought quickly. Did I want it? I remembered what Joan Honeyland had said about picking up any duplicates we ran across.

"Of course we want it," I said.

There followed a quick discussion on price. It was quick because I agreed to pay what he asked—or rather agreed that my client would pay. Miss Honeyland had given me carte blanche in these areas. When we were finished, Gresford-Jones seemed pleased, which he should have been.

It was enough money to keep him and Abner the Zombie Cat in sardines for a long time.

We said goodbye and left, with the record and with his promise to seek out any other memorabilia he might have pertaining to the Flare Path Orchestra or Colonel Honeyland. As he closed the door behind us and we walked through the garden gate Nevada said, "Glad you had your poker face on in there."

"Is that sarcasm?"

"Of course it is."

"Sorry. I couldn't conceal my disappointment when I saw it was the same record we already had."

"No kidding. He almost didn't sell it to us."

"I don't think there was much chance of that." We walked back past the hippie van to Tinkler's car and got in and drove off.

"You know what our next order of business should be?" said Nevada.

I said, "Seek out the little ferret of a local historian."

"Exactly. The one who knows all the details of the murder."

"All the sordid details."

"That's right. But we didn't get a name, did we? For the little ferret?"

"No. I don't think he would have given us one." I shrugged. "But how many of them can there be—local historians for this area?"

For some reason Tinkler had driven us up the hill, instead of down. And we now hit a cul-de-sac. "I was sure we could get out this way," he said, peering crossly through the windscreen at a blank concrete wall set into the hillside.

"Evidently not."

After laboriously turning the car around—we could have done with Clean Head and her wheel-spinning aplomb here—we finally drove back down again, into Gresford-Jones's street, heading in the opposite direction. As we coasted swiftly along, the Volvo's modest engine power supplemented by gravity, we passed a young woman strolling by in boots and jeans and a brightly coloured poncho.

Nevada turned her head and made a hissing noise that would have done credit to either of our cats.

She said, "It's that loathsome little succubus. The one who stole my Hermès scarf."

I said, "She didn't actually steal it from you and it wasn't actually your scarf."

"If you're going to tiresomely insist on details…"

"Yeah, if you're going to be tiresome," said Tinkler, gently applying the brakes, presumably to prevent us hurtling out of control to our doom. As I turned back to look at the girl, I thought I saw her turn and go up the path to Gresford-Jones's house.

"Do you know what I think?" said Nevada. "I think he was in love with him."

"Who was in love with who?"

"With whom," corrected Tinkler.

"Charles Gresford-Jones," said Nevada, ignoring him. "With Johnny Thomas."

"Perhaps it was the irresistible allure of his name," I said.

"Don't think I don't know that that's a penis joke," said Nevada. "But I'm perfectly serious. Did you see the way he reacted when he was talking about him? I think the bloke was the great lost love of his life."

"You know what *I* think?" said Tinkler. "I think that was one fucking weird cat."

8. SILK STOCKINGS

Much to Tinkler's relief, there wasn't time for a walk along the seafront in Dover. Having sat through Gresford-Jones's lengthy monologue, we were now running late and had to get onto the motorway again and hightail it back to Sevenoaks.

This necessitated driving past Canterbury, which was an occasion for more unwanted reminiscences from Tinkler about grave robbing, an episode that Nevada and I were both eager to forget, but which he couldn't seem to get enough of.

But he was the driver, so we couldn't tell him to shut up.

The sun was setting by the time we got back to Gerry's place and the wedding celebrations had moved into a new gear. A new gear that mainly consisted of being louder, more rowdy, and even drunker than before. Walking under red oriental paper lamps hanging in the trees—what had happened to the cowboy theme?—we managed to find the host without being confronted by a band of vigilantes this time, although Gerry's wife did give us a dirty look as we walked past her sitting at a table, eating cake with a group of little girls. She wasn't glad to see us back.

Somewhere behind the house a disco system in a tent was blaring out Jane Birkin singing 'Je T'aime' in a thunderous yet affectingly salacious voice, with loud and profane interjections from the revellers, and ensuing gales of laughter.

Gerry seemed, as ever, quite pleased to escape from the festivities and said as much as he led us back to the kitchen. Tinkler was crestfallen when he saw that the platters of food had been cleared away. "Don't worry, mate," said Gerry. "They're in the pantry. Through that door there."

"Oh, Tinkler, for Christ's sake," said Nevada, because it was her turn to say it. But I suspect, like me, she was ready for something to eat herself.

"No, that's fine," said Gerry. "Help yourself, mate. Fill your hollow leg. There's plates and napkins over there."

We sat down at the same table where we'd gathered before. Gerry sank into a chair and sighed. His tie was hanging loose at his collar now, and his smooth red face was more florid than ever. "So how was old Charlie-boy then?"

"Well," said Nevada, "to be frank he was a bit hit-and-miss."

"Hit-and-miss?"

"Yes. He was very voluble, but he didn't tell us a great deal. In particular we got the impression that he was holding back on one subject."

"What subject?"

"The murder," I said.

"What murder?"

"The sex crime in Kingsdown."

"Oh, Christ, that." Gerry shook his head. Suddenly he looked tired, showing his years. "He's got that bloody murder on his brain. I ask you, of all the people who got killed from our mob, in the air, during the war, all the blood that got shed. Thousands of our boys died. *Tens* of thousands. And he has to get a bee in his bonnet about *that*." He looked at us, pale blue eyes under bushy grey brows. In the dark garden beyond the window, the music was a muffled pounding. "You know what Charlie Gresford-Jones's problem is?"

"No. What?"

"He was ground crew. Do you know what he spent the war doing?"

"He was a rigger," said Tinkler, who had wandered back in with a plate of food—cold fried chicken, potato salad, and some kind of curry. "He looked after the airframe on the Lancasters."

"That's right, mate," said Gerry, gazing at Tinkler with new respect. "That was exactly what he was and exactly what he did. But what he *didn't* do was ever fly a combat mission or any other kind of bloody mission. He spent his war on the ground. And like a lot of the people who worked on the ground, he made a lot more bleeding fuss about the war in the air than the blokes what actually flew it." He looked at us. "He romanticised it. They all did. Everyone who didn't have to actually fly—or fight."

Tinkler sat down and joined us, gnawing on a chicken leg. The curry on his plate smelled good, even cold. "Do you know what he went and done?" said Gerry. "Old Charlie-boy wrote a number about us, about all us brave fly boys on our noble mission up in the air. A big soppy sentimental bloody tune it was too. Always had all the girls in tears. Lots of slushy strings everywhere. I never could be doing with strings."

"Can I make myself a coffee?" I said.

"Sure. Help yourself. There should be some in the pot over there."

As I got up I said, "So there's nothing to this murder?"

I heard him sigh behind me. "Well, there was a big fuss about it at the time. And they topped poor old Johnny for it." I found the coffee pot he was talking about. I gave it a sniff and it smelled all right. I poured one for myself and one for Nevada. I didn't think Tinkler would surface from his plate long enough to drink anything.

"Poor old Johnny?" said Nevada as I came back to the table and sat down. "What about the poor girl he killed?" Gerry shrugged.

"I understand it was a gruesome sex crime," said Tinkler, licking his fingers and setting a chicken bone aside. He seemed to have gnawed it completely clean of flesh. "But Mr Gresford-Jones wouldn't give us any of the details."

"She was strangled with her own stockings," said Gerry.

"So don't you think Johnny deserved to be hanged for that?" said Nevada. "It seems fairly appropriate."

"It's fairly appropriate if he *did* it, darling," said Gerry laconically.

No one else said anything for a while. Outside in the garden the music pounded away just at the edge of audibility, the tune not quite identifiable. He had good soundproofing in here. I broke the silence. "You don't think he did it?" I said.

"I'll tell you one thing, they hanged him as much for having it off with a bird who wasn't his wife as they did for any murder he might have committed. He got hanged for adultery." He looked at us and suddenly smiled. "You know, the other day one of the girls asked me what adultery was, and I was blowed if I could tell her."

"What *is* adultery?" said Tinkler. He was making a pretty good job of scooping up his potato salad with a piece of bread as his only implement.

"It's shagging someone you're not married to," said Nevada succinctly. "And if you tell me it should be 'someone to whom you're not married', Tinkler, I shall break a plate over your head."

"Fair enough," said Tinkler. "So it's having an affair with someone else when you're married."

Nevada frowned thoughtfully. "No. It's also sex out of wedlock. Pre-marital."

"So, basically, it's having sex in any form," said Tinkler.

"No," said Gerry. "Not if two people are married. To each other, like. Then they can have sex and it's not adultery."

"Though still morally wrong, I trust," said Tinkler. He stared down at his depleted plate and then looked hopefully towards the pantry.

Gerry chuckled. "So that's adultery. Between us we've just about sussed it out! If anybody asks me for a definition again I'm ready for them." His smile faded. "Anyway. That's what they hanged old Johnny Thomas for. And

Charlie Gresford-Jones never quite got over it." He shook his head despairingly. "Thousands of people dying every night of the war, and he got hung up on that one."

"I have a theory," said Nevada. *Here we go*, I thought. She said, "I think that Mr Gresford-Jones might have been in love with him."

"Old Charlie-boy gay, you mean?" said Gerry. He considered it. "Maybe. But if you ask me he always seemed *sexless*. Like someone's old-maid aunt. And I think it's what happened to Johnny Thomas what did it to him. I mean, I reckon it was the sex side of it, the scandalous nature of the whole thing. The *salacious* nature of it." He looked at us. "I think it scared old Charlie off it for life. Blew his mind, you might say. Gorgeous sexy girl, strangled with her own stockings. Silk stockings, they were. That caused as much scandal as anything else at the time. Where had she got those in wartime? They tried to make out that she was some kind of high-class prostitute or something. But she wasn't. Nothing like that. She was a lovely girl. Sweet girl. Smart as a whip, she was."

Gerry shook his head gloomily. He peered at Nevada. "You're right, love. Whoever did it to her *deserved* to have a noose round his own neck."

"Whoever did it?" I said. "It really doesn't sound like you think it was Johnny."

"Well, we'll never know now, will we?"

No one said anything. I sipped my coffee. It was lukewarm and bitter. I speculated on the possibility of asking him to let me make some fresh, and then I wondered if I was turning into Tinkler. Instead I said, "I understand Colonel Honeyland spent a lot of time with Johnny, just before…"

"Oh yeah, he did. He did everything he could for the kid. Lucky was a decent sort of bloke, for a stuck-up aristocratic prat. Charlie told you that too, did he?"

"Yes."

"So your visit wasn't a complete waste of time."

"Not at all," said Nevada.

"Although he only had one record," I said.

"Really? Which one?"

"'Blues in the Night' and 'Elmer's Tune'. But we already had it."

"Pity," said Gerry.

I looked at him. "Speaking of records…"

He wouldn't meet my eye. "Yeah, look, I'm sorry about that, mate."

"What do you mean, sorry?"

"They're gone. The records I had. All of them. I went up to have a look in the attic, like, so we wouldn't waste too much of your time when you got back here. And they was all gone. So imagine how baffled I was. I went down and asked Sheryll, asked the wife about it, and she said she'd got rid of them."

"Got rid of them?"

"Yeah. Just chucked them out. Months ago. Behind my back. Can you credit it?" He sighed philosophically. "Still, she's a good girl in lots of other ways. And they were just *things*."

"Just things?" I said. I felt like I'd been kicked in the stomach.

He took an envelope out of his pocket and set it on the table. "I know it must be a real disappointment and shock. It was to me. So let me try and make it up to you. Take these as a gift from me and the wife." I glanced at Nevada, then picked up the envelope.

Inside it were two tickets, to the Royal Festival Hall, for a concert by Daniel Overland and Orchestra. I showed them to Nevada. It was a nice gesture on his part. They were expensive seats.

"This is very good of you, Gerry."

"No, it's all right, mate. I'm sorry about the other business, the records."

Nevada had just twigged how much the tickets had cost. "Oh no," she said. "We couldn't possibly accept these, Gerry."

"No, go on, darling. Danny always sends me a couple of tickets whenever he's over here. Always very nice seats. For old times' sake, you know. And I used to make a point of always going up and seeing him. But now, me and Sheryll, we don't get up to London so often. The big city, traffic; it's all a bit much. So the tickets just end up going to waste."

He showed us out, arm on my shoulder, warm whisky breath in my ear. "And don't forget: those records we couldn't find—they're just things." He shoved the tickets into my hand. I took them gratefully. They might well prove useful. His philosophising I wasn't so sure about.

"It's people that count, son," he concluded.

I couldn't argue with that. I still wanted to put his wife in front of a firing squad, though.

"Firing squad, why a firing squad?" said Nevada a few

minutes later, when I told her as much.

"I envisage a proper military tribunal."

"That's very fair-minded of you."

"But the outcome will never be in question," I said.

The next day, spring seemed to decisively arrive. The sunshine poured in the windows of my little house, providing numerous places for cats to sprawl.

I'd decided to make pizzas for supper or, to put it differently, I'd managed to obtain a large number of ripe tomatoes gratis from a shady acquaintance in Wales. So now the only thing for it was to casserole them in the oven, tossed in olive oil, sliced garlic, fresh basil and thyme, and make a pizza sauce.

Judging by the mouth-watering aroma, the sauce was just about done by the time I'd rolled out the dough for the last of the pizza bases. I took the sauce out of the oven and put the bases in. I was smugly congratulating myself about the perfection of my timing when the doorbell rang. I flinched at the sound, then walked to the door like a condemned man.

I fully expected it to be Tinkler, having telepathically sensed that I was making pizza. He'd done it more than once before.

But it was Leo Noel. He was dressed in full cricket regalia, and additionally carrying some kind of large cricket bag with him. He'd evidently torn himself away from his beloved sheds full of 78s. I fleetingly wondered why—then noticed how smartly turned out he was, and concluded, with a sinking feeling, that Nevada had acquired another love-struck admirer.

"Good morning," he said, smiling brightly. My relief that it wasn't Tinkler began to fade and be replaced by a new apprehension. "May I come in?"

"Of course. Good to see you," I lied. I led him inside and down the hallway. Water was splashing in the next room as Nevada took one of her epic baths.

Leo peered eagerly around. "Where's your, ah… lady friend?" The way he said it confirmed my worst fears.

"Taking a bath." He nodded happily at this information, rather too happily I thought, as we walked into the sunlit sitting room. Sonny Rollins was playing on the turntable. The cats lay on the floor, stretched motionless in the sunlight like abandoned artefacts from a very successful cat simulation experiment.

"Oh, pussycats," said Leo, coming to a halt. "I didn't know you had pussycats."

"Yes. For years. Are you allergic?"

"No, not at all. I quite like pussycats."

We sat down at the table. He set the bag on the floor beside him, as if he didn't want it to get away. He nodded at the turntable. "Is that Coltrane?"

"Sonny Rollins. Good guess, though. And full marks for having heard of anybody after Louis Armstrong."

"Ha ha, yes, that is more my period, isn't it?" He smiled and sat back in his chair. He seemed quite at home, relaxing like a lizard in the morning sunshine.

I nodded at the bag on the floor. "Off to play a match?"

He leaned forward and looked at me seriously. "I don't actually *play* cricket. I just wear the clothes."

I said, "How long have I known you Leo? Ten years?"

"Oh sorry, of course. You were being ironic. No, not off to a match. Just thought I'd drop by for a visit. I hope it's not a bad time?"

"Not particularly," I said.

The bathroom door opened and Nevada stepped out in a wave of warm, damp, perfumed air. "Oh, hello," she said, staring at us. "I was wondering who you were talking to." She had just emerged from the bath with a bright red towel wrapped around her, and a matching bright red band in her hair. Bare shoulders emerging from the towel, hair wet and gleaming, she looked ravishing.

Leo certainly thought so. "Hello, Nevada. I was just saying I thought I'd drop by for a visit. I hope it's not a bad time?"

"No, of course not."

"And I brought something for you." He opened the bag and took out a bottle of Perrier. He handed it to Nevada, who accepted it, looking at me.

"How lovely. Thank you."

"I'll put it in the fridge," I did so. Meanwhile, the human palindrome's open delight at seeing a naked girl wrapped in a towel was enough to send Nevada scampering into the bedroom to get dressed. As potentially creepy as Leo was at home, he was potentially much more creepy elsewhere, out of his familiar environment and context. Fanny came wandering over and nosed around in his open bag. Leo studied her fondly.

"We used to have pussycats. I mean, Mum and Dad did. Here, pussy pussy pussy, lovely pussycat," he cooed. Fanny studied Leo cautiously for a moment, and then went back to delving in the bag. Leo said, "Lovely place you've got here. Lovely pussycats. Lovely girlfriend. She really is a cracker." Fanny now decided to actually climb into the bag.

I said, "Okay, Leo. What brings you here?" I might have sounded just a little sharp, but Leo didn't notice. He smiled at me and then abruptly reached down in the bag, causing Fanny to hop out and scoot.

"Do you remember when you visited me I got a phone call about an auction? Some records I'd purchased?"

"Scotland," I said. I felt the slow pulse of excitement start deep inside me.

"Yes, Glasgow, actually. And anyway I was looking through them when they arrived—it was a mixed lot; I had no idea what was in it and neither did the chap who was selling it—and I discovered this." From the depths of his bag he took a 78 in a paper wrapper. "By the Flare Path Orchestra." He squinted at the label. "A little number entitled 'Catfish'."

I was looking at him in astonishment. He seemed pleased with my reaction. He modestly refused to meet my gaze, looking instead at Fanny, who had returned to her place in the sun.

"How appropriate," he cooed. "Would this lovely pussycat like some nice catfish?"

9. THE EMBANKMENT

I still had the Stanton cartridge that we had bought from Lenny, which allowed me to play 78s.

So I stuck the record on the turntable, first flipping it over to read both labels. It was cold and heavy in my hands. Leo was grinning at me. One side did indeed feature a tune called 'Catfish'. The other had something called 'Whitebait'. The composer of both tunes was listed as D. Overland. I took this as a good omen, since it was undoubtedly the same guy we had tickets to see at the Royal Festival Hall.

From its title I had expected 'Catfish' to be an exercise in faux Dixieland or Deep South mannerisms. In fact it turned out an oddly cool, almost impressionistic piece. It was reminiscent of the Claude Thornhill band at its finest, but more intensely rhythmic. It was a compelling piece and created a sustained mood of combined elation and tension, only disrupted by a spurt of what I had come to think of as the Flare Path Orchestra's trademark wacky instrumentation, which almost tipped it over into the realm of a novelty number.

In this case, it was a jaunty intrusion by what sounded like a banjo and a triangle.

Towards the end of the piece the horns began to make an eerie keening that seemed oddly familiar—and disturbing. Then I realised that they were imitating aircraft sirens.

There followed violent, almost abstract blasts of percussion, scattered seemingly at random, like bursts of anti-aircraft fire exploding in the sky. It was a tour de force conclusion.

'Whitebait' was more playful and toe-tapping, though it showed the same moody complexity. There were no novelty intrusions here, though. No harmonicas, cowbells or xylophones. And it was all the better for it.

Nevada emerged from the bedroom, now fully dressed, and came over to sit beside me on the sofa in front of the speakers. We listened to the music together. Meanwhile Leo remained happily at the table, playing with Fanny, who was back in his cricket bag, her little head sticking out. She allowed Leo to stroke her between the ears. He seemed entirely besotted with the cat, and she was suffering his attentions good-naturedly.

When the record was over—all too soon—Nevada got up and went to the turntable and looked at it. "D. Overland?" she said. She looked at me. "Danny Overland?"

"So it would seem," I said. Mr Overland was evidently a very interesting musical mind.

I was looking forward to meeting him.

* * *

First, though, I needed to pay a visit to our client and update her about our progress. I filled Joan Honeyland in on our discoveries, and she was particularly pleased with the record Leo had turned up. But she was almost as happy about the duplicate 78 I'd got from Gresford-Jones. And she listened with keen attention to my summary of our conversation with him in Dover. I'd given her a sound file of the recording Nevada had made of our talk with him.

"All that will be very helpful for the standard biography," she said.

I didn't tell her about Gerry Wuggins in Sevenoaks. Not only had we not got any records out of him, we'd completely forgotten about recording any of his reminiscences. Nevada and I planned to visit him again and put this right.

What I *did* do was arrange for the agreed sums to be paid to Charles Gresford-Jones and Leo Noel for the records they'd sold us. Despite the large amounts I'd agreed on her behalf, Miss Honeyland did this without a qualm, typing expertly at her computer and transferring the money to their respective bank accounts.

The computer was set up on the dining table in the front room of her flat. The flat was tiny but nevertheless was no doubt worth a fortune. It was located above its own garage, another incredibly valuable asset, in a little mews in the middle of Soho. A location like this in central London was gold dust. All of Miss Honeyland's neighbours appeared to be media premises, film production houses and the like. Hers was the only domestic dwelling in the mews, and I had the strong impression that she owned it. Indeed, that it had been in the family for years.

This was the first evidence I'd had—apart from her car and clothes—that her dad's books for children really commanded the kind of wealth that she'd been talking about. The room in which we sat looked out over the narrow cobbled mews where the Mercedes gleamed. When I'd walked past it on the way in, it had seemed like some kind of a magic trick. The car was polished, immaculate, without a scratch.

I'd walked around it, looking carefully, but I could find no trace of the massive damage I'd seen last time. Some very expensive repairs had been effected, and damned smartly too.

Miss Honeyland smiled at the computer. "There, that's done," she said. She looked up at me. "Now I imagine you'll be wanting some cash yourself."

"Cash?"

"For out-of-pocket expenses. Walking-around money, as the Americans say. I'll go next door and get you some." She stood up, switching off the computer. As she crossed the small room she paused at the window and looked out with a fond, proprietary gaze at the Mercedes down below. Then she went out through a doorway hung with a clattering curtain of green and white beads. I was alone in the tiny place.

I was sitting in one of two armchairs. The room was too small for any kind of a sofa. A square wooden table in the corner beside the window had the computer on it and apparently also served for dining. Wooden chairs were tucked tightly away under it, their slatted backs close to the table edge. Another table took up most of the remaining space. This one was low and rectangular and stacked with piles of books.

Books for children. Mostly by 'Lucky', including of course *Farmer Henry Versus the Locusts*, but there were also quite a few classics by other kids' authors. Among these, and seemingly out of place, were a couple of yellowing Air Ministry pamphlets about the importance of the bombing effort in Europe, and a plastic folder of equally yellowing newspaper clippings. All I could see of the clippings were their edges protruding out of the folder.

But I suspected all of them were connected with Colonel Honeyland.

I turned to the bookshelves that lined the walls. Between these hung framed photographs of the famous man himself in his RAF days and, incongruously, a dartboard with bits of coloured paper stuck on it.

Listening to Joan Honeyland make mysterious noises in some remote corner of the flat, I felt a nice little glow of satisfaction. She seemed well pleased with our progress. And I certainly wasn't going to argue with her offer to give us some cash.

I took a closer look at the dartboard. The pieces of paper had been torn or clipped from magazines, newspapers, and apparently books. Each one bore the likeness of a famous children's character. There was Peter Rabbit, Thomas the Tank Engine, Winnie the Pooh, Paddington Bear and Mr Toad.

Peter Rabbit had a rather painful-looking dart stuck into his left eye.

I heard Miss Honeyland coming back and returned to

my chair. She came into the room with an envelope and two cardboard containers of coffee with the name of a famous Soho delicatessen on them. "I almost forgot," she said. "I'd asked Albert to go out and get these earlier. I understand you're quite a coffee drinker. I hope it isn't too cold." She handed me one of the coffees and the envelope. I put the reassuringly weighty envelope of cash in my pocket, resisting the urge to tear it open there and then. Instead I took the lid off the coffee and had a sniff. It smelled good. I took a sip.

"Is it stone cold?" said Miss Honeyland. She was standing in front of me, watching me eagerly.

"No, it's fine." It was. She remained standing in front of me, watching expectantly. I began to wonder if I was supposed to say or do something. I began to feel a little uneasy. There was, after all, a long history in Soho of people being expected to do all kinds of extraordinary things after being handed some money.

Finally she said, "Do you notice anything?"

I desperately hoped I wasn't supposed to say how youthful she looked with her new hairstyle or anything like that. Then I got it.

"No cane," I said.

She nodded approvingly. "It's my second day off it. I'm virtually back to normal."

"That's great," I said.

"Have to be careful on the stairs, though, of course."

"And no bicycling."

"No, ha ha. Not just yet." She pulled out one of the

chairs from under the table and sat down again, this time by the window. As we sipped our coffee she resumed gazing out and downwards into the mews below, with the same proprietary look as before. I assumed she was looking at the Mercedes, but when I said my goodbyes and stood up to go I saw that the Mercedes was being washed by Albert the chauffeur, who was stripped to the waist. As he sponged the vehicle, water gleamed on his rippling torso and chest. His powerful arms bulged as he swabbed energetically.

Nevada would have enjoyed the spectacle. And Clean Head would have appreciated both the car and the figure washing it.

Finally Miss Honeyland managed to tear herself away from the sight long enough to see me to the door of the flat, which led out to a very narrow echoing stairway and down to the mews itself. I walked out past the garage, avoiding the sudsy water on the cobblestones and nodding to Albert. I glanced up and saw his employer's pale face in the window. I waved but she didn't see me.

When we'd described Miss Honeyland to Tinkler, he had immediately remarked, "The old bat has a young chauffeur? She's probably shagging him." This was typical Tinkler. He hadn't even met them. If we'd described the woman turning up at our door with a Labrador retriever at her heels he wouldn't have been above positing an improper relationship between the woman and the dog.

I'd dismissed his comments.

But now something about her expression, and the deliberately exhibitionist nature of Albert's display, made me wonder if maybe old Tinkler was right after all. The whole car-washing performance seemed designed for someone's benefit. The car hadn't even seemed dirty.

Of course, I could have got completely the wrong end of the stick. We were, after all, in the middle of Soho, where the muscular young men were primarily interested in other muscular young men. Perhaps the chauffeur drove on the other side of the road, so to speak. And his employer's gaze signified nothing more than abstract admiration.

On the other hand, two people could live quite cosily in that flat above the garage.

As I walked through the short dark tunnel that led from the mews to the street I took the envelope out of my pocket and tore it open. Five hundred pounds in fresh new twenty-pound notes. Walking-around money indeed. Nevada would be pleased.

I noticed a man standing just outside the mews, waiting on the pavement. He was a skinny guy with a scraggly beard, in a green waxed-cotton jacket. He looked more like a yokel out for a day of poaching rather than someone trawling the sinful delights of the metropolis. Then I saw the camera around his neck and thought, *tourist*. He was staring quite intently towards the mews. But as I glanced at him he turned away, rather furtively, I thought. As I walked off, I glanced back over my shoulder at him. He was taking something out of his jacket. It glinted in his hand. A pair of spectacles. He shook them open and put them on.

I tucked the money deep into my pocket and walked away.

* * *

"You always get paranoid about someone following us, anyway," said Nevada. "So I reasoned that it would be better if we travelled in a taxi, because not only does it give us more control of the situation, the whole travelling situation—"

"Except when we're in heavy traffic," I said, peering out the taxi window at an apparently endless queue of stationary vehicles extending in both directions. I had suggested that we might have been better off making this journey by train to Waterloo. And I still thought the taxi wasn't a great idea.

"Except when we're in heavy traffic, granted. And also, this is the crucial thing, with Clean Head on the watch for us we're more likely to know if anyone is following us."

"True," I said. This was a good point. If someone was on our tail—and despite Nevada calling it paranoia, it had happened in the past—it would be better for us to know about it. And perhaps to draw them out.

"Which gives us the initiative, and puts us in control," said Nevada, completing my own thought. "Plus," she said, glancing at Clean Head in the compartment in front of us. Her bald head gleamed, a sculptural entity in its own right. You could see from the set of her neck that she was concentrating on the traffic flow in a reassuringly expert way. "And almost as importantly," continued Nevada, "we get to give a paying job to an old friend."

"Also true." We lurched forward, moving at last. I stared out the window behind me. I hadn't been paranoid before, but I was now. Were we being followed? We were just passing the London Eye, and every motor vehicle in London seemed to be here. I said, "We can get out anywhere around here. Can she hear us? Clean Head, have you got your sound system on at the moment?"

"I can hear you loud and clear, back there being a cheapskate."

"I know," said Nevada. "And it's not even his money."

Clean Head dropped us off outside Waterloo Station and we crossed the road among a throng of pedestrians. All of them, like us, were apparently heading for the South Bank Centre by the river. This was where the Royal Festival Hall was located, and it was where Danny Overland was rehearsing today. I had phoned the RFH and managed to get a number for Overland's management, where I'd spoken to a public relations person and arranged today's 'interview'. I hadn't corrected anyone's assumption that I was some kind of music journalist.

"Did you have to invoke the dreaded name of Stinky?" said Nevada. Stinky Stanmer was an old acquaintance of mine who'd climbed the slippery media pole with amazing alacrity and now had his own radio program. Sometimes even the television wasn't safe from his presence. In the past we'd used his name as an entrée to people in the music business we wanted to talk to, people I couldn't get at otherwise.

I shook my head. "It didn't prove necessary. They seemed quite eager to set up a meeting." We walked up the stairs, past the enormous bust of Nelson Mandela, and out along the windswept concrete of the Embankment. There was a cool breeze, but the sun was shining, glittering with blinding brightness on the Thames among the white riverboats.

At the coffee shop in the Royal Festival Hall we met Overland's PR, a pretty, suntanned Australian girl called Jenny. Overland was supposed to be there too, but all that remained of him was an empty coffee mug. "He's gone out for a smoke," she said, pointing back through the glass doors towards the Embankment. "He said you could find him and have a chat out there."

As we went back out the sliding doors she called, "Good luck." A remark that only later, in retrospect, took on significance.

We found Danny Overland standing by the river, smoking. He was a bald, wiry old man with a dark suntan and a deeply lined simian face. He was wearing flared jeans, which were either cutting edge or extremely dated, and a white shirt open at the throat, revealing grey curls of chest hair. Around his neck he wore a string with a white plastic clip on it that looked like it was designed to be attached to some kind of saxophone.

He didn't seem bothered by the cool river breeze despite only wearing the thin shirt. We were in jackets and scarves.

I said, "Mr Overland?"

He grimaced and nodded.

"If you don't mind, we wanted to ask you a few questions about Colonel Honeyland."

He took the cigarette out of his mouth. Smoke bled between his lips and was carried away on the wind.

"That fucking bastard," he said.

* * *

And our interview went downhill from there. Any notions of recording it and thereby gaining the delighted approbation of our client began to spiral down the drain.

I had assumed that the mention of Colonel Honeyland's name would be met with the same kind of glowing nostalgic approval that had greeted it at our previous interviews. Instead, it rapidly became clear that Overland had no time for the late children's author and air hero. No time at all.

"That son of a bitch," he said truculently. "Talentless dumb tosser." His Australian accent wasn't especially marked.

"So you don't rate him as a musician?" I said. Overland turned his face away from me disgustedly and stared at the river. "How about as a pilot?" He shot me a fierce look. I had his attention, anyway. I seemed to have touched a sore spot.

"As a pilot?" He shrugged. "The only thing he was worse at than flying a plane was leading a band." He turned away again, offering us his profile as he smoked his cigarette. I looked at Nevada. She shrugged helplessly. I decided to change tack.

"What about the Glenn Miller band?" I said.

He kept watching the river. "What about them?"

"I understand they were enormously popular here during the war."

He looked at me again. "The war?" he said. "What do you know about the war?"

"Nothing," I said, sensing an opportunity. "We were

hoping you could tell us about it."

"'Nothing' is right," said Overland with satisfaction. He looked at Nevada. "There was this girl who interviewed me in Melbourne for one of the papers. Did a very nice piece too. Lots of references to my experiences in World War One. World War Fucking One." He shook his head disgustedly.

"I do realise that's the wrong war," said Nevada. But he wasn't even listening.

"I like going to the pictures," he said, apparently apropos of nothing. "And whenever there's a film with a score by Johnny Williams I make a particular point of going along." I couldn't quite follow this sudden shift of logic and I wondered if it was a senior moment. But the steely contempt in his voice signalled a sharpness of focus that suggested otherwise. "And as a result of this," said Overland, "I've seen some of the damnedest movies. One of my favourites was one of those Indiana Jones pictures. It was the one where Indy runs into Hitler and a bunch of his brown-shirted goons."

"Was that the *Last Crusade*?" said Nevada, still trying gamely. But he ignored her again.

"And when he sees them, Indy says, 'Nazis—I hate those guys.' Do you know why he says that?" He didn't wait for an answer. "He says it so that people like you, children like you, kiddies who have never heard of Hitler or the Nazis or World War Two, will know what to think." He flicked his cigarette butt away on the wind. "I suppose someone has to tell you what to think."

"Look," I said, "why don't you tell us—"

"What do you know about strategic bombing?" he said. Another sudden shift of logic. I realised that, far from being a sign of vagueness on his part, these abrupt segues were actually deliberately calculated to keep us off balance and on the defensive. Like a prize-fighter crowding you to the ropes.

Certainly he seemed as combative as a boxer. "Come on," he said. "The strategic bombing campaign by the RAF in the Second World War." He looked at us, his dark eyes glittering. "What can you tell me about it?"

"Not a great deal," said Nevada brightly. "However—"

We never got to hear what brilliant idea Nevada was about to offer because he shook his head and said, with some measure of finality and disgust, "You just don't know the score." He turned away and looked at the river again. Gulls were wheeling and crying in the air above the bright water. "Send me someone who knows the score. I'll talk to them."

I said, "There isn't anyone else. Just us."

He looked at me. "Then come back when you can demonstrate you know your arse from your elbow." He took out a packet of cigarettes and a lighter. "If you ever achieve that." He lit a new cigarette and puffed on it. This, at least, seemed to make him happy. Then he turned back to his river view. "Because, until then, you're wasting your time. And, more importantly, you're wasting mine."

The following evening we got a phone call from Tinkler, who wanted us to come out and play. I told him that was impossible.

"Why not? I mean, why? Why impossible?"

I sighed and looked at the huge stack of library books in front of me. "Because I've got just about every book about World War Two that's available through the Wandsworth Public Library system. And I have to read, or at least look through, all of them."

"Why in god's name would you want to do that?"

"Because I've had enough of wading my way through the swamp of rumour, opinion, speculation, and occasional nugget of fact on the Internet."

I explained about our encounter with Danny Overland, the bastard, and his ultimatum. "If we want to talk to him, apparently we have to be able to prove that we know about the war and what he, and presumably other people like him, went through during it."

"Instead of doing all that reading, wouldn't it be easier just to go and talk to someone who is an expert in the field?"

I said, "Unfortunately, I don't know anyone like that."

"But I do," said Tinkler.

10. SATAN'S LADDER

We had first met Erik Make Loud—née Eric McCloud—
when we'd been researching the legendary British 1960s
rock chick Valerian. He had played in her band—indeed,
it had been Valerian who'd given him his name. But while
Nevada and I had remained on strictly business terms with
Eric—sorry, Erik—my old mate Tinkler had somehow
managed to strike up an implausibly close friendship with
the erstwhile rock god and lead guitarist.

So it was Tinkler who made the arrangements and
accompanied us on our visit to Erik's house beside the
river in Barnes. It was a modernist white residence with an
odd little moat around it, set deep in concrete. Erik feared
that the Thames might break its banks and wash his guitar
collection away. But if the mighty river did flood, I had my
doubts about how much good one little moat would do.

Erik himself opened the door. In fact, threw it open
enthusiastically and grinned at Tinkler as though he were
the prodigal returned. "Jordon, my old mucker. Come in,

come in." He slapped Tinkler on the back and led him inside, waving for us to follow. "Brought your friends, eh?"

"Yes, sorry about that. They're very annoying, too. We'll try and get rid of them as quickly as possible."

Erik laughed and pounded Tinkler on the back some more. "Good old Jordon. He was just joking. Jordon the joker. You're very welcome, all of you." After we came in, he stared at the open door in puzzlement for a moment, and then went and closed it himself, with the manner of a man unaccustomed to doing such things. "Very welcome," he repeated. Tanned and long-haired, he was looking fit and trim in an ornate Cuban shirt made of very fine cloth, and exquisitely faded jeans with strategic tears at the knees. He was barefoot, which made sense given the pleasant warmth of the heated tile floors.

"I got you that Faces LP you were looking for," said Tinkler. "With the original textured cover."

"Nice one," said Erik. He seemed genuinely delighted and gave Tinkler an energetic high-five. The sound of slapping hands echoed in the hallway.

"Yeah, nice one," burbled Tinkler, inordinately pleased with himself.

"Good to see you, mate."

"Good to see *you*, mate."

They hugged.

"It's a bromance," said Nevada in a voice that only I could hear. I put my mouth to her ear and said, "Just as long as they don't start talking about football."

Erik and Tinkler broke their manly clinch. "Where's Bong Cha?" said Tinkler.

"Setting up the audio-visual room."

"Nice one."

Bong Cha, whose name irresistibly suggested teenagers in their bedrooms furtively smoking controlled substances in bubble pipes, was in fact a rather strait-laced middle-aged woman who worked as Erik's housekeeper and live-in cook. Despite her dwelling full-time under the same roof as the priapic guitar hero, even Tinkler had been unable to impute a carnal dimension to their relationship.

Her name actually signified something like 'venerated daughter'. She was from South Korea by way of Birmingham.

She was waiting for us upstairs in the 'audio-visual room'. I hadn't been in this part of the house before, and I was impressed at how large it was. Our kitty cats could have spent days exploring the place. The audio-visual room was a rectangular space facing south—away from the river, and presumably towards a dense cluster of housing. A wide window that spanned the room would have given us a view of this, but it had been screened off by a highly effective blackout blind. The sunlight outside was just a remote subdued glow on its heavy cream fabric. Just below the blind was a long black sofa with a low table in front of it, and reclining armchairs on either side of it made of chrome and bright red suede. On the wall opposite was the biggest, flattest flat-screen television I'd seen in my life. There were no controls of any kind in evidence on it.

The table in front of the sofa consisted of an irregularly shaped, scarred slab of silver wood suspended over a smoked glass shelf on which were resting a large collection of remote controls. On the wooden slab was a bottle of peach vodka in a transparent plastic ice bucket and tall, ice-filled glasses. There was also a pile of black paper napkins, some white plates and gleaming cutlery, and a large tray covered with what looked like caviar and sour cream on blinis. They had served the same snacks to us last time. Perhaps it was the only food Bong Cha knew how to prepare.

She was in the process of putting napkins and cutlery on the plates as we trooped in, and she shot me a dirty look as if she'd sensed my thought. Perhaps I was being unfair to her. Perhaps it was the only one Erik allowed her to prepare.

"Sit down, sit down," he said. He ushered us over to the sofa and we sat. Meanwhile, Bong Cha moved around the table, to the opposite side from us, presumably to avoid contact with the guy who'd telepathically dissed her culinary skills, and continued setting out plates. "Back in a sec," said Erik.

He left the room and then came back with a pile of books. I recognised many of the same titles I had so recently borrowed from the library but these appeared to have all come from his own collection. So maybe Tinkler hadn't been entirely wrong about him being a World War Two specialist. He sat down on the armchair beside the sofa and slapped his knees. "Right. So you want to know about the air war in Europe?"

"Should I take notes?" said Nevada, taking out her smartphone.

Bong Cha snorted. Now that she'd finished setting out the food I expected Erik to send her from the room, but instead she settled into the other armchair. Obviously she was part of the discussion. Erik smiled at me.

"Bong Cha is the expert on the Yanks."

"And air warfare," said the housekeeper.

"No, *I'm* the expert on the air warfare."

Bong Cha shrugged contemptuously. "Ha."

"Well, let's just say it's one of the areas where we overlap. Where our areas of expertise overlap."

"Like the Blitzkrieg in Western Europe."

Erik nodded. "Yeah, like the Blitzkrieg in Western Europe. And like the North African campaign."

"Do you mind if I have some of these?" said Tinkler, reaching for the caviar blinis. Erik gave a start and lunged forward, snatching the vodka bottle out of the ice bucket so quickly that we were showered with fine drops of water.

"Where are my manners?" he said. He splashed large amounts of vodka into the waiting glasses and passed them around. Tinkler took his in one hand while industriously scooping up blinis with the other. Erik looked at me over the rim of his drinking glass. A slice of peach floated in the clear turbulence of the vodka, as did one in each of our glasses. It was a nice touch. I could tell Nevada was impressed. "Do you know the most fascinating aspect of the North African campaign?" said Erik.

"No. I don't really know much about World War Two at all."

"That's sort of why we're here," said Nevada. She fished the slice of peach from her glass and took a neat bite out of it. I suspected she wanted to dive into the caviar, but thought it was polite to wait. However, the way that Tinkler was going at it she'd have to get in quick if she wanted to claim a share.

"The most fascinating aspect of the North African campaign," said Erik, "was Rommel."

"General Rommel."

"See, you do know something," said Erik, leaning forward to punch me on the knee in a friendly manner—though not so friendly that it didn't cause half my leg to go numb. It seemed that my status as Tinkler's friend made me part of the inner circle. I was hoping he wouldn't try to high-five or hug me.

"Rommel was a military genius." Maybe so, but he had nothing to do with the war in the air. I knew that much about the subject. I sighed inwardly and braced myself for a long afternoon of being harangued about irrelevant specialist topics. Erik sipped his vodka contentedly, savouring his dissertation. "He was the greatest of the Nazi generals."

Bong Cha shook her head. "Rommel was nothing. Guderian was the true genius."

Erik looked at her and shook his head. "Yes, you would think that," he said, pityingly.

"You're always wrong about everything," said Bong Cha. "Who do you think was the finest Allied commander?"

"Patton," hazarded Erik.

"Patton? Ha! Slim of Burma." Bong Cha grabbed a blini before Tinkler could pick it up and ate it rapidly but daintily, with one hand under her chin. I noticed she had no use for the plates, napkins and cutlery she had so painstakingly laid out for the rest of us. "What does Erik know?" she said.

"Erik thinks the most important weapons system of World War Two was the Soviet T-34 tank."

"It was," said Erik, sounding a little stung.

"No." She shook her head. Now it was her turn to take pity on him. "The most important weapons system of the war was the US Mustang P-51 fighter-bomber."

Erik rose from his chair. I thought he was going to make a particularly important point about the P-51 but instead he held out a remote control and pointed it at the big screen on the wall opposite. "Anyway, let's start by showing you one of the documentaries from our collection. About the air war in Europe."

I was glad that we were back on topic. But the screen didn't come on. It remained gleaming and black.

This occasioned much confusion among our hosts. Erik tried another remote control from the shelf under the table. Then Bong Cha scolded him and tried a third one. Then they both went to the other side of the room and began to closely inspect the big screen, looking for a manual switch that was reportedly carefully camouflaged somewhere on the fascia.

While they did this I leaned over and spoke quietly to Tinkler. "They contradict each other about everything."

Tinkler nodded and smiled proudly. "I know. That's the beauty of it."

"Beauty?"

"This way you get a balanced view. Have you tried these blinis? They're magnificent."

* * *

Jenny, Danny Overland's PR person, seemed astonished that we wanted to meet him and try again. "No one comes back twice," she said. She had insisted on meeting us in the same café at the Royal Festival Hall and buying us coffee and cakes. Which was nice. She evidently wanted to make amends for our last encounter with the great man.

"It must be awful having to arrange interviews for him," said Nevada, at her most sympathetic and interested, "when he's so irascible."

"Irascible," said Jenny. "That's putting it mildly. But he's all right sometimes. It depends on what time of day you catch him."

I said, "Is now a good or bad time of day?"

She shrugged. "It varies. From day to day."

We finished our coffee and cakes, got advice on the irascible one's current location, then went out through the sliding doors like a couple of Christians entering the arena.

There was a book market by the riverside today, numerous stalls selling overpriced hardcovers and paperbacks. I noticed a box of vintage Penguins, easily identifiable by their orange spines, and thought of Clean Head, who was a devoted collector of them. There were art books, books on architecture, cars, and ballet. I saw a table of military history titles and flinched. It was our big audition, the final exam, but were we adequately prepared? We were going to find out.

Because of the book stalls, he'd had to move a little further downstream, but otherwise Danny Overland was standing in a similar spot to last time, and cutting a similar figure. Except now he was wearing a short-sleeved shirt. This was one old man who really didn't feel the cold. He was lighting a fresh cigarette as we approached him. He put his lighter away, exhaled smoke and said, "You two again."

"You said to come back when we knew what strategic bombing means."

"Did I? So, what does it mean?"

I cleared my throat. Nevada gave me a look of encouragement and squeezed my hand. I said, "Strategic bombing is fighting a battle from the air. Planes dropping bombs, not in support of the army or navy, but for their own purpose."

He nodded and said, "Which means…"

"Which means, well… it means the 'bomber barons', the ambitious air force chiefs, wanted to promote their own cause. So they argued in favour of strategic bombing. Because it would give them autonomy and power." I was paraphrasing what Erik and Bong Cha had told us the other day—amid much internecine bickering—and summarising wildly.

Danny Overland nodded and said, "Which means…"

"Ah, which means they had to stick to a policy of strategic bombing or they risked being subsumed into the army or navy."

He shook his head impatiently. "No, what does it *mean*? What does the bombing mean? The actual fucking bombing?"

I said, "Massive attacks on German cities…"

"Cities! Exactly. *Civilians* in cities. Ever since the First World War—and I do know a bit about the First World War despite the fact that I didn't actually fight in it, not being quite that fucking old." He'd obviously really been stung by that interview in Melbourne. "Anyway, ever since that war ended, there'd been a cult of air power. There were people who saw the future of warfare coming from the skies. And they always knew that would mean bombing civilians. That's what it was always about, though no one would say it aloud. You see, they thought that if you killed enough civilians it would bring a quick end to any war. It would lead to the collapse of morale. To surrender."

He sucked fiercely on his cigarette and stared out at the river. The brisk wind streamed his smoke away. It was a classic English spring day, which was to say, bright sunshine and biting chill. I was amazed he could stand here comfortably in his short-sleeved shirt, without so much as a goose bump on his skinny old arms, but evidently he could.

He said, "But when the Germans bombed you Brits, it didn't cause your morale to collapse. It didn't make you surrender. It got you *angry*. It made you fight *harder*." He looked at us. "So you can see why our strategic bombing campaign against Germany didn't shorten the war. Not by one minute. If anything, it made it go on longer."

I was glad we'd cleared that up.

He looked at the cigarette burning in his fingers and said, "Perhaps if we'd bombed other targets, military targets, it really would have shortened the war. We could have crippled the German war effort if we'd struck at crucial industrial centres."

"Like the ball-bearing factory at Schweinfurt," said Nevada.

He froze in the act of returning the cigarette to his lips. "Yes, like that, sweetheart," he said. "We could have bombed real targets instead of flattening hospitals and schools and people's homes. Melting women and children like candles by dropping white phosphorous on them."

Nevada shuddered, a little theatrically, I thought. But Overland seemed gratified with the effect he'd achieved. He said, "And your mate Colonel Lucian Honeyland, good old Lucky, he was one of the staunchest advocates of strategic bombing. He was one of Bomber Harris's closest advisers at High Wycombe. He supported the campaign; he propagandised for it. He wrote pamphlets and newspaper articles."

I remembered the yellowing pamphlets I'd seen in Joan Honeyland's flat, and the brittle old newspaper clippings. Now I knew why they were filed with Lucky's children's books. They represented the complete literary works of Lucian Honeyland.

Overland went on, "Bomber Harris made the decisions, Johnny Maze wrote the memos, and our old pal Lucky helped sell the idea of strategic bombing to the public, the carpet bombing of German cities and civilians. It was a well-oiled propaganda machine. And Lucky was the official mouthpiece. Bomber Command's champion of mass slaughter."

I said, "Did you feel that way about it at the time?"

"At the time? At the time all I cared about was getting through it alive. Do you know what a bomber crew's chances were of dying?"

"One in twenty," said Nevada. She'd been taking notes at Erik's.

He nodded. "And do you know how many missions we flew?"

"Thirty?"

"Forty." He puffed meditatively on his cigarette. "We flew forty missions. So we were dead men twice over."

"It must have been terrible," said Nevada. She seemed to be building up a rapport with him, so I was happy to leave her to it. "The sacrifices you made were incredible. You were all heroes." Was she laying it on a bit thick? Probably not.

"Heroes?" He chuckled. "Would you like to hear how they treated us heroes? When we went out on a mission we were issued with chocolate and sandwiches. And if we had to turn back for any reason without completing the mission—if we had engine trouble, if we were shot up by an enemy fighter, if we ran out of fuel—we had to give back the chocolate and sandwiches unopened." He grinned at us. "And if we didn't, we'd be up on a charge."

"That's appalling."

"That's nothing. It was typical. We were supposed to obey orders and go out and get killed like obedient little robots. Never ask questions. Keep a stiff upper lip. And die. One time some genius at Bomber Command sent down orders for us to try mixed loads." He looked at us steadily. "Mixed bomb loads. Do you know what happens if a bomber drops a mixed load of bombs?"

This was a rhetorical question if ever there was one. Nevertheless, I said, "No."

"Well, you see, some of the bombs will be bigger, heavier and different shapes than others. So when you start dropping the bombs they'll fall at different rates. Imagine a long strip of bombs dropping out of the bottom of your plane. And some of them are falling faster than others. So they'll hit the other bombs going down." He looked at his cigarette, which he'd smoked down to the filter. "And they'll explode. Which causes the bombs above them to explode. And the ones above them. And so on. Up and up the explosions go, like Satan climbing a ladder in the air. And when Satan gets up to the plane…"

I said, "It explodes too?"

He threw his cigarette butt away, over the embankment rail, into the river.

"So understandably we weren't too keen on mixed loads or those new orders. And we refused. Two of us refused. A British pilot and me. The Brit ended up in a military prison. They could do bugger all to me because I was Australian, but they made sure they made an example of the British boy." He looked at me. "Your old friend Lucky could have done something." He seemed to believe there was a deep bond of affection between me and the late children's author. It didn't seem worth correcting him. "He could have intervened on his behalf. But not old Lucky. He was far too conscious of his position as Bomber Harris's lap dog. He wasn't about to do anything to jeopardise his status."

"Is that why you hate him?" said Nevada, in that direct way that only women seem able to get away with.

"It's one of the reasons. But it's not even the main one."

"We found one of your records," I said, interrupting. I thought it might get him off the subject of how much he hated Lucky, and the myriad reasons for this hatred.

Overland had been taking a fresh cigarette out of the pack—it was far too long since he'd smoked the last one—but now he paused and swivelled his gaze towards me. "A record? Of mine?"

"By the Flare Path Orchestra. You wrote both the tunes, 'Catfish' and 'Whitebait', didn't you?"

He stared at me as he tapped the cigarette on the side of the pack, in an odd little musical rhythm. "You're kidding," he said. It was the first time we'd drawn a spontaneous reaction out of him, instead of well-rehearsed anger about old grievances. "I didn't think any of them still existed."

"Well, they're not too thick on the ground," I said.

He chuckled. "No, I bet they're not." Then his eyes narrowed. "Did you listen to it?"

I sensed he was setting a trap for me. "Yes," I said.

"What did you think?" There it was.

"I thought 'Catfish' was very effective," I said, "especially the anti-aircraft barrage at the end."

He chuckled again. "Well spotted. Did you like the horn section imitating the sirens?"

"Yes. That was another nice touch."

"Not really. It was banned from broadcast after the first couple of times it went out on the radio. It seems people were shitting themselves when they heard it. The siren sounds were all too realistic." He looked at me. "What about the other side? 'Whitebait'?"

"That was the better of the two, I thought."

He nodded decisively. "Right. Do you know why?

Because Lucky always fucking interfered with the music. I'd write a lovely little arrangement, just perfect the way it was, a little gem. And then he'd go and stick some fucking tambourine or xylophone or theremin or something onto it and ruin the whole effect." He grinned, showing teeth that were surprisingly white considering their age and the steady flow of nicotine across them. "But on 'Whitebait' he was called away to High Wycombe during the broadcast—it was recorded from a live radio broadcast—so I was able to remove his shitty interference. He hit the roof when he heard it. That was our parting of the ways. I didn't regret it. I only regretted I hadn't been able to also remove his shit from 'Catfish', which was the better piece. At least in conception."

He looked at Nevada. "You wanted to know why I hated him? That was the main reason I hated him. He always interfered with my fucking music." Nevada nodded as if this was a perfectly reasonable position. Which, come to think of it, it was.

He said, "Do you know what those titles mean? 'Catfish' and 'Whitebait'?"

"No."

"Code names. Catfish was Munich, and Whitebait was Berlin. They were bombing targets."

Nevada said, "We can make a copy of the recording for you, if you like."

"No thanks, darling. I'm trying to forget all that."

11. TP37

Despite what he'd so fiercely asserted, with smoke pouring out of his mouth like a pantomime dragon, I couldn't really believe Danny Overland wasn't interested in hearing his old records. After all, they were his own compositions. And they were very good. Plus he probably hadn't heard the damned things in over half a century.

What's more, I'd seen something in his eye when he learned that one of those rare fragile old discs had survived. He was interested, all right.

So I rang up Joan Honeyland. Thanks to Tinkler, I couldn't get the notion of her being banged by the chauffeur out of my head. I was almost reluctant to ring her number in case I interrupted some upstairs-downstairs carnal hi-jinks in their bijou flat over the Soho mews.

But Miss Honeyland picked up on the first ring, sounding composed and alert. Pleased to hear from me, in fact. I told her about meeting Overland and how he couldn't help us with any records. "Never mind," she said. "You've done remarkably well already in a very short space of time. I'm sure if there are any more out there, you'll find them for me."

I said I'd do my best. I didn't mention Overland's withering remarks about her father. When she asked if we'd recorded his reminiscences, or whether we even thought it was worth doing so, I said, "I think it would be worth it. But he's very busy and somewhat… cantankerous." She chuckled dryly. "So I've decided to offer him a bribe," I said.

"If it's a matter of money, you know I leave it entirely up to you."

"I don't think money will do it. What I think might do it is a copy of that record we found. The one with his own compositions. Frankly, I think it would appeal to his vanity."

"Ah, yes, I see."

"So I'd like to get a digital copy of it that I can send him. You said you were planning to make digital copies anyway…"

She hesitated for a moment, then she said, "I'm just thinking about the logistics. We've already given the records to a studio."

"A studio?"

"Yes, we anticipated you, I'm afraid. We've already started our own attempt to make digital copies."

"Well, that's useful," I said. Although I'd rather have made the copies myself.

"I hope so. Albert just dropped them off there. At a little recording studio in south London. The recording engineer there is said to be very good. He comes highly recommended. He's said to be excellent."

He'd better be, I thought. "And reliable?" I said.

"Oh yes. So as soon as he's digitised the record, I shall send you a copy of the two tunes. It's 'Catfish' and 'Whiting', isn't it?"

"'Whitebait'," I corrected her. And I wondered, if a radio operator had made the same slip during the war, would another German city entirely have been bombed by mistake? Random hell pouring from the sky in a nightmare torrent, all because of a slip of the tongue.

"Well, if you give Mr Overland a copy of the tunes, it will have to be in the form of a copy-protected compact disc. And he'll have to agree to return it to us once he's listened to it."

"I'm sure we can arrange that," I said.

"He can have a copy of the proper CD, of course, when it eventually comes out. The collected album of the Flare Path Orchestra tunes. But in the meantime he'll have to make do with the copy-protected disc."

She seemed obsessed with that phrase.

"And for that we have to wait on the labours of this recording engineer fellow." I couldn't argue with that. So I thanked her and said goodbye.

When I told Nevada about it I said, "I could have transferred the bloody record for her. I've still got the Stanton. I could have played it on my turntable and run it through an AD converter."

"I have no doubt."

"All I needed was the right cable."

She nodded. "And if you had done it, we could have *charged* her for it. Why on earth didn't she ask you to do it in the first place?"

I shrugged. "She wanted it done properly, by a proper sound engineer, and I suppose I can see her point."

"Well this joker better be good."

"That's what I thought."

"He better not turn out to be some kid with a computer in his bedroom."

"I'll look him up online." I sat down at the laptop and saw that I had mail. To be more accurate, I had a notification that someone had left a message on my blog. I went to see what it was. I felt a keen flicker of excitement as I read it.

> If you are looking for records by the Flare Path
> Orchestra I have one to sell.

There was no name, or any other indication of the identity of the sender, just the handle TP37, which might conceivably have indicated someone with the initials TP, who had been born in 1937.

Or not.

Of course, if they had been born in 1937, they certainly could have encountered a record by the Flare Path Orchestra, while those were briefly available. TP37 would be a little young—a mere child when the band was recording. But the discs would have been around in the post-war years for a while, when the person was older…

Or of course they could be mistaken, deluded, or a malicious time-waster. There was only one way to find out. I sent a message back asking for more details and waited. Or didn't wait, actually. Instead I went out with Nevada to Albert's, our local gastro-pub, and had a meal with Tinkler and Clean Head. It was a sort of mini celebration to commemorate receiving a recent cash injection from our employer. We ate and drank a little too much, taking turns buying rounds. And, at a certain point in the proceedings, we suddenly realised that we were all of us spending Miss Honeyland's money. Tinkler had been paid for his record, Clean Head for her services as a driver, and Nevada and I for the investigation we were doing. Everybody was, in some way or another, on her payroll.

For some reason this seemed terribly funny.

We got back from the pub quite late, just Nevada and I. Clean Head had gone home and, of course, Tinkler had failed to go home with her. We'd declined his offer to come home with us and regale us into the small hours with drunken self-pity leavened by sexual frustration, and put him on a bus home to Putney. The cats were waiting to reprimand us when we got in, Fanny lurking in a patch of shadow just outside the front door and Turk snoozing on our bed until we came inside, then thumping to the floor and trotting to confront us.

While Nevada plied them with high-end cat biscuits, I checked the computer for messages. I'd like to say I'd been able to put the matter of TP37 entirely out of my mind while we'd been making merry this evening, but in fact it had been a constant background concern. Indeed, one reason for going out to the pub in the first place had been the watched-pot-never-boils principle. I figured if I sat by the computer nothing would happen, but if I turned my back on it and spent the evening out in convivial pursuits, I would come home to find a message waiting.

Which was exactly what happened.

It is a 78rpm disc in a nondescript cardboard sleeve (no illustration or text). I will only sell for a substantial sum in cash. You must meet me at a time and place of my choosing. You must come alone.

I thought about this for a moment. Then I sent a message back and asked what tunes were on the record. Anybody who was actually in possession of such a disc would find this easy enough to answer.

Then I went to bed.

The next morning there was a new message waiting for me. It was commendably terse, as if the sender was getting impatient.

Fringe Merchant b/w Creep Back.

If this was a total fabrication at least it was an intriguing one. I checked these titles on search engines, but once again the mighty power of the Internet yielded nothing of use, though I did learn that a theatre company called Fringe Benefits were mounting a novel production of *The Merchant of Venice*. There was certainly nothing as helpful as a discography listing these titles as belonging to a very rare 78rpm disc of swing music recorded by the Flare Path Orchestra.

I considered my options and then got on the phone to

Charles Gresford-Jones. No reply and no voicemail. The phone just rang endlessly, echoing in that small front room in Dover, possibly with Abner the Zombie Cat listening in irritation. I hung up and tried Gerry Wuggins instead. He answered immediately.

"Oh yeah," he said, and burst into laughter when I read him the titles. "They were two of our numbers. Very popular they were, too. Dear me, I haven't thought about those for years. That brings it all back. It really does. It all comes rushing back."

"Then this wasn't one of the discs you had in your collection?" Before your harridan of a wife deep-sixed them, I did not add.

"Oh no. I must have missed out on that one. But it's a brilliant record. Lovely tunes."

I said, "What do the titles mean?"

"Eh?"

"'Fringe Merchant'," I said, "and 'Creep Back'."

"Oh." He laughed. "Fringe merchant. Yeah, you see, when you're on a bombing run and you're dropping your load, you've got a target. The centre of town or an oil refinery or what have you. And so the idea is, the theory is, of course, everyone's supposed to get as close as possible to dead centre on the target."

"And a fringe merchant is…"

"Somebody who is not dead centre, who is way out on the fringe."

"Because they're incompetent?"

"No. Because they're bloody sensible. Or a bit windy, depending on your point of view. Out there on the fringes there's a lot less chance of getting shot down, all of your anti-aircraft batteries being zeroed in right over the target."

"And 'Creep Back'?"

"Similar kind of thing, in a way. You've got your bomber stream—the stream of planes heading towards the target. And the nearer to the target they get, the hotter things get. More chance of getting shot down. So you want to start dropping your bombs as soon as you can, so you can get the hell out of there. Naturally."

"Naturally."

"So maybe you drop your bombs just a bit early. Then the bloke following you drops *his* just a bit early. And the bloke behind him does the same…"

"And so the bombing creeps back."

"Yeah, yeah. Getting miles and miles further away from the target. Creep back. It used to drive Bomber Command mad."

I tried to repress a rising feeling of excitement. It sounded like my anonymous seller's record had to be authentic. I couldn't imagine anyone cooking up such a plausible-sounding disc. "So you actually remember the band playing tunes with those titles?"

"Oh yeah. Like I said, they were cracking little numbers. Very popular."

"And do you know for certain that those tunes were recorded on a 78rpm disc?"

"Well, they must have been, mustn't they? I mean you've found a copy, haven't you?" He paused. "You have found a copy?"

"I might have done," I found myself saying, guardedly.

"Well, I'd love to have a listen to it, if you have."

"I'll see if I can work something out. Many thanks for the information." We discussed the possibility of Nevada and I coming down to his house and recording his reminiscences, as we had so notably failed to do last time. He seemed entirely amenable and we pencilled in a day.

Just before I hung up he said, "By the way."

"Yes?"

"'Fringe Merchant' and 'Creep Back'. They were both compositions by Johnny Thomas. Poor old Johnny."

"Really?"

"Yeah. Brilliant, they were. And I think they were the last things he wrote before, you know…"

He was hanged by the neck until dead. I thanked Gerry Wuggins and, on that unspoken note, we said our farewells. I immediately got in touch with TP37 and said I was very interested in purchasing the disc. This time I broke my own rule and spent the afternoon sitting around near the computer, in case I got a reply. Nothing. That evening I let Nevada drag me out to see a brace of foreign films at the Riverside. She was a sucker for anything not in English and vaguely arty, which had led us more than once into cinematic quicksand. Tonight we got a taut little Swedish thriller, and an interminable French epic about a prisoner who saw visions of deer jumping in front of cars and was then inexplicably and arbitrarily promoted to a criminal kingpin. There was, at least, a great Jimmie Dale Gilmore song at the end.

We returned home and I hastened to my computer, fully expecting a message.

Nothing.

Nothing the next day. Or the next. I was starting to climb the walls. Had I somehow bungled the negotiations? Had I put the seller off? I went back and reread the previous messages, all sixty-one words of them. Assuming you count b/w as a word. It stood for 'backed with' and was music industry speak for any record with just one track on each side. I started obsessing about what the use of this piece of jargon implied about my mysterious correspondent.

Or non-correspondent.

Finally, after I'd given up hope and reluctantly accepted that somehow I'd blown the negotiations, on Saturday I got a reply.

All right. We will meet next week. In London. I will
confirm the time and the place. You must come alone.

We then negotiated about price. This didn't take long. TP37 now seemed to respond instantly to every message I sent. We came to an agreement and signed off. I would wait for confirmation of the time and place of our meeting.

The final message from my correspondent read:

Tell no one.

I went and told Nevada. "I knew you were up to something," she said. "You've been all silent and moody."

I hadn't realised I'd given any such sign, but she could read me like a book.

"Have I?"

"Yes. It was obvious you were working on something and it wasn't going great and you didn't want to tell me about it until you had it sorted. Do you? Have it sorted?"

"You tell me." We sat down at the computer and she went through all the messages I'd exchanged with TP37. Then she looked at me. "Are you going to meet them?"

"Yes."

"Are you going to go alone?"

"No fucking way."

12. CHELSEA

TP37 turned out to be Toba Possner, a woman who lived in Chelsea, and had in fact lived there for the better part of half a century. I assumed she had indeed been born in 1937 but it didn't seem polite to ask.

Our first intimation that she lived in Chelsea came from Tinkler, or rather a friend of his who was able to trace the messages I'd received back to an Internet café on the King's Road.

"That's all right, then," said Nevada when she found out.

I said, "There being no psycho killers in Chelsea."

"Well, there are. But at least they have nice shoes."

I'd gradually talked Toba Possner away from her position of total anonymity, and of demanding that I meet her alone. I'd achieved this by explaining, truthfully, that if she didn't insist on a payment in cash that was physically handed over to her—say in a brown paper bag on a park bench—I could get her considerably more money for the record she wanted to sell. I suggested instead that she should accept an electronic bank transfer or, if she was old-fashioned, as seemed likely, a cheque. We'd make the payment to her on sight of the record.

I also added that if she'd personally known Lucian Honeyland, we'd be willing to pay her extra for any anecdotes or reminiscences she might have—provided we could record them. This seemed to swing it. She agreed to meet. I told her I wouldn't be on my own, that I'd be bringing my wife with me.

"Wife?" said Nevada.

"I thought she was more likely to agree if I said wife rather than girlfriend."

"Hot girlfriend. Extremely hot girlfriend."

"Extremely hot girlfriend."

She looked at me. "Are you sure this isn't a roundabout way of proposing to me? By lying to a total stranger? Because that would be so sweet."

I said, "Well, I don't feel like she's a total stranger to me anymore. And it isn't exactly a lie. You've been living with me for over a year, so you're my common-law wife."

"Am I? Good lord." She looked at the cats, lolling side by side on the floor in a slice of sunlight. "Hello common-law kittens," she said.

Toba Possner agreed to the terms of the meeting, provided we promise to make payment to her using a certified cheque made out to cash or a money order of some kind. "In fact, anything that doesn't involve giving away her name or personal details," said Nevada.

"That's right," I said. "Another one of her preconditions

is that she remains anonymous."

"She's got a lot of preconditions. And anyway, how can she remain anonymous? You already know her name and address."

"But our client doesn't. Toba made it very clear that it should stay that way. She doesn't want Miss Honeyland to find out who she is."

"Why?"

We found out when we went to meet her.

Toba Possner's address was in a side street just past Chelsea Old Town Hall. Clean Head, who was now officially on the payroll, dropped us off outside the big front gates of the estate where Toba lived. We walked under the shadow of a stone arch towards a tall metal gate, where we buzzed at a buzzer and were admitted into a large courtyard, with five storeys of dwellings rising above us in long stone ranks on three sides.

The estate belonged to the Sherman Trust, a charitable institution that provided affordable accommodation for those on low income. This meant that poor people could live even here, in the heart of one of London's most fashionable, and expensive, neighbourhoods.

Nevada was jealous. I could tell. "The cats wouldn't like it here," I pointed out. "They wouldn't have a garden and there's all that traffic right outside."

"That's true," she said, and took my hand. We walked up the dim echoing coolness of a concrete staircase to the top floor, arriving just a little winded. We then proceeded along a narrow walkway with front doors on our left and a stone wall on our right, slightly more than waist high, which looked down into the wide shadows of the courtyard. There were welcome mats outside many of the front doors, and numerous flower pots, and even some gnomes. Tinkler would have been delighted.

Toba's flat was at the end of the walkway. The canary-yellow front door sprang open as we approached. She'd buzzed us in and had apparently accurately estimated just how long it would take us to walk up here. She probably had experience in this area. She stood in the doorway, looking a little nervous.

She had disquieting amber eyes and jet-black hair in a short, helmet-style cut. I didn't need Nevada to tell me that the black had to be a dye job for a woman born in 1937. Toba was wearing drainpipe jeans, espadrilles, and a boldly striped blue and white sweater with a red batik scarf at her throat. The entire ensemble was strictly bohemian and rather chic.

She had a deeply and intricately seamed face. Another smoker, I thought. But apparently she had given up long ago, because when we went inside there was no sight and, more importantly, no lingering smell of cigarettes anywhere.

She closed the front door and showed us to the tiny galley kitchen where she offered us coffee. Nevada lifted the brown paper bag she'd been carrying, "What a coincidence," she said. "We've brought some. We got one for you."

Toba politely declined and proceeded to make a cup of instant for herself while we took the lid off ours and sipped.

The subtext of this exchange was that, at this stage at least, nobody trusted each other enough to accept any hospitality. Nevada and I, at least, had a sound basis in our personal experience to be skittish.

So we drank our own coffee while she drank her own. Which, ironically, verified that we each would have been fine drinking the other's. Paranoia is a terrible thing, but we hadn't exactly started this relationship under the most relaxed of auspices.

The little flat was crammed with paintings. Every wall, even in the kitchen, was literally covered with framed illustrations of all different sizes and media. They were hung from near the ceiling to almost floor level. Oddly enough, the effect of all these images was neither oppressive nor claustrophobic. Some clever discrimination had gone into positioning each picture and there was a sense of balance, proportion and harmony that made it all acceptable.

Not just acceptable, in fact, but rather pleasant.

As I began to get a feel for her aesthetic, I realised the yellow tint of the front door was no accident. The colour scheme had continued within. Underneath its layer of framed pictures, the front hall was painted a slightly more pale shade of yellow, and the further into the flat you went— as we found out later—the more pale the colour became, shading to cream in the kitchen and snow white in the three tiny rooms lying beyond.

Each of these was theoretically a bedroom but two of them had been converted, apparently permanently, into studies or work rooms. There were tables, desks, bookshelves and filing cabinets. Art materials were everywhere, and on an easel in a corner of the room where we sat was a half-finished pastel of a pastoral landscape. In its simple bold colours and forms it looked like late Hockney. It was an accomplished piece of work.

"You're an artist," I said.

"An illustrator," she corrected.

"Are all these yours?" said Nevada, indicating a wall full of framed pictures.

"Most of them. Many of them. A few are by friends."

The framed pictures, which included everything from large watercolours and oils to the tiniest pencil drawing, had apparently been grouped by period or mood, so that each piece seemed a close relative to those nearby. The ones in this room had an almost childish boldness of colour and form. And there was something oddly familiar about them.

I found myself wondering where I could possibly have seen her work before. Then I caught sight of a volume I recognised on one of her bookshelves and I put two and two together. I said, "You did the illustrations, didn't you? For Honeyland's book."

She gave me an ironic smile. "Lucky's book, you mean. Yes. That was me."

"Do you mind?" I said. I went to the bookshelf and took down the copy of *Farmer Henry Versus the Locusts* and showed it to Nevada. We flipped through the brightly coloured pages. None of the pictures from the book were actually present on the walls, but the stylistic similarity was unmistakeable. Toba Possner watched us closely, and nodded. Perhaps with approval.

She nodded at the wall. "The work in here is from the same period. Mid to late 1950s."

"It's marvellous," said Nevada politely. I finished flipping through the book and returned to the title page, which declared that the book was written by 'Lucky' but gave no clue as to who might have done the pictures that were such an important part of it. I turned to examine the fine print on the page with the publishing information and found a small legend: 'Illustrations specially commissioned from the Royal College of Art.'

I showed it to Nevada. Toba Possner came over to see what we were looking at. I said, "You didn't get credit for your work?"

"No."

"That was a shame."

She shook her head. "That was the least of it. The real shame was getting paid fifteen guineas and not a penny more. Never a penny more, after all these years."

"You didn't receive any royalties?"

"Of course not. But I'm hardly alone in that. Did E. H. Shepard benefit from the Winnie the Pooh millions? I think not. And, you know, the really gutting thing is that he got to keep the paintings. Lucky did. He kept my original artwork." She looked at us, dry-eyed and steady and ironic. "Do you have any idea what those paintings would be worth today?"

I said, "Considering the popularity of that book... a great deal."

"I could have a house in the country, a flat in London,

and a little place in France too. If I owned my own paintings and I could sell them."

Nevada glanced at me. If anything, the woman sounded mildly amused at her own predicament. But I wouldn't have been surprised if there was some volcanic anger lurking somewhere beneath the surface. She was certainly entitled to feel that way. But I elected to keep things neutral.

"Did you get to know Honeyland?"

"Yes. Oh, yes. I couldn't simply be commissioned to do the illustrations and go off and do them on my own. Oh, no. I had to meet the great man and be vetted by him in person. And he had to discuss his ideas with me in detail, giving me the benefit of his insights. And once I won the commission, he insisted on visiting me in my studio on an almost daily basis to consider and analyse the work in progress. He interfered constantly."

"How did he come to choose you?"

She shrugged. "He didn't choose me *per se*. He was looking for a starving student who would work cheap, so he put up a notice at the Royal College of Art." She smiled crookedly. "And I was the lucky girl."

"And you didn't even get credit for what you did," said Nevada.

"No." Toba came over and picked up the book. "And note the plural. '*Illustrations* specially commissioned from the Royal College of Art.'" She glanced at us. "It cleverly sows a subtle little seed of doubt in the reader's mind."

I said, "What do you mean?"

"Perhaps the *illustrations* come from different

illustrators. Perhaps it was a team effort. Perhaps dozens of people were involved. You see? Anything to dilute my contribution. The way it's phrased casts doubt on whether these pictures were even all executed by the same hand."

I said, "They obviously were. They're clearly all the work of the same person."

"And they're brilliant," said Nevada. "I think the pictures are the best part. Of the book, I mean."

"Thank you," said Toba Possner, who sat there quietly soaking up all this praise. "But unfortunately, because they were allowed to remain anonymous, over the years people, other illustrators, have been able to claim that *Farmer Henry Versus the Locusts* was their own work."

"That's terrible."

"Yes, it is. But anyone who was at the Royal College— at roughly the same time I was—could potentially claim credit for them."

As she said this, something crossed my mind and also, apparently, my face. Because she looked directly at me with her odd, pale brown eyes, and said, "You're thinking if other people could pretend to be the illustrator, perhaps I'm pretending too."

"No," I said, gesturing at the pictures hanging on the wall, the samples of her work that were so clearly related to the *Farmer Henry* illustrations. "There are all these…"

But she wasn't listening to me. She went over to a filing cabinet and slid open a well-oiled drawer. There was the brisk flapping of paper from inside as she looked for something, then she murmured with satisfaction and turned to us, holding a manila folder. She took out a scrap of vividly coloured paper and handed it to me. "I have this."

It was about the size of the palm of my hand and had been neatly clipped from the brightly coloured cover of what appeared to be a magazine, though on closer inspection it looked too crude to be a professional magazine. Perhaps more like a pamphlet of some kind. It depicted a cartoon of a locust with an enlarged head and vaguely human features. In particular the face featured a jutting, uncompromising Roman nose sprouting with unsightly hairs. It was primitive and coarse but it had a certain impact. I wondered if it was a caricature of a real person.

What was for certain was that it was a rudimentary version of the locusts that featured in *Farmer Henry*. "Mr Honeyland gave me this before I started work," said Toba, taking the clipping back and carefully replacing it in the folder. "You can see that my locusts in the book are based on this. He insisted that I use it as my model. He was very particular about how they should look."

I said, "Where did he get it?"

"I have no idea. He wouldn't tell me. But he was adamant that I had to work from this picture. This rubbish." She sighed. "In the end, I think I managed to make something decent of it." She flipped the folder shut. "Anyway, it's one more piece of evidence, isn't it, to prove my case?" She went back to the filing cabinet, put the folder in and slid the drawer shut. Then she turned and smiled at us. "Ironic isn't it, citing a naked example of someone else's stylistic influence to stake the claim that the illustrations are solely mine." She turned back to the filing cabinet and opened another drawer.

"Anyway, and perhaps more to the point, I also have this."

She took something from the drawer and handed it to me. It was a 78rpm record. As promised, one side was 'Fringe Merchant' and the other was 'Creep Back'. Both had a composer credit of J. Thomas.

I slid the heavy old record out of its cardboard sleeve and walked over to the window to inspect it in the daylight.

It was in remarkably good shape.

I turned back to see Nevada watching me expectantly. Toba Possner was smiling calmly. "It's very good," I said. "In fact, it looks fine. Where did you get it?"

"He used to play it during our so-called creative discussions. To get me in the mood, apparently. I had an old record player in my studio and he left it—the record—here. When the book was finished he said I could keep it." She looked at us. "Of course, I can't prove that. *She* could make the argument that the record is his, not mine, just as she insists that the paintings don't belong to me. *My* paintings."

"This is Joan Honeyland?" I said.

She nodded. "I approached her some years ago, making initial enquiries in an attempt to retrieve my original art. I asserted my moral right to ownership. But failing that, I thought we could at least have equal shares in the exploitation of the images." She looked at us. "Pictures from the book have appeared on posters, t-shirts, towels, kitchenware, god knows what. Even a tiny fraction of the revenue from that would have made enough to keep me in comfort for the rest of my days."

She looked away from us, out of the window. "In response I received a letter from her lawyer, threatening to sue me for everything I'm worth if I tried to make any such claim." She glanced around at the tiny flat, where she lived at the discretion of a charity. "Everything I'm worth," she said. She smiled, but I could hear the bitterness in her voice.

"So that's why you want to remain anonymous? Because you don't want Joan Honeyland to know it's you?"

She nodded.

"Let sleeping bitches lie," she said.

13. LOCAL HISTORY

The next morning over breakfast, Nevada and I sat discussing Toba Possner. The cats sprawled on the floor nearby, keeping us company and praying some silent cat prayers that a piece of bacon would fall on the floor. I said, "I was really thrown by her attitude to Miss Honeyland."

Nevada buttered a piece of toast. "I know. I noticed."

"I mean, in all our dealings with her, Miss Honeyland's been really decent. Generous and…"

"Nice?"

"Yes. Nice. But the way Toba Possner talks about her…"

Nevada crunched her toast. "Assuming she's telling the truth."

I looked at her. "You think she was lying?"

"No. Not especially. Do you?"

"No."

Nevada shook her head. "The thing is, you can't help siding with the exploited artist. I understand that. Neither can I. But look at it from Miss Honeyland's point of view.

She wants at all costs to protect and preserve her father's work. Any attempt to dilute his claim to total authorship—"

"Any claim to sharing his money, you mean."

"If you want to be cynical about it," said Nevada. "But she must see herself as protecting her father and his work. His heritage, in fact."

"Well, anyway," I said, "I managed to get a lot of money from her for Toba, for the record she had."

"Good. Toba deserves it. How much?"

I shrugged. "Perhaps enough for her to live on for a year, or maybe even longer. She doesn't look like the extravagant type."

"No, she certainly doesn't. I imagine all her money goes on art supplies and a bit of food."

"What about clothes?" I said. I thought she'd been pretty sharply dressed, for an old lady.

"That's the thing about reaching that age," said Nevada. "You've already bought all your clothes."

"And own an extensive wardrobe. Of fine vintage clothing."

"Exactly. Which I would be only too happy to ransack when she kicks the bucket. Not that I want that to be any time soon, you understand. I really liked her. So much so that when we successfully complete this job and collect our bonus from the generous Miss Honeyland—"

"*If* we successfully complete this job and collect our bonus."

"Think positive. So much so that, when we do that, I want to spend some of the money on commissioning a picture from Toba. A portrait, in fact."

"A portrait?" I said. "Of you?"

"No."

"Of me?"

"No."

The penny dropped. "Of the cats?"

"Of course."

"Okay," I said. "We'll see. When we get the money, we'll see."

"I love it when you lay down the law," said Nevada. "How did Miss Honeyland react when you told her the seller wishes to remain anonymous?"

"She was fine with it."

In fact, she'd been delighted and affectingly excited that we'd managed to find another record by her father's band. "You are doing splendidly," she'd said. And I'd found myself absurdly glowing with pride.

I remembered Gerry Wuggins's request for a copy of 'Fringe Merchant' and 'Creep Back'. I told her that someone else had asked me for a digital copy of one of the records we'd found.

"Would this be another person who has some useful reminiscences about my father?" she had asked.

"Exactly."

"You see? As I said, you are doing splendidly."

"You don't mind providing a copy for him?"

"Of course not. But first we'll have to get our man in south London to finish doing his work at the recording studio."

I was starting to get irritated with this guy and his so far purely notional recording studio. "He certainly seems to be taking his time," I said.

"He certainly does. I must make a note to call him and chase him. In any case, regarding this new disc that you've so cleverly found for me, I shall have Albert scoot around and collect it."

As promised, the chauffeur turned up shortly after breakfast. He took the 78, which I had swathed in bubble wrap, and handled it with every appearance of due, sober care. Nevada watched him through the kitchen window as he left. She said, "I wonder if Miss Honeyland really is shagging the chauffeur."

"Has Tinkler been talking to you?"

"He spews his filth everywhere."

I tried to keep any such thoughts from my mind when I spoke to Joan Honeyland on the phone again, later that day. She had followed up with the guy in the recording studio about the progress of his digital transfers. This clown, apparently based in Camberwell, now had the latest 78 too, Toba Possner's contribution, relayed to him by Albert the chauffeur. I was increasingly concerned about how long it was taking him to knock off a few simple digital copies.

So, by now, was Miss Honeyland. "It seems to have baffled him," she said. "Despite confidently promising that this was an area of his special expertise, it seems to have completely eluded him that at some point in the process he was going to need a 78rpm turntable to *play* the records in question. He has to play them if he's going to re-record them."

"I know," I said.

"This seems to have taken him entirely by surprise."

I said, "He probably thought he could just plug it into his computer." My mental picture of this chinless incompetent was gaining detail and resolution by the minute.

Miss Honeyland sighed. "Something like that, I fear, yes. So in any case he is now busy sourcing just such a turntable and promises that he'll have digital copies for us shortly."

I repressed the urge to tell her that I had just such a turntable and could have copied all the discs for her many times over by now. Instead, I said goodbye and hung up. Nevada came over and sat with me, carrying Turk in her arms. The cat settled contentedly into her lap as soon as she sat down. This was a trick I'd never been able to achieve. The only way I could guarantee that either of our cats would sit in my lap was by coming to a firm decision that it was time to get up and leave my seat. That would generally bring them at a run to install themselves more or less permanently.

"I fancy a drive to the country," said Nevada.

"Do you?"

"Yes. Southeast Kent. Guess who I would like to visit."

"A certain ferret-faced local historian? The one that Gresford-Jones so memorably evoked?"

"Yes. I definitely had the feeling that old Gresford-Jones was holding something back about the so-called Silk Stockings Murder." The crime that sent Johnny Thomas to the gallows.

I nodded. "I think he was holding something back, too. And he definitely didn't want us talking to Ferret Face."

"So it's decided, then," said Nevada.

* * *

We borrowed Tinkler's car and Clean Head volunteered to drive, so of course there was no chance of Tinkler not coming along, too.

"I can hardly wait," he said. "I've always wanted to plunge into the cut-throat world of local historians."

The ferret-faced party in question was actually named Jasper McClew. He had been easy enough to track down on the Internet, where he had a considerable presence as a remorseless, and amazingly boring, blogger. On his website he clearly stated that he was an authority on, among many other things, the Silk Stockings Murder. He was surprisingly taciturn concerning any details about the subject, though.

I suspected that this was because he wanted people to buy his pamphlets on the murder, which could either be purchased by mail order as a hard copy, or downloaded as a PDF for a PayPal payment. He also operated tours, for which he charged what I thought was an eye-watering sum.

Still, we were on expenses, so I booked one.

We drove down on a bright, clear Saturday morning after a night of heavy rain. The roads were still gleaming as Clean Head piloted us out of London. We drove down the M25 to Kent, skirting Canterbury and Dover and then a string of smaller hamlets. "Here's Ringwould coming up," said Tinkler.

"Great name," I said.

"I've always thought of it as a combination of ringworm and leaf mould."

"He's cheery today," said Clean Head.

"He's a local boy," said Nevada. "Local boy made bad."

"That's me," said Tinkler. "I'm *bad*."

Clean Head was still laughing at this as we drove through Walmer, heading towards Deal, and passed a petrol station with a minivan parked outside. On the side it had a trippy painting of a silver crescent moon against a purple background, spattered with turquoise stars. Across it was written, in flowing lettering: *Ms Moon is sending us to sleep with her healing silver rays.*

We all stared at it in astonishment, except Clean Head, who was reassuringly single-minded and intent on her driving.

"It's a companion piece," said Tinkler, "to that other stupid hippie van."

"What stupid hippie van?" said Clean Head. He filled her in as she negotiated the turn onto Walmer Castle Road. Walmer Castle itself, which followed shortly, looming up on the right as we drove beside the sea along Kingsdown Road, was an elegant and surprisingly modest structure of interlocking curves of stone. Clean Head explained that it was a classic 'Tudor rose' configuration.

She was obviously champing at the bit to go and look at the castle. And Tinkler was champing at the bit to be alone with her. So we got them to drop us in Kingsdown, turning down an alley and pulling up onto pebbles near a pub called the Zetland Arms. This was not our ultimate destination, but was near enough. We waved goodbye to them as the car pulled away and walked among the little lanes lined with houses, between the beach and the road.

We sniffed the salt air, heavy with the iodine tang of seaweed. It smelled good.

Jasper McClew's house was a mildewed little white cottage with a sign outside advertising TOURS, HISTORICAL WALKS AND LECTURES. His anxious bearded face was looming in a window, watching us approach, and the door clicked open as soon as we came through his gate. People seemed to be eagerly expecting us these days.

The ferret-faced local historian actually had a round, somewhat childish-looking face with an incongruous fringe of dark beard. He looked oddly familiar. Maybe he was just a familiar type.

He was wearing baggy brown corduroy trousers and a white shirt and a glistening tie with small black and bright green squares printed on it. On his feet he was wearing white socks and sandals. He ushered us into his small living room. It had a bay window that admitted a pale, watery light and looked out on other houses and, beyond them, the flat, pebbled beach.

After about ten minutes he remembered his manners and offered us some coffee, trotting off to the kitchen. Nevada and I sat and looked at each other.

There were books everywhere in the room, including some piled in precarious towers on either side of the armchair in which he'd been sitting. Nevada and I were in matching armchairs opposite, thankfully not hemmed in by books. Jasper's own chair was obviously his reading spot. There was a standing lamp stationed behind it, angled so as to provide a beam of light over the shoulder while books were carefully studied and absorbed.

All the books, as far as I could see, were about Kent. Southeast Kent.

Local history.

As he laboured in the kitchen over the coffee—for which I didn't have particularly high hopes—I leaned over to Nevada and said, quietly, "He reminds me of someone."

"He looks like E.T. with a beard," said Nevada. "Have you seen *E.T.*?"

"Yes."

"Then that's who he reminds you of."

I had my doubts about this thesis, but for the time being I wasn't immediately able to refute it. "He's not so ferret-faced," whispered Nevada. "Though he is a bit ferret-like in other ways."

This was true. The first words out of his mouth had been concerning our 'agreed fee' and he'd accepted the proffered cash with naked satisfaction, explaining, "I have to put this on a professional footing." He'd then put on a pair of spectacles and carefully and lovingly counted the bank notes in front of us.

Perhaps I was being unkind to ferrets, who were unlikely to exhibit any such uniquely human avarice.

He brought back the coffees on a tray. Mine was every bit as bad as I expected it to be, and after one polite sip I set it aside, resolving to never touch it again. Our host sat in his chair, ignoring his own cup. He took off his spectacles and put them on the nearest pile of books, on top of a handsome Victorian volume about the Goodwin Sands with a blue cloth cover embossed with gilt. There was an air of finality about the way he did this which didn't suggest he'd be getting up any time soon. This did not bode well for our promised tour.

"Well, should we get going?" I said. Nevada shot me a look. "As soon as we've finished our coffee, I mean." I noticed she wasn't drinking hers either. I wondered how long we'd have to sit here, all of us ignoring our hot beverages, before it would be decent to just abandon them and leave.

"We can't go just yet," said Jasper. "I took some laxatives this morning and I'm just waiting for them to kick in." He drummed his fingers on a pile of books, then gave a high-pitched laugh. "Don't want to step outside the front door and then—wham—have them suddenly take hold. We wouldn't want that."

I glanced at Nevada, who gave me a studiedly bland look. "No," I said. "We wouldn't want that."

"You know, it's funny." Jasper frowned thoughtfully. "My bowels have been giving me gyp all week. Bunged up. Bunged. Up. And at the same time I've been blocked with my writing. Not making my usual progress. I suspect there's some profound connection between the creative process and something as basic and primal and human as the digestive process. I wonder what would Jung have said?"

"He would have probably said to eat more fibre," said Nevada.

We sat there for a quarter of an hour, during which time I grew tired of studying the framed antique maps of the Kent coast on the walls and very nearly fell asleep. I was just nodding off when Jasper abruptly got to his feet and said, "All right, I suppose we'd better be going. It doesn't look like anything is going to happen."

We expressed our commiseration and tried to conceal our relief. "Just wait here. I'll get my shoes on." He went into the hallway where, through the open door, we watched him struggle to remove his sandals and then put on a pair of Hush Puppies. He was bent over at the waist, tying his shoe laces when he suddenly uttered a sharp, triumphant grunt as though he'd discovered a precious gemstone lying on the floor.

He hastily sloughed off his shoes again and trotted down the hallway in a semi crouch. Nevada turned and looked at me. A door slammed somewhere in the house, then silence. "The suspense is killing me," said Nevada. There was a pregnant pause, then the toilet flushed, a door opened and our host reappeared and hastily put on his shoes and beckoned to us.

As a mephitic stench came roiling down the hallway, we all fled out into the fresh air. Turning to lock his front door, Jasper took his glasses off and put them in his pocket. Then he squinted around and led us towards the main road. There, with much peering because clearly he could hardly see, he led us along Cliffe Road, which curved as it went uphill and became Upper Street. Luckily, even if he couldn't see much, he could hear the cars coming, and we made our way up the narrow lane without getting run over.

"This part of Kent has more pubs per capita than anywhere else in the UK," he yelled at us over his shoulder. "Though very few of them are the scene of such a famous murder." He was striding ahead of us, which gave us the chance to talk about him without being heard.

I said, "Why has he taken his glasses off?"

Nevada shrugged. "Vanity."

"You mean he thinks he looks better that way?"

Nevada shrugged again. "Whatever he does he still looks like E.T. with a beard."

Jasper McClew crossed the road ahead of us and paused at the entrance of a side street to our left. We caught up with him outside a pub called The Feathers. He stared up at it proudly.

"This is where it happened."

14. TOUR

The pub had a white stucco front and narrow, leaded windows. There was a crooked look to it thanks to it being built on a sloping hillside stretch of street. Jasper McClew led us inside and to the bar. Then he stepped back a little, to clearly signal that he had no intention of paying for anything.

I ordered drinks for Nevada and myself and, reluctantly, one for our tour guide. So far our tour had consisted of him hurrying up the street ahead of us, from his house to his local pub. Perhaps I did him an injustice—he had also shouted the occasional remark over his shoulder, to be lost in the wind. The barman pulled him a pint of some expensive-looking real ale then went off to find a bottle of the Rhône red Nevada had carefully selected from the pub's wine list.

While we waited for him to return, I looked around the bar and noticed a framed newspaper on the wall. I went over to inspect it. It was a yellowing front page.

'Silk Stockings Killer Hangs' declared the big ominous black letters of the headline. Nevada came and looked over my shoulder. "My god. He was so young." There was a photo of Johnny Thomas in his air force uniform. The portrait had obviously been taken long before the crime. He looked like a fresh young cadet. She leaned closer, peering at the picture in the dim light of the pub. "He looks so unhappy, he might have had some kind of premonition."

"That he was going to end up on the gallows?" Nevada nodded. "Or die in some other horrible fashion," I said. It was, after all, a time of war and sudden unpleasant death was not in short supply.

Jasper joined us, happily sipping the pint I had paid for. "Right up there," he said.

Nevada looked away from the picture of the terrified young airman. "I beg your pardon?"

"Right up there," he said, pointing at the ceiling. It was some kind of chunky textured white surface—now yellow with the nicotine of yesteryear—with dark old wooden beams running across it. Affixed to the beams were various allegedly antique objects—a lantern, a large pewter tankard, some strange agricultural tool—which represented a serious navigational hazard to anyone who was tall and especially, I imagined, tall drunks. Jasper was pointing to a nondescript patch of ceiling above us, an area free of such clutter.

"What's right up there?"

"The room. The murder room. The room where they spent the night together. Her last night on Earth." As Jasper warmed to his spiel Nevada glanced at me. It looked like we were about to get our money's worth from the tour. And I was beginning to wish we weren't.

"Johnny Thomas brought the beautiful young woman he was having an extramarital affair with to this very pub. And they slept together in the room above us. Although, as I understand it, there was very little actual sleeping taking place."

"What with all the sex and murder," said Nevada.

Jasper ignored her. "Johnny Thomas chose this particular pub because his uncle owned it. Indeed, young Johnny had come down here to work regularly in the pub during the many summers of his teenage youth before the war."

There hadn't been that many of those summers, I reflected. In fact, precious few.

Nevada looked at me and said in a stage whisper, "Isn't that a tautology? 'Teenage youth'?"

You kind of had to admire the way Jasper just kept ploughing on. "His uncle had promised him there would always be a room for him to stay whenever he visited. Even in wartime. Even when he was with a woman who wasn't his wife. His mistress. The mysterious and exotic Gillian Gadon." It was like listening to some kind of machine play back for the hundredth time a recording of the story. Except not as interesting.

"Johnny's uncle knew what was going on, everyone in the pub did, but they turned a blind eye. And when his uncle was castigated for this by the prosecutor during the murder trial—he was accused of running 'an immoral house'—he replied defiantly. He said, 'The lad was liable to die soon, like so many of the other brave lads'—there was applause in the courtroom at the mention of the brave lads and the judge had to call for silence—'so why not let them have a little fun?' And there was a murmur of approval throughout the courtroom and the judge had to slam his gavel and restore order."

I wondered if any of this had actually happened, though I had to admit that, despite myself, I was getting caught up in his account.

This ceased almost immediately, as he shot off on a tangent. "Note the way the uncle cleverly contextualised Johnny Thomas as one of a large body of brave young men for whom the public, and therefore hopefully the jury, would have admiration and sympathy. He did a surprisingly effective job of image control, or at least he would have done if it wasn't for the untiring efforts of the wife."

"What wife?" I said.

"Johnny Thomas's wife," said Nevada. "The wronged woman."

"Exactly," said Jasper, nodding vigorously. "And that's exactly the way she made sure she had herself depicted in the press. The wronged woman. Cruelly betrayed by her husband, the bestial sex murderer."

But apparently the uncle wouldn't let her get away with it. He wouldn't allow the stereotypes to settle. He kept insisting that Johnny was innocent, that he'd loved the girl, Gillian Gadon, that he would never have killed her. That someone else had killed her. An unknown third party. But when he tried to sway opinion in that direction, the wife responded by dragging her kids into the equation.

"He had children?" said Nevada. "Johnny Thomas?"

"Yes. Three. Ages two, four and six. All girls." Three little girls who got to see daddy going to the gallows.

"It's fascinating, really, the way the uncle and the wife shaped public discourse, and polarised it, over the whole sensational story of the Silk Stockings Murder. Their conflict and disagreement was widely covered in the press. For a few days the war was off the front pages, and the public of Britain actually welcomed the distraction. Meanwhile the wife and the uncle were struggling for control over who got to define the incident. In the terms of historiography, they were competing for authorship and interpretation of the agreed narrative."

Our eyes must have begun to glaze over at this juncture because he got back to the main event. "But, despite the best efforts of his loving uncle, Johnny Thomas was doomed to be hanged by the neck until dead for the very murder that took place in the very room above the very spot where we are standing now."

Luckily, before he could say 'very' again, the barman finally came back with a dusty bottle of hopefully very fine Rhône red. I'd thought he'd forgotten all about us. Jasper fell silent while Nevada carefully watched—supervised, actually—the barman as he opened the bottle and poured us both a glass of wine.

"That looks rather good," said Jasper. "Perhaps I should try some."

"Best stick to the beer," said Nevada. "You wouldn't want to mix. The grain and the grape, you know. Probably bad for the digestion."

"You here for Jasper's tour?" said the barman, giving us a sidelong glance as he carefully went through the wine list to make sure he hadn't undercharged us. He was plump and ruddy-faced, with a tonsure of thinning grey hair that made him look like a mad monk. We conceded that we were. "Nice to see some people with hair for a change," he said.

"Yes, thank you, Andy," said Jasper. He scooped up a tray and set all the drinks on it, bustling away from the bar. He didn't look back to see if we were following him, but we were. I was ducking to avoid the various lethal pieces of rustic ironware that were hanging from the ceiling. They were presumably there to give a period feel to the pub. Although the chief feeling they would impart would be a bruised skull for anyone not nimble enough to dodge them.

I caught up with Jasper. I'd thought he was heading for a table, but instead it seemed he was bound for the back door of the pub. I said, "What did he mean by that?"

He stopped and looked at me. "Mean by what?"

"People with hair."

He turned away again, shaking his head. "He didn't mean anything by it. He's an idiot. He resents anyone else taking an interest in local history. All he cares about is the money."

This was pretty rich, I thought, coming from a man who wouldn't let us across his threshold until he'd counted our cash. Jasper shepherded us towards the door. "Andy does very well out of my tours," he said in a low voice, glancing back at the barman. "People pay a premium price to stay in that room."

"People stay here?" said Nevada. "I mean, knowing what happened. They deliberately and specifically book that room?"

"Oh, yes. Frequently young couples. Sometimes honeymoon couples."

"Ugh." Nevada shuddered. "Maybe it's an S&M thing."

Jasper opened the door and we followed him out into the pub garden. He led us to a grubby white plastic table with a small puddle of dirty rainwater at its centre, and sat down. We pulled up chairs and joined him. It was a pleasant, mild day, and the sun was creeping over the concrete wall of the pub and beginning to peer into the garden, a small, grassed area with half a dozen other tables scattered around it. Standing in one corner was an old-fashioned wooden beer barrel with a hand-lettered sign pinned up over it. It was too far away for me to read the sign.

Jasper rubbed his hands together. "Well, what more can I tell you about the famous Silk Stockings Murder?" It seemed our tour guide had run out of spiel already. We were supposed to ask questions.

I said, "Did Johnny Thomas do it?"

"Well, if he didn't, he did everything possible to make everyone *think* he did. His every action seemed calculated to ruin any appearance of innocence. His biggest mistake was to try and get rid of the body."

"Get rid of it? I thought she was found in their bed."

"She was. Eventually." He set his pint down. "Johnny's story was that he just woke up and found the girl dead in the bed beside him, and he panicked. He knew he would be blamed for it, he said. So he decided the only thing to do was to try and dispose of her."

"Dispose?" said Nevada.

Jasper nodded. "We are, after all, right beside the sea. He thought if he could just get the body into the water no one would ever know about it. And he might even have been right. But before he could dump her—"

"Gillian," said Nevada. "She had a name. Gillian."

He nodded, agreeable but a little puzzled, clearly not getting it. "That's right, Gillian Gadon. He wanted to dump her into the sea. Exactly how well that would have worked is an interesting question. The water is shallow along the beach here in Kingsdown. There are no sudden shelves or areas of deep water easily accessible from the pebble beach. And there's no jetty that extends out any distance until you get to Deal pier, which is a considerable walk. It's the better part of two miles. An awfully long way to walk unseen in the middle of the night."

"Especially when you're trying to dispose of a body."

"Exactly. Anyway, as I was saying, he didn't have access to deep water. But perhaps he didn't need it. The currents around here are complex and unpredictable. The Goodwin Sands is a fascinating and multifarious region, ever-changing yet always dangerous. A palimpsest of shifting sands. I've written about them quite extensively, under the title *The Phantom Sands*. I have several pamphlets available back at the house or downloadable online. Did I mention that I accept PayPal? Anyway, the upshot is, Johnny Thomas might have been able to dispose of the corpse even in these shallow waters, just off the beach. The current might have carried it off. The barrel would have helped in that regard."

"The barrel?" I said.

"Yes. It would have tended to lend buoyancy—"

"What barrel?" said Nevada.

Jasper took off his spectacles and polished them with his tie. "Oh, yes, I see. I should have explained. Since Johnny knew the pub very well, having worked here in the summer, he was able to obtain an empty beer barrel from the cellar and put the body—ah, Gillian's body—into it." He put the spectacles in his jacket pocket.

Nevada and I stared at him. I said, "He hid her body in a beer barrel?"

"Yes. He obtained an empty one from the cellar, brought it into the deserted saloon bar of the pub—it was now about three in the morning and everyone was asleep. He managed to bring the barrel into the bar and bring her body down from the room without waking anyone. He then put the body into the barrel. His reasoning was that he might not be able to get down to the ocean carrying her body without being seen. But if he concealed it inside the barrel—"

"Back up a minute," said Nevada. "How did he end up with her dead body in the first place?"

"As I said, he woke up beside it. Beside her. They had both been drinking heavily in the pub. And then they'd gone up to the room and gone to bed and had sex. A number of times."

He seemed unwholesomely fixated on the sex lives of the long-dead.

Jasper continued. "Afterwards, Johnny fell asleep. And when he woke up, there she was. Dead and cold in the bed beside him, her flawless flesh an unearthly pale hue in the moonlight." I could tell we were back to the tour spiel.

I said, "Was there a moon that night?"

Jasper blinked at me and thought about it. "Yes, there

was. Of course there was. A full moon. That was another reason he was so concerned about being seen. If he carried the body down to the beach."

"So he put her in the barrel and he was going to *roll* her down to the sea?"

"Yes. Exactly."

15. BEER BARREL

Jasper McClew peered at us, his eyes watery without his spectacles. "And as you can imagine, that sort of cold-blooded calculation didn't help at his trial. Putting the body of his lover into a barrel. It spoke not of a panic-stricken innocent man but rather a shrewd and coolly calculating, *guilty* one. Anyway, that is the way it seemed as presented by the prosecuting barrister, who incidentally utterly destroyed Johnny Thomas during his cross-examination. Completely shredded him." He suddenly stopped. "That's the barrel over there."

He pointed at the other side of the pub garden.

We turned and looked at the old brown beer barrel standing in the corner with the sign pinned over it. Nevada said, "That's the actual barrel?"

"Uh, no, but one quite similar. Very similar. Almost identical." I got up and went over and read the sign. It had a jagged arrow pointing down to a slot in the wooden lid of the barrel and invited cash donations, 'To the memory of those who suffered in the tragic events of the Silk Stockings Murder'. There was no indication of how any such ensuing funds would be disbursed.

I was beginning to see what he meant about good old Andy the barman being all about the money.

I went back and sat with Jasper and Nevada.

"What happened?" I said. "When he tried to get her to the beach in the barrel? I take it he didn't make it."

"No," said Jasper. "If he had, no one might ever have learned of his crime."

"His crime," said Nevada. "So you think he did it."

Jasper sighed and corrected himself. "*The* crime, then. No one might ever have learned of *the* crime. But as fate would have it, he hadn't gone far, rolling the barrel down the hill, when who should he meet but a policeman."

"My god," said Nevada, apparently envisioning the events of the far-off moonlit night. We had just walked up that same hill. It was easy to imagine the setting. I wondered how Johnny Thomas had managed to stop the barrel rolling away from him. It was steep.

"Yes, he ran into the local bobby on the beat. Now, as fate would also have it, Johnny actually knew this constable."

"From his summers working in the pub," I said.

"That's right. So the policeman wasn't as suspicious as he might have been. And when Johnny spun him a story, he was inclined to believe it."

Nevada was leaning forward, literally on the edge of her seat. "What story?"

"He said that the barrel was full of beer that his uncle

wanted to donate to Johnny's band."

"The Flare Path Orchestra?" I said.

"Correct. Johnny told the constable that a lorry had been sent by the squadron and was going to come and pick him up along with the barrel of beer. So he was taking it down to the beach where he was going to be picked up, by some of his mates returning late after a mission. And the constable believed him. So much so that he offered to help Johnny with the barrel."

"Help him roll the barrel with the body in it."

"Yes. And furthermore, the policeman offered to wait with him until his ride came. To keep him company."

"Christ," whispered Nevada.

"Johnny naturally refused, said it wasn't necessary. He had no idea what time the lorry would arrive. There was no point both of them waiting. And so on. He convinced the constable to leave him there with the barrel, and the man was just about to go when someone else arrived. Another policeman."

"Shit."

"Yes. Only this time it was a military policeman. A so-called Redcap. He wanted to know what was going on. The constable explained to him about the donation of the beer and how Johnny was waiting for a lorry and so on. The military policeman joked about how lucky Johnny's orchestra was. The constable laughed and Johnny tried to laugh but by now he was ready to have a nervous breakdown."

"I'm not surprised," said Nevada. "I'm ready to have a nervous breakdown myself, just hearing about it. What happened?"

"Both the constable and the military policeman offered

to wait with Johnny for the lorry."

"The non-existent lorry," I said.

"That's right. The non-existent lorry. Which was never going to come. So, after much waiting around in the cold night, Johnny finally said that it was so late that he was certain that it wasn't going to come. If it *was* going to come, it would have been there by now. Something had obviously gone wrong. Some kind of cock-up. This was more than plausible during wartime, so the constable and the military policeman had no reason not to believe him. So, having established this, Johnny said he would take the beer back to the pub."

"You mean the body," said Nevada. "He'd take Gillian's body in the barrel back to the pub."

"Yes. Her body."

"And what would he do with it then?"

"I don't think he was thinking that far ahead," said Jasper. "He just wanted to get away from the constable and the military policeman."

"And did he?" I said.

Jasper shook his head. "No. They insisted on *helping* him roll the barrel back up the hill. All the way to the pub. So Johnny was back where he started, with Gillian Gadon dead and wedged tight in the barrel, said barrel now sitting outside the pub, with two policemen."

"What did he do?" said Nevada.

"Well, he went to get them each a bottle of beer, to say thank you for the help with the barrel. And, he hoped, to get rid of them."

"But he didn't?"

"No. When he gave them the beer they asked if they could drink it inside. They could hardly be seen drinking on the street when they were both, supposedly, on duty. So he was obliged to let them into the snug bar of the pub. While they sat there drinking their beers he made some excuse and hurried back to the barrel outside. He took Gillian's body out of it. While the policemen were drinking in the bar he managed to carry it back upstairs and into the room, where he put her corpse back into bed."

"Back where he started?" I said.

"Yes, exactly. Back where he started."

"What was he going to do?" said Nevada.

"I have no idea. I don't think he did, either. But it doesn't matter. When he went back downstairs to the bar to say goodnight to the policemen they put the handcuffs on him. They'd looked in the barrel outside, while he had gone to get them beers. They'd taken the lid off and they'd found her. Her contorted body jammed inside, her pale nude body with the stocking that had strangled her knotted around her neck, digging into the flesh. Her purple, contorted face—"

Nevada interrupted this gruesome word picture. "You mean, they found the body, then they put the lid back on the barrel and let him think…"

"Yes. They didn't give any indication that they knew."

"All the time he was getting them the beer."

"Yes."

"And while he dragged the body back upstairs…"

"And put it into bed, yes. I suppose they were playing cat and mouse with him."

"That was really sadistic of them," said Nevada. I tended to agree. However, Tinkler, when he heard about it all later, floated the suggestion that 'maybe they just really wanted a beer'.

"So the burden of evidence was completely against poor Johnny Thomas," said Jasper. "He never really had a chance, I suppose. His story was that someone must have come into the room while he was asleep and committed the murder. Strangled the woman he loved with one of her own stockings."

"Without waking him?" I said.

Jasper nodded dolefully. "That was the sticking point for the jury, too. Johnny claimed to be drugged, but it was no good."

"Drugged?"

"Yes. There was a half-bottle of whisky waiting for Johnny and Gillian in the room when they retired to bed that fateful night. It had a ribbon tied around it. Apparently a present for them. Of course, spirits were very rare in the war. They were hardly likely to look a gift horse in the mouth. Johnny assumed it was a present from his uncle. He and Gillian both drank the whisky. He later claimed it put them both into a heavy drug-induced slumber, from which Gillian would never awaken."

I said, "Was the whisky ever analysed?"

"No, the bottle had vanished. It was gone when he woke up and found the body."

I said, "Presumably removed by the same person who broke in and strangled Gillian."

"Presumably, yes. The defence barrister found a barmaid

who admitted to putting the whisky in the room. She said a man had given it to her, saying it was a gift, and asking her to leave it for Johnny that night. He had paid her to do so. But this mysterious man was never found, and when the barmaid herself disappeared before testifying in the trial…" He shrugged. "That was it for Johnny Thomas."

And that was it for our paid tour, apparently. Jasper McClew finished his pint and rose from the table, bidding us farewell. As he did so he took his spectacles out of the pocket of his jacket and shook them open before putting them on. It was an oddly familiar gesture and suddenly I knew where I'd seen him before.

He was the man who had been hanging around outside Joan Honeyland's mews in Soho. I hardly had time to register this when Tinkler came barging into the pub garden, followed by Clean Head. They had come out through the door as Jasper went in. They sat down at the table with us. "We left the car parked down by the beach," said Clean Head. "I made city boy here walk up the hill."

"It was both invigorating and terrifying," said Tinkler.

"So you managed to find us," said Nevada. "Despite the plethora of pubs in the locale. Did you know that this part of Kent has more pubs per capita than anywhere else in the UK?"

"Oh, we didn't have any problems on that score," said Clean Head. "We went into that petrol station at the bottom of the hill to fill up and, before I could say a word, the man said, 'Go up there, turn right, follow the hill, first left, and then you'll be right there.'"

I noticed her taxi driver's ability to repeat directions with exactitude.

"Right where?"

"The Feathers. This pub. He'd directed me to where you were waiting."

"That was nice of him," said Nevada. "But how did he know that we were together? That you were with us?"

"It's a tiny village," said Tinkler. "It's inhabited by a handful of inbred, banjo-strumming mutants."

"You have to get over this negative obsession of yours, Tinkler," said Nevada. "I think it's a perfectly lovely place."

"Anyway, the point is, *they don't see many strangers around here*." This last was uttered by Tinkler in a sinister and slightly moronic rural accent of no particular locale. "So of course they knew we had to be with you. The other strangers from the place called London."

Superficially this made sense. But only superficially. I said, "But how did they know we were going to this particular pub?"

"Good point," said Nevada.

Tinkler sighed. "Because they talk to each other. They *gossip*. That's all there is to do down here," he said. "Strum banjos and gossip."

I looked at him, then at Clean Head, beautiful and elegant with her smooth, shaved scalp gleaming. I got up from the table and went into the pub. Andy the barman was using a damp cloth to carefully wipe the dust off the bottle of wine that we'd ordered. He looked at me as I came in and set it aside.

"Excuse me," I said, "but what did you mean earlier, when you said it was nice to see someone with hair?"

"Oh, that? I just meant a lot of the people who come here for the Silk Stockings Murder tour, a lot of them, maybe even most of them, are skinheads. Like your friend outside." He glanced out the window at the garden, where Clean Head was sitting, laughing with the others. "Actually, not like her. They're usually a whiter shade of pale, if you know what I mean. Bovver boots, Fred Perry shirts, the Union Jack very much in evidence. All that lot."

I said, "Why?"

"Why, what?"

"Why do those people come here?"

He shrugged. "Because they're interested in the murder."

"But why them? Why those particular people?"

"I have no idea."

We went back down the hill and got in the car. Clean Head started the engine. "Let's go and visit Abner the Zombie Cat," said Tinkler. "Perhaps he'll fart for us."

"Abner the Zombie What?" said Clean Head, frowning as she turned onto the Dover Road. Tinkler explained in extensive detail, lingering on the effects of sardines on the digestive system of the poor cat.

"Wait a minute," I said. "Slow down."

"What is it?" said Nevada.

There, parked by the side of the road, was the van we'd seen earlier, with the nocturnal skyscape painted on its side and the logo *Ms Moon is sending us to sleep with her healing silver rays*. Clean Head pulled up beside it and I got out of the car. There was no one in the van. I walked around it and looked at the other side.

Of course, painted on this side was the big smiling sun shining its rays across a blue sky and the lettering that read: *Mr Sunshine is giving us some golden love today*. Nevada got out of the car and joined me. I said, "It's not a companion piece. It's the same van."

"Night and day," said Nevada. "Yin and yang. The great cosmic balance."

I made a note of the licence plate. I had no idea why, or what I'd do with it. Then we got back in the car and set off for London.

We told Clean Head and Tinkler the gruesome story we'd learned on our murder tour. This proved to be a mistake, at least in the case of Tinkler. All the way back he kept singing 'Roll Out the Barrel'.

"Roll out the barrel, we'll have a barrel of fun!"

He wouldn't shut up. Even when Clean Head told him to, he kept on quietly humming the tune. "I can't help it," he said. "It's stuck in my head now."

16. MUD ON THE PLATES

We got back to London to find two cats who thought they'd been criminally neglected and underfed. As soon as we started pouring biscuits into their bowls, the phone began to ring. So I left Nevada to make sure that Turk wouldn't steal Fanny's leftovers from her bowl. Or vice versa.

It was Joan Honeyland, who rang regularly at no particular time of day for updates on our quest. I told her I hadn't found any new records and was immediately met with her usual rush of reassurances that there was no hurry and that I was doing a fine job. This didn't lessen my regret about how little I'd so far achieved for her, and I weighed up whether I should tell her about our guided tour of the pub in Kingsdown.

The problem was, we'd spent quite a lot of her money on that little outing and it had yielded very little of direct value to her. It was turning out that the Silk Stockings Murder, as ghoulishly interesting as it might be in its own right, didn't seem relevant to the task at hand. This was because her father, good old Lucky, was utterly peripheral. All we'd gleaned from our local historian were some sound bites concerning the colonel's steadfast loyalty and support for Johnny Thomas, and those death cell visits. How he'd held Johnny's hand, literally and figuratively, on the night before the young airman went to the gallows.

But we'd already had all this from other sources.

Luckily Miss Honeyland seemed content to do most of the talking, so I didn't have to bring this up. She took pleasure in informing me that our half-wit recording engineer—my term, not hers—had finally managed to get hold of a turntable with a 78rpm speed setting and was now able to proceed with the much-discussed digital transfer of the Flare Path Orchestra records.

This cooled me down a little in regard to this chump and his endless postponements. In a way, I could see what the problem had been. Most turntables today are intended for club and DJ use. They are designed for scratching, mixing and backtracking, and only have 33 and 45 settings. There isn't much call for beat-matching on shellac.

Nonetheless, I didn't entirely understand the delay. There were still millions of turntables out there, old ones and new ones with a 78 setting, that he could have bought or borrowed.

Perhaps he simply wanted to do the job properly and had been looking for a suitably high-precision deck that really would go around at exactly and precisely 78 revolutions per minute without variation and allow the music to be most accurately and realistically harvested out of those antique grooves.

I wondered what the odds on that were.

As soon as I said goodbye to Miss Honeyland and hung up, the phone rang again. I thought she'd forgotten something and called back. But it was just my voicemail telling me I had a message. Nevada came and sat on the arm of the sofa as I dialled in to hear it. "Who is it?" she said.

"Gresford-Jones." I listened to the maddeningly measured nasal cadences of the old teacher.

"He must have heard us talking about him," said Nevada. "His ears must have been burning. *Abner's* ears must have been burning. What's left of them, his little decaying undead ears."

Gresford-Jones seemed to feel that speaking to someone's voicemail was like addressing a class full of particularly stupid children. Everything was painstakingly enunciated, to allow no chance of ambiguity or error. But eventually he concluded, and the gist of it was that he had some further reminiscences and anecdotal material that he thought might be vital for our purposes.

In other words, that we'd be willing to pay for.

He finished by asking if we would be interested, and if so to ring him and make an appointment. I rang straight back, but there was no answer. And no voicemail.

I tried him again just before we went to bed. No dice.

The following day I tried him again at regular intervals and began to curse his lack of any kind of mechanism for handling phone messages.

"Yes, you'd think he could at least train his zombie cat to answer it," said Nevada, when I groused to her about the situation.

The next day I tried to reach him five times before lunch and three times after. After the fourth attempt, I went out for a walk on the Common, resisting the urge to try him on my mobile. When I came back I sat down before I took my jacket off, picked up the phone and called him again. As if responding to my determination, Gresford-Jones answered promptly, and I made an appointment to see him at his earliest availability. I didn't think there would be too many other demands on his time, but it turned out he had to inspect his diary with microscopic care before he'd agree on when we could actually see him. But agree we did. Eventually.

As I hung up and went to report my triumph to Nevada— and finally take my jacket off—the phone rang again. I went back and answered it.

It was Gerry Wuggins.

He sounded strange.

We walked through the red metal ranch-style gate and up the hill towards Gerry's house. It was a cloudy day here in Sevenoaks. The air smelled nice, with a country sweetness. But there was a bite in it and the birds seemed to be huddling to keep warm in the trees above us. Where had spring gone?

"You said he sounded strange when he rang you," said Nevada. "Strange in what way?"

"Well, as if he was reluctant to be talking to me."

"But *he* rang *you*," she said.

"Exactly," I said. "He was reluctant, but also *relieved*.

He said he was glad to have reached me. And he sounded like he really was."

"Shh," said Nevada. "There he is now."

Gerry was indeed revealed as we walked around the bend in the driveway, standing in front of us. He was wearing tweed trousers and a checked shirt under an old green sweater with brass buttons. His ruddy face shifted from anxiety to a smile of welcome, and he waved his big hands in greeting, shoes scuffling eagerly as he came downhill to meet us.

"Good to see you again," he said, shaking our hands. "Bit different around here, isn't it, without a wedding going on? Quieter." He led us up the hill and across the lawn, into the gardens behind the house. We sat down at a folding pink metal table on the flagstone patio. He poured us glasses of Pimm's from a jug as we sat looking out at the vegetable beds, which were extensive and impressive. Green beans were much in evidence in the nearby greenhouse. I remembered his chutney and wondered if I should ask for a jar for Tinkler, for old times' sake.

Nevada took out her phone, switched it to record, and set it on the table in front of us. Gerry paused in pouring the drinks. "What's that for?" He peered at the phone.

"To record your anecdotes about Lucky Honeyland," I said. "As agreed. That's why we're here." Nevada gave me a look. Perhaps I spoke a little sharply, but we'd come all this way, driving the Volvo we'd borrowed from Tinkler, and I wasn't interested in changes of heart or other complications.

But Gerry just relaxed and smiled. "Oh, yeah, that. We can do that too." He handed us our drinks. "But first there's something else. Something I need to get off my chest." He took a deep breath, frowning and glancing down at the table in front of him as if searching for something there. I got the impression he didn't want to meet our eyes. "Do you remember what I said the last time I saw you, about my records?"

I looked at him. "You said your wife had thrown them away."

He raised his pale eyes to gaze into mine. He didn't look happy. "Yeah, look, mate, I'm sorry about that."

There was silence for a moment while this sunk in. We could hear the birds singing in the garden. I said, "You mean she didn't throw them away?"

He nodded. Nevada said, "You mean you've still got your records?" He nodded again. "But that's wonderful news," she said. She looked at me. "Isn't that wonderful news?"

"It is. Wonderful." I was watching Gerry, waiting for further explanation. The obvious question was: why had he lied to us? I could see he was struggling with something, and I waited.

Finally he said, "You see, what happened was, the night you came around, after you were gone—in fact, while you were still here—Sheryll had a word with me." Sheryll was the second wife. I remembered her calling him away from the kitchen and talking to him out of earshot. And then I remembered the look she had given us when we came back. She hadn't been glad to see us.

"You see," said Gerry, "she thought you were a bit dodgy. Not *you*, but the *situation*. It did seem a bit dodgy, what with you turning up like that in the middle of the night, the night of Belinda's wedding reception, and wanting to buy the records like that."

"It was only the middle of the night because you told us to come back later," said Nevada mildly.

He shook his head. "I know, dear, I know. But it's just that Sheryll thought you might be up to something, you know, trying to pull a fast one."

I said, "We offered to pay you whatever you wanted for them. We have a very generous expense account. It's hard to see how we could be pulling a fast one." I was a little nettled by his confession, but I thought that I was managing to sound civil and polite in spite of that. Anxious glances from Nevada suggested otherwise.

"I know, I know, but she just didn't want me to rush into selling them. She knows how much those records mean to me, and she didn't want me to rush into doing anything with them." I noticed that the records, which he'd previously said he didn't play anymore and indeed implied he might never play again, had suddenly become treasured heirlooms. I could see where this was going.

I sighed. "Okay," I said. "But it's all right with her if you sell them now?"

He glanced back over his shoulder, towards the house, as though expecting the ominous spectre of his wife to appear. "Yeah."

"What changed her mind?" I imagined her researching the records on the Internet and trying to work out how much money she could get for them. She'd seemed like the shrewd, organised type. But this wouldn't have proved an easy task.

The records were so rare they almost never changed hands, and there was precious little price data available on them. Probably the only thing she could find would be my blog about the 78 we'd discovered inside Tinkler's speaker.

And that, I reflected gloomily, had been a deliberate attempt to drive up the price of any and all Flare Path Orchestra records. So I braced myself now for Gerry's financial demands. I hoped Miss Honeyland wouldn't mind being taken to the cleaners.

But instead Gerry said, "We didn't change our minds. We had our minds changed for us, sort of. You see, we had a bit of a break-in."

Nevada and I looked at each other. "When?" I said.

"The other night. Someone broke in. Or they tried to." He sipped his Pimm's and stared into its ruddy red depths. "Came very bloody close, too." He looked at me. "And that's sort of spooked us. Spooked Sheryll and, I must admit, me too. So she suggested we should get rid of the records after all. Sell them to you."

I said, "Why would a break-in make you want to sell me the records?"

He blinked at me. "Because they were after them, after the records. That's what they tried to break in to get. So we figured we'd be better off selling them, and then we don't have to worry about them. Don't have to worry about security issues." He rattled the ice in his glass and took a sip.

"How do you know they were after the records?" I glanced at his large stylish house, rising in stacked blocks on the green slope above us. There were plenty of other things in there worth stealing.

"It was the ladder that gave it away," said Gerry. "They had a big folding ladder with them. Not the sort of thing you cart along on the off-chance. They definitely knew they were going to need it. And they went straight to the north wing of the house, which is the bit with the attic on top of it, and they put the ladder up beside the attic window." We all turned and looked at the house. I could see the section he was talking about, a two-storey unit set centrally in the rambling building. "If they just wanted to break into the house, there were a lot of other windows easier to get at. Doors, too, for that matter." He shook his head. "No, they were definitely heading for the attic."

"And the only valuable items in your attic are the records?" said Nevada.

"I don't think they're interested in my old beer-making kit."

"How did they know the records were in the attic?" I said.

Gerry shook his head mournfully. "You remember the day of the wedding? There was some blokes who crashed the reception."

I remembered the wedding crashers very well. I'd almost been beaten up on the presumption that I was one of them.

"Well," said Gerry, "it turns out that they'd been asking some odd questions. Though nobody ever thought to tell me until after the break-in."

"But they didn't get away with anything?" I tried not to let the urgency show in my voice.

Gerry smiled slowly. "No, we have a pretty good security system here. That is one thing we do have. They were detected as soon as they entered the grounds, and the alarm went off before they got anywhere near the window."

A sudden thought occurred to me. "You said you didn't trust us."

He spread his big hands in a helpless gesture. "Not me, son. The wife. And it's not that she didn't trust you, exactly…"

"But she thought there was something dodgy about our interest in your records."

"Yeah, that's right."

"So then someone turns up and tries to break in and steal those records."

He looked at me. "Yeah?"

"So why didn't you think it was us?"

"You?" he said.

Nevada nodded. "That's right. We would seem to be the obvious culprits. Why didn't you think it was us?"

"Oh," said Gerry. "There was never any question of it being you. Any of your mob. We picked them up on the surveillance cameras, our would-be burglars. They were hefty lads. Very hefty. And I'm very glad we didn't have a run-in with them. Anyway, they were a lot bigger than either of you or your friend who couldn't stop stuffing his gob."

"But you couldn't see their faces?" said Nevada.

Gerry shook his head. "They was wearing the traditional black ski masks."

"We could have hired someone," I said. He stared at me

in puzzlement. "We could have hired the hefty lads in the ski masks."

He shook his head again. "No, I never thought it was you. You're not the type. *They* were the type. Looked like they do this sort of thing for a living. They'd reversed their van in by our gate so it was pointing back up the street and ready for a quick getaway in case they needed it. Which, in this case, they did. When they heard the alarm they scarpered and got out of here, sharpish."

"A van?" I said.

"Yeah."

I felt a cold crawl of premonition up my spine. I said, "It was an old-fashioned Volkswagen van with a sun and a moon and a lot of hippie nonsense painted on the sides."

He stared at me as if I was mad.

"No, mate. It was a modern Hyundai CRDI 116 white diesel van with the twin side loading doors and nothing painted on it at all."

"Did you get the licence number?" said Nevada, while I pondered this information.

"No. The plates were covered with mud, accidentally-on-purpose, like."

We finished our Pimm's as we discussed a price for his records, and then he went inside the house and got them for us. There were a dozen of them, all 78s, in three cardboard albums each holding four discs. They were pristine, with glossy black playing surfaces.

After he wrapped them they made a heavy, expensive bundle under my arm. "Don't drop them," said Nevada, as we walked back down the hill.

"I'll try not to."

I glanced back at the house and I thought I saw the pale face of the wife, looking down at us from one of the upstairs windows.

17. FAMILY

Joan Honeyland was ecstatic about our latest discovery. She arranged for Albert the chauffeur to come and pick the records up the following day, first thing. We were still eating breakfast when he arrived, in complete livery including black gloves and cap. Normally at this time of the morning Nevada would still be in her dressing gown, but today she was fully and smartly dressed. I asked if this was the effect of a man in uniform.

"No need to be jealous. According to Tinkler he is occupied full-time in having a torrid affair with his employer." We watched him out the window as he drove off, the black roof of the Mercedes gliding past the top of the garden wall, then we went back to the table to finish eating.

Albert had been in too much of a hurry to even join us for a coffee. He was racing to deliver the records to the guy with the studio in south London, who would then presumably sit around for a few more weeks twiddling his thumbs before he made a digital transfer of them.

After breakfast we left the house, first putting out some biscuits for the cats. The idea behind this was that it would distract them from trying to follow us and throwing themselves under a speeding car on the main road—like some kind of urban lemmings. Actually, it was only Turk who was likely to follow us, being the bolder of the two. Her sister would only come as far as the garden gate and then fall asleep peacefully in the flower beds, awaiting our return.

We caught the bus into Putney and walked to Tinkler's house. He was at work but he'd left the car keys for us in the usual place, tucked behind a disused gas meter mounted on the wall by his front door. We collected them and found the Volvo, parked in the next street over, and drove down to Kent.

It was time for our interview with Charles Gresford-Jones. Tinkler had asked us to take a photo of Abner the cat while we were there, because Clean Head didn't believe he existed. "Preferably a picture of him slurping down sardines in tomato sauce. The more gruesome the better."

We reached Dover almost an hour early, the beneficiaries of remarkably light traffic leaving London, and decided to kill time with a walk along the seafront. We watched a huge white ferry drifting off towards France through the haze over the Channel, moving as silently as a dream. Then we checked the time and drove up to Gresford-Jones's place.

We were standing outside number eighty-seven on the dot. I opened the front gate and Nevada followed me through. We were about to ring the bell when the front door of the neighbouring house popped open. A woman looked out. She was plump, pale and middle-aged.

"Are you family?" she said.

"I beg your pardon?"

"He's in Buckland Hospital."

Apparently Charles Gresford-Jones had suffered a serious fall. The woman told us she'd found him lying unconscious on the floor of his front room. She had let herself in with a set of keys he'd given her, because Abner had been outside the front door, scratching to get in. Gresford-Jones didn't believe in cat flaps and had left the keys with his neighbour for just such an eventuality.

Luckily.

An ambulance had arrived promptly after her call and Gresford-Jones was now in hospital in a stable but critical condition and profoundly unconscious. "The big problem," said the woman, "is the cat."

"Abner?"

"Yes. You see, the thing is, my husband and son are allergic. I've been feeding him, but I can't take him in and give him a proper home, because of my husband and son, you see. And he does need a proper home. Deserves one. Poor old Abner."

"But what about his owner?"

She shook her head grimly. "He won't be coming out again. When you reach that age and start falling, that's it."

I said, "But he might recover."

She gave me a sceptical look. "Even if he does, we need someone to look after Abner in the meantime."

I looked at Nevada. We hadn't explained that we weren't family. Maybe we should now. Maybe it was too late. Maybe we looked too damned respectable and reliable. The woman watched us, almost visibly willing us to say we'd take the cat off her hands.

"It would be different," she said, "if there was anyone else to ask. If I could ask the people with that van."

"Van?" I said.

"Yes, they've been visiting Mr Gresford-Jones. But they haven't been around lately."

"What kind of a van?"

"Well it's got sort of a painting of the sun on one side."

"And the moon on the other."

"Yes, that's right," she said. "The hippie van. I've seen it parked outside his house often enough, but it hasn't been around lately. Otherwise I'd ask them."

"Them?"

"The people with the van."

"You've seen them?" I said. "Could you describe them?"

"Oh no, I've never actually seen them. Just the van. Parked outside his house." She looked at us. "It's such a shame they've gone away. It seemed they were always around, but now he's had his fall they've disappeared."

I glanced at Nevada.

The woman said, "I was thinking they could have taken Abner with them. It's a pity. The cat would have enjoyed that. Riding about the country in a van."

Actually, I thought, it was probably a cat's idea of hell. But I didn't say so.

The woman seemed to feel that the matter was decided now, because she found the keys and let us into the house. I wanted to search the place, but I couldn't very well do that with the woman watching. Gresford-Jones hadn't said he had any other records, but he'd insisted he had something that would be of considerable interest to us.

I'd assumed at first that it was some titbit of recollection, but you never knew. It could be a letter, a document, a photo...

Or even another record.

But there was no chance for us to look for it. Instead, under the watchful eye of the woman, we located a tin of sardines and a cat carrier and we used the former to lure Abner into the latter. I closed the front of the cat carrier and lifted it. He scuttled around inside, weight shifting from front to back. I carried it out to the car, which Nevada had gone ahead and unlocked. The woman watched me go, beaming with satisfaction. I opened the back door of the Volvo and put the cat carrier inside. It was easy to manoeuvre. It didn't seem to weigh much more than it did empty.

Abner's white-furred face peered at me from the darkness within, profoundly astonished at this turn of events.

I positioned the cat carrier carefully on the back seat, shut the door and got in the front beside Nevada. There was a wary silence from the back of the car.

Nevada looked at me. We were now going to have the discussion we hadn't been able to conduct in front of the woman. "What can we do with him?" said Nevada. She glanced over her shoulder. I followed her gaze. Abner had pressed his face to the bars at the front of the cat carrier and was staring out at us. His long white whiskers projected through the bars. Nevada looked away. "We can't have him with our two. Fanny and Turk wouldn't stand for it."

I was relieved. I agreed they wouldn't.

"And I rang Tinkler while you were in the house. He said, categorically, no. Or, said no categorically. I'm sure he'd be delighted to correct me."

I said, "He's not a cat person."

"I'm not so sure. I think he might be. But he said the prospect of sardine farts was the deal-breaker."

"He actually said 'deal-breaker'?"

"I'm afraid so. So what are we going to do? Honestly, I can't believe Tinkler. He keeps going on about those sardine farts and now he's managed to put Clean Head off, too. I gave her a ring but he'd already been in touch with her. He must have rung her immediately. Couldn't keep his big mouth shut. And I really think I had a chance to place him with her." She glanced at the back of the car again.

"Really? Abner the Zombie Cat."

She nodded thoughtfully. "Yes, I must admit that moniker didn't help. Still, Tinkler has now closed off two possibilities."

"Don't worry," I said. "I have a plan."

I started the car.

As we headed back for London, Nevada rang the hospital to find out the latest on Charles Gresford-Jones. They told us that they could only give out information to family, so we said we were his family.

Then they told us he was dead.

* * *

The news of his death seemed to add a strange additional velocity to the car as we hurtled along the motorway. Suddenly there was a curious finality about the journey. It had become a one-way trip, at least for Abner.

Now we knew we'd never be taking the cat back. His familiar places were vanishing behind him forever. And he seemed to sense this because, as soon as Nevada switched off the phone, he gave a long querulous cry.

It was an intricate, agonised sound, as though Abner was trying to tell us something complicated and painful. Nevada and I looked at each other. I said, "The hair on the back of my neck just stood up."

"Mine too. It's as if he *knows*, as if he somehow picked it up from us."

Or it could have just been the suspension on Tinkler's Volvo. It wasn't the most comfortable car in the world.

The sun was going down as we reached Enfield. We found a place to park in the street just outside the house. Nevada carried the cat while I rang the doorbell. There was a long wait and my stomach started to sink, then we heard sounds from within, approaching.

Leo Noel opened the door and blinked at us. "Sorry for the delay. I was out in the sheds. I've got a new consignment of 78s and I have to find room for them." He gestured for us to come inside and we followed him into the house. We stood in the hallway by the open door of the dining room, where the dozens of old gramophones gleamed under the subdued glow of the ceiling lamp.

Leo looked at the carrier Nevada was holding. It was

made of beige plastic with a hinged grid of white plastic on the front. Its contents were shrouded in shadow behind those bars.

"What's that?" he said.

I said, "We've brought something for you."

"For me?"

"Yes. Remember, you said you wished you had a cat." Actually, I couldn't remember if he'd said exactly that, but he'd certainly made a fuss over Fanny and Turk when he'd come to visit. And he'd reminisced about having a cat when he was young, and how he missed it.

Leo looked at me and blinked. "Did I?"

"His name is Abner," said Nevada brightly. She held up the cat carrier to eye level. I heard Abner scurry around inside the swaying plastic box, claws clicking as he hastened to maintain his precarious balance. Leo looked at her, looked at me, and then went to the cat carrier, bending his head as he peered apprehensively in.

From the shadows inside, the cat seemed to return his gaze with equal apprehension. Leo straightened up and cleared his throat.

Nevada said, "Just take him for a few days."

"A few days?"

"Yes, and see if you get along. If you aren't happy with the arrangement, then we'll think of something else."

This seemed to decide it for him. "All right," he said. "What do I feed him?"

"Sardines. Here, we've got some for you." I gave him the tins I'd put in my pocket at Gresford-Jones's house. At the time I thought I could always replace them. Now I knew he wasn't going to be missing them.

Leo accepted the tins gratefully.

"I'll give him some now. Do you think I should?"

"It won't do any harm."

"And a bowl of water. I'll have to get a bowl for his water. What about litter and a tray?"

"He went outside at his old home. You can let him into the garden."

"The garden?" Leo glanced worriedly out the window towards the darkness behind the house.

"It's all right," I said. "He won't harm the sheds."

"I suppose not. What did you say was his name?" He peered at the carrier again.

"Abner."

We left Leo looking for a suitable bowl to use for Abner's water. I wondered if he'd fill it with Perrier. As we walked back towards the car I looked at Nevada and said, "A few days?"

"Don't worry. After they've been together for a few days Leo will have utterly fallen in love with him."

"This is Abner the Zombie Cat we're talking about here."

We got in the car and started home. Nevada sat beside me in silence for a long while. Then she said, "He died of a fall."

"Apparently."

"He was certainly getting on. At his rather extreme age, it's not unusual to take a fall."

"That's true."

"And it's not unusual for a fall to prove fatal."

I said, "Absolutely."

"On the other hand, there was that van. Which was apparently there all the time."

"And disappeared when he had his fall."

Fanny was lurking in the shadows of the flower beds, waiting for us when we got home. As we opened the gate, Turk came dashing from some dark corner of the estate to join us.

The phone was ringing as we all came through the front door together. I went to answer it. It was the voicemail, with a message from Joan Honeyland.

"Call me immediately. Something terrible has happened."

18. CAMBERWELL GREEN

Camberwell Green is a region of south London that had distinguished itself for its extravagant levels of gang violence and gun crime. It was also the place where our sound engineer, Derek Roberts, had chosen to locate his studio.

Two days ago, first thing in the morning, Derek had followed his usual custom of going into the studio—where he worked alone—and opened up for his day's work. Having switched his equipment on and checked his email, he had then gone out again, locking the door behind him but not activating any of the heavy-duty security measures necessitated by his colourful neighbourhood. He didn't need to, because he was just going up the road to his favourite coffee shop to pick up his morning coffee, which he had waiting for him every day at this time, prepared to his exacting standard.

A man after my own heart.

He paid for this coffee and started back for his studio, carrying the paper cup in one hand and his phone in the other.

He paused in front of a cut-price booze emporium, which even this early in the day was doing a brisk business among locals who wanted to forget they lived in Camberwell. Derek didn't stop here because he was planning to buy any booze. Rather, it was his custom, because there was a litter bin outside the shop, to pause in this spot and take the lid off his coffee. He would then drop it in the bin, being a considerate and tidy sort of person, and take his first sip of the beloved brew. It was his habit to do this, and to make a phone call while he was standing there.

And as he was making such a call two days ago, he was apparently unaware of an approaching motorcycle coming up the street behind him at a considerable and illegal speed. The motorcycle slowed down as it approached him, coasting almost to a stop as the rider reached into his leather jacket, took out a handgun and shot Derek in the chest.

Everybody in the vicinity scattered or took shelter at the sound of the gunshots. There had been a shooting outside this very booze shop just three weeks earlier, and some of the residents recognised the noise all too well.

The motorcycle, which apparently didn't have a licence plate, speeded up again and took off. The rider was wearing a helmet with a smoked visor, so there was no chance of anybody identifying him even if they had been trying.

Derek, meanwhile, was down, spilling his coffee on the pavement.

He managed to retain his grip on his phone, though, and began to crawl back towards his studio, still clutching it. No one came to his assistance, either because they were still too busy hiding or because they were unaware that he was wounded. The spilled coffee on the pavement concealed any bloodstains, and the sight of a man crawling along on his belly made perfect sense in the context of everyone keeping a very low profile in an attempt to avoid getting shot.

No one knew if that motorcyclist was going to come around again and elaborate on his earlier visit.

Derek managed to reach the front steps of his building, having crawled there with agonising slowness, like an animal going home to die. He lay on the steps and tried to make a phone call to the emergency services. But after dialling the number, he dropped the phone.

But that didn't matter because one of his neighbours had realised what had happened and had already called for an ambulance, telling them that a man had been shot, and his location. The ambulance arrived in record time, but too late for Derek, who had already bled out and was declared dead on arrival at the accident and emergency unit at King's College Hospital.

The prevailing theory was that Derek, who was of West Indian descent, had been mistaken for a member of a local gang and had been gunned down by a rival gang. The quality control in such drive-by shootings was notoriously poor, and it was entirely possible his killing was purely a matter of mistaken identity.

So far no one had claimed responsibility for the shooting. Perhaps they were embarrassed at their gaffe.

It sounds terribly callous, but my first thought on hearing all this was—what about our records?

"That's the problem exactly," said Miss Honeyland when I confessed this to her. "He had completed making the digital copies, poor Derek, and he was supposed to have returned the originals to us—just the day before that appalling incident. But unfortunately it seems he hasn't. So presumably they are all still there at his studio."

"Did he even send you the digital copies?"

"No, he was going to email them to us, but apparently he never had the chance. The poor soul."

So we'd lost the originals and we hadn't even got the copies. I tried not to think ill of the dead.

"I am very concerned about the records," said Miss Honeyland.

"So am I."

"Anyone could just walk in there and steal them."

There was silence on the phone for a moment. Then she said, "I don't suppose you'd consider undertaking a job for me?"

My bungalow is, in theory, a three-bedroom house. Nevada and I have our king-sized bed in one of those rooms, while the other two are supposedly guest rooms. Both are equipped with sofa beds. But both are also currently used for other purposes and packed with other things. Nevada uses one to store all her clothes—her own stuff as well as the items she buys and sells. Her 'stock', as she's taken to calling it. The third room is used for general storage. In other words, all the junk we don't have any other place to put. It may not be surprising to learn that this includes several large boxes of records.

I shoved one of these boxes aside with a scraping sound of complaint—from the box, not me—and lay down on the floor so I could get an arm under the battered blue sofa. Fanny came in to see what was going on and lay down beside me as I scrabbled under the sofa, retreating cautiously when I began dragging out a dusty canvas bag. As it emerged from the shadowy space, Fanny came back and pounced on it, jumping on top of it as I hauled it out, giving it a thorough, savage going-over with her needle-sharp little claws.

Once she was sure the bag was good and dead, she hopped off and strode proudly away. Another job well done. I hefted the bag and carried it into the living room and set it down on the table with a heavy metallic clunk.

When Nevada and I had first met we'd collaborated on a project that had looked like it would involve breaking into a house in Richmond. In the event, it turned out we didn't need to do any such thing, but by that time Nevada had already made preparations in her usual methodical way. And since we had been bankrolled by a man of enormous financial resources and remarkably few scruples, this had involved assembling a state-of-the-art housebreaking kit.

Now I unzipped the bag, which had lain dormant in the spare room for years, and went through it. Just as I remembered, it contained everything needed to gain entry to a locked, well-protected property. Including the instruction manuals.

As I leafed through one of these, Nevada came and looked over my shoulder.

"You see?" she said. "Never throw anything away. You never know when it might come in handy."

Trident Studios was the name of a legendary music recording venue that had once existed in Soho. Great British rock and R&B acts had laid down tracks there, including the Beatles. If Tinkler had access to a time machine, this would be one of the first places he'd visit.

Trident Studios was also the name of Derek Robert's business in Camberwell. It had been an act of hubris for him to have borrowed it. And a particularly bitter irony because 'Trident' was also the code name of the Metropolitan Police campaign to stamp out gun crime in the capital.

Behind the Trident Studios in Camberwell ran a thin, winding maze of an alleyway that squeezed between two rows of business premises. The alley existed where there were gaps between the walled backyards of the various businesses. In some cases the yards shared a common wall, and at these points the alley reached a dead end.

Luckily it extended far enough to give us access to the rear entrance of the studio. Construction work was taking place around the mouth of the alley, with new brickwork rising in ragged and apparently random stacks. The entrance to the alley had been half-heartedly sealed off with a tall rectangle of weather-beaten brown fibreboard. It had been jammed tightly into the opening, causing a tall vertical crease in the damp board, but I was able to ease it aside, creating an opening big enough for us to squeeze through.

Nevada was standing behind me. She was carrying selected items from the canvas bag in a small rucksack. The instruction manuals we had left at home. The rucksack was black, as were the clothes we were wearing. We also had what Gerry had referred to as the traditional black ski masks, although as yet we hadn't put these on.

Nevada was speaking into the phone. "Yes, we're about to start now." Back down the street, Clean Head, who was sitting in a car keeping watch for us, said something in reply that I didn't catch. I grunted as I shoved the board aside.

Nevada switched her phone to silent and we went down the alley.

We eased along the dank, narrow passage. The only light came from behind us, in the street we'd left behind. The alley smelled sharply of urine. Empty beer cans crunched under our feet. I could see virtually nothing, and although we had torches, neither of us felt like turning them on yet. So I ran my hand along the wall to our left. I felt distinctly when it changed, the size and texture of the bricks altering perceptibly. This indicated that we'd passed one of the buildings and moved on to the next. Keeping count in this way, I was able to determine when we'd come to the fourth one. Trident Studios.

The biggest problem with the lock on the gate was getting Nevada to hold the torch beam steady enough to see what I was doing. Nevertheless, we were inside within five minutes. The gate gave access to a tiny courtyard with a green recycling bin beside a steel reinforced back door that looked considerably more formidable than the gate we'd just come through.

There was also the blunt metal box of a burglar alarm on the wall above and to the left of the door.

The heaviest item in the rucksack we'd brought was a drill, which would enable us to pierce the outer shell of the alarm housing and insert what the manual called the 'electronic countermeasures cluster'. This would be a ticklish business, not least because of the unavoidable noise of the drill.

So it was an enormous relief when I stood on the recycling bin and held a digital voltage detector beside the alarm housing which told me the alarm system was switched off. Derek Roberts must have done so after entering his studios for the final time, and the police had obviously not switched it back on—which, come to think of it, made total sense, since they wouldn't know the entry code and a constantly ringing alarm would just annoy the hell out of everyone.

I climbed back down from the bin and we went to work on the back door. This time Nevada wanted to try dealing with the lock. The subtext of this was that I should hold the torch and see how easy it was.

The answer being, not easy at all.

I had to hover behind her, moving when she moved, trying to keep the lock in the beam of light while preventing her body blocking it and also shielding it as much as possible from anyone who might be watching.

It took twenty minutes for her to open the lock, and I doubt that I could have improved on her time. We were both damp with sweat and shaking with relief when the door finally swung open to reveal a dark, quiet space that smelled of synthetic pine air freshener.

We didn't switch on any of the lights in the studio. As far as I could tell the windows were all shuttered and sealed, but we weren't taking any chances. We used our torches, probing the shadows and getting our bearings. We had moved through a storage area into the control room, which consisted of a long console covered with mixing controls and computer screens. There was a window above it that overlooked the recording studio proper—a small carpeted chamber with sound-absorbing panels on the walls and three microphone stands looking tall and forlorn and abandoned in the middle of the space. Inside the control room there was a secondary bank of equipment on the right and two doors to the left. We opened these.

One led into the studio, the other to a small kitchen area combined with an office and lounge and, beyond that, the front door of the building. Just on the other side of that was where the actual crime scene began, and where Derek Roberts had died on his front steps. We closed the inner doors and went to work.

We found the records almost immediately. Miss Honeyland had given me a list, but I didn't need it because every item was seared into my brain. I went through them quickly as Nevada held the torch.

Everything was there.

We had a bag thickly lined with bubble wrap ready to cushion the 78s. It would have been a terrible shame to go to all this trouble—and burglary—and then get home with a sack full of rattling shellac fragments.

As I packed the records carefully into the bag I noticed the bookshelf on the wall in front of me. Predictably enough, it held a number of volumes about electronics and sound recording. But most of the books were about statistics. I wondered if Derek had had any idea of what the odds had been of him catching a stray bullet in this neighbourhood.

One hundred per cent, as it turned out.

I was just packing the last 78 into the bag—'Catfish' backed with 'Whitebait'—when Nevada suddenly snatched her phone out of her pocket. It vibrated in her hand as she stared at it. "It's Clean Head," she said. "Someone's coming—"

At that moment we heard, from the other end of the building, the sound of the front door opening. We looked at each other for an instant and then I stuffed the last record into the bag and closed it. There was the sound of the front door shutting. Nevada and I quickly crossed the control room, the omnipresent carpet thankfully muffling our footsteps. Voices came from the other side of the door, in the office area.

Male voices, low, two of them by the sound of it.

Nevada went out of the back door of the control room and I followed her. She was already halfway across the store room and heading for the rear of the building as I came through. I turned to close the door behind me.

As I did so, the torch in my hand swung its beam across the control room and lit up something on the short section of the control console to the left.

I froze.

I couldn't believe what I was looking at.

On the other side of the door, the voices had come to a halt, somewhere around the office area, and were holding a low discussion. I stared at the thin beam of my torch, streaming back into the control room. Behind me Nevada had the back door of the building open. I felt a thin, cold stream of air flow over me from it.

I stepped back—into the control room.

Behind me I could hear Nevada hiss in astonishment.

I moved across the control room, following the beam of my torch.

There in front of me, built into the short section of the console between a reel-to-reel tape recorder and a rack full of headphones, was a turntable. It was a vintage EMT 930st studio deck. There was a thin patina of dust on the silver metal plinth of the turntable, which was set flush with the blonde wood of the console. I reached down and ran my finger through the dust on the plinth, and across the console. It left a long pale streak.

Then I switched the turntable on.

Through the door I could still hear the voices in low conversation. Were they getting nearer?

The platter on the deck started to spin, smoothly and silently.

The selector lever on the left allowed it to run at 33 1/3, 45 or 78rpm. I turned it all the way to the left, to 78. Then I switched on the small neon strobe lamp. Outside the door the voices murmured. It was hard to tell, but I thought they were indeed getting closer. Which wasn't at all surprising.

Behind me I heard a tiny sound and turned to see that

Nevada had come back into the room.

She was staring at me in utter terror.

I looked back at the turntable. In the eerie glow of the strobe lamp I could see the small black stroboscopic markings spinning on the outside edge of the turntable. There were three sets of these, one for each speed setting. Two of them were an indistinct blur as the turntable spun, but the third, which corresponded to 78rpm, appeared to be standing perfectly still.

Which meant it was running at exactly 78 revolutions per minute.

Outside the door, the voices were definitely getting closer.

I felt Nevada grab my arm and try to physically drag me away from the turntable. I pulled free and bent over it again. Out of the corner of my eye I saw her hesitate for an instant, then go back out the door.

The voices were very near now.

I took one last look at the turntable then switched it off, first the motor then the neon lamp. The strobe light went out. I heard the voices outside the door. I turned to go. I was almost out of the room when I realised that the turntable was still spinning. Although I had switched it off, momentum meant the platter was still rotating. I heard someone rattling the door of the control room.

I stepped back inside and went to the turntable. I reached towards the platter and put a finger on it to gently retard its progress without damaging the drive belt—the habit of a lifetime—then realised what I was doing and just grabbed it and brought it to an abrupt halt.

They were coming into the room as I left, silently closing the door behind me. Nevada was waiting for me in the outside doorway at the back of the building, her posture a pictogram of tension. She wouldn't look at me as we hurried out.

We locked the outer door silently behind us, went across the yard, through the gate, closed that and hurried down the alley.

I stuffed the tall damp panel of fibreboard back into the opening and we stepped into the street. "Wait a minute," said Nevada.

She reached into the rucksack and pulled out a checked jacket for me, and an elegant, geometrically figured sweater for herself. We hastily pulled these on, and suddenly instead of being two suspicious-looking figures all in black, we were a fashionably attired young couple strolling back from a night on the town.

Nevada still wouldn't look at me.

We got back to Clean Head's vehicle. She had left her taxi at home and had borrowed a silver Audi. She had a theory that silver cars were so all-pervasive as to be virtually invisible.

She was staring at us as we got in. "What happened?" she said. "Why did you take so long? I was shitting myself. Didn't you get my warning?" She looked over her shoulder at us as we settled in the back seat. "I told you they were going into the studio. Did you see them? Did they see you?"

"Just drive," said Nevada.

We pulled away, Clean Head smoothly slipping through the gears. Nevada looked behind us until we'd turned the corner, then she looked at me.

She hit me. On the shoulder. As hard as she could.

It was cramped in the car and she didn't have much room to manoeuvre, so it wasn't much of a blow, but nevertheless I grabbed her arm before she could hit me again and held it tight.

"What the hell is going on?" said Clean Head from the front of the car.

"He stopped to admire a fucking turntable," said Nevada. Her voice shook. Anger was turning to tears.

"What?"

"I didn't stop to admire it," I said. "I stopped to check it."

There must have been something in my voice, because Nevada calmed down immediately, wiping her face. "Check it for what?"

"It had a 78rpm setting. Our murder victim owned a working 78 deck."

"So what?" said Nevada. "We *know* he'd got hold of one. He told Miss Honeyland. That was the hold-up. He didn't have one, but just recently he managed to get hold of one."

"Not just recently," I said. "That turntable was integrated. It was built into the console." I looked at her. "It was installed the day they built the studio."

Nevada shook her head, putting it together. "So he didn't have to get hold of one... He already had one." She peered at me. "And it was definitely in working order?"

I remembered the ghostly glow of the strobe lamp, and

the precise dance of the markings. "Definitely," I said.

"Couldn't it have been recently repaired, the turntable? I mean, perhaps it was out of action and recently fixed. Or replaced? Or renovated?"

I said, "If it was, somebody managed to do it without disturbing the dust that had settled on it for years."

There was silence in the car. Clean Head was listening, too.

Finally Nevada said, "So that's what you had to check."

And Clean Head said, "And that's why you didn't come out when I warned you."

"Yes."

"Even though I gave you plenty of warning."

"Yes, you did. Thank you."

"They almost got you, you know."

"What did they look like?" I said.

She considered. "Two white blokes. Big."

"Police?"

"No."

"Hefty lads?" I said.

"Hefty? Yes. Did they see you?"

"No, but they were coming into the room while I was still there."

"That was a bit careless of you," said Clean Head.

"I was making sure the turntable had stopped completely after I'd switched it off. I had to. Otherwise they would have come in and seen it was still spinning."

"And they would have known someone had just been in there."

"Correct."

"Was it scary?"

"It was touch and go. But I had to do it."

Nevada took my hand. "That was very brave of you."

I said, "I noticed that you didn't take off, either."

"What do you mean?"

I looked at her. "You could have made good your escape as soon as things got dicey. But you didn't. You waited for me. You didn't bail."

"Oh, I wouldn't do that," said Nevada. "I have far too much invested in you. I've only recently got you to abandon your last bad habit. If something happened to you I'd have to start again with someone else. Imagine the *effort*."

"How romantic," said Clean Head from the front seat.

"Actually, it is," I said. I leaned close to Nevada and kissed her. I could smell her perfume and the tang of sweat. It was a lengthy kiss.

"Save it until you get home, you two," said Clean Head.

We moved apart. I looked at Nevada. Amber streetlights flared at regular intervals in tiny replica in her wide dark eyes. She said, "So the upshot of all this is that the sound engineer was a duplicitous individual."

"He was certainly a liar."

"And if he was given to lying, it was presumably for a reason. Which suggests he was up to something. Perhaps he was some kind of scam artist."

"Exactly," I said. "It kind of makes you wonder why he was killed, doesn't it?"

19. VIEW FROM THE BRIDGE

Having borrowed the necessary equipment from Tinkler—a Meridian AD converter and some cables—it took me less than two hours to make digital copies of all the records. This was grimly gratifying, but whenever I found myself reflecting with vindictive satisfaction on how favourably I compared to the spectacular incompetence of our chump of a sound engineer, I had to remind myself that this poor chump was dead.

I emailed the sound files to Joan Honeyland and received her effusive thanks. Then we discussed a time of arrival for Albert to collect the originals. He turned up in full chauffeur regalia again, including this time a sinister pair of sunglasses. I gave him the 78s and he drove off with them, and I had a sudden pang when I realised I'd never see—or hear—these recordings by the Flare Path Orchestra again.

I still had copies of them all in digital form, of course. But what the hell use was that to anyone?

"Someone on the phone for you," said Nevada,

interrupting my gloomy speculations. "I think it's the human palindrome, but he didn't try to chat me up so I'm not sure." She handed me the handset, which I took with some measure of trepidation.

"Hello? Noel?"

"Yes indeed. It is me. Listen, I'm ringing about Abner the cat."

I had a sudden sinking feeling. I'd half-expected this call. After all, we'd made the mistake of leaving a get-out for Leo when we'd given him the cat. We'd given him Abner on approval, so to speak.

If he didn't want to keep the zombie cat, I didn't know who the hell we'd turn to. I saw an elaborate cluster of complications stretching out before me like a Borgesian labyrinth.

I said, "So, how is Abner?" I might have sighed. Nevada certainly looked at me apprehensively.

"He's absolutely marvellous," gushed Leo. "He's such an affectionate little chap. Follows me everywhere and keeps me company while I'm sorting and cataloguing, purring constantly. And, absolutely the most important thing, he seems to have an innate and intrinsic respect for shellac and its uniquely fragile and vulnerable nature."

"That *is* the most important thing," I agreed. "So it would be safe to say you and Abner are getting along, then?" Listening intently on the sofa beside me, Nevada made a gesture of wiping sweat from her brow and sank back in relief.

"Absolutely. Absolutely. Very safe to say. Getting along famously. He's here right now, sitting beside me. Aren't you, little chap? Yes, you are. Yes, you are. You should hear him purring. Would you like to hear him purring?" Before I could say yes or no, the line went apparently dead.

Now, if I held my breath and I listened very attentively I could just about detect a faint susurration, like a rhythmic version of the indistinct miniature roaring you hear in a seashell. I offered the phone to Nevada. "The purr of the zombie cat."

She listened for a moment and handed it back to me. "Impressive."

Leo came back on the line. "Very impressive," I told him.

"Isn't it? He was a bit quiet when you first brought him here. He'd just spent a couple of hours in the back of a car in a cat carrier, of course. No wonder he was subdued. But he soon perked up and started nosing his way around, exploring the place. And he absolutely loves the garden. Spends half his time out there. Among the sheds."

"Among the sheds, of course."

"But he always comes in at night to sleep on the bed with Crystal and I."

My ears pricked up. "Crystal?"

"Ah, yes. Of course. I haven't told you about her. In point of fact, that's why I'm ringing you up. To tell you about her. To thank you for bringing Abner into my life. Because *he* brought Crystal into *mine*."

He spent the next five minutes giving me the details, which, I must admit, had me riveted. When he'd finished I hung up and looked at Nevada, who'd evidently been trying to piece together the conversation from my end of it.

"Leo's got a girlfriend," I said.

"So I gather."

"Called Crystal."

"So I gather."

"He met her at the vets when he took Abner in for a check-up. She's the secretary for the veterinary practice."

"Are they just dating or are they actually, you know, doing the thing?"

"Judging by his extensive complaints about the cost of condoms these days, I'd have to say that they are doing it."

"My god. And all thanks to Abner. Wait until I tell Tinkler. If he'd taken the cat maybe *he* would have got laid."

She got her chance to tell him that evening when he came over for dinner. This was the price he'd demanded for lending the kit I'd needed for the digital transfer. A small enough price to pay, although he had also insisted on planning the menu for tonight himself from among the recipes he called my 'greatest hits'.

"And I want the homemade Cointreau ice cream," he'd concluded.

That night he devoured the three courses with considerable satisfaction.

He wasn't so pleased when he heard about Leo. "You see," said Nevada, rubbing it in. "If you'd taken the cat, it could have been you who was shagging a gorgeous fit young veterinary secretary." The adjectives 'gorgeous', 'fit' and 'young' had not featured at any point in Leo's discussion of the woman from the vets. They were entirely Nevada's own embroidery. "It could have been you who met her."

"Well maybe I still can," said Tinkler. "When you go to see the vet about a cat, do you actually have to *show* them the cat?"

That night in bed, Nevada and I tried to plan our next move. Although the recent excitement in Camberwell had felt like a conclusive victory at the time, we were in fact pretty much back where we'd started, with no clear way forward. We'd found a number of records for our client, true, and recorded some oral history about her father.

But, apart from capturing Gerald Wuggins's recollections—something we always seemed to forget to do—we'd pretty much run out of leads to pursue.

I didn't know if there were more records out there. Or, assuming there were, how to find them.

Everything seemed to have come to a full stop.

Then Danny Overland phoned.

We met Overland some distance from his usual smoking spot along the Embankment outside the Royal Festival Hall. He was watching teenage skateboarders practising their art amid the brutal concrete forms of the South Bank. He grinned when he saw us approaching.

"Look at these kids. It's amazing what they can do." He smiled, squinting in the sun. It was a bright day, but an unforgiving, icy Baltic wind was blowing in across the Thames. Overland looked remarkably jaunty and full of beans for a man of his advanced years, and yet there was something incomplete about the picture. Then I realised what it was. He wasn't smoking a cigarette.

He seemed to read my mind because he instantly reached for his shirt pocket and pulled out a packet of Marlboros, took one out and lit it, inhaling with satisfaction.

"How do you stand the cold?" said Nevada.

"Come again?" He took his cigarette out of his mouth and squinted at her.

"Your short-sleeved shirt. You're always wearing them. And it's always bloody freezing." Nevada indicated his cigarette smoke, carrying briskly away on the icy wind.

He smiled and shrugged. "It's the war. I got so cold in those sodding Lancaster bombers, flying over Europe in the middle of winter at freezing altitudes, long night missions to Berlin; I just got so fucking freezing then that ever since nothing has ever really felt that cold." He puffed on his cigarette. "Does that make sense, dear?"

"It certainly does," said Nevada. "I can't imagine what it must have been like."

Neither could I.

I said, "You wanted to talk to us about something?"

Nevada shot me a look of annoyance. She obviously felt I was rushing ahead impatiently and being blunt just when we were building a nice rapport. But I was a little impatient, because I, sadly, *could* still feel the cold. I wanted to get inside somewhere warm and have a coffee, preferably a nice coffee.

Nevada needn't have worried. Overland smiled a crooked smile. "Straight to the point. I like that. Reminds me of home." He took his cigarette out of his mouth and studied it as though trying to remember what it was. "I asked you here because I wanted to say thank you."

This wrong-footed me. Sensitive expressions of appreciation were not on the list of things I was expecting from this man. "Thank you?"

"Yeah, for those records. The ones you digitised for me."

I'd completely forgotten about this. When I'd sent the digital dubs to Joan Overland I'd also posted CDs I'd burned—onto write-protected discs, of course—to Gerald Wuggins and Danny Overland. Or rather, to Overland's beleaguered PR person, Jenny.

But I hadn't expected any response. Certainly not this.

Overland was sucking on his cigarette, its tip glowing a hot bright orange, and peering intensely at me. "I didn't think I'd be interested in hearing them again, after all this time. Those old records." He exhaled smoke, pale ribbons in the cold streaming wind. "But you know what?"

"What?" said Nevada.

He grinned at us. "They *blew my mind*. Hearing them again. After all these years. Brought it all back to me. Those days. Gave me the chills in fact. I still get them now, just thinking about it." He indicated his bare arms. His deeply tanned, leathery old skin was puckered with goose bumps. They came and went, as if to decisively demonstrate they weren't being caused by anything as mundane as a freezing afternoon by the river in London. I was impressed.

"My god." So was Nevada.

Overland nodded. "Yeah. The music of those days.

Coming out of the past. Something I was part of. It brought it all back to me. Stronger than I could ever have imagined."

There was a long silence. At last Nevada said, "So, you liked the records?"

"Yes. You're doing a great job digging them up, and preserving them. It's good music—even with the fucking little idiotic vignettes that good old Lucky insisted on adding—even with those, it's still good music. Great music, in fact. It should be preserved. It deserves to be. It's important." There followed a silence that made the previous one seem brief by comparison, during which he stared at us with an unrelenting, analytical gaze, as though trying to make up his mind about something. Finally he said, "Anyway, I just wanted to say thank you."

He turned away and stared out at the river.

It seemed he had said his thank you and that was all we were getting. After a moment Nevada and I looked at each other, shrugged and started to walk away. I put my arms around her and she moved in close to me, sheltering from the wind. We walked back past the South Bank complex, then along the road and up the steps that led to the elevated walkway. "Well, that was weird," I said.

"It was certainly a bit of an abrupt dismissal."

I said, "I definitely got the feeling he was going to tell us something else."

"Exactly! And then he changed his mind." She looked at me. "What could it have been?"

I shrugged. "We may never know." We strolled along the elevated walkway through the Shell building. Then out again to where walkway formed a concrete bridge over the busy road, towards Waterloo Station.

As we strolled across the bridge, above York Road, I happened to turn to my left and saw a familiar vehicle navigating the roundabout by the IMAX cinema. A very familiar vehicle. It entered York Road and sped towards us. I gripped Nevada's arm.

"Look," I said.

It was the VW hippie van with the sun and the moon painted on it. There was no mistaking it. And in the clear afternoon light we got a very good look at its only occupant as it flashed by under the bridge where we stood.

The driver was a young woman.

A girl in fact.

"It's her!" exclaimed Nevada.

"Who?"

"That little harlot. The one who stole my Hermès scarf in Dover."

That night Tinkler joined us for dinner. I had by now finished paying him back with meals for lending me the digital conversion kit, but he came over anyway. It seems he'd got wind of the fact that we were cooking 'the thing with the artichoke hearts'. He arrived early so he could make sure and nag me about the correct use of fresh thyme. "You mustn't get any of the stalky wooden bits in like you occasionally do."

"Is 'stalky' even a word?" said Nevada.

"Don't start."

I had finished adding the thyme, all carefully de-stalked, and was just about to serve dinner when the phone rang. It was Leo Noel. When I saw the number I wondered wearily if he could be having second thoughts about custody of the zombie cat at this late stage. But as soon as I heard his voice, I relaxed.

He sounded jubilant, jazzed.

Nevada watched me with curiosity, Tinkler with impatience while I talked to the human palindrome. Or rather, while I listened to him. He didn't require much in the way of comment or response from me. The saga went something like this. Leo had discovered that Abner loved going in and out of the sheds and napping in them. Since he did no harm to the records, Leo was happy to encourage this practice. In fact, he was going out of his way to pamper the cat.

So instead of putting a cat flap in the door of one of the sheds to allow Abner easy access, he installed cat flaps in all of the sheds.

"All of them?" said Nevada, when I told her and Tinkler about it over dinner.

"Every one."

"What's the big deal?" said Tinkler, chasing an artichoke heart around his plate with a wedge of sourdough toast.

"He has a lot of sheds," said Nevada.

"And now a cat flap in every one."

"That must have been a lot of work."

"Yes, but not for Leo. He put an ad in the window of

his local newsagents asking for someone to do all the cat flap installing."

"An ad in the newsagent's window?" said Tinkler. "Why doesn't he just use the Internet?"

"The Internet hasn't made huge inroads on Leo's world. Anyway he got a response from one Leokadia, a Polish handy man. At least, he thought she was a handy man. But then she turned out to be a handy woman."

"A handy woman?" said Nevada.

"She sounds pretty handy, anyway."

"I trust she was at least Polish, this fraud," said Tinkler.

"She is Polish and she's no kind of fraud. And she is very attractive."

"According to Leo," scoffed Tinkler.

"Very attractive, and did a great job with the cat flaps. Such a great job that Leo invited her in for a drink afterward."

"A refreshing Perrier, no doubt," said Tinkler.

"And they got along extremely well, laughing and talking together over drinks, and one thing led to another…"

Nevada and Tinkler stared at me.

"They didn't," said Nevada.

"Please tell me they didn't," said Tinkler.

"I'm afraid they did. The human palindrome is now having a scorching affair with his Polish handy woman."

Nevada's eyes gleamed. "No."

"What about the vet?" said Tinkler. "I mean the vet's secretary or receptionist or whatever she was. Crystal?"

"Oh, he's still seeing her."

"You mean he's sneaking around behind her back?" said

Nevada. "Or do I mean sneaking around behind Leokadia's back? Sneaking around both their backs, I suppose."

"Oh no. He's not sneaking around behind anybody's back. They all know about each other."

Tinkler blanched. "They all *know* about each other? And they're all okay with it?"

"They certainly seem to be. And they all adore the cat. That's something they have in common."

"That fucking cat," said Tinkler. His face darkened. "Why didn't you let me adopt him? I could be having sex right now."

Nevada smiled. She seemed particularly gratified at this turn of events. "I did everything in my power to convince you to adopt Abner. But you wouldn't hear of it."

"Yes, I would hear of it. I would have heard of it. I would."

"No you wouldn't. And in fact you made some disgusting remark about sardine farts."

Tinkler shook his head. "Well, you should have pointed out how shallow I was being. I mean, how could you let an opportunity like that pass me by? The cat's obviously a chick magnet."

"He certainly is," said Nevada smugly.

"Actually I was going to say he was a minge magnet but I didn't think you'd let me get away with saying 'minge'."

"I definitely wouldn't. So it's a good job you didn't."

Tinkler pursed his lips thoughtfully. "What is it with that cat?" he said.

I said, "Maybe it's some kind of pheromones he gives off."

"Maybe it's the sardine farts," said Tinkler.

The following morning I was drinking my coffee in the back garden, Fanny sheltering underneath my chair, as was her custom, using my shadow to protect her from the pallid rays of the English springtime sun. I was reading an article about pink label Island first pressings in an old issue of *Record Collector* when I heard a hesitant knocking sound.

I looked up from the magazine and Fanny paused in washing herself under my chair.

The sound came again. A tapping on wood like the delicate application of a hammer.

I realised it was coming from the garden gate.

I got up, Fanny making a small sound of complaint at suddenly being deprived of her sun screen, and walked to the gate. I slid the bolt and opened it. Standing there, in the lane between my garden and the Abbey, was Jenny, Danny Overland's PR person.

"I'm sorry to bother you," she said. "I hope you don't mind that we tracked down your home address."

I wondered about her use of the word 'we' but then a voice said, "Of course he doesn't," and Overland himself stepped into view and shouldered past Jenny, into my garden. I moved back a little to let him in and he gave me a nod. Then he turned to Jenny. "You wouldn't mind leaving us alone for a few minutes, would you, dear?"

Jenny glanced at me and left. He closed the gate behind her and then turned to look at me. Fanny left her post under the chair and wandered across the gravel towards us. From somewhere nearby came the sound of a car door slamming. Jenny returning to their vehicle, I presumed.

"Listen, mate," said Overland. "When we met yesterday. There was something…" He paused and reached for his shirt pocket. "Do you mind if I smoke?"

"I'd rather you didn't."

"Fair enough." He dropped his hand to his side. His instant obedience surprised me. "Anyway, when I saw you yesterday there was something I wanted to tell you."

I felt a faint flicker of excitement but I didn't say anything.

"I wanted to tell you, but I bottled out." He looked at me. "You see, there's a record…"

There was a warmth rising in my stomach. "A record?" I said.

"Yeah, another one. By the Flare Path Orchestra. One you haven't got. It's a Victory disc. A V-Disc on twelve-inch vinyl. Probably the only one to survive the war."

"And you know where it is?"

He nodded. "Yes. But that's the thing. I know where it is, but I don't have it myself. Someone else has it. It's in the possession of these people. And they're some very dangerous people."

20. THE HOUSE IN ELTHAM

"Let me do the talking," said Nevada.

"Why?"

"Because you've been getting very impatient with people lately—'testy' is the word, I think. Testy and grumpy. And we don't want that. We don't want to alienate anyone." She pressed the doorbell. We were standing in a cramped alcove outside a big old house on a residential street in Eltham. There was a pair of grey plastic rubbish bins in the alcove with us, and a motorcycle shrouded in a blue plastic sheet that whipped and snapped. It was going to be a wild, windy night.

Nevada pushed the button again, and the bell echoed inside while grit circulated in the alcove at our feet, stirred by the breeze.

All I could see through the dusty slot of window in the door was a murky plane of shadows. Eventually, the shadows stirred and the door opened. A thin man with a bloodhound face and thinning brown hair peered out at us. He was wearing an expensively soft-looking grey sweater and baggy maroon trousers. Nevada smiled at him.

"Mr Pennycook?"

He nodded. "Yes?"

"Danny Overland arranged for us to—"

"Oh, yes, of course. Come in." He smiled and stood back so we could enter. I was expecting some kind of entranceway, but we stepped straight into a room. A bedroom. In fact, a teenager's bedroom—if the general level of untidiness and the numerous posters of heavy metal bands were anything to go by. I surveyed the posters. I didn't recognise most of the bands, though Tinkler would have been pleased to see that Led Zeppelin was still prominent among them. No sign of Erik Make Loud, however. Perhaps the grip of his electric guitar on the youth of today was failing.

There was also a music system, which seemed to involve an iPod docking station and some serious transistor amplifiers that were driving a pair of big black speakers with an accompanying pair of even bigger, blacker subwoofers. I didn't want to be around when anybody switched those suckers on. They would probably take the top of your head off in a lethal extravaganza of solid-state bass.

"My son's room," said Pennycook, who must have divined my thoughts. "Sorry about the mess. Bit of a shock to step straight into it when you come through the door from the outside world like that."

"No, it's fine."

"This used to be the sitting room, you see. But then when Billy broke his leg he couldn't get up and down the stairs very easily. So it seemed to make sense to relocate him down here. So we turned the sitting room into his bedroom. Would you like some tea?"

"Yes, please," said Nevada. "Although I expect *he* would prefer some coffee." She nodded at me as we walked through to the narrow galley kitchen that directly adjoined Billy-the-metal-freak's bedroom. We were now in the back of the small house. There was a window over the sink looking out on a narrow concrete yard with a table made from an oil drum. A bedraggled yellow and white polka dot parasol spread over it, twisting and contorting in the increasingly lively breeze.

"Coffee, then?" said Mr Pennycook. He was opening a cupboard on the other side of the narrow room, looking at me with his bushy brown eyebrows angled in enquiry on his high smooth forehead.

"Yes, please," I said. It couldn't be any worse than tea. Pennycook carefully set out three mugs. Two blue and one pink. The pink one was presumably for the girl among us. Then he unscrewed a jar and began spooning instant coffee into them. Nevada gave me a look to make sure I didn't kick up a fuss. Would I ever? Actually, it looked like decent instant—organic, fair trade and shade grown. It ticked all the boxes. Yet it would still remain something fashioned by an industrial process involving dry-cleaning fluid.

I said, "How did your son happen to break his leg?"

Pennycook was busy filling the kettle. "How did he…? Oh, on his motorcycle, of course. Or *off* it, actually. Yes, he came off his bike."

I remembered the shrouded motorcycle in the alcove. It

looked like no one had ridden it for a long time.

Pennycook switched the kettle on. "Who could have anticipated that?" he added bitterly.

"Is he all right now?" said Nevada. "I mean his leg."

"Oh, yes, he's fine." The kettle began to hiss. "In fact, he's going to university. Right here in London. I said I'd pay his student loan if he promised to stay off his motorcycle for the next three years while he's studying." The kettle began issuing steam into the tiny kitchen.

Nevada frowned. "But aren't you afraid he will just hop straight back on his bike the minute he graduates?"

"The minute he *hopefully* graduates," said Pennycook, peering into another cupboard. "I'm hoping, if he indeed does hop straight back on that bloody thing, at least his brain will have had a chance to mature a bit more." He took out a pack of chocolate biscuits. "And he'll be a bit more thoughtful and careful." The boiling kettle switched itself off with a click. Nevada was watching me with amusement. She knew that I'd had to repress an urge to switch it off a moment earlier. Coffee is best made with water a shade short of boiling. But I wasn't fanatical enough about the matter to start going around switching off strangers' kettles.

Pennycook stirred the hot water into the crunchy brown granules, releasing a smell distinctly resembling coffee, and he placed the mugs on a tray with some plates and the pack of chocolate biscuits. He was pushing the boat out for us. Mr Darren Pennycook seemed a peaceful, affable sort. "This way," he said. We followed him out into a cramped corridor that led to an awkwardly angled staircase. I realised that the house was actually half of a much larger building that had been chopped up decades ago. That explained a lot.

Pennycook started up the stairs and we followed him. "In a funny way, Billy is the reason you're here."

I said, "What do you mean?"

"Ah, come in. Since Billy moved all his stuff downstairs this has become our sitting room." He ushered us into a small room. There was a sofa and armchairs, but mostly it was crowded with books and records. A serious-looking hi-fi system lurked on a shelf of its own. Pennycook scored a few points with me for that.

The few blank strips of wall in the room were covered with pictures related to his central obsession.

I wondered what had happened to Pennycook's wife. Billy's mother. The uncircumscribed pursuit of male enthusiasms by father and son suggested a house without women.

In a way, this was a tidier version of the room downstairs. The difference here was that the walls weren't plastered with heavy metal posters. Instead there were framed publicity photos of our old friend Danny Overland. Nevada went over and peered at them avidly. I joined her. "He's so *young*," she said, gazing at a picture of Overland, grinning and looking dashing. He had gleaming, oiled hair, as they did in the age of Brylcreem, and he was wearing his air force uniform and holding a saxophone.

"Isn't that a great picture?" said Pennycook, setting the tray down and bustling over to join us. He talked us through the various framed portraits in great detail, giving dates and locations. There were several of the great man in the Flare

Path Orchestra, and one that also prominently featured Colonel 'Lucky' Lucian Honeyland. I made a mental note to see if we could get a copy of it for our client.

"What an amazing collection," said Nevada, perhaps hoping to draw his peroration to a close.

"There are even several pictures which don't show him holding a cigarette." Pennycook bent over and made a chugging, wheezing sound. After a startled moment I realised he was laughing. "Yes, he does smoke rather too much, doesn't he? I wish he wouldn't. I know he's already reached a massively ripe old age despite the cigarettes, but even if quitting now only bought him another year or two, that would be another year or two of the most marvellous music."

Personally, I suspected the nicotine was probably the only thing holding the old bastard together. But I let Pennycook ramble on, remembering Nevada's instructions not to be impatient. He resumed his inventory of the pictures on the wall, the most interesting of which showed Danny Overland with Frank Sinatra.

They were both holding cigarettes, of course.

"Australia in 1959," he said.

"When Sinatra was touring with the Red Norvo Quintet," I said. One of Old Blue Eyes's few purely jazz excursions.

Pennycook gave me a quick look. "Yes," he said. I had evidently scored some musical knowledge points myself. "They did an album together, Danny and Sinatra, very rare, only ever released on the Australian Calendar label. I have a copy here somewhere." He peered at a shelf of records, looked for the album in question, evidently couldn't find it, then in an apparent face-saving gesture, turned to the hi-fi system and began fussing with that.

It was a standard Linn-Naim setup, expensive and painstaking and considered by many to be the pinnacle of hi-fi. I wouldn't have minded giving it a listen, but not now. I opened my mouth, getting ready to ask him a blunt question concerning our visit.

But Nevada read my intention and spoke quickly, "So what is it you do, exactly, Mr Pennycook? I mean in the way of work?"

He glanced at us. It was just small talk, but he didn't seem to welcome the question. "Oh, I work in the local council planning office. All very dull really." Then he brightened. "But I also run dope."

Nevada and I looked at each other. "Oh, that's nice," she said. "Perhaps we can buy a quarter ounce from you later."

Pennycook flushed scarlet. It was quite a sight. The tips of his large ears flared brightly as if glowing with heat. He shook his head mournfully. "Not 'dope'," he said. "D.O.A.P. The Danny Overland Appreciation Partnership."

Nevada gave me a panicked, 'get me out of this' kind of look. I shrugged. I saw no way of backtracking. He didn't look like he was going to call the drug cops, anyway. "D.O.A.P.," he continued. "It's sort of a fan club and I'm the chairman and general manager."

"I'm so sorry," said Nevada. "I just thought—"

"That's perfectly all right."

"I mean, I was just being polite. I wouldn't really have used any. If you had any. If we'd bought any."

"Yes, she would," I said. "But *I* wouldn't."

Pennycook shuffled his feet and cleared his throat. "Well, anyway, you came here to ask me about something specific." It seemed Nevada's gaffe had had the happy side effect of getting him to cut the crap. "Danny Overland told you that I mentioned a certain record…"

"A Flare Path Orchestra recording," I said. "On a V-Disc."

He paused and stared at me. For a moment I had the odd but intense feeling that he was going to flatly deny it. But he said, "Yes. As I said before, my son Billy is the reason we know about this record. As you will have gathered from the trappings of his room downstairs, he is a big fan of the heavier variety of rock music."

"Yes, actually we did gather that."

"Well, this enthusiasm has led him to some odd places. Travelling around the country to listen to little-known bands in obscure clubs." I thought of Lucky Honeyland, in another century, tooling around wartime Britain on his motorcycle, racing through the blackout in his quest for a quite different kind of music. "And it has also led him to some very odd people. He has quite an eccentric collection of friends." He hesitated, and I wondered if we'd reached a sensitive subject. But he picked up a chocolate biscuit and crunched on it hungrily as he spoke.

"Last year he was in Gloucestershire to see one of these esoteric bands that he so admires. He just goes to gigs on his motorbike with no thought as to where he is going to stay afterwards. He's driven by the sheer love of music. He doesn't care where he ends up spending the night. He takes a sleeping bag and bedroll with him. Sometimes he sleeps in ditches, for all the world like a tramp. On other occasions he's lucky enough to be taken in by somebody he met at a gig. As I say, he makes friends, and sometimes they invite him back home."

He finished his biscuit and licked the crumbs off his fingers. "This particular time he'd been to see a band called Necker Cube. And he met a young bloke, about his age, in the audience and they hit it off. Shared enthusiasm and so on. After the gig the young bloke invited him back to his home. Or rather, the home of his older brother, which proved to be a farmhouse in the middle of nowhere."

He went in search of another biscuit. As he was levering it out of the packet he recalled his duty as a host and offered the biscuits to us. We shook our heads. "It was a dump of a place, but big, the farmhouse, and Billy was given one of their many empty rooms to unroll his sleeping bag in and use for the night. He was duly grateful, and knackered, and when everyone else retired he went to sleep. Apparently a few hours later he woke up and needed to do a wee. He got lost and wandered through the house. It was very late and no one else was around. And he happened to open a door and find a room full of certain... unusual memorabilia. He went in for a closer look. And while he was looking he saw an old gramophone, and on it was a record." He looked at us. His eyes had a kind of pleading intensity. "He knows about my passion for the work of Danny Overland, of course."

"Of course." I looked around the room at the dozens of pictures. How could anyone miss it?

"So when he saw that the record was one of Danny's he took careful note of it. He knew I'd be interested, especially if it was one I didn't have. Which indeed it turned out to be."

I said, "And he's sure it was a V-Disc?"

"Yes."

"And you're sure he's reliable? I mean, it was late, the middle of the night. He was tired. You're sure he definitely saw the record?"

Pennycook nodded. "He did more than just see it." He reached into his pocket and took out a phone. "He photographed it. With his phone." He showed me the image. It was a close-up of the record label and was admirably clear. Red, black and blue lettering on a white background.

It read:

Army—Navy—Marine Corps—Coast Guard
V-Disc
Produced by the Music Branch
Special Services Division
Army Air Force
OUTSIDE START 78RPM
This record is the property of the War Department of the United States and use for radio or commercial purposes is prohibited.
No. 719A
DEEP PENETRATION
D. Overland
The Flare Path Orchestra
BB 1821 Swing Band

"DD" RELEASE

I looked at him. He must have read the excitement in my eyes. "Amazing, isn't it? What a discovery. And what an astounding coincidence. Or perhaps I should say, piece of synchronicity. I mean, my son was one of the very few people who was in a position to recognise this record and realise its importance, and he happens to stumble on it in this godforsaken farmhouse, in the middle of the night."

"What kind of memorabilia?" said Nevada.

His enthusiasm abated. "I beg your pardon?"

"You said your son was drawn into the room by the unusual memorabilia. What was it, exactly?"

He cleared his throat again and shuffled nervously. "What you must realise," he said, "is that the sort of music he listens to, it is played by all sorts of people, all sorts of bands, and certain bands attract a certain type of listener." He paused. "Including some people on the far right, politically speaking. In fact, rather to the right of the far right. Extremists. The lunatic fringe, not to put too fine a point on it."

I said, "So what he found in the room was…"

"Nazi memorabilia. Swastika flags. Portraits of Hitler. That sort of thing, I'm afraid." He said it as if it was somehow his fault. "I explained all this to Danny Overland when I told him about the discovery of the record. It made matters quite… complicated. Normally I would have simply approached the people, these people at the farmhouse who owned the record, with an offer to buy it." He looked at me for moral support. "It's an extremely valuable artefact."

"Yes, it is," I said.

"Priceless, in fact. But these people weren't exactly approachable."

"How do you know they're not just some harmless

nutcases?" said Nevada. "I mean, presumably Nazi memorabilia is sometimes collected by harmless nutcases. In fact, most of the time it is, I imagine."

"Presumably most of the time it is," said Pennycook. "But not in this case. When Billy got back in touch with this boy, the one he'd met at the gig, to say thank you for putting him up, he discovered he'd been savagely beaten up."

"What?"

"Yes. By his own brother. For bringing a stranger to the farmhouse."

"Wow," said Nevada.

"They're incredibly private people, not to say paranoid."

I said, "Were they skinheads?"

"Sorry? Skinheads? Oh, yes. Naturally. And apparently this boy violated some kind of rule of theirs by letting Billy stay. Even though Billy didn't see anything."

"But he did see something," I reminded him.

There was silence for a moment. Then Pennycook said, "So I told Danny Overland about the record, and about the kind of people who had it in their possession. I still felt we should try and obtain it, for the archive, for posterity. But he said not to worry about it—when he heard who had it. He said to forget it. It wasn't worth the risk. Also, at that time he looked down his nose at his own records from that period. He didn't think they were worth preserving." He looked at us. "He really hated Colonel Honeyland's interference."

"Yes, he has mentioned something to that effect."

"But then he heard the digital copies, the ones you made, and he changed his…"

"Tune."

"I was going to say his mind, but yes he did indeed change his tune. Now he is very eager to get hold of it. If we can do so safely."

"Which is why he told us to talk to you," I said.

"That's right. Perhaps I can get a copy?"

"Sorry?"

"Of the digital copies, of the recordings by the Flare Path Orchestra. The other ones you've found." He smiled shyly.

"Of course," I said, making a mental note to check with Miss Honeyland that this would be okay. I looked at the picture he had on the wall featuring her father and speculated that, if necessary, we could do some horse-trading.

"Oh, thank you. That would be excellent."

"So, how should we proceed?" said Nevada.

He blinked at her. "Proceed?"

"Perhaps we could start by getting the address of these people at the farmhouse," I said.

"Ah, I see. Of course. Well the thing is that Billy never gave me the exact address. He was concerned, as soon as he heard about his friend being beaten, concerned that I might do something foolish. In an attempt to secure the record. So he's been protecting me by not giving me the full information. But now this is rather a different situation."

Yes, I thought, *because it won't be you going after these dangerous fascist lunatics. It will be us*.

"I will get all the details from Billy and then get back to you."

"Okay," I said, and we all rose to our feet.

"Thank you for your time," said Nevada politely. I think she was still trying to recover lost ground after offering to buy dope from him. We trooped back down the stairs and into Billy's heavy-metal den. As we walked towards the front door I said, "By the way, when did Billy come off his bike?"

"When?"

"Yes. Was it soon after he visited the farmhouse?"

Pennycook stopped dead and stared at us. "Yes. Quite soon after. You don't think—"

"What happened exactly?"

"The usual thing. The all-too-usual thing. He was knocked off his bike by a car." He peered at me. "You don't think these people could have—"

I shrugged. "I don't know." We shook hands in a glum silence and left. It was dark now and the wind was howling with an unnerving ferocity. We could hear the sound of dustbins rolling in the street somewhere and the clatter of anonymous things being blown past us in the night. Nevada was huddled against me as we leaned into the gritty gale and hurried back towards the street where we'd left Tinkler's car.

"Do you really think the Nazi skinheads from the farmhouse knocked Billy off his bike?" said Nevada, shouting against the wind, which seemed to be building to an apocalyptic intensity.

"I think it falls into the large category of things we'll never know for sure."

"Yes, that is a large category." She tucked herself in tight beside me, sheltering from the gale as we plodded forward.

We were halfway to the car when we heard the scream.

21. OPAL

It came to us loud and clear, over the banshee howling of the wind. A human scream sounds like nothing else, especially when it really means business, when it's a cry of genuine terror. You know it's not kids larking about or someone whooping with idiot glee. It's the real thing. It raises atavistic hackles.

Without a moment's thought, both Nevada and I turned and ran towards the sound. I had a very clear idea of what we were going to see—some accident, potentially horrible, probably caused by the savagely gusting wind that was currently hurtling around objects.

That isn't what we saw.

What was waiting for us when we rounded a corner was a scene of strictly human mayhem—an assault in progress. Two men were attacking a woman in a vehicle.

The vehicle was our old friend: the VW hippie van with the sun and the moon painted on it.

And the victim of the assault was the girl we'd seen driving it the other day.

The two men were both large, dressed in black leather jackets, grey hoodies and jeans. It was like a uniform. They had thrown open the sliding side door of the van and they were both reaching inside, bent over at the waist, grabbing at the girl. She was lying on her back on the floor of the van, kicking at them. She wore black leggings over her slender legs and incongruously heavy boots—Doc Martens. In some distant corner of my mind I noticed that the men wore Doc Martens too. And then I didn't have time to register anything else. They must have heard us over the wind, because they turned and faced us.

In doing so they released the girl. We came to a halt in front of them. The men stared at us. The girl lay on the floor of the van, sobbing and panting.

We were in a residential neighbourhood, in what had once been a street of small shops. The recession had wiped out half the businesses here, leaving blind, shuttered storefronts. It was late and the few shops that were still functioning had now closed for the night. Directly behind the van was a building site, apparently abandoned, in a stretch of wasteland dotted with scattered planks, mounds of earth and random piles of brick. The place was utterly deserted, except for us.

One of the men's hoodies had fallen back, revealing a shaved head. His face was fat, but his body looked bulky and hard and well-muscled. His companion was whippet-thin but tall and broad-shouldered. His eyes peered at us from within the hood, cavernous and shadowed in his pale narrow face. He gave an impression of lean, latent violence.

The men stared at us and we stared at them.

For a moment no one moved. Then everyone moved at once.

The girl bounced off the floor of the van and scrambled forward, heading for the driver's seat. Fat Face spun around to pursue her, saying, "You sort them." The Whippet moved towards us—or, rather, towards me, because Nevada chose this moment to disappear, promptly trotting around the other side of the van.

The Whippet kept coming towards me. I didn't move. I kept watching his face, thinking it would give me some warning of whatever he intended to try. In the van the girl was now sat in front of the steering wheel and reaching for the ignition. Fat Face grabbed her from behind before she could turn the key. She screamed again, the sound almost instantly lost in the wind. Then her scream turned to a snarl as she struggled with him.

Meanwhile the Whippet was reaching inside his open leather jacket, into the pouch of his hoodie. His hand came out with something hanging from it, loose and gleaming. It was a dog chain. I felt my stomach turn cold. I suspected he wasn't going to be using it for walking the dog—a suspicion immediately confirmed as he began to spin it over his head in a circular, scything motion, cutting through the air with a metallic, almost musical sound that mixed crazily with the howl of the wind.

He was clearly planning to use the heavy chain to lash me to a gory ruin. Inside the van, the girl and Fat Face were struggling in a tightly confined version of hand-to-hand combat. They suddenly twisted and rolled across the width of the vehicle, slamming against the window beside my head.

I saw their contorted faces, his hand pressed to her mouth.

Meanwhile the Whippet was building up speed with the whirling chain. It flashed in the streetlight. The chain was dangerously long. It would provide him with a lethal reach.

So I took a quick step *towards* him.

There was very little he could do with the chain at close quarters, unless he proposed smacking himself in the face with it.

Inside the van I saw the girl's mouth suddenly open wide, revealing a set of laudably white and even teeth with which she proceeded to bite her attacker on the hand, hard.

The Whippet was staring at me in surprise, taken aback by the fact that I'd advanced on him. He'd obviously expected me to start hastily backing away from the threat of the swinging chain. Perhaps that was his standard strategy, to provoke a retreat that would leave his opponent open to a devastating attack.

There was another piercing scream within the van—this time from Fat Face. The scream seemed to further wrong-foot the Whippet, who now backed away from *me*. I quickly followed him. If he managed to put any distance between us, he would use it to deploy the dog chain.

Fat Face came bursting out of the van. He was holding his right hand in his left. Blood was flowing copiously from the right hand, which he was holding contorted at a very strange angle. The position of his fingers didn't seem quite right.

"Me fucking finger," he shrieked. "She bit me fucking

finger off!" Then he pressed the bloody hand tightly under his left armpit and turned and ran. The Whippet stared after him as he continued to back away from me and I continued to advance on him, making sure I kept the gap between us closed. He was still whirling the chain above his head with athletic vigour, but an expression of perplexity had begun to cloud his features.

"Hello!" shouted a voice close behind him and he spun around to see Nevada standing there. She was holding an item she'd just scavenged from the building site—a concrete block about the size of a loaf of bread. As soon as the Whippet turned to look at her she threw it with surprising strength and force, right in his face.

The block struck him accurately, with a solid sound of impact, bouncing off and dropping to the ground and landing on the toe of one of the Whippet's boots. It must have hurt like hell, but nothing to compare with what had just been done to his face.

That face was now terribly white and, to my admittedly rather overexcited gaze, actually looked somewhat concave. He reached his hand up just as the blood started to flow, to delicately touch what had once been his nose. Then he put his other hand there, made a low moan, and ran off with blood coursing down the front of his hoodie turning the grey material a gleaming wet black.

He vanished into the howling night after his friend.

Nevada looked at me. "Next time, pick up something heavy and hit him with it." She touched my arm. "But otherwise… nice work standing your ground, Tiger."

* * *

"You're kidding," said Tinkler, his voice unwholesomely excited even over the phone. "You've got the teenage slut at your place? She's staying at your place?"

"Stop calling her that."

"I seem to remember it was your lovey-dovey who first used the expression. Who coined the name."

"It's not her name," I said.

"What is her name, then?"

"I don't know."

"You don't know?"

"There wasn't exactly time for formal introductions when we met. And then she was out like a light when we brought her back here."

"Why did you bring her back to your place?"

"We couldn't just leave her there. And she refused to go to hospital. Or to the police."

"Well, what's she doing now? Now that you've got her there?"

"She's sleeping. She's been asleep virtually since she arrived."

"Who can blame her?" said Tinkler airily. "Being attacked by neo-Nazis is very tiring."

I said, "We're only guessing they're neo-Nazis."

"Oh, come on. I think we can safely assume."

Or unsafely, I thought glumly.

"So where is she sleeping?"

"Where? In the spare room."

Tinkler chortled. "You mean the room where you keep your overflow record collection?"

"You're behind the times, my friend. It's now where Nevada keeps what she calls her 'inventory'. In other words, her clothes collection."

"Now, that's ironic," said Tinkler. But before I could ask him what was ironic about it, there was the sound of the handle turning on the door of the guest room. "I've got to go," I said quickly. "She's getting up." I hung up and the girl came out of the room.

She was wearing a baggy white t-shirt many sizes too big for her with bold black lettering on it that read FRANKIE SAY RELAX. That's a classic, I thought. On her legs she was wearing the same black leggings as the night before, but her feet were now bare. They were dirty, with the toenails painted a metallic lavender.

Her face was puffy with sleep, and her lightly freckled cheeks had for the moment a distinctly chipmunk aspect.

She had frizzy, toffee-coloured hair that hung around her face in untidy waves—a Pre-Raphaelite mess. "Good morning," she said in a croaky voice. "Or is it afternoon?" She peered blearily at the window, trying to glean something from the daylight, then looked at me. "Evening?"

I said, "Late afternoon, early evening."

"He never likes to commit himself." Nevada came through from the kitchen and sat down between us, close beside me on the sofa. As if this was a signal, the girl sank into one of the armchairs. She settled into it with such utter boneless relaxation that I thought for a moment she'd gone back to sleep.

But she opened her eyes and looked at me, then at Nevada. "Thank you for letting me stay at your place." She glanced around our sitting room. "It's very nice."

"Thank you," said Nevada.

The girl stretched her feet out in front of her, studying her grubby toes in the square of sunlight that spread across the floor. "You just let me sleep?"

"You looked like you needed it," said Nevada.

The girl yawned. "Your cat came in and slept with me. I hope that was all right?"

"Oh, did she?" said Nevada. I wondered if I could detect a note of annoyance in her voice. She glanced towards the half-open door of the guest room and right then Fanny emerged hesitantly, as if sensing that she was being discussed. I had been wondering where the little turncoat had got to. She trotted across the floor, came almost close enough to pat, then veered ostentatiously off towards the kitchen and her food bowl, glancing back at me to see if I'd taken the hint.

But I stayed where I was. As soon as the small talk was decently concluded I had a long list of questions for our guest.

"The cat was making this snuffling noise," said the girl. "Sort of snoring and wheezing while she was sleeping. Is there something wrong with her?"

"No," said Nevada, sounding distinctly defensive. "There is not anything wrong with her. The vet says it's perfectly normal. She just has an unusually narrow breathing passage."

"It was quite sweet," said the girl. "Almost like snoring."

I said, "I hope you don't mind me asking, but who are you?" Nevada shot me an annoyed look. But I'd had enough of small talk, and sometimes bluntness is the best policy. The girl stared at me for an instant then got up and padded back to her room on her bare feet, emerging again a moment later clutching a small rectangle of plastic. It was her driving licence. She handed it to me.

Her photo showed her smiling brightly, revealing the even white teeth that had served her so well the night before. In it, her hair was a Rossetti fright wig. She was deeply suntanned—unlike her winter pallor now—and looked young and happy, with not a care in the world.

Her name was Opal Gadon.

Her address was given as Bridgnorth Road in Stourbridge in the West Midlands. Her birthdate was also listed, and I did a quick calculation. She was eighteen.

I passed it to Nevada, who passed it back to the girl without apparently even glancing at it. But I knew she'd studied it as carefully as if she'd given it a prolonged scrutiny with a magnifying glass. "We weren't asking for ID," said Nevada.

"You should," said the girl. "You've got a right to know who someone is if they're staying under your roof. You've got a right to know."

"Opal?" I said.

She glanced at me. "Yes." She nodded. "Opal, like the precious stone, but with the stress on the second syllable. Oh-*pal*."

"Oh-*pal*," said Nevada. "How fascinating. So distinctive."

But it was the girl's surname that interested me. "Gadon," I said.

"Pronounced in the French fashion," said the girl. But I was only half-listening. It was a name I'd heard before. Where?

The Silk Stockings Murder—what I now irresistibly thought of as the Beer Barrel Murder. The girl who had died in that pub by the sea, one forgotten winter night during a long-ago war…

"Gillian Gadon," I said.

Opal nodded. She looked me in the eye and said, "She was my great-grandmother."

22. DISSERTATION

"So, she's what," said Tinkler, "writing a book?"

"No, a dissertation."

"About her great-grandmother?"

"Well, it's an important event in cultural history, or so she seems to think. Which throws light on all sorts of significant sociological phenomena of the period. Or something." Actually, although her jargon was almost as bad as I was making out, I thought the girl was right about this. She was onto something.

I wasn't about to say so in front of Nevada, though.

"And she's travelling around the country researching it?"

"Yes," I said.

"In her hippie dippy sun and moon van."

"Yes, she lives in it, more or less. She has a foldaway bed and pots and pans and a little cooking stove arrangement."

"Which is probably lethally dangerous," said Nevada.

"So she's been talking to a lot of the same people we've been talking to," said Tinkler.

"Correct."

"Which is why she's been suspiciously turning up wherever we go?"

I liked the way Tinkler saw himself as part of the investigation. I said, "Exactly. And asking people to keep quiet about having spoken to her."

"That's her story, anyway," said Nevada. "I actually think she's been following us—she must have followed us to Pennycook's, at least."

"And this dissertation," said Tinkler, "it's for, what—a university degree?"

"Yes," I said. "A master's, I think she said."

"She must be really smart if she's doing that when she's only eighteen," said Tinkler. "Wise beyond her years."

Nevada snorted but said nothing. She was studying the menu. Our local gastro-pub was run by an affable egotist called Albert—not to be confused with his namesake, the 'granny-shagging chauffeur', as Tinkler had dubbed him. Albert the publican was a good and interesting cook, although far too lazy to do anything much in the kitchen himself. Consequently he hired a string of other people to do it all for him, and luckily had the happy knack of choosing people who were also good and interesting cooks.

So now Albert mostly sat around behind the bar and served drinks in a leisurely fashion. He ran a pleasant and convivial establishment, and we were lucky to have it just around the corner. Or across the main road and over the railway tracks, if you wanted to be exact about it.

We had spent many pleasant hours here. In fact, Albert's

only real flaw was his unaccountable enthusiasm for Stinky Stanmer, an old colleague of mine and personal nemesis. You never knew when a peaceful evening of food and drink at Albert's pub might suddenly be interrupted by Stinky on the radio or, much worse, television, which Albert would insist on playing to his clientele.

He was always enraptured by Stinky's taste in music, blissfully unaware that any good idea Stinky ever had was first stolen from me.

Anyway, the food at Albert's was invariably good. Whenever he introduced a new menu Nevada and I made a point of coming out to dinner. Tonight had the added advantage of getting us away from our houseguest for a few hours. However, Tinkler inevitably got wind of these new menus, and always invited himself along, too.

So now he sat opposite us, beaming, and sabotaging any hope of a quiet evening with his barrage of questions about Opal—whom he now insisted on referring to, thankfully less immoderately, as the 'teen temptress'.

Tinkler perused the menu. "That pork crackling sounds good."

"I feel sorry for the poor piggies," murmured Nevada.

"They'd eat us if they got the chance," said Tinkler succinctly. "In fact, if they had the option of eating my delicious body fat cooked to crispy perfection with the judicious addition of sea salt and select herbs from Provence, I have no doubt they'd devour it in a trice."

"A trice?" said Nevada sourly.

"Yes. With relish. A trice with relish." He set the

menu aside. "So the teen temptress is already writing her dissertation. She must be pretty bright to be at such an advanced stage of post-graduate education at her early age."

Nevada snorted again and scrutinised her menu ever more closely.

"Oh, you know, it's probably just one of those Mickey Mouse masters degrees," said Tinkler in a conciliatory tone. "Not like when we were at university. When we were at uni we actually had to study something concrete."

"Nevada helped someone study something concrete the other night," I said.

Nevada chuckled. I could tell I'd cheered her up. She set the menu aside and looked at me. "We shouldn't joke about it, really."

"Yes, you should," said Tinkler. "It's not every day you get to address a neo-fascist with a breeze block. As a matter of fact, I think that entitles you to another large glass of red wine." He got up and moved towards the bar.

"That's very decent of you, Tinkler," said Nevada. "Make sure he gives us the Chapoutier."

"Yes, yes, the bottle with the Braille on the label. I know."

We got back home quite late, having successfully loaded Tinkler into a taxi on the Upper Richmond Road. As we walked through the estate there was an abrupt flurry of activity behind us: Turk came racing out of the darkness with heart-stopping suddenness, falling in at our heels and joining us as we approached our gate. "Hello, girl," said

Nevada. Turk followed us in through the gate. When we opened the front door it wouldn't open all the way. I peered down curiously as we squeezed inside.

Opal's bright pink backpack was leaning against the wall just inside the door. This was odd because she had previously taken it into the guest room and left it there. She was living out of it. It contained her clothes and most of her personal belongings.

I went into the living room and found Opal sitting on the sofa, hands neatly folded on her lap. Her jacket—a tattered bright red leather item with many zippers—was spread on a cushion beside her. As I came in she picked it up and began to put it on. "Hi there. I wasn't sure when you were coming back."

"I'm sorry we're so late."

"No, it's fine. I was just waiting for you because I wanted to say goodbye before I left."

"Before you left?" We hadn't even had time to properly quiz her about what she'd found out during her researches.

She began to zip up the jacket. "I think it's time."

My heart leapt with relief. "Are you sure?" I said. "I mean, do you feel well enough?"

She continued zipping the jacket. It was a lengthy procedure. "Oh, sure. I'm fine. I just wanted to say thank you. You've been so kind to me."

Nevada walked in. She was holding a pale grey silk scarf with little red flowers printed on it. She said, "Can I ask what this is?"

Opal stared at her. "Have you been looking through my backpack?"

Nevada turned the scarf over in her hand. "I was going to say, what a coincidence. I have one just like it." She held up the scarf to show me a little price tag attached to one corner. "But, in fact, this is my scarf. With my price tag, in my handwriting, still attached to it."

She threw the scarf so it landed neatly beside Opal on the sofa. The girl made no move to pick it up. She was staring at the floor. "If you want it so much, then take it," said Nevada.

Opal raised her face, her eyes filled with tears. "Why don't you go and look on your bed?" she said, then got up and surged from the room. I heard her in the hallway struggling into her boots. Nevada and I stared at each other. There was the sound of the door slamming. I went and looked. Opal and her backpack were gone.

Behind me Nevada said, "Go and look on our bed?" She went into the bedroom. A moment later she came back with several bank notes. She handed them to me. They came to exactly the price on the scarf. I looked at her.

"I feel terrible," she said. "And yet I'm still relieved that she's gone."

"I know what you mean."

"Which makes me feel even more terrible. I feel I should chase after her and apologise. And yet…" She hesitated.

"We've got her money and we've also got her scarf," I pointed out.

"I'll phone her," said Nevada decisively.

"You've got her number?"

"Of course. Where's my phone? I left it in the bedroom." She turned and walked out. I sat there looking at the money and the scarf, and feeling bad even though I'd had nothing to do with the accusation of theft. I suppose I'd been so eager to get rid of her. That was what I was feeling guilty about.

There was a sudden explosive clattering of the cat flap and Fanny came streaking in from the back garden, the hair on her back standing up in spikes and her tail fat with panic, swollen to four times its normal thickness. She stared at me and gave the strangest yowl. Something had given her a hell of a fright.

I stared out the window into the darkness of the garden. I could just make out the wall.

And, beyond it, the silhouette of Opal's van.

I grabbed my shoes and went out the back door, pulling them on as I moved. I hurried across the gravel to the gate in the back garden wall. Opal's van was parked immediately outside. I opened the gate, and there it was, with the sliding door open, truncating the message of the painting with the silver lunar crescent, so that it appeared to read: *Ms Moon is sending us to Ealing.* An even stranger slogan than before.

In the shadows within the van, two figures were engaged in a ferocious struggle.

Opal's bright red jacket made it easy to distinguish her from her attacker. I climbed into the van. Neither of the figures writhing on the floor seemed to notice me as I stepped around them gingerly. This time I was following Nevada's advice. I was looking for a suitable implement.

There was a pile of cookware in a cardboard box on the back seat. I selected a cast iron frying pan.

It was a proper, old-fashioned pan. It was so heavy I

could barely lift it one-handed, but I did. It came out of the box, which was jammed with other pots and pans, with a clatter. This must have alerted Opal's assailant, because he suddenly rose up from the floor, lifting his head.

He was a large and powerfully built young man in a black puffer jacket and combat trousers. He had a skinhead haircut, but he wasn't either of the men we'd encountered the other night.

He was still holding Opal down as he turned towards me. She was lying on the floor with him sitting on her hips, pinning her legs down with his weight and holding both her hands with his. Her mouth had already been taped shut with silver gaffer tape. She was struggling like a wildcat but, given his position, there was nothing she could do.

However, by the same token, given his position, there was very little *he* could do.

So I hit him in the head with the frying pan.

I hit him good and hard, the sound of impact on his shaved skull echoing in the confined space of the van, and the shock of impact radiating back along my arm.

He shook his head, stared at me in slow-focusing surprise as I lifted the pan to give him another good one. Then he released Opal and lurched to his feet. Moving with commendable alacrity for a man who had just been hit in the head with a cast iron pan, he scrambled out of the van and fled.

I only managed to deliver him a glancing blow on the shoulder as he slithered past me, out into the night.

I quickly checked that Opal was all right—she was

sitting up, delicately peeling the adhesive tape off her mouth—then I got out of the van and looked around.

He was gone.

The garden gate opened and Nevada stepped out, holding one of the large ornamental stones from our garden. No points for originality, but I suppose if you have a good trick, you might as well stick with it. She looked at the frying pan with approval. She said, "How many times did you hit him with it?"

"About one and a half."

"Good on you."

We helped Opal back into the house, replacing the stone in the garden along the way.

23. THE HOUSEGUEST

There are a number of single-vehicle garages on my estate, some concealed underground, others tucked in beside residential blocks. Luckily we knew a neighbour who owned one of these, which was moreover unoccupied at the moment. Our kind neighbour was willing to let us use it at short notice, late at night.

They charged us a bit extra for the late at night aspect, but it was worth it. We moved Opal's VW van into the garage and shut the door on it. As soon as it was out of sight, we all felt better.

Now any interested parties might get the impression that she had driven off in it, destination unknown. Meanwhile, the safest thing seemed to be to keep the van in the garage and Opal in our guest room. This wasn't an ideal setup, since even with the scarf situation resolved—Opal got it for a twenty per cent discount, an unusual concession from Nevada, who believed in preserving what she called the 'price integrity' of her stock—there was still a certain tension in the household.

Indeed, in private, Nevada had taken to referring to our guest as 'Go Pal', like the dog food but with the stress on the second syllable. Though she did also confide in me that she was impressed with her skills in a scrap—"The girl can take care of herself," she grudgingly admitted. "She's got lots of pluck, at least. Especially considering she's been attacked *twice* by hulking thugs."

"Twice that we know of," I said.

But still, like I say, there was a certain tension…

So we fell into a routine of leaving the house as early as possible, and staying out until the evening. It reminded me, with twisted nostalgia, of the days when I hadn't been able to afford central heating and had stayed out of my freezing crypt of a house as much as possible, roaming the streets of London in search of vinyl.

The difference now was that I had a beautifully heated home, occupied during daylight hours only by our two cats, who no doubt spent their every waking moment fraternising with, and being fawned over by, an unwanted eighteen-year-old neo-hippie houseguest. Of course, we could have just kicked Opal out. But neither of us had any intention of doing that when her life might be in danger. Plus we were still trying to find out if she'd discovered anything useful to us in her travels. Whenever we tried to draw her out on this, however, she'd change the subject.

So, since we were in waiting mode on all fronts of our investigation, Nevada and I spent our evenings in the pub and our days hunting through charity shops. It had been a while since we'd done this together, and it was actually quite a nice nostalgia trip. Nevada found various exciting items of clothing, and I found a Bonzo Dog Doo-Dah Band album, the double LP compilation with the booklet still attached.

So there was an upside to things.

On Wednesday Nevada left the house even earlier than usual because she wanted to be present for the grand opening of a new charity shop in Sheen. It was intended to be an outlet that would sell only clothing—they call it 'fashion'—with no books, DVDs or, most important, records. This was, from my point of view, a worrying new trend in the charity shop community. Didn't they realise all anybody really wanted was vinyl? Preferably rare jazz? Particularly first pressings in mono on the Blue Note and Prestige labels?

Anyway, the upshot was, I was still tidying up after breakfast—a very tasty and simple Spanish omelette; I'd got the recipe from an Australian website, surreally enough—when Nevada set off. Having finished with the breakfast things I planned to get dressed and get out the door.

I would meet Nevada for coffee after she'd fully sated herself on fashion and continue our joint explorations, probably in Hammersmith and Shepherd's Bush, through lunch and the rest of the afternoon.

First, though, I had to talk to our client.

I hadn't spoken to Miss Honeyland for some days now, and I'd started to grow a little concerned. I sat down on the sofa and rang her on the landline. I got her voicemail again. I considered leaving another message, but decided that two was plenty, and just hung up. I wondered if I should go over to her little mews flat and see if everything was all right.

Or was that just giving in to rampant paranoia?

I went to get dressed. I could hear Opal in her room—I'd begun, worryingly, to think of the guest room as *her* room—talking to one of the cats. I was glad Nevada wasn't around. This perhaps annoyed her more than anything else about our visitor. Opal talking to our cats. And, of course, Nevada had to know what was said.

If she had been here it was very unlikely I could have stopped her listening at the door, using a wine glass. "This actually works, you know," she'd said, her ear pressed to the base of the glass, its bowl pressed to the door. "Pass me one of the Riedel's, would you, darling? I might get better reception on it."

She just had to know what the girl might be saying to our cats. When she'd used the wine glasses a few times, and decided that the Riedel, Eisch and other expensive brands actually did enable better eavesdropping, I asked her what Opal was saying to our pets.

Nevada had just shaken her head dismissively. "Oh, you know, just cutesy cat gushing. Darling this and Miss Soft Paws that. Puerile, vomit-worthy nonsense."

This was pretty rich coming from a woman who did her own fair share of cutesy cat gushing, but I decided I wasn't going to say as much. Despite this, though, Nevada remained obsessed with what our guest might be saying to Fanny and Turk.

"Do you suppose it's possible she could turn them against us?"

"No," I said firmly. "Unless, of course, she offers them food."

Now, alone in the house with the cat whisperer, I resisted the urge to reach for a wine glass, and instead headed for the shower. I was wearing my bathrobe and nothing else. So when the doorbell rang, I felt a tiny bit reluctant to go and answer it. But my bathrobe was a natty vintage blue-and-white striped cotton item Nevada had recently bought for me on eBay. And the only other person in the house was far too busy trying to suborn our cats.

So I answered the door.

It was Stinky Stanmer.

Someone once said—actually I think it was me—that Stinky looked like a fish with lips. Certainly there was something odd and not entirely human about his face with its bulging eyes and doughy pale contours. Yet somehow the public, or at least a significant portion of it, had taken him to their hearts. It seemed beyond belief.

He was currently sporting hair that had been dyed an aggressive peroxide blond to conceal its mousy brown norm. It had been cut in a deliberately nerdy manner, as though he was a member of a 1960s pop band that had wrongly considered itself ironic.

Smiling and not quite looking me in the eye, he said, "Salutations, citizen." With a sinking feeling I sensed the arrival of a new catchphrase. He made a move to enter the house and I made a move to block him.

"Who's there?" said a small, frightened voice behind me. It was so unlike Opal that I looked around in surprise to confirm it actually *was* her. It was. She was wearing a silk dressing gown, also recently sourced from Nevada, though this time only at a ten per cent discount. My honey-pie's contrition was wearing thin.

She peered at me in fear, and I realised she had good reason to be afraid of strangers at the door. "Don't worry," I said, "it's no one."

"No one?" said Stinky, attempting jocularity as he took advantage of the fact that I'd turned around to shoulder past me and enter the house. He goggled at Opal—nubile young girl wearing a clinging silk robe and nothing else—and she stared warily back at him.

"It's just a… friend," I told her. The truth would have taken far too long to explain.

"Okay," said Opal uncertainly.

"Stinky Stanmer at your disposal, citizen-sister," said Stinky. Did someone come up with this stuff for him? If so, they needed to be fired with extreme prejudice.

"Okay," repeated Opal, nodding at him vaguely. She turned and went back into her room.

Stinky glanced at me. "A bit shy, is she? She'll come out later and ask for my autograph, when she's summoned up her courage."

"Look, Stinky," I said, "I'm just on my way out the door."

He lifted his arms in the air. "No problem, no problem." He walked into the living room and sat down on the sofa.

"You really can't stay."

"That's fine, that's fine," he said, hastily looking through the books on my coffee table. Turk came in through the cat flap and stared at Stinky. She must have heard our voices. And recognised his. There had been a time when Stinky had bribed her on a regular basis with salmon and prawns. Clearly there was nothing wrong with Turk's memory.

She came over to Stinky, who grinned and said, "Hello, Fanny!" He tried to pat her and she retreated, coming back however to sniff his fingers. But as soon as she failed to detect any hint of expensive seafood, she very sensibly went back outside.

I looked at Stinky, sitting on my sofa in my house, utterly uninvited, and felt myself getting angry enough to tell him exactly what I thought of him, preferably while dragging him to the front door and physically projecting him from it. Then I remembered that Stinky Stanmer had once almost certainly saved our lives.

So it seemed the minimum possible civility to at least offer him a coffee. It went against every fibre of my being, but there you are. Then I had an inspiration. "Listen, Stinky. I've got to go out. We can't stay here. But I can buy you a coffee. There's a very good café in the high street."

With a bit of luck I could get rid of him before I rendezvoused with Nevada.

"Fine, fine," said Stinky. But he'd risen from the sofa and was now heading towards my turntable. This was far from fine, and I moved in to intercept him, but then the door of the guest room opened behind me and Opal stepped out.

She said, "Can you help me get something down from a shelf in here? It's too high for me to reach."

"The Charles Sharp 6," sneered Stinky. He was now

standing at my turntable and staring down at the record on it. "Never heard of them."

I hardly registered what he was saying. I was too distracted by Opal's sudden request. It had thrown me considerably, because there weren't any shelves in her room, at least no high ones. None above waist height, as it happened. "Weird instrumentation," said Stinky, reading the record sleeve.

"Perhaps the only welcome instance of the vuvuzela in modern jazz," I said. "Excuse me." I went into the guest room where Opal was waiting for me. She immediately closed the door behind us. She was still wearing her dressing gown. It was a bit big for her and had an alarming tendency to fall open below the neck, so I kept my eyes studiously on her face.

"There's not really anything on the shelf," she said. She had unusual eyes. They were a pale shade of brown. Almost amber. Almost gold. "I just wanted to say something. I haven't had a chance to see you on your own since the other night, and I wanted to say thank you. For saving me. The other night."

"That's fine, I just—"

"And not just that. For letting me stay in your home. And cooking for me…" She stared up into my eyes. She was still warm from the bath. I could feel the warmth coming off her.

"Okay, that's great. I mean, you're welcome. I mean, I just have to get back to my friend."

"Of course."

I got out of there and back with Stinky. He was sitting on the sofa, holding his phone and trying to look casual. But the cover of the Charles Sharp 6 album was in front of him, and I knew he had just photographed it. "Stinky, listen, I've just got to quickly throw some clothes on and then we can go for that coffee."

He rose to his feet, ostentatiously putting his phone away. "No, don't worry, mate. Not to worry, I've got to shoot off. Things to do." He gave me a big phoney smile and a broad wave of his hand, as though cleaning a window. "So long, citizen." He ambled down the hallway to the front door.

I stared after him. He really had just come to check up on what I was currently listening to. And, now that he'd found out, he was gone. I don't know why I was surprised. Surprise was as futile, and as irrelevant, as the sudden fury rising in me.

The front door closed, signalling Stinky's exit.

Opal immediately came out of her room.

"Is he gone?"

I sighed. "Yes, thankfully."

"Who was he?"

"If you don't know, you're better off never finding out." I wandered back into the living room, worn down by this encounter. I picked up the phone and tried Miss Honeyland's number again. Voicemail. I hung up. Opal came and sat beside me on the sofa.

She said, "I never finished what I wanted to say to you. I wanted to thank you."

"You already have."

"No, I haven't. Not for cooking for me, and taking care of me." Her head was close to mine on the sofa and her hair smelled nice. I started to get up and she caught hold of my arm. "I really mean it," she said. She leaned towards me and her robe fell open. She kept moving towards me, and before I knew it she was in my arms, treacherously fragrant and warm. She drew my head down towards hers.

Her robe was fully open. She gently guided my head down and all at once her bare, warm breasts were soft against my face.

A terribly bad idea suddenly began to seem like a terribly good idea.

Her nipples brushed across my lips and they felt like electricity. It was the second most difficult thing I've ever done in my life not to just open my mouth and begin kissing and gently nibbling at them.

The most difficult thing was putting my hands on her shoulders and pushing her away from me. I forced her back. We stared at each other. I felt a writhing pain in the pit of my stomach as physical desire did a handbrake turn in my body. I said, "Look, I'm sorry—"

But my rejection had not gone down well with Opal. She rose from the sofa and lurched away. Then she stopped and turned, her hair swinging, a look of pure savagery on her face.

Hell hath no fury, I thought glumly.

Just then the front door opened and Nevada's voice announced, "You have no idea what a complete disappointment that new charity shop is." With a few strides she was in the room with us. We stared at her. She stared at us.

Opal started to close her robe, then abruptly she let it swing open. Her pert breasts jiggled as she pointed at me. "Nevada," she croaked. "He just screwed me."

Nevada stared at us.

"Or rather," said Opal, "I just screwed him. I started it because he was too timid to try. He wanted to, oh so badly. But he was too timid. But then once he got started, once I got him started, he couldn't get enough of me. I'm sorry it happened under your roof." She shrugged and decorously closed her robe, putting her breasts away. "But there's no point trying to hide it from you now it has happened."

Nevada looked at us both, her expression unreadable. Then she said, "Really?" Her voice was cool. "That's very good of you."

"Is it?" said Opal. "Well, good or bad, it is what it is."

"He couldn't get enough of you, you said?"

"Yes."

"You just had passionate sex with my boyfriend?"

"Yes."

Nevada shrugged dismissively. She set her bag down on the table. "I don't believe you. Do you know why? Because a silly little schoolgirl like you would have been put off by his tattoos."

"I love tattoos! I love *his* tattoos. I kissed them, and licked them—"

I relaxed. Nevada relaxed. She smiled at the girl.

Opal immediately sensed the shift in mood between us. She looked at me bitterly. "He doesn't have any tattoos, does he?"

"You'll never find out," said Nevada.

Opal fled into her room, slamming the door behind her in classic teenager fashion. We heard the muffled sound of sobbing. Nevada looked at me. "How on earth could you have been foolish enough to allow yourself to be alone in the house with that creature? With neither of you dressed?"

"Stinky Stanmer."

"Enough said."

"Why don't you have any tattoos?" said Tinkler. "Is it because you're a total wimp?"

"Lucky for him he is," said Nevada. We were back in Albert's gastro-pub, sitting in our usual booth. She kissed me on the cheek. "Still, well done. Seven out of ten for resisting. I should have known I could trust you even if a hormonal little honey was waving her hot little fanny in your face."

"You paint such an attractive picture," said Tinkler.

"Her tits, actually," I said. "Waving her tits in my face."

"Fanny," said Tinkler forlornly. "Tits. Why does nobody ever wave anything in *my* face?" Nevada kissed me on the lips. "Oh, for Christ's sake," moaned Tinkler.

Nevada kissed me again. She said, "I'm glad you didn't complicate our lives by doing anything stupid."

I said, "Are you sure you don't just think I'm boring?"

"*I* think you're boring," said Tinkler.

We finished our drinks and Nevada went to buy the next round. As soon as she was gone Tinkler said, "And she's still living with you? Opal?"

I said, "She's not living with us. She's *staying* with us."

"She's still staying with you? After what happened?"

"After what nearly happened."

"But, still, you're letting her stay with you?"

"She has nowhere else to go. No parents. No guardian. No aunts or uncles or close friends. Believe me, we've checked."

"And so she's living with you for the foreseeable future?"

I shrugged. It was true. Tinkler hitched himself closer to me. "Maybe you can have a threesome," he said. "With both of them."

"Yes, that's what a threesome usually means."

"When you say 'yes'…" said Tinkler excitedly.

From the bar Nevada called, "Hello, Tinkler, I can hear every word you're saying."

"Well, somebody should," said Tinkler. "Otherwise a great opportunity is going to waste."

"You've got threesomes on the brain," said Nevada, returning with our drinks. "It's too much Internet. That's what it is."

There was a sudden burst of music from behind the bar. I looked over to see Albert standing there with his hand on the radio and a foolishly beatific expression on his face. The music blared out. It was a familiar piece, and normally I would have enjoyed it. But not now. Not by a long stretch of the imagination.

"What happened to the no music policy?" said one of the drinkers at the bar. A question I would have happily seconded.

But unfortunately I knew the answer all too well. Albert waved the drinker to silence. Finally the music concluded and the voice of Stinky Stanmer came over the airwaves.

"Perhaps the only welcome instance of the vuvuzela in modern jazz," he said.

Albert switched off the radio and said, in an awestruck voice, "That Stinky, he's always got his finger on the pulse."

Just then the door opened, let in a gust of wind and rain, and Opal came in. She walked across the pub, coming straight to us. Tinkler said, "Is that…?"

"Yes."

"The brazen hussy," murmured Tinkler. But he immediately moved over to make room for Opal as she reached the table, and she sat down beside him, smiling across at us.

"I hope you don't mind me joining you."

"Why would we mind?" said Nevada blandly.

"I just had to get out of the house. I put some biscuits out for the cats so they wouldn't follow me across the main road." I could see this sincere concern for the wellbeing of our cats really getting Nevada riled, but luckily at this point Tinkler changed the subject.

"My name is Jordon Tinkler."

"Hello, Jordon." They shook hands.

Tinkler waved a magnanimous hand at us. "My friends here have been telling me all about your dissertation. It sounds fascinating."

"It is," said Opal. "It's going to be dynamite."

"Oh, really?" said Nevada.

"It must be, uh, fascinating," said Tinkler, "to, uh, research it. It must be really hard work. Doing all that research."

Opal nodded. "Oh, it is. I've been driving all over the country. But it's been worth it."

"You've made a lot of fascinating discoveries, I imagine," said Tinkler. He seemed stuck on the word fascinating.

"Oh, yes," said Opal. "For instance, I found the barmaid."

For the moment I wasn't sure I'd heard her correctly. "The barmaid?" I said.

"Yes. From The Feathers. You know, the pub in Kingsdown. Where my great-grandmother was murdered. The barmaid who was working there that night."

"You found her," I said. "The witness?"

"Yes."

"The missing witness?"

"Yes," said Opal. "She told me all about it."

24. THE BARMAID

I said, "This is the barmaid who was supposed to have turned up at the trial, but didn't? The crucial missing witness for the defence?"

Opal sighed theatrically. "Yes."

"She was the one who put the bottle of whisky in the room," said Nevada.

"Yes."

"What whisky?" said Tinkler.

I said, "Johnny Thomas claimed that they'd been given a bottle of drugged whisky. It knocked both of them out, and when he woke up, the girl was dead." It occurred to me that 'the girl' in fact was Opal's great-grandmother. It was a strange and somewhat unsettling thought. I looked at Opal. It was the first time I'd looked at her so squarely since our close encounter. She met my eyes with a level gaze. I was completely thrown. I'd lost my thread. "Uh," I said.

"So, while they were unconscious, someone entered the room and killed her," supplied Nevada. "This was the cornerstone of Johnny's defence."

"Such as it was," I said.

"Such as it was."

"So where did the barmaid get the drugged whisky?" said Tinkler.

"She claimed it was a present from a mysterious stranger."

"The same one who killed Opal's great-grandmother, presumably," said Tinkler. He'd made the intellectual leap from anonymous victim to blood relative without having to be hit over the head, I'll give him that. Opal rewarded him with a smile of approval. "Would you like a drink?" he asked her.

"Yes, thank you," said Opal. "A bottle of cider please. Organic, if they've got it."

"Oh, I'm sure they've got it," said Tinkler, rising and scurrying towards the bar. This left me and Nevada alone with Opal, which could have been awkward, but it wasn't. We all had something new to think about, something that effortlessly eclipsed recent events on our sofa.

I said, "Where did you find her? The barmaid?"

"Stoke-on-Trent." Opal seemed pleased with herself, which she had good reason to be. "Just outside, in Shelton, near Newcastle-under-Lyme. I met her there and we went out for a walk, and I recorded her."

"You've got a recording?" said Nevada.

"Yes. I'll make a copy for you if you like. We talked for hours. We walked through the cemetery there, which is huge. Hanley Cemetery. We walked along Cemetery

Road while she told me all about it. Which I suppose is appropriate. Cemetery Road." I thought that indeed it was, rather spookily so. "Anyway, it's nice and green in there. Lots of trees."

Tinkler came back with drinks for himself and Opal. I noticed he hadn't got anything for us, but perhaps it had genuinely not occurred to him. The Tinkler in rut is a single-minded creature.

"So what happened exactly?" I said.

"Well, this man gave her the bottle of whisky—"

"What did he look like?" said Nevada.

"She said she never got a good look at him. And even if she had, after all these years—"

Nevada snorted. "Never got a good look at him. That's very convenient."

Opal seemed to take this personally. "Esmeralda was telling the truth."

"Esmeralda?"

"Esmeralda Paynton. It was the name she assumed, after she dropped out of sight and started again."

"Great choice."

"It was easy to start again like that," said Opal, "during the war. In all the confusion. She said she'd lost all her papers when her house was bombed out, and got new ones. Under a new name."

I said, "She claims she never got a good look at this guy? The one who gave her the whisky."

"Yes." She was defensive again. "Why does everyone find that so hard to believe?"

"Because he must have been near enough to her to give her the whisky. And hence near enough to get a pretty good look at."

Opal's face took on a stubborn set. "She said it was night time. There was a blackout."

"Of course."

"And he was wearing an army cap. And goggles."

"Goggles?"

"Like they used to wear when they were driving one of those old-fashioned cars with the open tops. Apparently they also used to wear them when they were driving jeeps and other military vehicles of the period."

"I repeat," said Nevada, "very convenient."

"What about his voice?" I said.

Opal looked at me, suddenly unsure of herself for the first time since she'd strode into the pub and joined us. "His voice?"

"Yes. She didn't get a good look at him, because he took great pains to make sure she didn't. But she must have heard his voice."

"I didn't think to ask her that," said Opal. She took out her phone. For a moment I thought she was about to call Esmeralda, but instead she typed in some text. "I must make a note to ask her next time I speak to her."

Nevada gave me a look. I said, "You're still in touch with the barmaid?"

"Yes," said Opal.

"That could be very useful." I made a mental note of my own to draw up a list of questions for Esmeralda Paynton. Opal put her phone away. I said, "Did anyone else have access to the whisky? After she accepted the bottle from the mystery man?"

"In goggles," added Tinkler.

"After she accepted the bottle from the mystery man in goggles," I said patiently, "and before she left it in the room, as a present for Johnny and your great-grandmother?"

"No. No one else could have tampered with the bottle."

"You're sure of that?"

Opal nodded vigorously. "As soon as he gave it to her, she took it down to the cellar. And when she was sure no one would see her, she decanted half the bottle."

"She did what?" said Nevada.

"Decanted it. It means to transfer it from one bottle to—"

"I know what it means. Why did she do that?"

"To keep it for herself," I said.

Opal nodded again. "It was very good whisky, and very scarce in wartime. She wanted to keep some for herself. It was understandable."

"It was theft," said Nevada.

Opal immediately flew to the defence of her friend. They must have really bonded during that cemetery walk. "It was totally understandable. It was wartime, a time of scarcity and shortages. She felt she was entitled to something nice when it came her way."

"Entitled, eh?" said Nevada.

"She felt that everyone should share and share alike. It was a time of national emergency."

"Didn't they notice that it was half empty?" said Tinkler. "Didn't Johnny Thomas—I love that name—and your great-grandmother, didn't they notice their gift bottle was half empty?"

Opal shook her hand. "No. She filled it up again with a much cheaper, inferior brand of whisky they used at the pub."

"How generous of her," said Nevada.

Opal shot her a look. "She said she felt she *was* generous leaving them half."

But Nevada wasn't listening. She was frowning thoughtfully. She looked at me. "It was topped up with whisky from another source."

I said, "Which means we no longer know where the drug—if there was a drug—where it came from. It could, as we first believed, have got there in the bottle from the mysterious stranger…"

"With goggles," said Tinkler. Opal giggled. Tinkler beamed, and Nevada shot him a sardonic look.

"The mysterious stranger with goggles," I said wearily. "Or, on the other hand, it could have been in the whisky which Esmeralda used to top up the bottle."

"The replacement whisky."

"Right. We can't be certain which one was doped."

"Oh, no," said Opal. "We can certainly be certain! Esmeralda told me they continued to serve the replacement whisky to the customers in the pub, and no one ever had any ill effects. Even the landlord drank it, and he was fine. And besides…"

"Besides, what?"

"She tried some of the good stuff."

"You mean the stolen whisky?"

Opal seemed to have trouble accepting this word in connection with her friend Esmeralda. It was a little odd that she'd conceived such a strong attachment to someone who, after all, had been complicit, however unknowingly, in the murder of her great-grandmother. But she nodded.

"She drank some right after she finished her shift that night. A 'stiff tot', she called it. And woke up, very disorientated, twelve hours later with a terrible headache."

"Serves her right," said Nevada.

Something else occurred to me. "That's why he woke up."

They all looked at me. "What do you mean?" said Opal.

"Johnny Thomas. He woke up and found the girl—your great-grandmother, sorry—dead in bed with him. And he tried to dispose of the body. And he almost got away with it. He might well have done if he hadn't had such bad luck." Some of the worst bad luck any human ever had, it seemed to me.

"So?"

"So he might well have wrecked the plans of whoever was trying to frame him—I think we're all pretty certain someone did frame him. And Johnny almost spoiled their scheme when he woke up like that. He wasn't supposed to wake up until the following morning. Late in the morning, if the barmaid's experience based on her stiff tot was anything to go by. Probably he would have been found in bed by the pub staff when they tried to rouse him. Apparently dead drunk and, tucked beside him, the dead girl." It was hard to imagine a more incriminating scenario. The half-empty whisky bottle, Johnny groggily coming to consciousness, staring at the aghast face of whoever woke him, with Gillian's dead body beside him, silk stockings in a terminal ligature around her throat. *I don't remember doing it, honest. I don't remember anything after we drank all that whisky.*

"But by substituting the cheaper whisky she'd inadvertently diluted the stuff in the bottle," I said.

"And reduced the effect of the drug," said Nevada.

"That's right. So he woke up. Which was definitely not in the game plan."

"Yes," said Nevada. "But whose game? And what plan?"

I looked at Opal. "Why didn't she turn up for the trial? The barmaid—Esmeralda, or whatever her real name was."

"It seems she received some threats."

"Threats?"

"Yes," said Opal, "I suppose it was only natural."

"Really?" said Nevada. "What was natural about it?"

"Well," said Opal, "during its day the Silk Stockings Murder was quite a cause célèbre."

"Ah," said Nevada, who tended to take a proprietary, not to say possessive, view of any Indo-European tongues other than our own. She was the language expert around here and didn't like anyone else infringing on her turf. "A *cause célèbre*. Of course."

"So she got these threats, and then someone sent her some money, on the condition that she made herself scarce. It was enough money that she could drop out of sight and start again. And she decided this was a good idea."

"Someone sent her some money," I said.

"Yes. Through the post."

"An anonymous someone."

"Yes."

I said, "Like the anonymous someone who gave her the whisky."

There was silence at our table for a moment. Then Tinkler clapped his hands so loudly that Albert looked up from his sudoku behind the bar. "My god, that's brilliant," said Tinkler. "And you researched all that yourself?"

Opal nodded modestly. "Yes."

"You're really great at what you do," said Tinkler fervently.

Opal inched closer to him. "Why, thank you!" She smiled up into his face.

I looked at Nevada. Nevada looked at me.

"What did she do with the rest of it?" I said.

Opal blinked. "I beg your pardon?"

"The rest of the whisky. What did she do with it?"

"Oh, she poured it away. Down the drain."

"She did what?"

"I know," said Opal, her face and voice grave. "And with it she poured away forever any chance of Johnny Thomas being proved innocent and spared the gallows."

"That's a classy sentence," said Nevada. "You should use it in your dissertation."

"Oh, I intend to."

"I think it's a great sentence," said Tinkler.

We all walked back from the pub together. I walked beside Nevada, and Tinkler beside Opal. Before we reached my bungalow Tinkler insisted on taking a detour to the garage we'd rented and having a look at Opal's van. "I've never really seen it properly," he said. "I've only ever been able to admire it from afar."

"Really? You admired it? What did you admire about it?"

"Ah, the duality, the brilliant notion of the sun on one side, and you know, the moon on the other. That kind of thing."

So we all crowded into the damp little concrete cubicle and stared at the van under the buzzing glare of the flickering fluorescent light. "And you did the paint job yourself?" said Tinkler, walking around the vehicle like a general inspecting his troops. "That's amazing. You're so multi-talented."

"Thank you," said Opal demurely. "You can't really appreciate the colours in this artificial light. You need to see them in daylight."

Tinkler squinted and nodded. His serious look. "No, true, the lighting conditions in here don't begin to do justice to your work. I definitely need to see them in daylight."

"I can take you for a ride," said Opal, looking at Tinkler.

"I would like that, that would be fantastic, I like it, hey let's do that," said Tinkler, more or less coherently.

"Sometime," said Opal, in a qualifying way.

Nevada and I looked at each other again and said nothing. We locked up the garage and all trooped back to the house for a coffee. Normally I would have said we were night owls. But on this occasion we were sitting around yawning and longing to get to bed for what seemed like endless hours while Opal and Tinkler chatted away, showing no signs of tiring.

Finally, thankfully, they ordered a taxi to take them back to Tinkler's house in Putney. "Opal wants to hear my hi-fi."

"Of course she does."

The phone rang to announce the arrival of the taxi and we said goodnight and they left. We finally went to bed. Opal had a key so she could let herself back in when she returned.

But she didn't return. Staring into her empty room the next morning Nevada said, "You don't suppose she and Tinkler…"

"Stranger things have happened."

"Really? Have they? Have they really?"

But I was more concerned with trying to ring Joan Honeyland. I still hadn't been able to reach her, and I was becoming seriously worried by now. I made my morning coffee and carried it straight into the living room and sat down with it beside the phone.

She answered on the first ring and I felt a warm plunging sensation of relief. After some small talk I got around to the first of the questions that had really begun to gnaw at me over the last few days.

I said, "You remember when you were run off the road?"

"Yes. All too well. It was shortly after we first met, wasn't it?"

"Was it by skinheads? I mean, the men in the car. Were they skinheads?"

There was absolute silence on the line. Then she said, "Yes, they were. How did you know?"

"Why didn't you mention it at the time?"

"Well, it hardly seemed relevant. Also, I suppose, it would have seemed like I had some sort of prejudice against… some particular segment of society. Which I don't. At least I hope I don't. You didn't answer my question."

I said, "What question?"

"How did you know?"

It was my turn for silence on the line. I said, "Can we meet?" There were some things I preferred not to talk about over the telephone.

Most things, in fact.

"And discuss it in person?" said Miss Honeyland in her efficient, clipped way. "Absolutely. I was just about to suggest that."

We arranged a time and she hung up.

25. BACKFIRE

I was getting ready to go out when the doorbell rang. "Dozy trollop has forgotten her keys," remarked Nevada. But it was Tinkler. He came in looking relaxed and happy, beaming at us.

"Opal stayed the night," he said. "At my place."

"So we surmised."

"It got really late, so we just thought, you know."

"Of course. We know."

"And she's going, ah, to stay with me, um, for a few days. So I came over to collect her stuff."

"Yes!" said Nevada, punching the air. "Here, Tinkler old fellow, let me help you gather up the little darling's belongings."

They went off to the spare room together and emerged a few minutes later with Opal's pink backpack, bulging and full. "I swear, Tinkler," said Nevada, "you're wandering around the place like Turk after she's caught a pigeon. All puffed up and proud of yourself."

"Can you blame me? Do you know how long it's been since I last had sex? I'll give you a hint. They were knocking rocks together and inventing fire."

Nevada held up both hands in front of her, as though warding off an invisible assailant. "I don't want to hear about it." She went back into the erstwhile guest room, presumably to carefully inventory her stock and make sure nothing was missing. Tinkler wandered into the living room to join me.

He addressed me confidentially, in a man-to-man way. "Oh my, she's naughty."

"I'm very happy for you," I said. "But I don't particularly want to hear about it, either."

"Oh, yes, you do."

"Was she impressed with your hi-fi?"

"She certainly was," said Tinkler. "She also loves my collection of folk records." I laughed. "Why are you laughing?"

"What folk records?"

"I have folk. I have John Martyn. I have Cat Stevens. Sorry, Abdullah Ibrahim. I mean Yusef Lateef."

"You mean Yusuf Islam," I said. "You see? You don't even know his name."

"They're all fine musicians. And devout theologians. In any case, Opal loves folk music, and she happens to think that I have a very impressive collection."

"You mean the box of LPs you acquired by accident when buying job lots of rock and blues and now keep permanently stashed away in the cupboard under the stairs?"

"Well, it's not stashed away under the stairs any more. And Opal loves those records. We have the Incredible String Band, we have Lindisfarne, we have Fairport Convention."

I noticed his use of 'we' and wondered how long it would take for this romance to crash and burn. Perhaps I was just being cynical.

"Is she listening to them now?" I said.

"No, I left her using the CD player in the kitchen. John Martyn *Live at Leeds*."

"Are you sure she's satisfied with that?"

I saw a shadow of doubt and alarm cross his face. "Of course she is."

"Perhaps even now she's switching on the Thorens, dropping the needle onto a record without using the damping device…"

"Stop it, you varlet. Stop playing on my deepest fears."

"Anyway, I've got to go out now. I have an appointment in town. Are you ready to go?"

"Sure. Do you want a lift? I could drop you at Putney station. It will save you some time."

"It will save me some time if we don't hit traffic."

"And it will give us a chance to talk," said Tinkler.

"All right, but no sexual boasting. I've already had a visit from Stinky Stanmer this week."

Since I was going into the West End anyway I decided to drop in at Styli. The shop did still occasionally surprise me by turning up some interesting records, so it paid to keep an eye on them. Today was a case in point. They had a great collection of Jasmine reissues on vinyl, classic British jazz of the 1950s including Dizzy Reece, Tony Kinsey and Victor Feldman. But I already owned copies of all of them, indeed in some cases I was blessed with the originals. And there wouldn't be enough margin to make them worth reselling. So I reluctantly left them there for some other lucky customer.

I wandered through the maze of smaller thoroughfares near Harley Street, paralleling Oxford Street but avoiding the crowds of shoppers. A high, clean blue sky stretched over London. There was fresh air mixed in there somewhere among the traffic fumes. I strolled along Cavendish Place feeling pleasantly detached from everything. At the last possible moment I turned left, crossing Market Place and finally, having delayed it as long as I could, entered the bustling maelstrom of Oxford Street. A moment later I was in the quiet back streets again. I walked towards Soho, heading for Miss Honeyland's mews.

I was crossing Great Marlborough Street when I saw him.

To my eyes he instantly stood out from the passing crowd, with his look of someone up from the country and out of place in the big city. He was wearing his green waxed-cotton jacket again, his familiar face peering out over it with a kind of goggle-eyed bafflement. *E.T. with a beard,* I thought.

It was our ferret-faced local historian, Jasper McClew.

He saw me and immediately turned and started walking briskly the other way. I hurried after him. I called his name. He ignored me and increased his pace. I increased mine.

We hurried across Poland Street into Noel Street and

turned right into Berwick Street Market, where I finally caught up with him outside a tattoo parlour and touched him on his elbow. "Hey," I said. He turned around and stared at me, eyes blinking, feigning mild surprise.

"Oh, hello there."

"I was calling you."

"Were you? I didn't hear you. Sorry." He started walking again and I fell in step beside him. I tried to maintain our conversation on the move, although he seemed far from anxious to talk to me.

"Why did you hurry away when you saw me?"

"I didn't hurry away. I didn't see you."

"This is the second time I've bumped into you around here." We had turned off Berwick Street and were now very close indeed to the mews where Miss Honeyland lived. Coincidentally, my destination. Or perhaps not so coincidentally.

"No, it isn't. I mean it couldn't be. I mean you must be mistaken."

I said, "No, it was you all right."

"I don't think so."

"Are you saying you weren't here a few weeks ago, hanging around?" We were now standing beside a trendily funky diner, on the corner of the street that led into Miss Honeyland's mews.

"I'm saying it's highly unlikely."

I laughed. "What the hell does that mean?"

He seemed a little stung by my laughter. "It means," he said, "even in the unlikely event that I was here, if you did happen to see me here, I didn't see you. I wouldn't have."

"Why not?"

He lifted his hand to his glasses. "I wouldn't have recognised you if I wasn't wearing my glasses."

I said, "But you *were* wearing your glasses."

"Was I?"

"And you had a camera."

"Did I? I don't recall. Well, it's been nice running into you…" He started to walk off again. I followed him, easily keeping pace now that he no longer had a head start.

"Are you saying you've never been around here before?" I said.

He stopped and looked at me. "I will concede that I have been here, in this neighbourhood, previously, in the past, on more than one occasion."

A dispatch rider thundered past us on a powerful motorcycle, his visor gleaming in the sunlight, rendering his face invisible. A common enough sight here in Soho where people constantly felt the need to urgently dispatch something important to someone else, even in this age of email. I looked at Jasper. "Doing what?" I said.

"I'm not just a local historian, you know." He puffed up inside his waxed-cotton jacket. "I am working on other things. I do have other projects. Certain, specific, other projects."

I sensed a disclosure in the offing. Perhaps we were finally getting somewhere. "For example?"

He peered at me craftily. "For instance, a biography of Millicent Cavermann." He apparently expected this to be a major revelation, but the name meant nothing to me. I shrugged.

"And who is that?"

He looked crestfallen. "Millicent Cavermann née Honeyland, family nickname Taffy, because of her fondness for that sweet snack, a chewable boiled sugar confection, what is known in our country as toffee. She acquired a taste for it when her family was living in America. Her father was a diplomat who was stationed over there for a period between the wars."

I waited for him to stop talking long enough for me to say something. "Did you say Millicent Honeyland?"

"Yes."

"The sister of Lucky Honeyland?"

"Yes."

"Joan Honeyland's aunt."

"Obviously." Some of Jasper's natural confidence, and general snottiness, had returned.

"She was the Nazi enthusiast," I said.

"And notorious anti-Semite. Yes. 'Mitford in a minor key.' Have you heard that appellation?"

"As a matter of fact, I have."

"Did you know it was I who originated that phrase? In an article published some three years ago. Since then many others have falsely laid claim to it. It's now become an Internet meme. It's enormously frustrating, to have created such a memorable and euphonious phrase and to have others repeat it ad infinitum with no mention of its creator, no credit where credit is so manifestly due, as if it were some workaday form of words worn smooth by commonplace usage."

I was about to insincerely offer my condolences.

But that was when we heard the gunshot.

I left Jasper McClew standing where he was and ran down the street, past a man who was confidently assuring his girlfriend, "It was a car backfiring." As they disappeared behind us I heard him add, "I know the difference between a car backfiring and a gunshot."

So did I, and unfortunately I'd formulated quite the opposite conclusion.

The sound had seemed to come from Joan Honeyland's mews. I ran out of the bright sunlight into the cold shadow of the arched entranceway, the sound of my footsteps ringing urgently off the flagstones. The Mercedes was parked there, pristine, lustrous and glowing. I went through the door, which was open, and suddenly came to a lurching halt.

What was I doing?

I was running towards a place where I thought a firearm had been discharged. Running *towards* it. I was standing just inside the dim, musty entrance hall, where a narrow staircase led up to Miss Honeyland's flat. There was a movement in the shadow at the top of the stairs. I jerked back instinctively. As I did so I caught a glimpse of a man's face, peering down at me.

It was Albert the chauffeur. He looked more scared than I was. Something glinted in the air above his head, a small, smooth distorted blob of metal. It bobbed erratically, catching the light, and I realised it was the head of a golf club. He was holding a golf club, ready to use it as an offensive weapon. Or perhaps a defensive one.

I called up the stairs, "It's me."

His voice was unsteady. "What are you doing here?"

"I have an appointment. Then I heard a shot. And I came running."

There was a moment of silence at the top of the stairs and then he said, "All right. Come on up." He waited at the top of the stairs as I came up, feeling a little apprehensive about the golf club, which he was still clutching tightly. But I wondered if he'd even have room to swing it in this confined space. My nerves being on edge, I tensed up in readiness, but he stood aside to let me by and slowly lowered the club.

"Did I hear a shot?" I said. "I mean, was it a shot?"

"Yes."

"Someone was shooting at you?"

"Yes. Someone was shooting at us."

We walked into the tiny sitting room. Miss Honeyland was standing there, composed and calm and opening a bottle of champagne, of all things. I didn't think this was a woman who had just been shot at, but then she turned to look at me and her face was white as milk and she looked spectacularly aged, every flaw and wrinkle cruelly deep-etched.

And then there was the bullet hole in the window.

It was a neat perfectly circular hole punched in the lower pane of the window overlooking the courtyard. There was an odd frosting of the glass around the perfect hole, which I suspected on closer inspection might prove to be an aura of microscopic cracks radiating outwards.

But somehow I wasn't tempted to make that closer

inspection. I wasn't sticking my head anywhere near that window. In fact I skirted the whole area carefully as I entered the room.

"That's all right," said Miss Honeyland calmly. "They're gone now. Whoever they were."

"You didn't see them?"

"No, just heard them. First the gunshot, of course, and then the sound of someone running across the cobbles from the courtyard, out onto the street. By the time we looked out the window—as you can imagine we were, like you, reluctant to show our faces near it for a moment or two—by the time we looked, they were long gone."

"But I came in through the entrance," I said. "I didn't see anyone."

"No, there's a side passage," said Albert scornfully, as if anyone who wasn't an idiot was expected to know this. "They went out the side passage."

"Ah," said Miss Honeyland in an odd voice. She had carefully removed the foil and the cradle of wire from the cork of the champagne bottle and was now staring at it. "You know, it's absurd," she said. "You're both going to think I'm a complete amoeba, but I don't think I can bear the sound of the cork popping." She held up the bottle and stared at it hopelessly.

"I'll put it back in the refrigerator," said Albert, moving towards her.

"Don't do that," she said sharply. "I want a drink. I want it opened. I just want it opened *carefully*." He obediently took the bottle from her and, clutching the cork in the solid slab of his fist, he began to struggle with it. "You hold the cork stationary and twist the bottle," Miss Honeyland advised him.

Nevada would have been proud of her.

So instructed, Albert managed to open the champagne, easing the cork out with just the slightest hint of a sound. Miss Honeyland nonetheless flinched. While Albert carefully poured a glass for her, I edged over to the other side of the room to see what had happened to the bullet. It took me a moment to find it. I was working from the position of the hole in the window and a rough guess about where the gunman must have stood outside.

They had fired upwards and so the hole on the wall had to be higher than the one in the window.

A rising trajectory.

I finally found it. Right on the dartboard with the pictures of famous children's book characters pinned to it. The bullet had left a deep gouge, furrowing through the yellow painted wood of the board and into the wall behind it. It had decapitated Peter Rabbit and narrowly missed Winnie the Pooh.

I felt a cold tingling in the muscles of my back as I looked at it. It was either a wild fluke, or a terrifyingly accurate shot.

Miss Honeyland looked at the glass of champagne in her hand, then at me. "You probably think I'm mad. I mean, drinking champagne now. In a situation like this." I tried to protest politely, but she rattled on too quickly for me to interject anything, her voice wavering with a kind of frenetic gaiety. "But it's sort of a family tradition, you see.

Be they happy occasions or sad, light-hearted or solemn. We always marked them with a glass of bubbly. Some think it's a bit macabre, but it made perfect sense to us. We even opened a bottle in memory of my father when we got word that he died."

Suddenly there were tears flowing down her raddled cheeks. Albert moved towards her, but she immediately said, "I'm fine." He moved back again, watching her carefully. She looked at me, her eyes sparkling with tears. "And anyway, what better excuse for a celebration than the fact that we're alive? We're still alive."

Miss Honeyland said they were going to ring the police, of course, but perhaps I didn't want to hang around for that. I didn't. They poured a glass of champagne for me before I left, though. I took a polite sip, but it tasted like battery acid to me. There was nothing wrong with the vintage. It was the after-effects of fear.

It was just hitting me now. My legs were like jelly going back down the stairs, jolting me jauntily from side to side in the narrow, shadowed space. I staggered out into the daylight and across the cobbled courtyard like a drunk. I paused to look back up at the window with the bullet hole in it, just about visible from where I was standing.

I realised that this must have been where the gunman had stood.

For some reason, with this thought, my legs began to steady and I was able to walk quite normally back into the street. Jasper McClew was gone, of course. I didn't blame him.

I wouldn't have hung around either.

But I still wished I could have talked to him. There were suddenly a lot of things I wanted to ask him. I turned south and headed towards Piccadilly Circus. I'd get the Tube to Waterloo and then a train home. I was feeling a sudden powerful yearning to return safely to my home place and just sit there. Any sudden noise—a motorcycle accelerating, a blast of music from an upstairs window—set my heart racing.

I crossed the streets with great care, watching carefully for traffic. Recent events had given me a bruised awareness of mortality and made this seem like a particularly stupid time to get run over. So I paused carefully at the edge of the pavement, waiting for every van, car and bike to go past before I crossed the road.

Which is why I was standing outside the sushi bar in Brewer Street, waiting for a truck to rumble by. And I happened to glance inside, and I saw him.

Jasper McClew.

He was sitting with someone at a table just inside the window. His companion was an elderly woman. She was small, sharply dressed in a vivid bohemian style and wearing a beret like the artist that she was.

Toba Possner.

Jasper was leaning across the table towards her.

They were deep in animated conversation.

26. BOVINE TB

"So what did they say when you just walked into the sushi bar and joined them?"

"Well, Jasper didn't say anything. He just stared at me, very upset. He clearly thought I'd painstakingly shadowed him to his secret rendezvous and he was plenty pissed off about it. After all, he'd last seen me running in the opposite direction. And as soon as he was sure I was gone, he'd promptly scarpered."

"He vamoosed."

"Correct. So now he couldn't figure out how I'd managed to find him."

Nevada passed me the colander. Small yellow shells of pasta lay in it, soft and warm. Steam was rising from the sink. She said, "Did you tell him it was sheer chance?"

I added the pasta to the mixing bowl. It was a big white mixing bowl, which nicely set off its contents: bright green shards of herbs and red slivers of Alaskan smoked salmon, all swimming in a layer of golden olive oil.

"No, I let him think I was a master sleuth. Which pissed him off even more."

"So he wasn't pleased to see you."

"No, but Toba Possner was. She seemed perfectly pleased to see me. Relaxed and—"

"Convivial?"

"Yes. Exactly. She was all sort of, 'sit down and have some sushi with us'." I spooned some fromage frais into the mixing bowl and stirred it in. I picked up another spoon and tasted a sample. It was too salty. The smoked salmon was still too dominant. But that was what the fromage frais was for.

"Did you have any sushi?"

"No."

"Did they explain why they were meeting?"

"She said Jasper was interviewing her."

"For his book about the sister? The fascist sister?"

I added a bit more of the fromage frais. "Yes. Millicent Honeyland. Also known as Taffy."

"And did she? Know the sister?"

"No. She only knew the brother. Our friend, Lucky Honeyland. And she only knew him briefly. In the days when she was an impoverished art student and he was visiting her cold-water studio and bullying her about the illustrations for his book."

"Farmer Henry and the Frigging Locusts," said Nevada. "You know, I loved that book when I was a kid. Did you ask Toba about doing a portrait for us?"

"A portrait?" I said. I tasted another sample from the mixing bowl. It was delicious. Perhaps still a shade too salty. A bit more fromage frais was called for.

"Of the cats."

"No, as a matter of fact, I didn't," I said. "I merely established that she was there talking to Jasper—"

"E.T. with a beard."

"The ferret-faced local historian, right. She was talking to him about Lucky Honeyland. For background material. For his tome about the sister."

"And you don't think he was the shooter? Wait a minute. He couldn't have been, could he? He was talking to you when you heard the gun fired."

"That's right." I liked the way she used the word 'shooter'.

Nevada frowned. "But what about her? I mean Toba Possner herself. Could it be her?"

"The shooter?"

"Yes."

I served up, and Nevada clattered a few saucepans into the sink. We carried our plates out of the kitchen and sat at the dining table.

I was thinking. "Yes," I said finally. "It could possibly have been her. She was in about the right place at about the right time."

"You really think she could have done it?"

"Well, she certainly has a reason to want to put a bullet in our client."

"For swindling her out of the revenue from her own artwork, yes. I must commission that painting from her."

I said, "You still want it, even if she's a potential assassin?"

"In fact I'm all the more eager. We need to get it from

her before she's slung into prison."

"Assuming she's guilty."

"Always assuming that."

"Anyway," I said, "I have a feeling that was just a warning shot."

"Why?"

"Because they didn't hit anyone."

Nevada shook her head. "That doesn't necessarily follow."

I tasted my dinner. I'd added too much of the fromage frais. I cursed myself. Now there remained only a tantalising hint, a delicious ghost, of the taste it had possessed a few short seconds ago.

"What are you sulking about?"

"Too much fromage frais."

Nevada tasted her meal. "Don't be ridiculous. It's absolutely delicious."

I started to dig in. It wasn't bad.

"Oh, and by the way," said Nevada, "before I forget, what's-his-name rang. The bloke with the son who came off his motorbike. Penny something. Pennycook."

I said, "Oh, the guy who runs dope."

"Don't you dare remind me of that. I get thrills of mortification every time I think of it even now."

"What did he want?"

"He wouldn't tell me. Presumably because I was only a woman."

After dinner I rang Darren Pennycook. He sounded pleased to hear from me. After the usual polite greetings he said, "You see, the thing is, I spoke to Billy."

"Your son."

"Yes. Initially he was very reluctant to tell me the location of the farmhouse. You remember the farmhouse?"

"Yes," I said. "It was full of Nazis."

"Yes. Well, full of Nazi paraphernalia."

"And more to the point, a record I want."

"Exactly. The V-Disc recording of 'Deep Penetration'. Incidentally, that's not a sexual reference. It actually refers to bombing missions. Specifically the deep penetration into Germany required to bomb Berlin. Danny Overland told me all about that."

"Yes, that's the record all right," I said. "And your son is willing to tell us its location?"

"Assuming it's still in the same place, yes."

That was a point I hadn't considered. Perhaps the record was no longer there. "Anyway," said Pennycook, "he has given us the address of the farmhouse. As I said, he was very reluctant to reveal the information. He kept saying that they are dangerous people and I kept saying that you understood that. So he finally agreed."

"Good. Okay. Can I have the address?"

Pennycook paused. "First, there are a couple of things." He sounded like he was consulting a written list. It seemed he was as reluctant to reveal the information as Billy. "If I give you the address and you manage to obtain the record, I would like to listen to it."

"All right."

"I mean, you have to play it for me. At least once. Before

you pass it on to your employer."

"Of course."

"It's just that I have to hear it."

"I understand."

"It's probably the rarest collector's item of any recording featuring Danny Overland."

"It's okay," I said. "I understand." I really did. Being a music nut myself. "Is that all?"

He hesitated. "No. Billy also made me promise to tell you something. If I give you this address and you insist on going there and trying to get the record."

"Okay," I said. "What did he want to tell me?"

He hesitated again.

"He said, it's your funeral."

"They don't have any of the Domaine de Thalabert left," said Nevada. "That's a real bugger. We can order the Châteauneuf-du-Pape and that will be fine, I suppose, if a bit pricey. But it won't have the whole blackberries-and-cream thing going on." She sighed and set the wine list aside, studying the pub with scepticism. She clearly felt let down by the fact that they'd run out of her favourite wine.

The pub was located in a village outside Tewkesbury. It was an allegedly ancient inn called the Crispin and Crispinian, a weird name only rendered slightly less weird by a little historical plaque on the wall that explained that Crispin and Crispinian were twin brothers and saints, the patron saints of tanners and other leather-workers. The pub had once been a monastery guesthouse, then later a tannery.

We had chosen the place on the Internet and booked a room here because of its reputation for providing decent accommodation and superior food and wine. And also for its proximity to our ultimate destination.

Just a few kilometres along the Tewkesbury Road, on the other side of Bredon's Hardwick, was the farmhouse.

The Nazi farmhouse.

Nevada continued to study the wine list with disapproval. We were sitting on a padded bench in the corner of the saloon bar nearest to the fireplace, which luckily wasn't currently in use. It was a warm, humid night, and the place was relatively empty with most of the other customers outside in the beer garden.

Besides ourselves, there was a middle-aged couple with two Scots terriers who had brought their own water bowl for the dogs and set it down under their table. They must have been regulars because no one had batted an eye. Other than the well-hydrated dogs' owners there were half a dozen teenagers who looked barely old enough to be drinking, a young but clinically obese couple who were rather embarrassingly in love and all over each other, and a pair of unreconstructed hippies in the traditional uniform of jeans and army surplus jackets with hair down to their shoulders, hunched quietly over pints of real ale.

It was a peaceful, relaxed place and it would have felt good to get out of London and come here, if it wasn't for the tight feeling in the pit of my stomach. I couldn't get our mission out of our mind, even if we weren't going to make any kind of start on it until tomorrow, when Tinkler and Clean Head would join us. I found this thought reassuring. Clean Head was enormously reliable and competent, and even Tinkler, surprisingly, had proved himself cool-headed and resourceful in a crisis. Once in Canterbury, in a very perilous situation, he'd saved us all.

So there was no question of Nevada and I doing anything until these reinforcements arrived.

We had driven up that afternoon in Tinkler's Volvo. He would be following with Clean Head in one of the many cars she had access to. Opal would not be accompanying either of them. Ostensibly this was because her van was far too conspicuous. The truth was that we didn't want her along, because none of us trusted her. Well, none of us with the possible exception of Tinkler. But then, as Nevada said, he was love-struck.

Although instead of 'love' she had used a blunt old English noun for a portion of the female anatomy.

So Tinkler had been left to make up a story for Opal about why he had to leave London for a day or two, and why she couldn't join him. He had been on the phone to me immediately, partly to expiate his guilt about having lied to his honey-pie and partly to tell me about Clean Head. Apparently she had called at his home to discuss our strategy for the whole Nazi farmhouse operation.

"She just dropped by without phoning first," he said. "She never does that. Come to think of it, she never drops by. And it was incredibly embarrassing because Opal and I were, ah, having a little nap."

"You're becoming strangely circumspect."

"No, seriously, that's what she calls it—napping. We've been napping so much lately I can hardly walk. Anyway, there we are in bed with Clean Head knocking at the door. And she just kept knocking. She wouldn't go away, so I had to answer it. So there's Opal and me, undressed, just out of bed, and Clean Head is there. And it's totally obvious that she's just interrupted us, and it's all terribly uncomfortable. Don't you think it's weird?"

"What?"

"That Clean Head just happens to turn up, drop in on me for the first time ever, when I happen to be in bed with someone. You know, I think women have a sixth sense about these things."

"Or Nevada phoned her," I suggested. He clearly hadn't thought of that.

"So, anyway, what do I do?"

"About what?"

"About Clean Head and Opal."

I sighed. "It isn't as though you've been unfaithful to her."

"All the same, she seemed pretty upset. Clean Head, I mean."

"I doubt if she's that upset."

"She certainly seemed it, when we were all standing there awkwardly in the kitchen."

I said, "You didn't suggest a threesome, then?"

There was a pause on the other end of the line. "Do you think I should have?"

"I suspect not."

"I'd hate to think I missed an opportunity."

"I suspect you didn't."

"Well, anyway, I was wondering if you could try and get some sense from Nevada about how Clean Head feels. About the whole situation. About me and Opal. The next time they speak."

"They've already spoken," I said.

"So what did she say? What did Clean Head say?"

"She said, 'At least it proves he has one.'"

"I have one!" said Tinkler proudly. "At least I have one. That's great. She means a penis, right?"

So the upshot was that Opal would be staying in Tinkler's house, hopefully not destroying any rare vinyl or expensive and delicate hi-fi equipment, while Tinkler and Clean Head came north to join us here for however long it took. We had already booked rooms for them.

Two separate ones, naturally.

They were bringing with them an assortment of useful equipment. Some of this we had stored at my house in what was now, once again, the spare room. Other items had been newly purchased by Nevada and would be charged to Joan Honeyland as part of the cost of retrieving the V-Disc.

Nevada had downloaded instruction manuals for some of this newly purchased kit and printed them out to bring with us. She was studying these now while we waited for the landlord to serve our wine. I said, "How many of those Tasers did you buy?"

"Four of them."

"Four!"

"Yes," she said, a little defensively. "Three of them aren't really Tasers at all. They're purely handheld short-range electroshock weapons. With these you need to make physical contact, deployed by hand, to stun the subject." She'd clearly been busy with those instruction manuals. "Whereas a proper Taser fires two electrode darts. So I'll be the one using that, because I'm the only one of us who can shoot worth a damn."

I couldn't argue with this. I said, "So there's one that shoots and three handheld?"

"Actually, to be perfectly honest there's one that shoots and four handheld." She smiled demurely. "Because I wanted both kinds for me."

"And Clean Head is bringing all these up?"

"Yes."

"Did we bring anything up ourselves?" We certainly had come with enough bags.

"Of course we did," said Nevada in exasperation. "We brought the night-vision binoculars and our new wide-range electronic countermeasures detector, which I purchased at the Spook Store."

"Jesus. I thought we had all the electronic counter-measures detectors anyone could ever need."

"Not a wide-range one."

"And what do we need that for?" I said.

"The farmhouse, of course. We want to sneak up and keep it under surveillance from a considerable distance. But if they're clever and well-equipped they might just have some kind of detection and alarm system that will alert them to intruders even at just such a considerable distance. Out among the fields and woods. And this device will enable us to find out if they have anything like that."

"It will enable us to detect their detector."

"Yes."

"What if they have a dog?"

Nevada looked at me with approval. "I didn't think of that."

"It seems the sort of thing you might find at a farmhouse."

"It does indeed. I'll phone Clean Head and tell her to pick up some pepper spray, too."

I said, "So the idea is we just hang around and watch the place."

"The idea is to establish a well-concealed vantage point and *surveil* the place. Is that even a word, surveil? I suppose it's rapidly becoming one."

"And then we watch their comings and goings and wait for a moment when everyone is out of the farmhouse, and then we go in and get our record." I'd already started thinking of it as *our* record. Perhaps I just had larceny in my heart. At least where vinyl was concerned.

"Exactly. Although hopefully we'll have more than a moment." Nevada set aside her Taser manual and picked up the pub menu.

I said, "You know what the problem with that is?"

She nodded, flipping through the menu, which was lengthy. "Yes. The problem is making sure that we know exactly how many people are in the farmhouse so we can make absolutely certain they're all out when we go in."

"Billy Pennycook seemed pretty certain that it was just the bloke and his brother who live there full-time."

"Big skinhead and little skinhead. Yes. The relevant phrase there is 'full-time'. We have to make damned sure that the brothers and also any potential houseguests who might be visiting—to practise Heil Hitler salutes or something—are all out of the place when we go in."

We stopped talking while the landlord brought us our glasses of wine and asked if we were ready to order supper yet. We said we were still looking at the menu. I waited until he was out of earshot before I said, "And what if we can't get everybody out of the farmhouse at the same time?"

"We will create a little diversion to draw them out. I couldn't help noticing—good old Google Maps—that there's a large propane tank attached to the farmhouse. Any kind of fire in the vicinity would be likely to draw their immediate and full attention. One doesn't want fire near a propane tank."

"A bit dangerous," I said, "don't you think?"

"You mean if we got it wrong it could result in blowing up lots of Nazi regalia and one extremely rare record?"

"Not to mention potential injury or even loss of life."

"Well, it's only a last resort," said Nevada defensively. "Shall we order supper? Even they shouldn't be able to screw up roast beef. Or we could just order bread and cheese. That should be pretty comprehensively foolproof." She really hadn't forgiven them for not having her favourite wine.

* * *

We went out to the beer garden to wait while they prepared our meal. Nevada had decided that the pub could probably be trusted with roast beef, although she had made a point of telling them at least six times that it had to be rare, thereby laying the groundwork for sending it back to the kitchen with a grim sense of satisfaction if it turned out to be overcooked.

It was a pleasant spring evening, the sky just starting to darken. You could smell the countryside around us in the gathering gloom. A bee buzzed past my ear, on its way to an important meeting with a flower. There were a lot of people in the beer garden, sitting on deck chairs or on long wooden benches beside long wooden tables. There was a sort of gazebo or bandstand made from weather-beaten silvery wood at the far end of the garden.

A rotund, hairy man in a bright green tweed jacket and red corduroy trousers was standing on the bandstand holding a microphone. Behind him hung a banner that read SAVE THE BADGERS. It featured a cartoon of a smiling badger on either side of the slogan. They looked very cute with their black masks and their white snouts.

Most of the deck chairs in the garden were clustered around the bandstand, as though they were waiting to hear the badger man. He cleared his throat, and the guttural sound reverberated all around us.

I realised that there were large outdoor speakers mounted in the trees at all four corners of the garden. Whatever he had to say—I'd concluded by the lack of backing musicians and his general demeanour that he wasn't going to sing us a song—there would be no escaping it.

"Shall we go back inside?" I said, rising from the table where we'd sat.

"Wait a minute," said Nevada. "I want to hear this."

I sat back down.

The man cleared his throat again, thunderously, then started talking. "In the eighteenth century," he said, "hedgehogs were slaughtered here in England en masse. They were deliberately, cruelly massacred by country folk wherever they could be found. They died in their millions." There was a murmur of subdued horror from the seated audience, and I saw Nevada wince. The poor little hedgehogs.

"Why did they do this?" said the man. "Because it was believed at the time, in the eighteenth century, that hedgehogs suckled on sleeping cattle." There was incredulous laughter from the audience. "That's right," said the man. "Suckling on cattle and therefore stealing the farmers' milk. And you do well to laugh at the foolish fantasies and hysteria of an earlier age. But now, once again, in our own century, farmers' paranoid fears for their precious cattle are prompting them to slaughter innocent wild creatures. And I use the word 'innocent' advisedly. The argument for culling badgers to prevent bovine tuberculosis has an equally sound scientific basis as the quaint eighteenth-century annihilation of our nation's hedgehogs."

He reached down and picked up something from the floor of the bandstand. It was a fat document. He held it in his hands and shook it at us as he spoke, like a priest sprinkling holy water. "What I have here," he said, "is the government's 'Final Report on Badger Culling', subtitled 'Bovine TB: The Scientific Evidence'. Over three hundred pages of carefully considered scientific research. And do you know what it says? It comes to two main conclusions." He thumped the report in his hand. "It states that although badgers are indeed a potential source of cattle TB, culling them—by which of course they mean killing them—does *absolutely nothing* to control TB in cattle."

He flipped through the document. "The exact wording is 'can make no meaningful contribution'. In fact, culling badgers is likely to make the situation *worse*. That's one of the two main conclusions. The other one? Let me read it to you. 'Cattle themselves contribute significantly to persistence and spread of disease in all areas where TB occurs.'"

He closed the document and thumped it again. He had a pretty good oratorical style. "That's right. The *cattle themselves*. In other words, if anything we should be culling cattle, not badgers!"

There was applause from the audience. I noticed the hippies from the bar had come out into the garden to hear the speech. Now they, too, clapped enthusiastically, even though they had to set down their pints to do so. The Badger Man modestly accepted the approbation, then waved his hands for silence.

"So there you have it. Scientific proof. Common sense. But do our farmers listen? No. Instead they persist in their misguided belief that badgers are somehow to blame for the consequences of their own foolish factory farming and overcrowding and exploitation of animals. And these misguided farmers, in the countryside around us, in our own community, are taking the law into their own hands, locating badger setts and sealing them off and pumping in exhaust fumes to kill their inhabitants. Whole families of badgers are being massacred, illegally culled, even now. Right now! Trapped and gassed in their homes with no chance of escape."

"That's horrid," said Nevada. Tears gleamed in her eyes. "The poor badgers."

"We are asking for your help to stop this happening," cried the Badger Man. "We need your support. Both in the form of financial contributions—yes, we'll be happy to take your money for a good cause—but also in the form of your personal involvement. We are planning a campaign of direct action to support and assist the badgers. If you feel you can donate your time and dedication and courage, we would like to speak to you." He lowered the microphone, then raised it again. "But money would be nice, too."

There was laughter from the crowd. The sky above the garden had darkened with night, and lights had come on in the trees. They were red and orange Chinese-style plastic lanterns, in bright clusters in the dark branches. Presumably they were on some kind of time switch. Either that or they were designed to come on in response to pro-badger rhetoric. The Badger Man left the stage, and three men and two women rose from the deck chairs and went to him. They were all wearing badger t-shirts, so I assumed they were already part of his team. But other people now began to join them. New adherents.

"Well, we can't give them our time," said Nevada, "but we can certainly give them some money. How much cash have you got on you?"

"About three quid in coins. Plus credit cards and a bank card."

Nevada glanced at the milling crowd of badger fans at the far end of the garden. "No, I want to give them cash, and a decent amount. But I've got even less on me than you."

I shrugged. "Then we'll have to go find a bank machine."

"No," said Nevada. "I've got a bankroll in the car."

"What? Since when?"

"Even in the finest hotels you don't want all your cash in the room with you. So I concealed some in our vehicle. Underneath the spare tyre, as it happens. I put it there when we packed the car this afternoon." She rose from the table. "I'll go and get it."

"No, that's all right," I said. "I'll get it. I have to go to the loo anyway." I got up and Nevada sat down.

"You are a darling," she said.

"Aren't I just."

"And perhaps when you go in you could remind them one more time about making sure the roast beef is rare."

"I could," I said, "but I suspect I'd end up with a serving fork through my throat."

I went in to the pub, visited the toilet, then went out to the car park. This was located across a narrow winding road, beside some kind of municipal building which backed onto a wide open field.

Absurdly, there was a large tree in the middle of the

concrete car park. I suppose it was admirable of them not to have simply chopped it down and paved over it, but it had called for some nimble manoeuvring when we'd arrived. The car park had been almost full and very busy.

Now there was no one else around, although it was still cluttered with vehicles. A narrow access lane ran from the road past the municipal building on one side and some houses on the other before broadening out into the car park.

I walked down the lane. As I passed the tree someone approached from the other side of the shadowy car park. One of the hippies from the pub. He was clutching a wad of pamphlets with pictures of badgers on them. When he saw me he came towards me, holding out the pamphlets.

I reached out to accept one—Nevada would probably want to peruse it at length—when he threw the whole pile of them in my face. I was too startled to react for an instant, and by then he was on me, grabbing for me.

I wrestled with him desperately, driving an elbow into his chest and tearing free. As I hit him, the top of his head slipped off.

His entire scalp sloughed off horribly in a single piece.

But it wasn't his scalp. It was a wig. The long hair fell to the ground revealing a smoothly shaved bald head.

And, as if just to hammer the point home, he had a swastika tattooed there. I started looking around for something heavy to hit him with—a frying pan would have been my preferred choice—but before I could even register the lack of any such useful implement nearby, I saw movement in the shadows.

Someone else running towards us out of the darkness.

It was the other 'hippie'. He had something in his hands. A wide, dark, shapeless object. I fought savagely but between the two of them they drove me to the ground and held me down, helpless. They reached into my jacket and searched my pockets.

They pulled out my phone. Then they stopped searching me and one of them held me down while the other one picked up the shapeless object. It was a large sack.

They pulled it over my head.

27. SACK

I shouted for help.

But what was the point?

I hadn't seen anyone else in the street when I'd been coming from the pub. It was a quiet village. Anyone who was out at this time of the evening was sitting in the beer garden, on the other side of the pub, on the other side of the road.

On the other side of the world.

And now they had pulled a sack over my head. Halfway to my knees, in fact. On the outside of the sack they'd cinched a belt around my waist, tight. So not only could I not see, I couldn't even use my arms. They were bound too tightly to my sides in the close-fitting sack.

The sack itself was made of some kind of heavy, rough cloth that would have muffled the sound. So now I stopped shouting and saved my breath—and waited for an opportunity. They were moving close beside me, one on either side, shoving me roughly along, blind and stumbling.

I waited for my chance. To escape.

But it didn't come.

We abruptly stopped and one of them punched me in the stomach, and while I was doubled over in agony they pushed me over. I hit something—hard, metal—with the back of my legs and fell and kept falling to slam down on my back. I was in a small metal space. They shoved my legs in after me and something heavy and metallic slammed down above me. I smelled oil.

I was in the boot of a car.

Helpless, tied up in a sack, in the boot of a car.

I heard the engine start, and the exhaust pipe throbbed under me through the metal bed of the vehicle. We drove off.

I started working my arms, pushing out at the sack so that it was dragged up past the belt. If I could get the bottom of the sack past it, I could pull it off over my head. But before I got very far something snagged and the sack wouldn't move any further. All I'd achieved was a fraction more room in which to move my arms.

I don't know how long we drove for. It seemed like an eternity but was probably no more than a quarter of an hour. Finally we turned off onto a rough, rutted road, jolted along for some distance and then stopped.

They switched off the engine. Doors slammed. They came for me.

The lid of the boot opened and cool air rushed in. I'd already decided what to do when this happened. With my arms pinioned there was no way I could overpower them and make a break for it. Indeed, with my arms tethered so close to me in the sack I could hardly get my balance and stand up straight.

So instead, I lay there limply as if I was unconscious. This didn't seem to bother them. They dragged me out and carried me.

Even through the sack, the cool night air was nectar after the hot, oily, airless space of the boot.

They walked along, carrying me over what felt like rough, uneven ground. We moved as a unit in eerie silence. Then one of my captors spoke.

"You got the leaflets?"

"The what? Oh, yes."

They kept walking. They were strong; the two of them didn't seem to have any trouble carrying me. I tried to simulate a dead weight. I heard twigs crunching underfoot. We were among trees and bushes. I could feel us brushing past the shrubbery.

"He hasn't said anything."

"Shut up."

I heard an owl call. We were deep in the country.

"What if he's dead?"

"Just shut it."

Gradually we began to move uphill—a gentle slope.

"No, listen, if he's dead, if he's already dead, it isn't going to work, is it? I mean, it won't look like—"

"Shut. Your. Gob."

"I'm serious. It won't look all right if he's already dead. We have to check if he's dead."

My heart raced in my chest. They were going to examine me. They would open the sack. They would have to. And then I would—

"He's alive all right. I just felt his muscles tense up."

"Yeah, me too."

"He's thinking about trying something clever."

"Well, it's too late for that."

We came to a sudden halt and they let me drop. I slammed to the ground. The wind was knocked out of me and before I could recover they were kneeling on me. I struggled, but there was nothing I could do. I felt them loosening the belt, then they picked me up again. The sack was flapping loosely around me now. My feet and legs were suddenly free—at least in theory. But my escorts still gripped me tightly, one carrying me by the elbows so he controlled my arms, the other holding onto my legs.

I started to kick, but it was too late. They were lowering me towards the ground and I felt my feet go into a hole. Then my legs. It was a tight, narrow hole. As I kicked out, my feet almost immediately made contact with the sides of it. A hole in the ground, roughly circular in section, and narrow.

But wide enough for my body.

"It's a tight fit."

"He'll go."

They shoved me and down I went—legs, hips, wildly struggling arms. They forced my arms to my sides, and shoved my torso in. As my head and shoulders went in, they whipped the sack off my head.

Then they pulled the sack out of the opening, retrieving it. I caught a moment's glimpse of their pale faces against the night sky, then I was in the hole.

It was a tunnel, slanting down into the earth. I slid down

it with the impetus of their final shove until I came to a halt. I was perhaps a metre below ground. I heard them shove something in after me—a rustling sound—and then they slammed something down on the hole, and I felt myself cut off from the world above.

I was sealed in the darkness.

The tunnel was so narrow that my arms were trapped at my sides. I was utterly unable to move them. I felt a sudden wave of panic and twisted wildly around. But as I twisted, I inadvertently drove myself further down the tunnel, and as I slipped further down I found that it widened. I could move my arms. I breathed a fervent thanks and kept moving downwards.

My feet were moving into a much larger space. I descended into it. I could actually move now, arms, legs, everything. I couldn't stand up, or even sit up fully, but I was grateful for what I'd got. I was in a dark chamber about twice as long as my body and wide enough so that I could stretch out both my arms and my fingertips would barely brush the sides. Kneeling, I could almost, but not quite, sit up fully. I was in utter darkness. I felt roots brush my head. They must be coming through the ceiling of the chamber.

It was an irregular space, roughly dug out of the sandy earth. It had a thick covering of what felt like dried grass on the floor. There was a sweetish smell, like a dry compost heap, but I didn't think it was coming from the grass. It had a musky, animal edge to it, but it was not unpleasant.

I tried to get my bearings, feeling my way back to the tunnel where I'd come in. As I ran my hands along the dirt walls I felt other openings, of all different sizes, some much too small for me. I managed to orientate myself and locate the spot where I'd made my entrance. I began to climb back up it, arms in front of me this time. This made for a much more controlled ascent, and gave me more room to manoeuvre. I didn't feel any of the claustrophobic panic I'd experienced coming down. As I went up I felt something under my fingers.

Pieces of paper. I remembered the rustling sound as they'd shoved something in after me. Square pieces of paper, several of them. I folded them and held them in my hands as I kept crawling.

Now I knew what to expect, I managed to scrunch myself up so I could slither back up the narrow tunnel with surprising speed. I was moving towards the opening where I'd come in—or what had been the opening.

They had sealed the hole very thoroughly. I rapped my knuckles on something hard. A large sheet of wood. I pressed my palms against it and pushed. It didn't budge. I exerted all my strength until my shoulders creaked. Nothing. It appeared that a very substantial weight had been placed on top of the sheet of wood.

I went back down the tunnel, wriggling backwards feet first, my hands trailing behind me. I felt a sense of relief to get back into the chamber. Home again. I realised I was still holding the pieces of paper clenched in my sweaty fists. I stuck them in my pocket. I wouldn't be able to read them any time soon.

They had taken my phone, so I couldn't use it for a light source. For once I felt a regret that I didn't smoke. With a cigarette lighter I would be able to shed some light on my surroundings, at least until it ran out of fuel or I used up all the air—

The air.

My heart thudded with a shock of panic that rocked my whole body. When would the air run out? Instantly I felt it getting hard to breathe. I couldn't suck in enough oxygen. My heart was pounding, my pulse thick and heavy in my head, behind my eyes. I couldn't breathe…

I was going to suffocate here in the darkness.

I forced myself to calm down.

Gradually my heartbeat slowed. My breathing eased. There was enough air. There was plenty of air. In fact, now that I'd calmed down I realised I could feel a thin cold draught weaving around me, leaving a chill even now on the sweat on my face.

There was air coming in from somewhere.

Which meant there might be a way out.

I began to explore. There were at least seven holes in the wall of the chamber, not including the one I'd come down. Of these, four were too small for me to get through. Of the three larger ones, two gave access to rapidly narrowing tunnels. I didn't travel too far down these before turning back. I still had a morbid fear of getting stuck.

The final tunnel led to another chamber, about half the size of the first one and with a much lower ceiling. There were a half-dozen holes in the walls here, none of them big enough for me to get through. I returned to the first chamber.

Home again.

I crawled into the darkness of this small space, its contours already becoming familiar to me. There wasn't much more I could do. It was still the middle of the night. I would have to wait until morning before I could do anything else. As soon as the sun was up, I'd go looking for any hint of light. Somewhere above me there were—thankfully—holes letting in air.

They would also let in light.

If I could see them, I could move towards them. Even if it meant enlarging the diameter of one of the narrower tunnels. Somehow I would dig myself out of here. Could I dig with my hands? Maybe I could snap off one of the roots from the ceiling, use it as a shovel. My mind whirled with possibilities. I forced myself to relax, to stop speculating. For now, there was nothing I could do. Except conserve my energy.

Exhausted, I curled up on the bed of sweet grass and went to sleep.

I had no way of estimating how long I slept, but I was awakened by the muffled thudding of an engine somewhere on the surface above me. My heart surged with hope. I listened to see if the vehicle would come nearer. Perhaps I could signal somehow. Hammer on the wooden lid that sealed the entrance.

But the engine didn't come any nearer. As far as I could tell, it didn't move in any direction. It wasn't a passing car, because it would have passed by now. And it wasn't a tractor working back and forth across a field, because it didn't seem to move at all.

It just stayed in one place.

Perhaps it was a generator. Running a pump or something. I lay down again; in my excitement I'd risen to my knees. As I lowered my face to the dried grass I smelled something odd. The sweetish fragrance was gone. Something else was there. I sniffed. Suddenly the air in the chamber was smelling insidiously less fresh.

I sat up immediately. Higher up, the air wasn't so bad, but something was still clearly wrong. Had the breathing holes been sealed? But I could still feel the draught circulating around me. If anything, it was a little stronger— warm and insistent.

Warm.

And now it carried an itchy, choking smell with it. A faint odour of petrol.

Suddenly I knew exactly where I was.

I was in a badger sett.

And they were pumping in exhaust fumes.

28. UPWARDS

I didn't know how long it takes for carbon monoxide to kill you, but I knew it wasn't long.

I forced myself to think. What were they doing to me? They were pumping exhaust fumes from an engine on the surface. They must be using a hose or something, and getting it into the sett through a breathing hole.

A breathing hole. Possibly not the only one. Come to think of it, there was bound to be more than one breathing hole, if only to give proper ventilation. This sett struck me as a well-engineered structure, fashioned by creatures who knew what they were doing, at least when it came to sett building. There was certain to be another breathing hole.

Sensible, clever badgers.

I scrambled down one of the wide tunnels to the second, smaller chamber. The air in here seemed cleaner. I searched the walls, feeling them like a blind man reading Braille. As I found each hole I stuck my head into it and breathed, searching for that incoming breeze, clean and pure and cool.

Instead what I found was dead, stale air. I groped from one hole to the next, already certain that I'd visited them all already, but seeking them out again with my hands in the dark, desperate—

In the dark.

In the absolute, total darkness. There was no tiny hint of light. And the sun must be up by now. So no light meant no openings.

If there were other breathing holes, someone had closed them.

I was sealed in.

The air in this chamber was starting to become hot and heavy with the smell of exhaust.

I crawled back down the tunnel into the larger chamber.

The air in here was now very bad.

I couldn't just stay here and die. Maybe I could batter my way out through that piece of wood over the main entrance. I hadn't been able to shift it last night. But now I had slept. I was refreshed. I was…

Suffocating.

Up the tunnel I went, worming my way towards the opening, the promise of life, and the all too solid barrier I knew was waiting for me there. I surged and slithered upwards. I was becoming accustomed to the strange manner of motion required, and I was now moving very quickly.

So quickly that I slammed right into the wooden barrier, a painful collision for my urgently questing hands. I crawled up as close to it as I could, my face against the wood. I could smell it. Just cheap particle board, but solid enough to seal my fate, with whatever weight they'd placed against it. It smelled of formaldehyde. Embalming fluid. How appropriate.

It took me a moment to identify the crazed laughter as my own, and at that moment I realised just what an easy thing to lose a mind can be. Your sanity blowing away like an unsecured toupee in a high wind.

I took a deep breath. The air in the tunnel was still relatively clean. The exhaust would be heavier than oxygen. It would sink most thickly to the deepest part of the sett— the big chamber. That was the lowest point. This tunnel I was in was the highest. And I was at the highest point of the tunnel.

The air wasn't going to get any better than this.

I took a deep breath and braced myself. Then I pressed my bruised hands to the wood and pushed. I pushed for all I was worth. I braced myself again and pushed again. I heard the blood roaring in my ears. I pushed for my life, desperately trying to lever up the wood, even the tiniest fraction. Even a hairline crack would be enough. I'd be able to breathe. I could suck in the cool air.

But the piece of wood didn't budge. Not even a hairline crack. I pushed and pushed, and red lightning began to flash in my head. I was sure it was going to budge. I knew it would budge. It had to.

It didn't.

It wasn't going to move. Not by the tiniest fraction. I couldn't do it. I was too weak. It was too late. I kept pushing at the wooden barrier, giving it everything I had, but that was no longer very much. My arms were cylinders made of damp twisted rags.

From the darkness below, the fumes rose towards me.

Nevada—

Nevada was staring down at me. I realised I'd heard the sound of something shifting, something dragging and thudding, just before she lifted away the big square sheet of wood and looked down at me. The sky behind her was pale blue, denim just starting to fade. Dawn.

We stared at each other in the early morning light.

I realised another sound had stopped. The engine.

"Come on out," said Nevada. "Can you move?"

"Yes."

"You're not too affected by the fumes?"

I slithered out of the hole, the cool air embracing me, and then Nevada embracing me. She kissed me. "Poor you, you smell like an exhaust pipe." She helped me to my feet.

I said, "You smell wonderful." She did. She smelled like life. Over her shoulder, silhouetted against the rising sun, I saw the big purposeful shape of a tractor. That was the engine that had been running. It was silent now. I saw a long red hose snaking from it, lying on the ground in coils, running up the gentle hillside slope to wherever the badger had put its breathing hole.

I turned back and looked at the entrance hole. A small dark opening, a squashed circle tucked under some tree roots in the side of the hill. It was so tiny I couldn't believe

I'd fitted in it. Beside it lay the square of plywood and a heap of sandbags that had been piled on the plywood until Nevada had dragged them off.

I breathed the sweet air and looked at her, smiling and sweaty from recent exertions, a lock of her raven-black hair plastered to her forehead. All I wanted to do was sit there and look at her, but I had to get up. "I need to pee," I said. "I've been holding it in all night. It's funny, but I'm almost more relieved that I didn't wet myself than that I didn't die."

"It wouldn't have mattered if you had wet yourself," said Nevada.

"I know. I think it's just that I can wrap my head around the humiliation of pissing my pants, and wetting the badger's nice clean bed—"

"Was it nice and clean?"

"Relatively speaking. But I can't wrap my head around being dead."

"Who can?" said Nevada. She held my hand while I pissed a smoking stream into the cold morning air as the sun came up and the birds began to sing. A pastoral landscape. Urinating city-dweller and girlfriend. It was a moment of utter peace.

At least it was until I turned my head to the left, towards the tractor, and noticed someone lying there. It was a skinhead, the smaller of last night's 'hippies'.

"He was operating the tractor when I arrived," said Nevada, following the direction of my gaze. I zipped up and stared at the unmoving figure.

"He didn't just set it running and leave it?" For some

reason, this is what I'd imagined they'd done.

"No, he was keeping a close personal eye on things. Maybe because he wanted to make sure he did a good job. Anyway, I had to deal with him."

I took a few steps towards the tractor, then stopped. He was lying there on the ground with his face in the dirt, mouth open and eyes shut. He looked very young, as people sometimes do when they're sleeping.

Or when they're…

I said, "Are you sure he's all right?"

"No."

"Did you hit him hard?"

"Yes."

To me he looked terribly, terminally inert. I averted my gaze. "What did you hit him with?"

Nevada nodded. "There's a tool box on the other side of the tractor, full of all sorts of useful implements. I think this was something for removing tyres. It was big and it was made of metal, that was the main thing."

I said, choosing my words carefully, "Do you think you hit him too hard?"

"You know what? I don't really care."

I turned away from the tractor. The sun was coming up over the fields, the light watery and orange. I stared into it, feeling its warmth on my face. I said, "How did you find me?"

"They got hold of your phone."

"Yes, they took it from me."

"Well, they sent a text message pretending to be you. It said you had found something vitally important and you needed to meet me. In the middle of the night, in the middle of nowhere. It was obviously a trap, but I played along and arranged a rendezvous. When they got there I was already in place, in hiding, watching them. Then I texted to say that I couldn't make it, that I was going to be a few hours late. So they went back to wherever they'd come from."

"And you followed them?"

"Yes. First back to their farmhouse, where they split up and the little one went off, and luckily I followed him."

I looked at the body lying by the tractor. "Here."

"Yes. I saw the tractor and saw the hose and the sett and everything, and I worked out what he was doing."

"Thank god."

"Thank god."

I felt something in my pocket. A damp, tightly folded piece of paper. It was the piece of paper from the tunnel, which they'd shoved in after me last night. I unfolded it.

It was one of the leaflets the badger man had been handing out. I read it with interest. I'd wondered about it all night long, unable to decipher it in the dark. It spoke of solidarity with the badgers. And suggested that volunteers could chain themselves to machinery and even occupy setts.

"Occupy setts," I said.

Nevada nodded. "It's what gave them the idea."

I said, "That's why they left me with the leaflet."

"So you'd seem to be a save-the-badger activist."

"Exactly. Like chaining myself to a tree to stop it being cut down." I looked at the dark mouth of the sett, the morning sunlight probing at it. "It would have been a tragic accident."

Nevada nodded again. "It certainly would have muddied the water in any murder investigation."

I looked around; the golden sunlight was stealing over the fields, moving the shadows of trees.

"Even so," I said, "they were crazy to do it on their own farm."

"This isn't their own farm."

"Isn't it?"

"No. Their place is a couple of miles away."

That made sense. I looked at Nevada. "Do you know how to get there?"

"Of course I do."

"Let's go."

The rising sun was growing brighter and more intense, ambushing us with bursts of brilliance between clusters of trees as we drove along winding country lanes. At the wheel, Nevada was wearing sunglasses. I said, "I'm not going home until we get what we came for."

She studied the road. "That's the spirit. Just because you were nearly gassed to death, you're not going to pass up the opportunity of obtaining a rare record."

"That's right. I'm made of sterner stuff than that."

"Indeed you are."

We parked the car half a mile from the Nazi farmhouse down a narrow side road. From there we walked over fields. Nevada had scouted all this last night. "It looked very different through the night-vision binoculars. But I think I remember the way." She did indeed, and after a pleasant ten-minute walk through the countryside we were sheltering behind a barn opposite the main building of the farmhouse.

It was no longer a working farm, just buildings and several acres of land surrounding them, consisting of hedges, woods and overgrown fields. Some fairly new-looking fences demarcated the edge of the property. I guessed that what had once been extensive land belonging to the farm had now been sold to the neighbours, who would actually be able to work them. Meanwhile, no one here was earning a living through the honest sweat of their brow.

"Judging by last night, it's just the two of them," said Nevada.

"And no dog."

"And thankfully no dog."

I peered around the edge of the barn at the farmhouse. It was rather a pretty building made of irregularly shaped grey bricks. A motorcycle was leaning up against the wall and a white Hyundai van and a blue Range Rover were parked outside. I said, "Do we just wait for him to leave?"

"Of course not," said Nevada. She took out a phone.

"What's that?"

"His brother's phone. I took it from him when I knocked him out. Just like they took yours from you. I thought, *Two can play at that game*."

"Good thinking." I watched while she composed a text: *Come quick*. To be more precise, the message read: *Kum kwik*.

"That's the way they actually spell," said Nevada. "I made a point of studying the style of their messages—

something they weren't bright enough to do when they stole your phone and pretended to be you."

She was about to press send when the phone suddenly came to life in her hand, vibrating and flashing and playing a jaunty tune. We both nearly jumped out of our bodies.

The ring tone was 'I Get Around' by the Beach Boys, of all things. A message flashed on the screen. *Caz calling*. Nevada stared at me, waving the phone in the air as if it had suddenly grown red hot.

"What do I do?"

"For god's sake, don't press answer."

She peered at the phone. "No. Ah, it's all right, it's going to voicemail."

We let it go to voicemail and then we dialled the voicemail number and listened. An angry male voice rattled from the phone, with just the trace of a country accent. I thought I recognised it from last night, but then I'd been listening through a sack, so I couldn't swear to it. It said, "You should be done by now. Answer the bloody phone." There was an angry, strained sigh before it cut off.

Just then there was the sound of a door slamming. We looked around the edge of the barn and saw the bigger of the two skinheads—the 'hippie' who'd lost his wig in the car park. He came out of the farmhouse and climbed into the blue Range Rover and started the engine.

He pulled away.

As soon as he was gone, we went in.

29. NAZI FARM

The door wasn't even locked, much to Nevada's disappointment. She had purchased some kind of new electronic lock-picking device she wanted to try out. We stepped inside the farmhouse. Outside it was warm and the sun was rising fast. In here it was all cold, dank shadows. There was a smell of damp in the narrow hallway that ran the width of the house. To one side of us was a washing machine, apparently no longer in service, just abandoned there in the hallway. There was a pile of cardboard boxes on top of it containing ill-assorted muddy rubber boots. These guys knew how to live.

Further down the shadowy hall to our right were five really big cardboard boxes, each about the size of the washing machine. We went to look at them.

The first four were full of Golden Eagle cigarettes. Cartons and cartons of them. They were apparently manufactured in Vietnam. "I wonder if the full and correct import duty has been paid on all of these?" I said.

"They're obviously selling them on the black market," said Nevada.

I estimated the number of cartons sitting in this hallway and did a quick calculation. "And making a lot of money from it."

"To spend on what?" said Nevada, looking at me. We went and looked in the fifth box.

It was full of guns.

"Question answered," said Nevada. I left her looking through the firearms while I went in search of the record.

I turned left down the hallway. There was more light here, from the windows at the front of the house. I could see that the floor was covered with what had once been handsome green and white tiles, now layered with overlapping muddy footprints. I followed the heaviest flow of footsteps and they led me to a large room at the far end. This room was long and dark and ran the length of the farmhouse. There were several sets of windows in the wall to my left, but they were all heavily sealed with brown drapes.

I had been expecting Nazi flags, but the denizens of the house had gone one better. The entire room was painted red, with fierce crude brushstrokes, except for one perfectly executed circle of white at the far end, containing a precisely incised black swastika. The circle and swastika had clearly absorbed all the decorators' energies and all their concentration. After they'd done it they'd obviously got bored doing the rest of the job. All that fucking red paint.

And, now that I noticed it, they'd actually missed a corner of the ceiling, up above the door and to the right, at a difficult-to-reach angle, which showed the previous lime-green floral wallpaper underneath.

It rather spoiled the dramatic effect.

But I was far more interested in the record player. It was tucked in beside the fireplace, not an ideal position from a temperature point of view, but it provided a handy alcove. Beside it was a long wooden sideboard displaying carefully placed, if dusty, artefacts. Included among these was a German army helmet, a rather phoney-looking dagger with *SS* on the handle, a book—*Mein Kampf* of course—and a rack of records. I quickly looked through the records. They were mostly the speeches of Hitler and other luminaries, but there were also some recordings of Wagner, old Decca mono pressings, which deserved a better home.

The record player was some kind of German make, appropriately enough, with 78, 45 and 33rpm speed settings.

And there it was, on the turntable.

The twelve-inch vinyl Victory Disc of 'Deep Penetration' by the Flare Path Orchestra, composed by Danny Overland. It looked like it hadn't been touched since Billy had taken that picture with his phone all those months ago.

They didn't use the record player much. It was basically just for display.

The record was thick with dust. That didn't matter. A quick cleaning would sort it out. I lifted it off. The other side—the underside—was perfectly clean. It featured another Danny Overland composition, entitled 'Wanganui'. I needed something to wrap the record in, to protect it.

I looked around the room. It was a strangely empty

space. The concrete floor wasn't carpeted, but there were several large frayed rugs spread across it. These were Indian, and I assumed they had been chosen because they had some patterns resembling swastika motifs. These guys never let go of a theme.

Standing clustered on the rugs were several ill-assorted old leather armchairs. These were perhaps chosen to give the atmosphere of an exclusive gentleman's club. If so, it was an atmosphere rather undermined by the large tottering stack of colourful and pornographic wank magazines stacked to elbow height in easy reach of one of the armchairs. In another armchair someone had left a tattered beige sweater.

I put the record in the sweater, folded it carefully, and turned towards the door. As I turned I saw a phone on the sideboard, plugged into a charger. It looked like my phone. I went and picked it up.

It *was* my phone.

I tugged it free of the charger and stuck it in my pocket, feeling disproportionately happy. It was good to know that such a personal possession was no longer in the hands of the enemy. As I pocketed it, something caught my eye. It was the copy of *Mein Kampf*.

What I had thought was a bookmark sticking out of it was actually a pamphlet. And something about the colour of the pamphlet's cover was familiar. I pulled it out of the book. I'd lost their place now.

It was entitled *The Crucial Racial Question* and featured a crude cartoon of an insect with semi-human features.

I stuck it in with the record and got out of there. Nevada

met me in the hallway. "Did you get it?"

"Yes, it's here," I said. "What did you glean?"

"They've got a lot of cigarettes and a lot of guns."

"Everything that's bad for the health," I said. "Let's get out of here and go home."

"Agreed."

We were just making our way to the front door when the blue Range Rover came back.

It pulled up in the driveway and stopped right outside. We stepped back from the door, moving away from the window. Nevada looked at me. We edged back down the hall and paused by another window, peering out through the mildewed curtains to check on the situation again. They weren't getting out of the car.

"What do we do?" said Nevada.

"Go out the back way?"

"Are we even sure there is a back way?"

Just then the skinhead brothers got out of the car. The smaller one, last seen lying on the ground by the tractor, was holding his head and looked pale and very much the worse for wear. But he was alive. I felt relieved—then ashamed that I was relieved. The fucker had tried to gas me like a poor fucking badger.

Then the two of them started towards the front door.

I looked at Nevada, then at the doors along the hallway leading to various rooms—all potentially dead ends. We had to choose one. I picked one and took Nevada's hand and pulled her towards it. She pulled back. I looked at her. She nodded eagerly at the window. I looked out.

The younger, smaller skinhead had paused halfway to the front door to turn and puke all over his brother. There was suddenly vomit all down the brother's jeans and spattering copiously onto his gleaming boots. His brother stared at him in horror, then at himself in even greater horror, then dragged him away. We heard the distant tortured screech of a rusty tap being wrenched open, then the sluggish juddering of water pipes in the wall.

They had gone around the corner of the house and were using a hose to wash themselves down. We heard them splashing as we crept out the front door, a sound weirdly reminiscent of children's summer parties and inflatable paddling pools, though those would be without the steady stream of frenzied cursing. We hurried across the driveway and took shelter safely behind the barn.

While they were occupied cleaning up, we got out of there. We walked through the fields back to where we'd left the car. The sun was high now and the birds were singing. "By the way," said Nevada. "I was being unfair to the hotel. Their roast beef was really good. Or at least it looked really good. I couldn't eat a bite because you'd disappeared and I was too worried about you." We stopped walking and kissed.

"Thank you," I said. "For saving my life."

"Always a pleasure. I had them put the roast beef in a doggy bag for us. Plus the vegetables. All the trimmings."

Back at the hotel, we discovered that Tinkler and Clean Head had arrived. When I'd gone missing Nevada had asked them to join us as soon as possible, and they'd got here a couple of hours ago and had been waiting tensely in the hotel for us to return ever since.

Nevada had already phoned them with an account of what had happened, and Clean Head and Tinkler looked at me like a man who had risen from the grave.

Which in a way I suppose I was.

It only took a few seconds, though, for Tinkler to return to form. "I hope you don't mind," he said. "You know they put that roast beef dinner in a doggy bag for you last night when you couldn't eat it? Well, I have a confession to make."

"He's eaten it," said Clean Head, succinctly.

"It was delicious," said Tinkler.

"That's really not on, Tinkler," said Nevada crossly. "Because both of us are ravenous. And we were looking forward to that fucking roast beef dinner. And my beloved here nearly died."

"I'll make it up to him. I'll make it up to you. I'll buy you breakfast."

"Breakfast is not the same."

"I'll pour syrup on things for you. The bacon will be crispy. My god, now I'm making myself hungry."

"Not again," said Clean Head. "Not already."

"It must be all this sex I've been having," said Tinkler.

"Oh, please," said Clean Head. "No need for details."

Tinkler beamed at me, looking a little manic. "And just think," he said, "now *you* can go on having sex, too, because you're not dead."

"There is that," I said.

"That's the crucial thing. Not being dead."

"Profound words."

Tinkler looked at Nevada. "By the way, what if he hadn't been in the sett? I mean you cold-cocked the guy on the tractor and everything."

"Cold-cocked him?"

"Knocked him unconscious. What if you'd looked in the hole and found he wasn't in there?" Tinkler glanced at me. "What if it was just badgers?"

"Then at least I would have saved some poor badgers," said Nevada.

We ate breakfast in the beer garden and then drove back to London.

"They were setting you up," said Tinkler in the backseat. "Do you get it? *Sett*ing you up…?"

"Shut up, Tinkler."

"All right."

He was silent for a moment then leaned forward again. "If Nevada hadn't got there in time, it would have been game, sett and match."

"Tinkler, shut the fuck up."

30. NATIONAL NEWS

To Nevada's delight, the story made the national news. We heard it on the car radio driving back to London.

"Responding to a telephone tip-off, police in Gloucestershire have today raided a farmhouse, seizing a large cache of illegal firearms. A substantial quantity of contraband cigarettes were also found. Police sources say they believe the weapons may have been used in a number of recent high-profile crimes. Two men have been arrested."

"Amazing what you can do with one little anonymous call," said Nevada happily. I was equally pleased at the thought of those two jokers cooling their heels in a police cell somewhere. The report went on to identify the men as brothers and name them as Carroll and Vivian Weston.

I noted the girlie names and wondered if they had spent a lifetime being mercilessly teased about them. Was it a reaction against that that had put them on the path to fascist thuggery?

Tinkler dropped us off at our house and then drove home to Putney, presumably to an emotional reunion with Opal.

We went inside and as soon as I was through the door I had an emotional reunion of my own; the cats were all over me. I managed to sit down on the sofa with them both struggling to climb into my lap, sniffing at me eagerly. Nevada stared at us.

"They're behaving so strangely towards you. Isn't it extraordinary? It's as if they know what happened. They must be able to sense that something terrible almost happened to you."

I said, "Either that or they can smell the badgers."

Eventually I managed to detach myself from the worshipful cats and went and took a shower. I stood under the hot cleansing spray and just let it wash everything away. I stood there for so long that Nevada knocked on the door to see if I was all right. I said I was. Finally I turned off the shower, towelled myself dry and put on a bathrobe.

I sat in the living room while Nevada made coffee, and I tried to summon the energy to ring Joan Honeyland and report on recent events. It was going to be a long report. At length, I sighed and reached for the phone and, as I did so, it started to ring. I picked it up.

It was Tinkler.

He said, "Opal said to tell you she spoke to the barmaid."

"What barmaid?"

"Did those badgers destroy your brain? Do you remember the Silk Stockings Murder? Opal's great-grandmother dead in a beer barrel? The mystery man and the bottle of drugged whisky?"

I did remember. "And she spoke to the barmaid again?"

"Yes. She asked that question that you asked her to ask."

This, I didn't remember. "What question was that?"

"I really do think those badgers did something to you."

"There weren't actually any badgers in the sett with me. They had very sensibly vacated it for the evening."

"Well, we've been reading about badgers. Opal and I. She's fascinated. Because of your recent experience we are thinking of painting one on the van."

"We?"

"That's right," said Tinkler. "Opal and I are thinking of painting a badger on the van. Maybe two badgers. One by day and one by night. Anyway, we've been researching them and apparently they even have toilets, special badger toilets, among the chambers in the sett. Did you find the badger toilet?"

I sighed. "No, Tinkler, I didn't find the badger toilet."

"And apparently they take their bedding, which is made of hay, straw, bracken and grass, up onto the surface to air out and be cleaned by the sunlight."

"Yes, it was pretty clean. It smelled all right."

"So you don't think you've lost your memory because of exposure to toxic badger poo? I think it's still a strong possibility."

"Tinkler, remind me why you rang?"

"You see what I mean?"

I sighed. "What did the barmaid tell Opal?"

"Well, you remember—or perhaps you don't—that the barmaid never got a good look at the mystery man's face. But you said she must have heard his voice. And Opal said she'd ask about that."

I remembered now. I was all ears. "And what did she say?"

"She said he sounded posh."

"Posh?"

"Yes."

After Tinkler had hung up I sat there, staring at the phone.

I didn't ring Miss Honeyland. Instead I went and looked through the pile of clothes I'd taken off, which were in a plastic basket in the spare room waiting to be washed. I dug through my pockets and took out the pamphlet. The one that had been used as a bookmark in *Mein Kampf*.

The Crucial Racial Question. I studied the cover with the crude cartoon of an insect depicted on it.

The insect was, of course, a locust.

"These are very good," said Toba Possner, looking through the photos. "These will do very well." They were colour photographs that Nevada had printed off our computer, featuring our cats. Perhaps not surprisingly, we had quite a few photographs of the two of them stored on our hard drive.

"I'm glad you like them," said Nevada, leaning forward eagerly. The three of us were sat in Toba's tiny front room in her flat in Chelsea, which meant all our knees were virtually touching. "I tried to choose the best ones."

"They're lovely. The colours are excellent. Look at those exquisite turquoise eyes."

"That's her name, actually, Turquoise. We call her Turk for short."

"And their coats as well. Lovely markings. I shall be

able to make great use of the interplay of the colour of their coats, the way I juxtapose them in the composition according to their posture and the way they are lying against each other, the contrast of their markings as they follow the contours of their bodies."

She set the photographs aside and looked at us shrewdly. "But that isn't what you came here to talk to me about, is it? Commissioning a portrait of your cats?"

Nevada looked at me. "Ah, not exclusively, no."

I said, "Do you remember showing us the clipping that Lucky Honeyland gave you before you started work on the illustrations for his book?"

She looked at us steadily with her strange pale brown eyes. "Yes, of course. The one he gave me as a guide. Do you want to see it again?"

"Yes, please."

She went to the filing cabinet and took out the manila folder, extracting the fragment of coloured paper from it. She handed it to me. I was already holding the pamphlet I'd stolen from the farmhouse. I took the fragment and placed it on the cover.

It seemed to vanish, blending in with the background.

A perfect match.

I turned the fragment over and opened the pamphlet and repeated the process with the inside front cover, but it was already a foregone conclusion. Another perfect match. "So you found where that clipping came from?" said Toba. "That was clever of you. I've always wondered where Mr Honeyland got that image. I've been wondering about it, on and off, now and then, for the better part of my life. May I look?"

I hesitated. "Of course you can," I said. "But I'd better warn you that it's the most virulently anti-Semitic propaganda you can imagine."

She smiled at me. "You wouldn't believe what I can imagine."

"Basically it depicts the Jews as a scourge sweeping through Europe, sweeping across the world..."

"Like a plague of locusts."

I nodded. "Exactly, yes."

I looked at the cartoon on the cover, the grotesque locust head with the semi-human features. The jutting, hooked, hairy nose that I'd thought was supposed to be Roman but was now clearly a clichéd caricature of a Semitic stereotype. I handed her the pamphlet. She leafed through the pages, not bothering to read the text, just glancing through it.

"And does it propose a solution to this plague of locusts?"

"It makes it pretty clear that the best thing to do with locusts is exterminate them."

"Naturally," she said. She set the pamphlet carefully aside and went to a bookshelf, where she pulled down a copy of *Farmer Henry Versus the Locusts*. She returned to her seat and flipped through its brightly coloured pages, beloved of generations of children, depicting the evil locusts being crushed, impaled, spattered and, of course, baked in ovens.

Crunch, crunch, crunch.

She handed the book to me. I opened it to the title page, which had a dedication printed opposite. *For Taffy—who hates the locusts as much as I do.* "Do you know who was responsible for this pamphlet?" said Toba. I nodded. I'd done some research online. There weren't any images of the pamphlet's cover art, but its title cropped up in places, with appropriate historical and political commentary.

"It was financed by something called the Cavermann Foundation. Herman Cavermann was an American, a wealthy right-wing nutcase who lived in London where he met and married Millicent 'Taffy' Honeyland."

"Lucky Honeyland's sister."

"That's right," I said. "They lived here until the war came, her and her rich American fascist, and then they fled to Argentina."

"But you don't know who actually wrote it?" She picked up the pamphlet by one corner as if it was contaminated. I was hoping she didn't plan to do anything dramatic like tearing it to shreds, because I needed it.

"I have my suspicions," I said. She gave me a piercing look.

"Would you care to share them with me?"

"Well, Lucky Honeyland wrote a lot of highly dramatic propaganda for Bomber Command during the war." I shrugged. "Maybe he had some practice before that." Toba Possner was silent for a long moment. Finally she spoke.

"When I finished doing the illustrations for his book, Mr Honeyland was very pleased with them. He gave me a bottle of wine as a present. It was obviously a very good and very expensive bottle of wine. I remember at the time wishing it was money instead, because I needed money and I didn't need wine. He was in a very good mood, I remember. High spirits. I believe he had already drunk some wine himself. He kept referring to me as a 'daughter of Abraham', by which he meant Jew. This was his way of being tactful. He said he was delighted with the pictures I had done for him. And he was especially delighted because I was a daughter of Abraham. Because I was a Jew." She picked up the copy of *Farmer Henry Versus the Locusts* and peered at the cover, or rather into it, as if it was a looking glass.

"It turned out I was a good Jew," she said. "A clever, resourceful one. Shrewd at business. Because after making some enquiries I sold that bottle of wine he gave me. I sold it for a considerable sum. Rather more than my commission for doing the illustrations, in fact."

"Good for you," said Nevada. I admired her restraint in not asking what kind of wine it was.

Toba put the book down and picked up the pamphlet again. She smiled a crooked smile. "Now at last I know what he meant, why it was particularly pleasurable for him to have a Jew doing the pictures for his book, and her not even knowing what it was really about. It must have been— how can I put it? *Piquant*."

When we got back to the house Tinkler was waiting for us, sitting on the raised concrete edge of the garden bed by our front gate. Fanny was lying among the flowers beside him, allowing him to rub her ears. "What are you doing here?" I said.

"I was waiting for you to come home. It's certainly taken you long enough."

We unlocked the front door and Fanny hopped out of the flower beds to follow us in. "But why, pray tell, were you waiting in the first place?"

"I came over to get some stuff from Opal's van in the garage." Tinkler followed us in.

"But you can't get into the garage without a key."

"So I realised."

"And we've got the key."

"That's why I'm so glad to see you," said Tinkler.

We gave him the key and he went out again, heading for the garage area. Nevada fed the cats while I started to prepare dinner. We heard the front gate open and saw Tinkler there, holding a precarious pile of boxes. He'd evidently got what he wanted. Nevada opened the door for him and he tottered into the kitchen, still holding the boxes. There was a precarious stack of books protruding from the one on top.

"Got what you came for, then?" I said.

"Yup. Yes, indeed. Just thought I'd check in to see what's cooking for dinner. If it's something nice—"

"Is it ever not?" said Nevada.

"If it's something nice," continued Tinkler pointedly, "I thought I might grace you with my company."

"What about Opal? Surely you will want to dine with your turtledove?"

"I thought I could take her a doggy bag," said Tinkler. "She says she misses your cooking."

"Enough with the doggy bags," said Nevada and hit Tinkler between the shoulder blades. It was only a playful blow, but it carried sufficient force to cause the boxes to tremble in his hands, and consequently the book at the top of the stack toppled off and fell to the floor.

"Ouch," said Tinkler. "That hurt. I'd be rubbing my back if my hands weren't full."

"Here, I'll rub it for you," said Nevada. "You big baby."

I bent down to pick up the book. It had a curiously familiar cover. "Put it back in the box, then," said Tinkler. I ignored him, studying the book. It was a statistics text. I realised where I'd seen it before.

In the recording studio in Camberwell Green. The one that had belonged to the guy who'd been shot down outside.

I reached for the box of books and carefully lifted it off the stack Tinkler was holding. "Hey, what are you doing?" he said. "Put that back. I may never get this stuff stable again."

I looked through the books. "These are Opal's?"

"Yes," said Tinkler.

I didn't recognise any of them. I certainly didn't remember any of them being on the shelf in the recording studio. But they were all books about mathematics or statistics. I looked at Tinkler.

"She asked me to pick them up because she needs them for research," he said. "She's working on her dissertation about her great-grandmother."

"And her great-grandmother was a statistician?"

"No, she was a code-breaker. And you need statistics to break codes."

31. SIGNAL FLARE

"A pleasure to meet you, darling," said Gerry, taking Opal's tiny hand in his two enormous ones. "I knew your gran and she was a lovely girl. Really lovely. What happened to her was terrible, just terrible." I was a little alarmed to see that there were tears gleaming in his rheumy old eyes.

There were suddenly tears in Opal's eyes, too. "Thank you, sir," she said. "It's so nice to meet someone who met her, who remembers her."

"Remember her? I could never forget her. Have a seat." He gestured towards the white plastic table and chairs in a flag-stoned corner of the garden. It was a warm, glorious spring day and I was glad we were sitting outside.

Since I'd been buried alive, I'd acquired a new appreciation for fresh air.

We all sat down and looked around at the garden. It was quite a garden. There was sensibly little lawn, mostly just narrow strips of grass for access between the flower beds. We were basically sitting among flowers. "It's a lovely place you've got here," said Opal. I could see that Nevada was a little annoyed that she was doing all the talking, but the teenager had clearly established a rapport with our host and Nevada wasn't about to interfere.

"It's not bad, not bad," allowed Gerry Wuggins, looking around.

"I really like the cowboy theme you've got going on."

"Southwestern, love, it's called Southwestern. Or ranch style."

Nevada rather pointedly waited for Opal to stop talking so we could get down to business. There was still an undercurrent of hostility among us, between Nevada and Opal and, to a lesser extent, between Opal and myself. Tinkler seemed quite oblivious to it, and indeed to the beautiful day around us. Butterflies were dancing above the flower beds. But Tinkler looked bored.

Gerry got down to business.

"It was terrible what happened to your gran," he said again. "But we never believed it was Johnny Thomas what done it."

"I don't believe it was either," said Opal. Gerry's eyes widened.

I said, "In fact, we have an idea of who it really was." Gerry stared at me, moist eyes wide with surprise.

"You know who the killer was?"

"We think so," I said.

"And it definitely wasn't Johnny?"

"No, it wasn't."

He sighed and leaned back, as if a great weight had

been lifted off his shoulders after all these years. Then he laughed a strange, bitter little laugh. Shrugging, he said, "I don't suppose it matters any more, though, does it? I mean, what with it being over half a century ago now and with poor Johnny being dead all that time."

Hanged for something he didn't do, I thought.

"It matters a great deal," I said.

"We know who the killer is," said Tinkler smugly. "By the way, when is lunch?"

"Soon, mate," said Gerry.

"More importantly," I said, "we know why the killer did it."

"Why he killed my great-grandmother," said Opal.

Gerry shook his head. "Why would anyone want to kill that lovely girl? Her face used to light up when we played. You could always spot her in the audience. She loved our music. What was her favourite number?" He wrinkled his forehead. "What was that now?"

"You're right," said Opal. "She loved swing music. And she thought your band was the best."

"We *were*, darling. We were the best." He frowned and shook his head, an old man trying to remember. "What was that one she was always asking us to play?" His eyes were on other days. Gillian Gadon lived again, in his mind.

"Her favourite piece of music?"

"Yes."

"By the Flare Path Orchestra?"

"Yes, love. Who else?"

"It was called 'Cookies'," said Opal. "I came across that

in my research. She mentions it in a letter."

Gerry snapped his fingers. "'Cookies'! That's it. That was her favourite tune. And do you know what the name means?"

"Not a sweet biscuit-like confection?" said Tinkler hopefully.

"No, mate. It was a 4,000-pound bomb."

"Four thousand?" said Nevada.

"Yes, dear. We used to call them cookies. No one can say we didn't have a sense of humour."

"Four thousand pounds? Of high explosive?"

"Yeah, but don't worry, we didn't drop many on the enemy. They were ruddy great useless things. They just weighed the plane down. The idea was to dump them in the ocean as soon as you could after take-off—so you could gain some decent altitude and avoid the bloody night fighters. But high command got wind of it, us dumping the bombs. Somebody told them I suppose, somebody who went to the right schools and learned to do the proper thing. And after that the bastards went to diabolical lengths to stop us wasting their precious cookies. The buggers rewired the bomb release circuits so that the photoflash system would go off whenever we dumped one."

There was silence in the garden for a moment. "Oh look, a squirrel," said Tinkler. A small squirrel hopped across the lawn, passing near our table. It didn't seem at all alarmed at our presence. "He's probably on his way to lunch," suggested Tinkler.

"That was the reason it all happened," I said. "Because Opal's great-grandmother loved swing music. Because she loved your band." *That's why she got killed,* I thought.

Opal nodded. "That's why she became interested in the puzzle in the first place."

"What puzzle?" said Gerry.

"My great-grandmother was a code-breaker. A junior code-breaker. A code-breaker's assistant. After all, she was just a woman. She worked at Bletchley Park. You have heard of Bletchley Park?"

"Of course I have. Enigma and all that. She was one of their mob?"

"Yes. A cryptographer. She was always good at crossword puzzles, number puzzles—she used to call them 'brainteasers'—all that sort of thing. So they took her on. Of course she was basically just a secretary at first, but then they realised how smart and talented she was." Opal positively glowed with pride. "When they realised her abilities, they moved her into one of the huts where the real work was being done."

"But it wasn't all work," I said. "Even during the war people had to take a break, even if it was only listening to the radio at night."

"That's right," said Opal. "They called it the wireless. And my great-grandmother never missed a broadcast by the Flare Path Orchestra. That's why she began to notice some strange things."

Gerry's big grey eyebrows angled up. "Things?"

"Patterns. In the music. Music and cryptography were her two passions. And a puzzle that combined them both was irresistible."

Nevada leaned over and casually whispered in my ear, "Another sentence from her thesis."

"Dissertation," I murmured.

"Dissertation. Whatever."

"The only problem," said Opal, "was that no one would listen to her. No one believed she was on to something. So she set out to investigate it herself. She attended live concerts by the Flare Path Orchestra and met the men who were playing the music. She knew that one of them would have the answer."

Gerry suddenly stood up. I realised he was looking down at the far end of the garden, where the driveway snaked up among trees from the front gate. A figure was standing there. A small, suntanned man in a short-sleeved shirt. His stance, even at this remove, was aggressive and cocky. It was Danny Overland. He paused and stared at us, ostentatiously shading his eyes with his hands.

"Come on, then," shouted Gerry. "You took bloody long enough to get here."

Overland shouted back, "You shouldn't live so far out in the fucking sticks, should you?" He ambled from the drive, among the flower beds, to join us.

I stood up and shook hands with him. "I'm glad you could make it."

He pumped my hand energetically. "Sorry I'm so late. I got lost. That happens when you leave the city and venture into the outback." Then he turned to Gerry, and the two old men embraced and grinned at each other. Overland looked around at the extensive gardens, the rambling ranch-style house. "You've done all right for yourself, Airman Wuggins."

Gerry sighed contentedly, surveying his domain. "Not too shabby. Not too shabby at all." He pushed out a chair, and Danny Overland sat down at the table with us.

"You drove down on your own?" said Nevada.

Overland nodded. "Jenny is out of action. Sick." We all made sympathetic noises, even Tinkler, who'd never met her.

"I'm sorry to hear that."

"Yeah, no, very sick. Food poisoning. Really serious. They say she's only still alive because she's young and strong." Overland grimaced. "If it had been me I'd be dead. And it could have been me."

"Don't be such a miserable old bugger," said Gerry. "Can I get you a beer?"

Overland looked painfully conflicted for a moment but finally shook his head. "Best not."

Gerry nodded, full of understanding. "Because you're driving."

"Not just driving. Conducting. You won't have forgotten it's my concert tonight." He nodded at us. "I know they've got tickets. You gave them yours."

"Uh, well," said Gerry Wuggins, "you see, me and the missus…"

"Never mind explaining. You gave them your fucking tickets. Gave them away. Didn't even *sell* them. Well, here are two more." Overland slapped them on the table. "Now, I expect you to be there tonight. With the missus. No excuses. And here's two for you." He took out two more and gave them to Opal and Tinkler. Ticket sales obviously weren't too brisk.

"Thank you," said Opal, taking them.

"I can't stay long," said Overland. But he leaned back in the chair and smiled up at the sky, the sun on his face, like a man settling in for an extended stay. "I've got to get back early. It's total chaos. Like I said, Jenny is out of action. I'll have to leave soon."

If that was the case, I thought I'd better move things along. "Opal was just telling us about her great-grandmother at Bletchley Park discovering that there was some kind of code being sent out in your broadcasts with the band."

"Our broadcasts with the band? Our radio broadcasts?"

"Yes."

Overland looked at me. His eyes gave nothing away. "The Flare Path Orchestra? Some kind of code?"

Gerry chuckled. "Yeah. They think we were sending messages to the enemy."

"Not knowingly," I said. "Only one person knew about it."

"Two, if you count my great-grandmother," said Opal.

"It's ridiculous, though, isn't it?" said Gerry.

"Actually embedded in the music?" said Danny Overland. "The message actually in the music?"

"Yes."

"In existing tunes?" said Overland, giving me a hard stare. "Including well-known tunes?"

"Yes."

"You're not taking this seriously, are you?" said Gerry.

Overland looked at me. "The Flare Path Orchestra was

like Glenn Miller's outfit. It was an arranger's band. If you wanted to plant codes in the music, you'd have to do it through the arrangers."

"Exactly," I said. "If Lucky Honeyland wanted to send a message, he had to get the arranger to make the necessary changes."

"Lucky?" said Gerry. "Colonel Honeyland? You must be joking."

"Without realising what they were doing, of course," I said. "The arrangers were completely innocent."

Danny Overland nodded thoughtfully. "At least that would explain why Lucky always insisted on interfering with my arrangements. And everybody else's. We all thought he fancied himself as some kind of master orchestrator, which was a bit of a tragedy because he couldn't tell a baritone sax from a banjo on his best day on earth…" He trailed off, thinking. "But it would also explain something else," he said slowly. "Why he always insisted on adding such jarringly inappropriate instruments." He looked at me. "Because it wasn't the musical message he was interested in."

"No," I said. "He was more interested in the message being sent to his Nazi masters." I'd already begun to formulate a very negative view of old Lucky.

"You're not taking this seriously, are you?" said Gerry. "You can't believe *any* of it. Lucky sending messages to the Germans?"

"More than that," I said. "He killed Opal's great-grandmother. He was the one who strangled her." The Silk Stockings Murder, solved at last.

"Oh, come on, now."

"Let me ask you something, Gerry," I said. "Do you remember Lucky riding around the country at night on his motorbike?"

"Yeah."

"Do you think he could have got to Kingsdown and back in the course of a night?"

Gerry paused to consider this. "Yeah," he said finally. "Sure. It would have been a long run, but Bomber Harris had got him a special pass so he could use any road he wanted, and he always had priority. He was probably the fastest thing on wheels in England. But so what?"

"Let me ask you something else. Did he wear goggles when he was riding the bike?"

"Of course he did. So what? Why would he have killed that girl?" He looked at Opal. "Her poor gran?"

"He must have got wind that she'd found him out," I said, "found out that he was a traitor and a Nazi spy. And she was on the verge of exposing him."

"How?"

"From Johnny Thomas."

Danny Overland nodded. "Johnny was the weakest of us arrangers. He wouldn't stand up for himself. He would always do exactly what Lucky wanted him to. If someone wanted to find out what Lucky was up to—"

"Lucky wasn't up to anything. He wasn't a Nazi spy!"

"If anybody wanted to find out," said Danny Overland gently, "Johnny would have been the man to talk to. Because he did most of his so-called musical work through Johnny."

"That was why my great-grandmother got to know

him," said Opal. "That's why she was with him."

"She was pumping him," said Tinkler, "for information, among other things." And she'd ended up dead in his bed.

Gerry shook his head stubbornly. "You don't really think Lucky was the Silk Stockings killer? And that he let poor old Johnny go to the gallows for it?"

"It would have been a neat way of silencing everyone who might be in a position to implicate him," I said. "Two for the price of one."

"But he went down there to be with that boy in his cell, right up to the minute they took him away to be hanged."

"Maybe he had a guilty conscience," said Nevada.

"Or he wanted to make sure Johnny Thomas didn't tell anyone anything he shouldn't," I said. "Keeping an eye on him right up to the end. Or maybe he was just gloating."

"Oh, come off it now," said Gerry. "Lucky might have been a stuck-up toffee-nosed bastard, but he wasn't a sodding spy, and he certainly wasn't a bleeding cold-blooded murderer."

None of us would meet his eye.

Danny Overland took out a cigarette, looked at it, and then carefully put it back in the pack. He smiled at us. "Trying to cut down. My official fan club has asked me to stop."

"The man from dope," I said.

"Don't remind me," said Nevada.

Overland squinted at me. "If Lucky *was* sending messages to the Germans, how did they get messages back to him?"

"In the same way, I imagine," I said.

"In musical broadcasts?"

"Why not?" I said. "I seem to recall he was fond of listening to German broadcasts of a certain Berlin swing band."

Gerry Wuggins stared at me. "That's right. He did."

Overland was nodding too. "He got a bollocking when someone found out, but the big man himself, Bomber Harris, intervened on his behalf."

"And so Lucky was allowed to go on listening to the German broadcasts?" I said.

Danny Overland and Gerry looked at each other. "Yeah," said Gerry. "As it happens, he was."

Overland shifted his chair closer to his old friend. "Gerry," he said, "do you remember when Lucky went after those records?"

"By the Berlin band? Yeah, I remember. We all had a good laugh about it at the time. He went all the way to Germany to get them, didn't he? Some rare records by some Huns. We just thought he was a jazz nut."

"I know one of those," said Nevada, looking at me.

"That's right," said Overland. "Our boys were sweeping into Berchtesgaden, ransacking Göring's house, taking all the plunder he'd accumulated during the war. Looting Nazi loot."

"Re-looting," said Tinkler. "It's like re-gifting."

"People were taking silverware, fine wine, paintings and tapestries. And all good old Lucky wanted was those records by the Berlin jazz men."

"These would have been transcription discs?" I said. "Of radio broadcasts."

"That's right."

"So they would have been unique. They would have been the only copies."

"Right again."

"I wonder what happened to them?" I said.

Danny Overland looked at Gerry. "We know what happened to them, don't we?"

Gerry nodded. "Some poor bastard dropped them and broke them. Delivering them to our airfield. Swore he didn't know what happened to them. Said he'd been ever so careful. Our boys almost beat him up." He looked at me. "Because poor old Lucky had lost his beloved records."

I remembered the story Gresford-Jones had told us. I said, "Curiously enough, the same thing happened to the transcription recordings of the Flare Path Orchestra that had been stored at High Wycombe. It seems Lucky wasn't very lucky where his records were concerned."

"It's all very convenient," said Nevada. "All of the evidence getting destroyed like that."

"But he flew with us!" said Gerry.

"I doubt he was taking any chances," I said. "I've checked the dates of the missions he flew." They were all on an RAF memorial website. "And I correlated them with the dates of broadcasts by the Flare Path Orchestra."

"Actually, I correlated them for him," said Tinkler. "It was a fascinating database merge. I can tell you all about it over lunch."

Danny Overland was looking at me. "And…?"

"And he always flew on a mission the night *after* a broadcast."

"So what?" said Gerry.

"Very unlikely, statistically speaking," said Tinkler.

"We were always broadcasting. And always flying bloody bombing missions."

"Not Colonel Honeyland," I said. "He flew very few missions. And always the night after he'd made a broadcast with the band."

"You think he was sending a message?" said Overland. I nodded.

"What message?" said Gerry.

"'I'm coming tomorrow, don't shoot me down.'" I looked at Gerry. "You said yourself he was like your good luck charm. When he flew a mission with you, you knew you'd all come back safely."

"But not that one time," Gerry said. "Not the time we got shot to pieces by the Junkers."

"No, not that one time," I said. "Of course, I checked that date, too." I looked at Danny Overland. "It was the night after a broadcast, of course. And it's a broadcast you might remember." Overland began nodding vigorously. He was way ahead of me.

"The night I refused to make Lucky's changes," he said.

"That's right," I said. "When you performed the tune called 'Whitebait'. You told us Lucky was called away to High Wycombe during the session."

"That's right, summoned to see Bomber Harris."

"So he wasn't there to supervise the broadcast."

Danny Overland nodded thoughtfully. "And while the cat was away, the mice did play. I was able to change the orchestration. I removed the steaming heap of shit he'd added."

"And when you did that," said Nevada, "you removed his message."

I studied Overland. "I guess he was upset when he heard it," I said.

"Yeah, he hit the fucking roof. I remember now. He was at Springfield House with Bomber Harris, receiving the benefit of the commander's wisdom. And of course they knew what time the band was being broadcast, so they switched on the radio and had a listen." Overland grinned savagely. "It was a ritual. Apparently Harris always listened, presumably smoking a pipe and tapping his toes in a restrained manly manner."

He took out a cigarette. "And all the while in the music were the coded messages Lucky was transmitting to the enemy." He lit the cigarette.

"But not that time," I said.

Danny Overland breathed smoke. "No, not that time. And when he found out, he went fucking spare. Because he'd committed to flying a mission the following night. He couldn't back down."

"And now he had to face the same risks as the rest of you."

Gerry was looking very pale. "Oh my god," he said.

"What's the matter?"

"The first time you came here, the night of the wedding, remember? I told you all about that mission, us getting shot to bits by the night fighter, Lucky flying home on one engine, how he won the DFC… But there was something I didn't tell you."

Gerry sighed and shifted uneasily in his chair, as though it had suddenly grown uncomfortably constraining. "I stopped myself telling you. Because it was top secret. Seems a bit silly doesn't it, worrying about something being a secret all these years later? But I had never told nobody, and I suppose it was a hard habit to break."

"Tell us now," I said.

"Well, like I said, we were being shot to bits by the Ju 88C. It looked like we were done for. Then Lucky opened this satchel he had brought with him and took out this flare. Special emergency flare, he said. We dropped it out of the bomb doors."

Gerry paused, staring out not at the sunny garden around him but some unimaginable inner landscape, a night of terror in the skies over Germany more than half a century ago. "And the flare went off. It was the strangest colour. Sort of a pale purple. Like lilac or lavender. I'd never seen one like it before. And as soon as the flare lit up, the Junker broke off the attack."

He came back from that night over war-torn Europe and was looking at us again. "Lucky told us the flare was some special new device that was being developed. Something that interfered with the instruments of the enemy planes. It was a prototype. Top secret." He sighed. "That's what he said it was." He looked at me, blinking sadly. "But there never was a top secret device like that, was there?"

"No," I said. "It was a signal flare to tell the German fighters that they were attacking one of their own. And to desist immediately."

Gerry sighed again. "I always wondered why we weren't all issued those purple flares." He shook his head. "I also wondered, if it interfered with the German's instruments, why it didn't also interfere with ours."

Danny Overland puffed fiercely on his cigarette, then exhaled smoke. "And all because I monkeyed with that broadcast." He glanced at Gerry. "Sorry, mate."

"And I don't think he was just telling them when he was flying a mission," I said. "There were far too many messages for that. I also believe he was providing vital information to try and help his masters win the war."

Gerry looked at me. "Like what?"

"Like warning them of missions being sent to bomb important targets. I suspect he was busy at Bomber Command, too, using his influence to make sure that most of the targets chosen were as unimportant as possible."

"Encouraging Harris to bomb civilians," said Overland.

"Exactly. Doing everything he could to try and help Germany win the war."

Gerry glared at me. "Well, he didn't manage it, did he?"

"No, he didn't," I said. "But he was still a very valuable asset to them. Too valuable for the Nazis to risk losing. So they had a contingency plan in place, in case he was in danger. Hence the purple flare."

Tinkler rubbed his hands. "Well, that's settled," he said. "Colonel Honeyland was a treacherous code-sending Nazi spy and also the Silk Stockings murderer. Now how about lunch?" A look from Nevada and he quickly fell silent.

"But that's just the start of it," I said.

Danny Overland frowned through cigarette smoke. "What do you mean?"

"I mean, it's not over. People are still being killed." Including, almost, me.

"Who?" demanded Overland. "What people?"

"There was a sound engineer who ran a studio in Camberwell Green. He was gunned down on the street."

"What does a sound engineer in Camberwell Green have to do with anything?"

"He was making digital transfers of your records," I said, "and he discovered they contained a code. He was shot dead in front of his studio. The police think it was a gang shooting, but I think that was just a convenient cover for the real killers."

Overland tapped ash off his cigarette. "And who are the real killers?"

"People working for Joan Honeyland."

"Oh come on now," said Gerry.

I nodded. "She's the one who hired us. She set the whole thing in motion. She wanted us to find the records so she could suppress them. But it backfired. The recording engineer noticed something." I remembered the books about statistics that had lined the wall of his studio. "He seemed to be taking forever to do the transfers. There was a very good reason for that. He was holding onto the records, stalling for time, until he had enough samples to prove his theory. When I got the last batch of records from Gerry here, he had enough. And once he knew what he had, I suspect he was going to blackmail her."

"Joan Honeyland? Lucky's daughter?"

"Yes. So she had him killed."

"She did what?" said Gerry.

"Why would she be willing to do that?" said Danny Overland. "Just to protect the reputation of her old man?"

"More than his reputation," I said. "His children's books are worth millions. Providing she can sell them to the right media giant. And evidence of murder, treachery and rampant anti-Semitism would tend to dramatically reduce their market value."

"Wait a minute," said Tinkler. "So you're saying Joan Honeyland killed the recording studio guy?"

"She arranged to have him killed."

"It still doesn't make any sense," he said. "She has him killed and then she hires you to go in and steal back the records from his studio."

"Yes," said Nevada. "What doesn't make any sense about it?"

"Well, if she's going to hire someone to kill him, why not just get them to steal back the records as well?"

"Would you trust a hired goon with something as fragile as an antique disc of shellac?" I could see I'd scored a point with him. "Besides, Miss Honeyland knew she could depend on us to return the records to her. I don't think she could trust the goons. In fact, I think there was serious conflict between her and the goons."

Danny Overland was looking at me. "What sort of serious conflict?"

I said, "Judging by the fact that they fired a shot through

Miss Honeyland's window…"

"You think that was them?" said Tinkler.

I nodded. "They also ran her car off the road. Combined with the fact that they were holding onto one of her father's records, which she must have wanted for herself, I get the picture of two parties who have shared interests, and occasionally shared actions, but who don't trust each other and don't like each other."

"What shared interests?"

"Making a shit-load of money out of Lucky Honeyland's children's books," said Nevada.

"You think the Nazis want a piece of that action?" said Tinkler.

I nodded. "I think it would buy a lot of guns."

Overland considered all this. Finally he breathed out smoke, then waved his hand in the air to clear it away. He grinned at me. "Ah, you're full of it," he said. "You almost had me going for a minute there. But I don't believe it."

"What don't you believe?"

Danny Overland shook his head. "Joan Honeyland isn't a murderer."

"What makes you sure of that?"

"If she's so worried about those recordings, why did she make me a copy? I never liked her old man. And in all modesty, nobody in the world knows more about arranging than I do. What if I'd noticed something on those recordings?"

"The disc she provided for you was write-protected," I said. "You couldn't make copies. And she asked for it back, didn't she?"

"Yeah, and I've given it back to her. I gave it back the other day at lunch…" He stopped. He took the cigarette out of his mouth and looked at it as if he was surprised to see it there. Maybe he was. He was supposed to be quitting.

"Lunch…" He frowned. "She invited me out for lunch the other day. And I took Jenny with me. And Jenny got sick afterwards." He paused, then looked at me. "But you see, we've had this running joke in restaurants, Jenny and me, that whatever she orders turns out to be shit and whatever I order is great. So that day we switched. Switched meals. We'd been talking about doing it, and we finally did it."

"And Jenny ate the food that was intended for you."

"Yes."

"And she got sick."

We all looked at each other.

"I think Joan Honeyland is tying up loose ends," I said.

Danny Overland shook his head. "You can't be sure. You don't have any proof, mate. All we've really got is a case of food poisoning."

I said, "There's one way to find out."

32. ROYAL FESTIVAL HALL

"This is nice," said Nevada. "Why don't we go out and hear live music more often?" It was a beautiful spring evening, warm but fresh, with the river wind blowing in on us as we navigated the modernist concrete blocks of the South Bank.

"Because it sounds just like my hi-fi system at home," I said.

"Yes, true, but at home there is no ordering of drinks for the interval. I love ordering drinks for the interval. You just order them and then go in and enjoy the music and then you come back out for the interval and they're there, the drinks, waiting for you. They have appeared, as if by magic."

We made our way to the bar of the Royal Festival Hall and proceeded to order drinks for the interval—a lengthy procedure given Nevada's close scrutiny of the wine list and subsequent suspicious questioning of the bar staff before coming to a decision. But eventually we chose, ordered and paid.

The warning bell went off, and we filed towards the auditorium for the performance.

The crowd was mostly older people and largely casually attired, so we stood out on at least two counts. Nevada was dressed to the nines in a black strapless evening gown, stockings and stilettos, and she'd carefully selected my own outfit—a Woodhouse suit bought at a Red Cross shop in Chiswick and an Armani shirt from Oxfam in Hammersmith. I'd been allowed to choose my own shoes, provided I shined them.

We had evidently ended up a little overdressed for the occasion, but there had been no alternative. Nevada had got the bit between her teeth as soon as she'd heard that Opal was planning to dress up for the concert. Personally, I was surprised that she and Tinkler were even going to use the tickets Danny had given them. I couldn't imagine it was the kind of music that would appeal to either of them.

We glimpsed them behind us in the crowd as we filed into the auditorium. They'd arrived characteristically late. Tinkler waved to me happily. Opal was on his arm, and a fair man would have had to admit she did look quite ravishing. She was wearing some kind of jade green tie-dyed silk creation that appeared to be wrapped around her body in somewhat the manner of an Indian sari. There was no evidence of anything holding it together except for a few strategic folds and also, even at this distance, no evidence of any underwear lurking beneath it. She was causing quite a stir, and Tinkler looked uxoriously proud.

"Just look at the gaudy little fox," said Nevada. "Doesn't she look ridiculous?"

"What do I know about women's fashions?"

"A transparent evasion."

"That's not all that's transparent," I said.

"You're going to pay for that, chum. No drinks in the interval for you."

It was cool inside the auditorium with the happy buzz of conversation you get when people are finding their seats before a concert. I liked the Royal Festival Hall. I liked its wide, open spaces and its natural wood. It had a tradition of jazz going right back to when the South Bank had been created.

Over the years I'd heard Nina Simone, Dewey Redman and Lalo Schifrin here.

It wasn't jazz tonight, though, at least not immediately. The first half of the concert consisted of Danny Overland's acclaimed light orchestral music, written in the 1940s and 1950s. The second half would see some jazz surface, including the big band material from the war.

We edged to our seats, easing past those already sitting down with the usual cheerful apologies, and past the occasional difficult bastards who wouldn't stand up so you had to graze their knees to get by. As soon as we were seated, Nevada was craning around to see if she could spot Tinkler and Opal. They were at the back.

"Good grief," said Nevada, "they're *all over* each other. He can't keep his hands off her. And vice versa. They're kissing. They're pawing. Thank god we're not sitting beside them. She'll probably give him a blow job during the concert."

"At least it will keep him awake," I said.

The music in the first half wouldn't have been Tinkler's cup of tea, and it wasn't really mine either. Light orchestral was what our ancestors had before easy listening was invented. I could admire the nimble playing and the witty orchestrations, but ultimately it left me cold.

The second half was what I was waiting for. Jazz. Swing. The Flare Path Orchestra.

"Look there," said Nevada suddenly.

Along the wall to our left were the boxes where the well-heeled elite sat. In the one nearest the stage was Joan Honeyland. Beside her was a neatly dressed young man. It took me a moment to recognise Albert without his chauffeur's uniform.

They waved at us.

We waved back.

Despite her threats, Nevada did let me have a drink in the interval, in fact she sent me to fetch them while she went out onto the embankment to meet the composer and conductor, who was busy furiously smoking. She was standing upwind of him when I arrived. It had grown dark and a night wind was rippling along the Thames. The giant art-deco alarm clock of the Shell Mex building glowed at us from the other side of the river.

I was carrying two glasses of wine.

"Nothing for me, mate?" Overland looked dapper in his formal black conductor's outfit.

"I thought you weren't drinking because it was the evening of a performance."

"No drinking *before*. Lots of drinking halfway through."

"Really?"

"After the interval you'll notice a marked new level

of energy from the brass section." I offered to get him something from the bar, which was now crammed and heaving, but thankfully he shook his head. "So what did you think of the music?"

Nevada convincingly gushed with praise, but Danny Overland was looking steadily at me. "Thanks, darling, I'm really glad you liked it. But I sense your boyfriend here has some doubts."

"Well, he's just a terrible music snob. That's his problem."

"So, mate?" said Overland, looking at me.

"It's just not really my kind of stuff."

"You don't like light orchestral music?"

"No, not really."

"Why not?"

"It's a slippery slope," I said. "And waiting at the bottom is Mantovani."

He laughed. "Mantovani had his moments, you know. Fucking brilliant use of strings. He got all that from his arranger Ronald Binge." He turned away from us and stared out at the river for a moment. He took a final drag on his cigarette, stubbed it out and then put the spent stub back in the pack that went back into his pocket. His jacket must have smelled like an old ashtray.

He checked his watch. "Oh, well. You'll like the second half. Which reminds me, have you got it for me?"

I handed him the slip of paper.

He read it and gave a short snarl of laughter.

"Very good," he said. He folded it and put it in his pocket.

* * *

The second half of the concert began with some excellent modernist big band jazz directed by Danny at the piano. The compositions gradually devolved into 1940s-style swing. The auditorium grew darker and lights danced across the stage, and then began to angle upwards, probing the dark ceiling. I realised they looked like searchlights, hunting the night skies for enemy planes.

The horn section made a convincing imitation of aircraft sirens.

They faded to silence and Danny Overland left the piano and came to the microphone. A spotlight stabbed down on him. He seemed entirely at ease.

"During the Second World War—our war—the Royal Air Force chaplain, Reverend John Collins, was once forced to attend a lecture on 'The Ethics of Bombing'. He sat through it patiently. Well, not so patiently. And when it was finally over he stood up and said, 'Sorry I misunderstood you.'" Overland paused dramatically here. "'I realise now that your lecture was actually about "The Bombing of Ethics".'"

There was laughter from the audience.

"He was against the atom bomb, too," said Overland. "That's the sort of nutcase he was."

More laughter.

"In Australia we love it when you come over and test your atom bombs." Laughter, cheers and whistling from fellow Australians. "We like a bit of politics," said Overland. "But what we prefer is a bit of music. In this case, the sort of dance music we used to play with a little outfit called the Flare Path Orchestra."

Tumultuous applause.

"And after that we will conclude with a world premiere performance of a new piece I've written especially for the occasion." He glanced casually into his hand, curled on the edge of the lectern. I doubt anyone else would have noticed anything, but I knew he was reading from the slip of paper I'd handed him.

"It's a little number called 'Bletchley Park Girl Comes Good in the End'." He stared into the audience. "It's part of a suite entitled *Coded Messages to the Enemy*."

There was polite applause.

I looked up at the box.

Miss Honeyland was hurrying out, followed by Albert.

33. CHAMPAGNE

We had just arrived home from the concert and were unlocking the front door when my phone rang. It was Danny Overland. "You need to get over here right away," he said. Then he told me where he was.

The cats stared at us in astonishment as we turned around and headed back out the door, pausing only to pour them a few biscuits. "The poor darlings," said Nevada. "Did you see their little faces? They thought we were home for the night."

"So did I," I said. As we hurried back towards the Upper Richmond Road we phoned Clean Head. It so happened she was working that night. She was currently in Bayswater and just clearing a fare. We arranged to meet her in Hammersmith and caught a 33 bus across the bridge. It was after midnight by the time we arrived. Clean Head was waiting for us in the road behind Marks & Spencer. We climbed into the back of the cab and set off, streetlights flashing by above the dark, busy streets.

We hit traffic twice and got to Soho in about half an hour. Clean Head dropped us off in Berwick Street. "I'll be driving around in a circle," she said.

"Thanks."

"I've got your back."

"We know. Thanks."

She drove off, her engine chugging in the night. The streets were full of people, many in a party mood, most a little drunk. Friday night in the centre of London. It was as busy as high noon. Around the corner, Danny Overland was waiting for us, in the entrance to Joan Honeyland's mews.

"You took your time," he said.

"We could have got here quicker on the Tube," I said. "But we preferred to get a friend to drive us."

"She's a very reliable friend," said Nevada.

"Never mind. Anyway, you're here now. Come on." He turned towards the dark entrance of the mews.

"Wait a minute," I said. "You haven't told me what you're doing here."

"She invited me here," he said, his voice echoing in the dark passageway. "For drinks."

"She invited you for drinks?"

He shrugged. "After the concert. She sent me the invitation a few days ago."

Nevada said, "And you came? After she tried to poison you once already?"

I said, "Knowing all that, you came here? On your own and unprotected?"

Overland smiled. "Not unprotected. I've got this." He

took out a Taser. I knew what it was, because I'd seen one just like it. One exactly like it, in fact.

"I wonder where you got that?" I said, and looked at Nevada. It was hard to tell in this light, but I think she had the good grace to blush. She'd probably rented it to him.

"Anyway, I didn't need it," said Danny Overland. He put the Taser back in his pocket. "Come on." We followed him down the dark passage and out into the cobbled courtyard where the Mercedes gleamed in the darkness. I remembered Albert's male-stripper routine as he'd washed it here, a million years ago.

We went through the open door and up the narrow staircase that smelled of dust. The dark apartment above us radiated a silent sense of emptiness, and Overland wasn't making any attempt to be careful. I knew now what he wanted to show us. The place was deserted. They had flown the coop.

We came to the landing at the top of the stairs and advanced into the tiny sitting room. It wasn't so dark in here. There was a small red and green art nouveau lamp glowing on the corner of a desk, its light doubled by its reflection in the window. I searched the panes for any trace of the bullet hole I knew had been there. It was as if it had never happened. Nice window repair.

I remembered their car, destroyed one day and like new again the next. She certainly knew how to get good service.

The one lamp provided enough light to see a pile of records—all 78s—with a piece of notepaper on top with some handwriting on it. I picked it up. It read 'For Daniel Overland, to make use of in any manner he sees fit. *This music must live.*' The last four words were emphatically underlined. Overland and Nevada watched as I looked through the records. They were all the ones we'd found—with the exception of the Victory Disc, which was still at my house—and a few others I'd never seen before.

"Miss Honeyland's collection," I said, and handed Overland the note. "They're all for you."

"There's that, too," he said, nodding at a white envelope on the desk. It was narrow but bulky and had my name written on it.

"But first you have to see what's through here," said Overland. He led us into a room I'd never entered before. The bedroom. There were two more lamps on in here, discreet spotlights over the bed. They created a dramatic light in the small shadowy cube of a room. Joan Honeyland was lying in the bed.

She wore an elegant pair of dove-grey pyjamas with yellow piping. Beside her, in a matching pair of pyjamas, lay Albert the chauffeur. The former chauffeur. He lay half on and half off the bed, his body twisted. His legs were still on the bed but his face and shoulders were on the floor, his torso bent like a man frozen halfway in the act of rolling over.

My mouth went dry. Nevada made a little sound in the back of her throat.

"They're—"

"Oh yeah," said Danny Overland. "As cold as the fucking grave."

There were roses strewn all over the bed, red and white and yellow roses. They had evidently been originally placed with great care, but now a number of them were disturbed, scattered and spilled on the floor. All on Albert's side of the bed.

"Where do you get flowers this time of night?" said Danny Overland.

"This is Soho," I said. "You can find anything, any time."

There was a silver tray on the dressing table with a bottle of champagne and two glasses on it. Nevada went over and looked at it. "Don't touch that," said Danny Overland. "And for god's sake don't drink any of it."

Nevada looked at the bottle of champagne, then at the bodies on the bed. "Suicide pact?" she said.

"Well, suicide pact-ish," said Overland.

"What do you mean?"

He nodded at the body of Albert, lying half on the floor. "If you look you can see that bloke's got a t-shirt and boxer shorts on under his pyjamas." I saw what he meant. Albert's pyjama top was in rumpled disarray and had crept up his back, revealing shorts and a shirt. Danny Overland looked at me.

"When's the last time you wore a t-shirt and boxers under your pyjamas, mate?"

"Never," I said. I didn't wear pyjamas, but I knew what he was getting at. "You think she put them on him?"

"Yeah, after he was unable to do so."

Nevada was staring at the bottle of champagne. "You mean…?"

"She gave him a drink first," I said, "and waited for it to take effect on him."

Overland nodded. "And then put him on the bed and put

the pyjamas on him. And then she did all the—" he waved his hand at the flowers, the discreet lighting, "—all the set decoration for her little tableau."

"Then she took a drink herself," said Nevada, looking at the glasses. One of them had a bright red smear of lipstick across it.

"And then she lay down beside him," I said, moving towards the bed. It wasn't an easy thing to do. "But later, after she was unconscious, he must have woken up." I peered down at Albert lying on the floor. Luckily his face was deep in shadow.

"It had a different effect on him, whatever they took," said Danny Overland behind me. "He's young and strong. I mean was."

As my eyes grew accustomed to the darkness I saw what was on the floor by Albert's pale hand. "There's a telephone here. He was reaching for it, but he didn't quite make it."

"He didn't want to make the journey with her," said Overland, "or maybe he changed his mind."

"Poor bastard," said Nevada. She went back into the sitting room and I followed her. She had picked up the envelope with my name on it. She gave me a questioning look.

"Open it," I said.

It contained a wad of banknotes. Nevada counted them. She looked at me. "It's our bonus, for the successful completion of our task."

There was also a note.

34. NOTE

The note was written on several sheets of Joan Honeyland's monogrammed notepaper, neatly numbered.

Can you imagine what it's like to work your whole life towards a purpose and to see your goal finally within your grasp and then to watch it being snatched from you?

Well, I can't.

And I have no intention of finding out.

However, I mustn't go without thanking you for all your efforts on my behalf. You and Nevada were extremely industrious and dedicated to your work, and I can't begin to tell you what rare qualities those are in young people in this day and age. You were also courteous and efficient and showed loyalty to your employer.

If only Roberts, the recording engineer, could have displayed similar merit. Instead he tried to extort money from us and had to be dealt with. Unfortunately this involved us getting more deeply involved with people I had been trying to distance myself from for some time.

I make no apologies for my father's beliefs and loyalties. They didn't lie in the same direction as the prevailing beliefs and loyalties of his day, but that is a tragedy and I believe an error of history, and one that I sincerely hope will be rectified one day in this great nation.

I am deeply sorry that I destroyed the journals of my father. But having read them I realised what a vulnerable position his literary estate was actually in. So I set about making sure that no one would learn of those aspects of his character that might damage the value of his books.

Our books.

That is why I hired you to collect all the remaining copies of his records. I knew there would be few enough of these, and once I had them all in my control we would be safe for posterity.

Unfortunately, however, I am not the only one who is devoted to keeping my father's memory alive.

She meant the Nazis at the farmhouse. I turned to the next page of the letter.

By a bitter irony, these people, whom he would regard with nothing but deserved disdain, know the truth about his heroic wartime effort.

And they rightly venerate him for it.

But this veneration comes hand in hand with a desire to share in the revenues flowing from his books. They seem to believe that they are continuing his work and my father would, if he were alive today, want to fund their efforts.

In fact, if he were alive today, he would put them in chains and make them dig ditches, which is about all they are good for. Perhaps after twenty years of hard labour he would let them join the fine new world he would build.

But if my father were alive today, everything would be very different.

Perhaps he could have succeeded at my task.

I have failed.

I turned to the next page of the letter.

I realised what I was doing wasn't enough. That obtaining all his records, burning his journal, and suppressing the last copies of some pamphlets he wrote in the flush of his youthful enthusiasm wasn't enough. It would never be enough.

Even silencing that recording engineer wasn't enough.

What followed was a series of bullet points.

- *There was Daniel Overland, with his contempt for my father, and who knew what dangerous memories of the war lurking behind those low brows of his.*
- *Then there was that illustrator trying, like so many others, to chisel a share of my father's rightful earnings. He was always very proud of how he had*

dealt with her, making an agreement with her that only paid her what she was worth and not a penny more. "I out-Jewed a Jew," he liked to say.

• *And there were others, a seemingly unlimited supply of them. Like the little man with a beard who's been hanging around our street, taking photographs.*

The bullet points ended.

They all needed dealing with.

And I began to suspect that it would never end.

And then the announcement tonight at the concert, telling me that the Australian music-maker did indeed know exactly what transpired during the war. That was the final straw.

I reached the last page of the letter.

And so we take our leave of you.

The champagne has been poured and now I have penned this note.

Before closing I find myself wondering if I should give you the details of our 'associates'. You could pass them along to the relevant authorities.

But I see they've managed to get themselves arrested on firearms charges, and I think I can trust to their incompetence and the efficiency of the police to see that they get what they deserve.

Farewell.

I don't regret anything we've done. I do regret, keenly, that we didn't succeed.

Joan Honeyland.

EPILOGUE

Danny Overland kept the records, including the Victory Disc, which I gave to him. I'd almost died getting hold of it, but I'm not really into playing 78s. And he made good use of it, and all the others. He had them properly remastered, and released an excellent Flare Path Orchestra CD with an authoritative booklet.

He gave Jenny a co-producer credit on the project. She had recovered from her 'food poisoning'—which, come to think of it, really had been food poisoning—but I think he still felt guilty. He sent me a copy, and Nevada and I enjoy listening to it on those rare occasions when we listen to CDs.

It probably would have earned respectable sales among vintage jazz and swing enthusiasts.

But by the time it was released, the story had broken. It was all over the media and caused sales of the CD to go through the roof. Of course, this was mostly motivated by ghoulish interest in the 'secret Nazi code', as the tabloids dubbed it. Someone even released an unauthorised cash-in single which cobbled samples of all the alleged coded passages together and connected them with a techno beat and rap vocals. This aberration was attributed to a pseudonym—Nasty Honey Man—and, since the single sank without a trace, no one ever tried to claim credit for it.

However, I suspect the involvement of one Stinky Stanmer.

Joan Honeyland's 'lethal passion pact' (the tabloids again) attracted quite a lot of attention on its own merits, complete as it was with a May-December romance and a possible whiff of murder. But when the truth about her father was made public, it became a complete sensation.

Jasper McClew, the ferret-faced local historian, broke the story.

Or at least he tried to.

In his research he had pieced many of the facts together. And, crucially, he had photographs of Joan Honeyland talking with some known neo-Nazis. He'd planned to write a book about the Honeylands, but events moved too fast for him to complete it. Instead, he came to a deal with a television company to make a documentary about the subject.

But then the TV people discovered Opal. And Jasper found himself completely marginalised. No one was interested in taking shots of E.T. with a beard when they could instead film a pretty young girl who had pluckily travelled around the country, trying to track down her great-grandmother's killer. And her hippie van made for great visuals.

We watched the documentary with a disconsolate Tinkler. The van did indeed look pretty distinctive. In addition to the sun and moon it now featured badgers. "I painted that badger," said Tinkler. "Well, I painted the tail. And the whiskers. Most of the whiskers."

Opal had moved out of Tinkler's place as soon as the television project beckoned, leaving Tinkler alone in his house with only ten thousand records and a huge, extraordinary hi-fi system to comfort him. He had hoped she'd return when the documentary was complete.

And indeed she had. But only to say goodbye. "She's dumped me to go backpacking in the USA," he reported to us.

"Why on earth didn't you volunteer to go backpacking *with* her?" said Nevada.

"I did. She said it was a journey of self-discovery. And she wouldn't be able to discover herself if I was with her. I said I understood."

"Do you? Understand?"

"No. She lost me at 'self-discovery'."

So, after a brief burst of carnal bliss, Tinkler reverted to his status as what he called our designated sexual loser.

One welcome effect of the publicity was the clearing of the name of Johnny Thomas. He was exonerated of murder. Much good it did him; in his grave all these years, neck broken by a hangman's knot.

A happier beneficiary was Toba Possner. The story made her a hero, and she was emphatically rediscovered by the public and the art world. She was much in demand for articles and programmes about art and morality, and her paintings began to sell.

The price of her work sky-rocketed and she bought a

large house in Crouch End. Luckily, Nevada had already commissioned and paid her for our portrait.

"We got in just under the wire on that one," said Nevada.

So we no longer have any of the money Joan Honeyland gave us, but we do have a very nice painting of our two cats.

Miss Honeyland's faith in the efficiency of the police proved justified. They discovered that one of the guns taken from the Nazi farmhouse had been used to kill Derek Roberts outside his studio in Camberwell. Other weapons were linked to other serious crimes.

Consequently, Vivian and Carroll Weston were sent to prison for a very long time. I trusted that their girlie names would serve them in good stead in the penal system.

It didn't take long for some intrepid journalist to make the connection between *Farmer Henry Versus the Locusts* and a certain rancid anti-Semitic pamphlet. Consequently Lucky's work began to vanish off the kids' shelves of bookshops and libraries. And thankfully not in a suddenly-in-demand way.

As far as racism in vintage children's literature goes, it definitely made Enid Blyton's golliwogs seem mild by comparison.

These days you meet far fewer people who admit to having adored Farmer Henry's adventures when they were kids. And as Joan Honeyland predicted, the value of her father's literary estate plummeted, and some venture capitalists were able to pick up all of his assets for a rock-bottom price.

Which may yet prove to be a smart move. I understand

there is an initiative in Hollywood to rehabilitate and reinvent his children's classics in an acceptable form. In fact, there's an animated feature in production.

Coming soon, to a movie screen near you.

AUTHOR'S NOTE

Controversy still surrounds the British bombing campaign in Europe during World War Two. One thing is for certain: too many died on all sides, both combatants and non-combatants.

Anyone interested in the historical background to this novel should read Max Hastings' brilliant work of non-fiction *Bomber Command* and Len Deighton's equally brilliant work of fiction *Bomber*.

There have been a number of releases of Glenn Miller's wartime band on vinyl, and later on CD.

But if you're after the music of the Flare Path Orchestra, I'm afraid you're on your own.

AC

ACKNOWLEDGMENTS

Thanks to my splendid editor Ella Chappell, my unparalleled publicist Lydia Gittins and my ingenious cover designer Martin Stiff. And of course to the usual suspects: Guy Adams, without whom these books would have remained on my hard drive, and Miranda Jewess who was the first to believe in them and make them a reality. To my old friend Ben Aaronovitch for unfailing encouragement and help, and insisting I put the cats in. To my super ninja agent John Berlyne. To Sebastian Scotney at London Jazz News for outstanding support and patronage. To Mike Gething for lots of lovely records and suggesting the Vinyl Detective LP, and helping to make it happen. To the formidable Andrew Wilk for being my jazz and vinyl mentor. To Alan Ross of Jazz House records for enabling my habit. To Jean-Michel Bernard for making fantastic music and introducing me to the maestro, Lalo Schifrin. To Joe Kraemer for driving me to Lalo's house in Beverley Hills, for composing amazing music of his own, and for being my friend. To Penny

Winchester, Dimitri Del Castillo and Lenore, my friends in Los Angeles. And especially to Howard Hayes, the most generous man I know. Happy trails, amigo.

ABOUT THE AUTHOR

Andrew Cartmel is a novelist and screenwriter. He is the author of the Vinyl Detective series, which was hailed as "marvellously inventive and endlessly fascinating" by *Publishers Weekly*. His work for television includes commissions for *Midsomer Murders* and *Torchwood*, and a legendary stint as script editor on *Doctor Who*. He has also written plays for the London Fringe, toured as a stand-up comedian, and is currently co-writing a series of comics with Ben Aaronovitch based on the bestselling *Rivers of London* books. He lives in London with too much vinyl and just enough cats.